Ste_____n By_____ school at sixteen to join the Merchant Navy. He now lives with his family in Bedford, where he teaches English.

By Stephen Bywater

The Devil's Ark
Night of the Damned

STEPHEN BYWATER

NIGHT OF THE DAMNED

headline

Copyright © 2015 Stephen Bywater

The right of Stephen Bywater to be identified as the Author of
the Work has been asserted by him in accordance with the
Copyright, Designs and Patents Act 1988.

First published in 2015 by
HEADLINE PUBLISHING GROUP

1

Apart from any use permitted under UK copyright law,
this publication may only be reproduced, stored, or transmitted, in
any form, or by any means, with prior permission in writing of
the publishers or, in the case of reprographic production, in accordance
with the terms of licences issued by the Copyright Licensing Agency.

All characters in this publication are fictitious and any resemblance to real persons,
living or dead, is purely coincidental.

Cataloguing in Publication Data is available from the British Library

ISBN 978 1 4722 1041 8

Typeset in Sabon LT Std by Palimpsest Book Production Limited,
Falkirk, Stirlingshire

Printed and bound in Great Britain by CPI Group (UK) Ltd, Croydon CR0 4YY

Headline's   policy is to use papers that are natural, renewable and recyclable
products   and made from wood grown in sustainable forests and other
controlled   sources. The logging and manufacturing processes are expected to
confo   rm to the environmental regulations of the country of origin.

For my parents

I will knock down the Gates of the Netherworld,
I will smash the doors and trample them down.
And I will let the dead go up to eat the living!
And the dead will outnumber the living!
            The Goddess Ishtar in the *Epic of Gilgamesh*

So with curious eyes and sick surmise
We watched him day by day,
And wondered if each one of us
Would end the self-same way,
For none can tell to what red Hell
His sightless soul may stray.
            Oscar Wilde, *The Ballad of Reading Gaol*

Prologue

He had no idea why she'd shot him. At first he couldn't believe she had, couldn't, for a split second, connect the hammering in his ears with the copper-capped slug which had flown violently into his chest. It was only as his torso buckled backwards that his mind came to accept what she'd done, how hate or fear or a combination of both had torn through his shirt. The bullet had split his flesh, chipped his sternum and buried itself deep inside. He was ripped, seared, falling; reduced to nothing more than a hefty weight. All it took was an inch of lead to knock him off his feet. Thoughts ricocheted round his skull; was it for the man she was with, sitting there impassively watching? His mind registered the cane chair behind him, falling with him. The hard wooden floor, his head racing to meet it. This wasn't how it was supposed to happen. Not in this godforsaken corner of the world, not at the hands of a young woman he hardly knew.

Scenes flickered in quick succession: the freak show on Coney Island, the breakfast table with Mother, tears of condensation on a bedroom window, the shudder of the ship's engine. They brought no comfort and served only to taunt him by showing how miserable his life had been. His eyes were open to the ceiling above, the soft, amber wood rising

1

as he fell. But he didn't see any of it. He was blind to everything except the receding pictures in his mind of his recent arrival. Outside was the muddy river bank, the dark, malevolent jungle, the incessant rain. There were no thoughts of revenge or what might happen to her. The future was becoming sparse, disconnected.

The chair hit the floor, his back falling hard against it. In his ungainly flight his neck had begun to twist. His right cheekbone shattered on impact. He was conscious of his head rebounding. There was even the expectation of pain, but the fire in his chest had overwhelmed his ability to feel anything else.

He couldn't bring his hands up to the wound. He didn't know if he was bleeding or not. Frayed slippers down at heel, her red satin slippers, registered sharply for a moment and then, just as quickly as they'd appeared, they were lost in a thickening haze. Darkness was descending. He welcomed the numbness, dousing the ripping fire. He knew he was dying, but still refused to accept that he'd soon be dead. He was letting go, but not forever. This wasn't the end. The last spark was neither a thought nor an image. It floated somewhere in between. A contraction of the self and yet a fanfare of colour and emotion: maternal love, the airless office, the vast expanse of the plantation.

1

The Carson Motion Picture newsreel plays in the movie theatre in Detroit, the flickering light intermittently illuminating the audience, most of whom are waiting patiently for the main feature to begin. In grainy footage the Brazilian settlement shifts on a yellowing screen of cotton muslin. The camera pans, from a vantage point above the bunkhouses, across the corrugated roofs and dusty roads. In the distance, beyond the park and its tall, fluttering palm trees, is the municipal hall, the hospital and the row of stores. Labourers walk along Main Street, machetes swinging beside their loose linen trousers. The sweeping movement of the camera slows to a stop as the jungle creeps into view. The voice is calm and authoritative, a Midwestern burr wrapping itself around the listener. 'The settlement was Sinclair Carson's own idea, and his plan was simple: to carve out a vast rubber plantation in the Amazon for the tyres, piping and seals required by the automobile industry; an industry which in the United States is now churning out over six thousand motor cars a day.'

The image switches to the head and shoulders of a young woman standing beside an orange tree. Behind her is one of

3

the clapboard bungalows for the Michigan managers and their families. She stares at us, or rather slightly to the side. She has a smooth, oval face and dark eyes. Sunglasses are perched above her brow and she is squinting a little. A hand goes up to shade her eyes, but it only remains there for a second or two as though she's immediately instructed to lower it. 'With other raw materials under his control, it was only latex which eluded him, but not any more. Now, with Brazil's full co-operation, Mr Sinclair Carson has his very own township in the heart of the Amazon jungle, and our dependence on rubber from British and Dutch plantations in South-East Asia will soon be history.'

The woman's oval face expands until it is almost filling the screen. She is smiling, but it's a mildly impatient gaze. She's quite young, more a girl than a woman. Her skin is clear, her hair short and blonde. No matter how hard she smiles, her almond-shaped eyes are sad and glisten like reflected teardrops above her freckled cheeks, the result of a hard-bitten childhood or a broken heart. The camera lingers for several seconds, the cinematographer dwelling on her prettiness. The next shot shows a man. His skin is pale in comparison to the woman's. He's much older, somewhere in his late thirties, and wearing a collar and tie, but he's unshaven and his brow is damp with sweat. His thinning hair is lank and dark. Unlike the woman we assume to be his young wife, he is standing in the shadow of the bungalow and ignores the camera. He's not happy, but neither is he angry. He refuses to look into the camera and you sense that he's impatient for the shoot to finish.

'His men from Southfield and Granite Mountain manage the plant. Brazilian workers help to keep it running, and tap the trees for their latex. Yet this isn't just a factory or a business opportunity he has created alongside one of the most famous rivers in the world. No, it is an idea he is exporting. Carsonville is a settlement unlike any other, a plantation created to feed a different kind of hunger.'

4

The next shot of the young woman shows her at full length. She is wearing a simple cotton dress with horizontal grey lines. The dress is tight around her waist and her head is bowed, as though the sun is still troubling her eyes. The slight mound of her abdomen posits the idea that she's pregnant. The girl turns to the camera and slowly moves towards us, still staring calmly into the lens.

In amongst the movie audience is Vernon Miller. At just over six foot he sits slouched in his seat, a cowlick of blond hair, a square jaw which, at thirty-nine, is beginning to turn jowly. Like most Carson employees, he watches the familiar story unfold with a mix of satisfaction and disquiet, though unbeknown to him his fate is being fixed three thousand miles away.

While Miller scratches at the stubble on his chin, the blood of a fellow agent drips between the floorboards. It is the plantation in full swing. This is where Leavis has gone, where coincidentally his corpse is being dragged out of the room. The short, coppery hair smears a semi-circle of scarlet lines across the wooden floor. Miller shifts in his seat. The people are smiling, or industrious, moving briskly, striding over furrowed earth, pointing at saplings, the jungle, the sawmill. The reel is selling a vision. Cost and competition has driven its creation, but there is something more behind the idea, a zealous force which lies hidden. Miller idly wonders how Leavis is coping with the insects in Brazil just as his lifeless body slumps forward, folding over itself like a discarded puppet. A freckled hand hangs down off the porch. Rain cleanses the fingers, droplets of translucent pink falling into blackness.

2

Earlier the same evening rain had started to fall in Carsonville. Thick charcoal-coloured clouds had tumbled through the dusk, bringing with them a premature darkness. Heavy rain and a hushed stillness in the trees; the squawking of birds and the howling of monkeys in the jungle having ceased as if in accord, as though holding their breath in anticipation of what was about to happen.

On Cherry Drive Frank Leavis, his face almost feminine in its untested delicacy, stood under a covered porch and, with arms outstretched, shook droplets from his coat. He hadn't been in Carsonville long enough to appreciate the relative quietness of the evening. Instead, he softly cursed the tropical rain and rapped his knuckles impatiently on the frame. Behind the fly screen the bungalow's door was ajar and a dim light, as though from a candle, lit the polished floor. Leavis called out again. At his back, water was beginning to pour off the roof like shattered glass. He inched closer to the door. 'Can I step inside for a minute?'

A woman shuffled towards the screen. 'We don't let in anyone after dark.' Her face was hidden, but he sensed her resentment at having been disturbed.

7

'It's not yet five, and this is an official visit.' The voice was soft, almost whining.

'Sullivan sent you?'

'I'm with the Sociological Department. Here to see Mr Sam Halliday.'

'The socio-what?'

'I just need to ask you a few questions. Make sure everything's OK.'

There was a pause. 'Dr Masterson know you're calling?'

'Yes, he does,' came the reply, a little louder on account of the rain.

Through the screen door Estelle looked the stranger up and down. He wasn't tall, yet he stood straighter than most men, particularly those who'd become bowed beneath the tropical heat and constant irritations found in the Amazon.

'It's just a short survey, that's all,' prompted Leavis. His manner was calm, unaggressive. He smiled his practised, plaintive smile.

Estelle paused again, as though weighing up the consequences of sending him away. 'We got company,' she hollered over her shoulder. 'You better be sitting.' Trying to disguise her unwillingness, she pushed open the screen door and tilted her head, motioning him to enter. 'Might want to hang your coat on the hook. We don't want it dripping all over the rug.'

Leavis, suave and smiling, did as he was told while his eyes adjusted to the gloom inside. He took out his notebook and fountain pen. 'I was just going to bed,' said Estelle. 'Sam, I'll switch on the lamp.'

'I didn't realise people retired so early. We're on Detroit time here, aren't we?'

Estelle nodded. 'I just like to read, and the more you're covered up, less chance of them bugs taking a bite. You new, ain't you?'

'Yes, I am. All the way from Southfield, to help as best I can.'

'Well, not everyone goes so early, but when it rains there's precious little to do. You just hope it's eased off before dawn.' She straightened up from the lamp, the light catching her short blonde hair as she did so, and stepped in front of Halliday. Leavis expected him to tell her to stand aside so he could see their visitor, but he remained silent while she continued to talk. Her wary tone had made her sound older than she was, but now Leavis saw that the woman had barely stepped out of childhood. Hanging from her slender shoulders was a worn-out dressing gown, tied low at her waist and held by one hand tight across her heavy breasts. There was something rudely wholesome about her, though in the lamplight her oval face betrayed a measure of suffering he'd only ever seen in women twice her age. 'Now what is it you want?' Estelle asked. 'Have you really been sent here to help?'

'My name's Frank Leavis.'

'You've already said.' She swapped hands across her chest to allow her right to be shaken, but otherwise showing no inclination to put her visitor at ease. 'What is it you want?'

'They're just questions I have to ask all employees from Michigan. Mr Carson's keen to avoid the kind of labour unrest we've had in the past.'

'You mean like the riot they had here or back in—'

'Take a seat,' interrupted Halliday in a slow drawl.

'My,' said Estelle, turning round, 'aren't you talkative tonight.'

Leavis sat down facing the couple, daintily lifting his damp slacks an inch higher on his thighs. Between them was a small, low table with a copy of *The Phantom Detective* and a label-less bottle with a tumbler beside it. The girl said something about the drink being medicinal yet he knew enough to know it was cachaça; had smelt it on her breath as he'd brushed past her.

Suddenly conscious of how she was eclipsing Halliday, Estelle moved to the side. As her shadow fell away from the man behind, Leavis saw enough to know that there was something wrong with him. His face was deathly pale and he sat slumped in such a way that he appeared almost corpse-like. The man was

9

thirty-one according to the records, yet he appeared to be in his fifties. Before calling, Leavis had gone over what few papers they had on him and, as he'd suspected, little of what he was seeing made any sense. The drink alone was enough for a serious reprimand, if not to send them packing. And as for the girl, well, the fact that he hadn't seen anything referring to a Mrs Halliday put her in a very vulnerable position. He had his official line of questioning, but he thought it might be worth teasing out one or two stories while he tried to ascertain their true status.

The agent studied the man sitting in his grubby overalls. He was staring straight ahead, rather than at Leavis, and what hair he had left on his narrow head was dark and thinning. Estelle saw Leavis looking and moved the standing lamp away from the chair. Even in the shadow, though, the agent couldn't get over the paleness of the foreman's skin. It was his understanding that Halliday was one of the men in charge of cultivating the rubber trees and therefore must have been spending most of his time outdoors, and yet in comparison to the girl he looked as white as chalk.

'Are you ill, Mr Halliday?'

'My husband's as good as he's goin' to get.'

'You look washed out. Dead beat.'

'Happens with the shift,' said Estelle. 'You've spoken to Masterson, haven't you?'

'Yes,' replied Leavis, though he thought it wise not to elaborate.

'Well, he's been doin' the shift for the last month or so. Doctor says he can stay in the house. I mean, that's why you're here, isn't it?'

Leavis nodded, simply to put her at her ease. In the distance thunder rolled across the treetops. Neither paid it any heed. He thought he knew what kind of a girl he was dealing with: the sort who started out with a surly politeness, became irreverent and hot-tempered in the blink of an eye, and ended up sullen and unfriendly. Yet he couldn't quite fathom her husband, if that was what he was. While Leavis had been talking she'd been gazing

10

unsteadily at his bow tie. Outside the rain was driving hard into mud and in the distance thunder rumbled again as if the night sky itself was cursing the swollen land.

'You like the bow tie?' asked Leavis.

'It's all right, I guess.' The pastel print looked strange on a man, but she wasn't drunk enough to say it. Instead she made some loose comment about how the rust in it matched his hair, then she shivered, despite the warmth, and tried again to talk like a grown-up. 'When you say unrest, you mean here?'

'Here and at the factory in Ferndale. We certainly don't want a repeat of the riot. They're questions which will give Southfield some indication of how things need to improve if this is to succeed.'

'Well, we've been here less than a year. You should talk to Bell. He's been here since the start.'

'And Bell works . . .?'

'At the payroll office. Lives just up Riverside with his wife and kids.'

Leavis made a note of the name to satisfy her. 'I'll be speaking to everyone over the next month or so.'

'Including the blacks and those Indians they have working out in the fields?'

The scratching of the nib stopped and the agent looked up. 'As many as possible.'

'Indians are fit only for a sideshow – everyone says so – you won't get much sense out of them. Say, what are you writing?'

'Just a reminder about Bell.'

'Least that's what Sam says. I ain't never had no trouble with them.'

He closed his notebook, though the tip of a finger kept his place. The girl was sitting forward in her chair. Her dressing gown had fallen loose across her frayed nightdress, which lay taut over her swollen belly. The sight of it made Leavis uneasy. Despite the rain, it was unbearably warm in the house. The heat had pooled during the day, the metal roof turning the bungalow into an oven. There was a smell as well, something lurking beneath the cheap

11

perfume. The stench of garbage, or rotting meat. Halliday sat motionless, his dark hair plastered across his forehead.

'This isn't going to take long, is it?' she asked.

'No more than five minutes.'

'And it's not about rubber production? I don't know a thing about how much they're supposed to be producing.'

'No, Mrs Halliday.' The girl seemed pleased to be addressed as such. 'This has nothing to do with the amount of rubber being produced. Perhaps I should explain. As I'm sure you're aware, Mr Carson's ambition is to create a harmonious settlement for all employees. We're here not only to export rubber but to create an irradiating centre of civilisation in this neglected corner of the Americas, to set an example to the natives and to harness, in as efficient a manner as possible, what natural assets the land and people possess.'

'Those are high-faluting words.'

'No different to the sentiment your husband's heard a dozen times before.' The agent looked at Halliday, but the man still didn't say anything, nor had he even looked at the agent.

'And I'm guessing you haven't spoken to anybody else.'

'I thought I'd start with the botanists this afternoon, then those at the powerhouse, sanitation, sawmill . . .'

'Then why Sam?'

'He's involved in the planting.'

'Not any more. Masterson should have told you that.' Estelle looked a little confused. 'You say you're here to help?'

'That's right.'

'And how you figuring on doing that?'

'Well, one of Southfield's biggest concerns is the number of labourers we're losing.'

'You mean dying or getting sick?'

'No, not exactly.' Leavis reopened his notebook. 'Last year was better than the year before, but we're still finding it hard to keep men.'

'We ain't planning on going nowhere, I can tell you that,

12

though the heat and the bugs don't exactly make it a delight. And the Indians don't like work, that's the short of it. They're lazy, most of them, or sick. And then there's the shift, of course. It frightens them. Then there are all kinds of crazy stories.'

'Like what?'

'Just stories. You know Masterson doesn't like us talking too much. These Brazilians aren't company men. They must have explained that to you.' Estelle poured herself another drink. She'd forgotten how fine it was to talk to someone who wanted to listen. 'Do you want one? I can get you a glass.'

'No, thanks.' Leavis was gratified to see her relaxing. 'From what I've heard it sounds like some silly superstitions are taking hold. There's nothing you can think of that perhaps could bring them round to our way of thinking, help to develop a sense of belonging?'

'*Companhia Carson* don't mean much out here, other than a free hospital and a roof over their heads. Money don't mean much neither, unless they're buying cane alcohol.'

Leavis nodded as though he sympathised with the girl sitting in front of him. 'And the men and their families from Michigan, they still see themselves as part of the Carson family?'

'As much as they ever did, though some find it harder than others. Folk here are dying all the time. If it ain't fever it's snakes or spiders, and then there are things in the river that make swimming as dangerous as flying. Bloodthirsty fish, Sam used to call them.'

'There's the pool,' said Halliday, as though emerging from some sort of reverie at the mention of his name. 'We like the pool,' he slurred. Leavis glanced again at the cadaverous figure slumped in the chair; he was either ill or some sort of dope fiend.

'One for us, and one for those whose skin ain't as lily-white,' Estelle explained. 'I don't want you to think we ain't civilised.'

'And you've been here for how long?'

'I said, less than a year.'

'Can you be more specific?'

13

She turned towards Halliday, more from habit than expectation. He didn't seem to be inclined to speak. 'It was last June,' said Estelle. 'A rotten time to arrive, though better than those winters back in Chicago. Saying that, this summer's something else, what with the heat and the rain and neighbours becoming delirious and shooting off about all kinds of crap.'

'Before you arrived you worked in Chicago?'

'He did.'

'I'd like Mr Halliday to tell me in his own words.'

'Yeah,' he replied, though the word was grunted rather than spoken.

'Ain't there a file up in Sullivan's office?' asked Estelle.

'There may be, but this is for my records. It makes my job easier if you just confirm what I need.' Leavis sensed a growing uneasiness but continued with the questions which had been agreed upon back in Southfield. Part of the reason why he'd been sent to Carsonville was to root out any irregularities. In the few days he'd been on the plantation he'd come to suspect there was some sort of scam being perpetrated, though he wasn't sure how far it stretched. 'What was your address in Chicago?'

'216 Oakfield Avenue.'

'A fancy neighbourhood?'

'Apartment 27. It wasn't that fancy.'

'And how long did you live there?'

'Say, is this about here or what we did back in Chicago?' asked Estelle.

'Believe me,' said Leavis, 'this is just a formality.' Perhaps he should have waited a little longer before launching into his enquiry, but now there was no going back. 'You ever lived in Texas?'

'Ain't never been anywhere else, till we come here.'

'It's just you sound more the southern belle than anything.'

'What you saying? That I don't know where I'm from?' The girl was wary now. There was the feeling he was out to trip her up.

The agent shrugged. 'Where did Sam work before he came here?'

14

'Grant Park, Chicago.'

The answer was too slick, the city superfluous. 'You know most of those working in the fields are engineers. Carson figures engineers are bright enough to plant a few rubber trees.'

She wasn't saying anything.

'Where did you meet Halliday?'

'That's none of your business.'

'How long have you been married?'

No answer.

'Are you married?'

'Of course we're married!' There was too much righteous indignation for her outburst to be anything other than phoney. 'Now if you ain't here to help me, if you're not asking me about how the crawlies make me cuss, or what it takes to survive in this godforsaken place, then I suggest you leave.'

He briefly regarded the girl with ill-disguised disdain before asking Halliday what exactly his work entailed.

'You know he can't answer questions like that.'

'What do you mean?' asked Leavis.

'You've spoken to Masterson, ain't you?'

'I met him briefly and he checked me over. A courtesy I believe he extends to all new arrivals.'

Estelle kept her face composed as best she could, but her eyes seemed to flare with anger and alarm. 'Then you know nothing about what's been happening?' In a drunken act of realisation she slapped her forehead with the heel of her hand and kept it there until she started shaking her head. 'You haven't been sent by Masterson, have you?' It was an accusation, more than a question.

'No. As I've told you, I'm here to find out why we're losing men, but I also want to make sure that those who are employed are here legitimately. At the moment all I can see is a man who's not fit to work, let alone care for his wife, if that's what you are.' Leavis looked pointedly at Estelle. 'Is it drugs? Is that what he's taken? Is it heroin?'

15

'It ain't drugs,' she snapped.

'You want to tell me the truth?'

The girl glowered back at him. He assumed that she'd been taken in by his boyish looks; had thought she could fool him, even entertain him with a fluttering of her eyelashes. An Eagle Scout doing a man's job was how they perceived him, but he knew he was twice as hard as Miller. Other agents were susceptible to their charms, but not Leavis.

'Well, child, are you going to answer me? Why don't we start with the easy stuff? You have a marriage licence, any sort of paperwork? Because I tell you, there's precious little in Sam's folder.'

Estelle angrily pulled her dressing gown over her exposed knee and stood up. On her face was the look of one whose trust had been abused too many times by all sorts of men. 'I'll give you what you're looking for,' she said before shuffling purposefully into the bedroom, her scarlet slippers making a soft hushing sound over the wooden boards.

Leavis quietly rose up from his chair and took the opportunity her departure offered to have a better look at Halliday. Further checks would be required to ascertain whether any of Halliday's credentials were in order. It wouldn't surprise him if he was wanted in at least one State. 'Mr Halliday,' Leavis said, then repeated his name. In response he turned his head slightly, but remained gazing into space. The rubber plantation had yet to come close to matching its predicted output and suspicion had fallen on those in charge of planting. Whether or not they were suitably qualified to carry out the work was one of the things he'd been sent to investigate. Looking at Halliday, it seemed to Leavis that he wasn't qualified to do anything.

From the bedroom there came the faintest rasp of a drawer being opened, but the agent wasn't listening. There was something wrong with Halliday's eyes, the irises so pale it was hard to detect any colour. Was he blinking? Leavis snapped his fingers in front of Halliday's face. Nothing. An insect, which must have been lodged behind his ear, fell to the floor and beetled its way beneath the cane chair.

He took hold of the wooden lamp stand and leaned the shade towards Halliday. The man in the chair squirmed away from the light. Leavis caught the stench of spoilt liver, saw the puckered face and its reaction to the lamp: his skin was lime-white, his lips gnarled and twisted, his unblinking eyes dulled, gelid and sunk in his head. His wasting flesh was anaemic, an incurable type of anaemic and fatal looking. This was no white-knuckle drunk or dope addict, but a man who was seriously ill. A fly landed on Halliday's bottom lip and sauntered in and out of his gaping mouth. It was a sorry, repellent sight: a man so absent from the world that he was no longer capable of reacting to anything.

Leavis straightened up at the sound of Estelle returning. Her hips swayed a little with her languid shuffle. There was a yellow square floating in front of her: a nicotine-stained pillow. She was holding it folded over her right fist. He'd been about to share his thoughts concerning her husband, but the sight of it folded like that made him forget what he was going to say. Her face was fixed, her dressing gown hanging open. In her lowest voice she whispered viciously, 'You get away from him.'

Leavis saw the pillow thrust out, saw her cleavage, made manifest by her pregnancy and almost monstrous in one so young. As she stepped forward she looked up at him between her thick lashes. He moved away from Halliday and then winced instinctively. Her hidden hand was only inches from his chest when the irresistible urge to squeeze the trigger, to punish the cowering man in front of her, overcame what little self-restraint was left. Ever so lightly she squeezed, just the lightest of touches, and a searing hole blew through the greasy cotton. The thunderous retort reverberated in the living room and between narrowed eyelids she saw the agent thrown back over the cane chair. His red hair and freckled cheek falling hard against the wooden floor; the deafening thump of the Colt 45 almost

17

instantaneously followed by the dull, wet thud of flesh against floorboard. Grim satisfaction and horror was beating through her veins as she glanced over her shoulder. Halliday was sitting as though nothing had happened. Her lips were trembling, but she managed to smile. 'You know I had to,' she said before turning back to the corpse, the fingers of which were drumming on the boards as though death was still busy wringing out the last drops of life. In her nose was the acrid smell of gunpowder while small grey feathers floated in front of her. They were settling on the agent's blood-soaked shirt, sticking to it and turning crimson.

Estelle couldn't stop herself from flinching at the sight of what she'd done, yet she couldn't afford to be afraid. Her face turned ugly as she grimaced, a brashness which belied her waning courage. She told herself again that she had to do it, that she should have listened to what he'd said, that they should never have allowed themselves to be filmed. Estelle knelt down at Sam's feet and pressed her shoulder hard against his shins. She began to bawl like a child; snivelling, wailing and sobbing with such abandonment she felt as if she was losing her mind all over again.

3

The following morning Vernon Miller sat smoking at his desk in Southfield. He was reading a report by a floor supervisor at one of the factories owned by Carson Industries and trying to ascertain whether there was any suggestion of an unspoken grievance or political allegiance, something which might have unconsciously surfaced in the carbon copy delivered to the Sociological Department. Glancing up from the lines crippled by misspellings, Miller caught sight of himself in the office window, the hunched shoulders, the crooked elbows, the smouldering cigarette. He couldn't make out the faint creases at the corner of his mouth, but he knew they were there. They'd always been there when he smiled, but he'd recently noticed that now they stayed there when his face was relaxed. In the pane was the portrait of a man slowly drowning, though he knew he lacked the habitual gloom of the depressive. Life dealt you one hand and you had no choice but to sit in. Through the light blue tobacco smoke he gazed at his cold reflection; a shrewd, open look which was as contradictory as his bluff yet affable manner.

He thought back to the newsreel he'd caught at the movie theatre the day before. In some ways Miller envied Leavis his assignment. He knew Carsonville was a sociological experiment almost as much as an industrial one, the intention being not only to cultivate rubber but the rubber gatherers as well. 'This project is a work of civilisation,' the voiceover had said, echoing his own impression of what Carson – rightly or wrongly – was trying to create. 'This town, on the edge of nowhere, needs to have the traditional essentials for health and happiness. Flower gardens and square dancing.' Yet Miller found it hard to champion the vast rubber plantation. Was it because Harvey Firestone was enjoying more success in Liberia with half the land, or did he know, in the pit of his stomach, that there was something not quite right with Carson's scheme? All through little Miss Fay Wray's performance his mind had been troubled by what he'd seen. Why he'd felt uneasy he couldn't say and he'd had no inkling that, as he'd been staring at the grainy pictures, his friend Leavis had been shot. No, he couldn't put into words what it was that had stirred his own misgivings. Perhaps it was seeing the plantation on the screen and knowing what false dreams movies peddle. He'd found himself wondering what lay behind the fixed smiles, the nervous grins on the faces outside the hospital, the thoughts which must have been passing through the young woman's mind as she laughed at herself in loose derision while her husband stood hiding in the shadows. The man in particular had bothered him. It wasn't just the reluctance to be filmed, which he could understand, but the way he'd endured it.

There was something which struck him as dishonest about the vision Carson was selling, and Miller was tired of lies. Lies were what he had to deal with every day, from the manager massaging production figures to the dope-brained clerk batting his eyes and coughing the dry addict's cough politely into his palm. Deception was his speciality and had been since he'd moved to Detroit to study experimental psychology, though he'd only really become something of an expert after he'd married Dolores. Before Dolores and the war he'd believed in truth and beauty, but his experiences in

France and his subsequent homecoming had closed his heart to men and women. Within six weeks his wife had run off into the arms of a man Miller had never liked; a change of life so swift he could only assume the blueprint had been agreed upon whilst he'd been away serving his country.

To make it easy for her and their daughter he'd moved out of their apartment and had graduated from bar to morphine den in under a month. A year best forgotten, and another to get back on track; costing him a large chunk of his raw optimism and crushing most of the dreams he'd been foolish enough to share. When Dolores finally left for Florida she took with her not only their daughter but also what he'd always assumed was going to be his best shot at happiness. He wanted to write to her, but she'd warned him against it; and only birthday and Christmas cards were ever acknowledged by Dolores. Yet recently Jessica had started to write to him. A bitter-sweet reminder of what he'd lost. In her last letter she'd enclosed a photograph of herself out on the lawn: socks round her ankles, skinny legs, long wavy hair, grinning just like her mother. A woman Miller could never quite get out of his mind.

4

The discovery of Leavis's body caused some consternation within the administrative offices on the plantation and quickly overtook the collapse of one of Detroit's largest banks as the topic of conversation. For once the talk in the canteen had nothing to do with the outside world and the labourers spoke almost in accord. In the humid, fluttering darkness there had been fights before, drunken brawls outside bunkhouses or in the straw-roofed bordellos which had sprung up along the river. Even after the riot in 1932, the death of a peon, as the Americans called the native worker, wasn't that uncommon, though no one from Michigan had ever grieved over what was for them no more than a rough copy of a man. They may have built the industrial arteries of the south with their canals and railroads, but the managers at Carsonville were always keen to stress in their reports that drinking and fighting was to the Brazilian labourer like breathing in and out. No, the murder of a peon wasn't uncommon, but the death of an agent sent from Southfield was another matter altogether. And though the agent had had his queer ways about him, he'd been generally liked and even admired by a few for what he was trying to do. For Leavis to have been savaged in such a horrific fashion was hard to comprehend.

Under the seven-watt lights in the compound's clubhouse three men in open-necked shirts sat quietly playing cards. On a brightly lit service hatch, behind the polished wooden counter, there was the occasional soft clatter of a plate as a dark hand landed a steak dinner. Managers preferred the clubhouse to the canteen. They could eat for free in the canteen, but only in the clubhouse could they be guaranteed the choicest cuts, the unfaltering deference they expected. On the counter there was the coffee machine, toaster, covered cakes and pies, a paper-napkin holder; paraphernalia which comforted the men by merely being. In the canteen they served stringy stews and cold, damp doughnuts. In the clubhouse there was the glimpse of home, the warm and salty, the pink and blood-oozing, the sugary-slick taste of Michigan. But of the three playing cards only Tom Pinion, the curly-haired engineer-cum-botanist, had eaten in the clubhouse that night. The other two had waited patiently for him to finish. There had been little merriment that evening. It wasn't in their nature to grieve openly for any fellow, yet the hushed tones in which they spoke signalled a conscious effort on their part not to appear too callous as they, like countless others in English and Portuguese, went over the finer points of the gruesome discovery of Leavis's body.

'Shocking,' said Curtis Bell, the largest of the three, in sorrowful judgement. 'And God only knows what they'll make of it.' The Texan's brow glistened, and he wiped it every few minutes with a handkerchief given to him fresh every morning by his wife. Like all of Carson's managers, Bell's dark hair was cut short, though his pencil moustache, a trim black stripe at odds with his round, fleshy face, set him apart from his clean-shaven colleagues up at the counting house.

Although Bell and Garret hadn't ordered anything other than cream sodas, the table was furnished with a small plate of dried meats, nuts and savoury little pastries. This little acknowledgement of their status on the plantation flattered Bell, whose early life had been one of deprivation and hardship. His protuberant

24

eyes carefully watched the other two while his hand fed his mouth with a mechanical action. He didn't stop to chew, but kept on cramming his cheeks. Pausing between mouthfuls, he leaned forward and filled the lull in conversation with his own opinion. 'It must have been a machete,' he said solemnly. 'The agent was too trusting.'

'You think they took advantage?' asked Pinion.

'What else?' replied Bell, flicking a crumb of corn from the table. 'He shouldn't have been out after dark.'

'You didn't see what was left of him,' said Garret, a man of sinew and bone and little tact. 'It wasn't like any machete had been at him. His flesh was pulverised.' He gnawed thoughtfully on a toothpick. His front teeth, snagged and chipped, had a prominence about them which gave his face a horse-like appearance. In charge of the sanitation squad, having served as mess sergeant during the war, Garret was the plantation's sharpshooter and the nearest thing they had to a sheriff. Older than the other two, he was the authority when it came to alligator-like caimans, panthers and large snakes. It had been his job to bring back what was left to be buried.

'So what do you think happened to him?' asked Bell.

Garret lifted his head and stared back at the Texan. He knew better than anyone the dangers that lay outside the compound. 'It must have been an animal of some sort.'

'Like what, a big cat?'

'No, his flesh was all mushed up. Like it had been eaten and then spewed out. Could have been a caiman, but too far from the river to say for definite.' For the second time that week thunder rolled across the night sky and the men shook their heads almost in unison at the summer storm, as though admonishing something over which they had an element of control or responsibility.

'What was he doing out in the jungle after dark? That's what I'd like to know,' said Bell. 'And what does Sullivan say?'

'Well, he's cabled Southfield. Let them know we've found

their agent.' The end of his sentence was punctuated by a single gunshot from somewhere outside.

'That wasn't thunder, was it?' said Pinion.

'You got someone else out there shooting jaguars?' asked Bell, frowning at the hand he'd been dealt.

'Not me,' said Garret. 'Though that don't mean Ferradas ain't becoming trigger happy.'

'Shouldn't you go see what it was?'

'What was it last week?' asked Pinion.

'I told you, Ferradas thought he saw something at the end of Cherry Drive.'

'Bit early to be firing at anything, as I recall. What was it, six o'clock?' The Texan laid his cards down with the look of a man who'd given up playing. 'I mean, kids are still playing outside at that hour. A shot in the middle of the night makes sense, but before curfew . . .'

'What's your point?'

'Just don't want your man firing at any child, that's all.'

Garret looked at his watch. 'Well, it's not far off curfew now, so I'm guessing all your kids are tucked up in bed.' He lifted his Stetson from the chair beside him. The hat was a dark, tobacco brown, though the sun and the dust had tarnished much of the richness of its colour. 'If Ferradas has shot at something, he's either killed it or it's run away again. Or he's been eaten by it. Ain't nothing I can do to rectify the matter.' The sharpshooter stood up and cradled the crown of his hat between his arm and his side. 'But I'll take a look if that makes you sleep any better.' He pulled a dollar bill out of his battered wallet and threw it down on the table next to his cards.

5

When news of Frank Leavis's death was cabled to the office in Southfield, Miller was the obvious replacement. Like Leavis, there was something which set him apart from the other agents, though in manner and dress he was very different to his short, debonair friend. Miller was somewhat slovenly in appearance, elbows and knees shining on his suit and rarely clean-shaven. That he was well read often surprised those meeting him for the first time, though some men in positions senior to his own tended to think of him as a smug son of a bitch. It was also common knowledge around the offices in Southfield that he'd enjoyed some luck in the past with pool typists and waitresses and that he'd once courted a society dame a couple of years older than himself. With his candid, albeit somewhat curt, smile most people liked Miller, and he'd the enviable ability within the Sociological Department of putting people from all walks of life at ease.

It therefore didn't surprise Miller when his bald and bespectacled manager told him that he was sending him to Brazil to replace Leavis. There was little talk of anything suspicious having happened, but if it required an investigation then Miller was the ideal agent to undertake the preliminary work. It was sold to him as an adventure, a chance to escape the Michigan winter and the dull office days. Sure, Carsonville could be a hostile place, but Southfield, with its deep snow drifts and grey, washed-out streets, wasn't any place for a man like Miller.

His manager spun him a persuasive spiel and later, in his icebox of a boarding room, he couldn't stop himself from picturing a warm green paradise with brightly coloured birds and overblown flowers. Disease and deprivation were mentioned, but only as justification for the allowance which was paid to agents operating outside of the country. 'Hell,' said the manager, squeezing Miller's arm as he was wont to do, 'within six months you'll be back with enough dough to take that long vacation in Florida you're always going on about.' And it was true. He'd have enough leave owing to visit Dolores and his daughter. Brazil would be good for him. He'd maybe even write to her from Carsonville, just as he'd done in France. It was exotic and she'd like that.

6

Outside, bats were swooping through the night and the jabbering of monkeys had almost stopped. With only a candle burning, Estelle sat at her small dressing table in the semi-darkness and looked at herself in the mirror. She was seventeen and pregnant with a child she kidded herself was Halliday's. The man most took to be her husband stood silently beside her; no more than a crumbling mannequin. A breeze ruffled the curtain which lay undrawn across the window's screen. Dr Masterson had explained what would happen. It was for the good of the plantation. 'You had it coming to you,' she said to the dim face in the mirror. 'Maybe Mama was right. Maybe I am just the worst kind.' It was a voice that now always seemed to tremble before it came to the end of a sentence. 'But no more gallivanting around for you, Sammy-boy. No, sir.' She looked up at the man who stood beside her. As usual, his eyes appeared to be staring into space. Estelle took hold of his hand, which in colour reminded her of papier mâché and to the touch was stone-cold. His fingers instinctively closed round her own. 'Say something, Sammy,' she said, though her gaze had returned to her own reflection. Craning forward, she studied her young face critically.

'Bed. Window. Wall . . .' The words, slurred but still recognisable, tumbled out above her head.

Her eyes were still red from crying and there was a mosquito bite above one dark brow, but her complexion didn't seem to have suffered at all. The only make-up she had on was lipstick; a shade of crimson so dark it was almost black. She liked how it contrasted with the dirty lace on her slip.

Estelle withdrew her fingers from Halliday's hand and stood up. Putting her ear next to Sam's lips, she listened for him breathing. She held her breath and waited as she'd done countless times before. When she couldn't hold it any longer she inadvertently inhaled the putrid smell coming from his mouth. Estelle cursed his foulness. Perhaps a drop of bleach would help. Maybe later. 'Close your mouth,' she ordered. With a clunk of teeth he obeyed. Estelle went over to the bed and threw herself down upon it. She thought of telling him to undress, to come over and caress her, but she knew it wouldn't work. It was something she didn't like to dwell on. Not that he'd ever been a considerate lover. Instead she picked up the tumbler on the bedside table and, being careful not to touch it against her lips, she dabbed her tongue against the bottom of the glass. Like the child she was, she savoured the last drop of the syrupy liquor. With Papa's death and Sammy's estrangement from his daughter, it didn't need a shrink to tell her what their relationship had been built upon. Funny how, despite him being such a brutish man, he'd liked to pick dresses for her to wear and how she'd humoured him. And now he was her toy. It beats all, she thought to herself. But for how long was this to last? She rolled over and looked again at her man. He hadn't moved. His overalls were dirty. There were dark stains over the knees. She should have them washed, but what was the point? 'Hey,' she cried, 'come over here.'

He turned, his dusty boots shuffling on the wooden floor. A ponderous step and he was at the edge of her bed.

'Open your hand.' He did as he was told and she pushed the glass against his palm. 'Close it.' She watched as his fingers wrapped themselves around the tumbler. 'Tighter,' she whispered, as though afraid of her own thoughts. Estelle watched as his knuckles blanched. She saw the sinews in his forearm tighten. 'Tighter,' she said, her hands hovering over her ears. Nothing happened and she was about to repent. Perhaps he couldn't do it. Then it happened; deep in the palm, dampened by the fist. The sound of it cracking was a disappointment. He didn't flinch, though Estelle winced. 'Let it drop.' The glass fell heavy against the floor. 'Show me your hand.' He held it out to her, a few inches from her face. She held his fingers and studied the circular gash, tilting it towards the light. His palm was damp, blackened as though by an oily rag, but there was no blood. 'You need a bandage,' she said, but didn't get up from the bed.

He was hers to command, but it didn't make her happy. There was a time when it would have done. When she would have lorded it over him and would have had such wicked fun. 'God damn you!' she cursed. Her eyes were hot and moist and her feelings were all jumbled up. She started to bring his hand towards her mouth, but it stank like stagnant water. She flung it from her face. The thought of kissing it made her retch. She could still smell it. 'Go back to the door,' she cried. He was repulsive. There was nothing left of the man she'd run away with; nothing to desire or cherish or even care for. Yet there had been days and nights, all those tear-stained, liquor-ridden times, when she'd wished for him to be like what he was: docile and dumb.

7

A gentle breeze stirs the treetops and carries the trailing clouds towards the Brazilian coast. In the jungle, howler monkeys with fur flat and damp squat in restless agitation and cling with swollen fingers to clammy branches as black as night. Leaves flicker and fronds swirl and fold in the splintered moonlight. Water trips, slides and sidles down trunks, dripping from leaf to leaf, falling rhythmically to the sodden floor where tiny coronets of mud burst over scurrying beetles.

A rippling centipede begins its ascent. Insect legs crawling over the smooth grey knuckles. The cold, slender hand, an unfamiliar barrier, yields imperceptibly to the silent patter. A moth lands momentarily on a thin ankle. It turns, advances an inch towards the pale calf and then takes flight. Nothing disturbs the girl lying half submerged on her side: the mud-splattered dress, once a dark fuchsia pink, clings to the narrow chest and trails behind her back. Her bare legs are splayed as though she's tripped, arms thrown out as if marching. Flecks of ghoulish silver dapple one cheek, while the other lies hidden an inch beneath the muddy water; rainwater ripples against her teeth. No wound visible. She rests motionless, veiled in decay.

The stench of death has yet to spread. The rain has dampened all, smothered the putrefying flesh. Motionless, and yet

33

the eyes are open, staring with a vacuous viciousness. Below and above. The humid air, the stagnant water. At first only the gnats react, the invisible cloud lifting from the corpse. Then what was still begins to stir. A finger lifts and the centipede makes haste to the muddy floor. A tremor of despair passes through her frame, followed by a shivering motion, as if all the bones, muscles and nerves are readjusting themselves, and after this comes the sudden convulsion.

The girl sits bolt upright, her sodden dress spreading across her pale thighs. From one side of her distorted face mud drips like molasses onto her velvety frock. She is abnormal, detestable, putrid. An abhorrent travesty dripping in the darkness. Her black memory begins to quiver, reverberating with the sound of a gunshot fired several nights ago, and not far beyond the spiny ferns and creepers. It lifts itself up from the slime and stands as though listening to the breeze, staring into the darkness with unseeing eyes. The soles of her shoes are worn through and yet they cling to her feet. She shuffles in the mud, squelching as she readjusts her direction. Again she stands in her own silence. Then she begins to walk. She lifts her worn knees high over the undergrowth, thorns snagging her dress, scratching her legs of wax. Vines slide across her narrow frame. The girl walks on, oblivious to the vegetation that conspires against her or the endless single melody, the lullaby composed to celebrate our mortality.

In the Amazon there is no such thing as the soundless dark. In the Amazon the predator takes its nocturnal promenade.

8

Ferradas always started his patrol down at the dock. He was
a familiar sight at night, always visible with his white woolly
hair, always happy to talk about the heat, the mosquitoes, the
jungle, so long as it wasn't past curfew. Big white teeth in his
skinny black face. Mixing his rum with sugar cane juice, mixing
his Catholicism with a great deal of Macumba, or 'dumb-ass
magic' as Garret kept telling him. Folk were always happy to
see Ferradas, a watchman always willing to pray to his gods
for their protection.

He liked the sound of the inky water lapping beneath his
feet against the wooden pillars. The pier was large enough now
for the biggest of freighters that could make it this far up. He
walked across the uneven planks, away from the water tower
and towards the small jetty which ran from the end of the
dock and jutted out into the river. With his flashlight on the steps,
he descended to the narrow walkway. There were three boats
tied to its struts: two of the plantation's covered launches and
a small fishing smack which had been there for a couple of
days. The latter was filling with rainwater. He'd speak to Garret
about it, otherwise it was liable to disappear beneath the murky
river. He stood listening as the hulls bobbed up and down, the
launches rubbing themselves against the tyres which were

hanging half submerged from the wooden frame. Beyond either end of the dock the jungle had started to reclaim the river bank, and from along its muddy shoreline he could hear the soft croaking of countless frogs. Occasionally they'd fall silent. There were frog-eating snakes out there and it didn't take much imagination to figure out what was happening.

Ferradas had been taught long ago by his father that there was a snake for every creature: bird, fish, monkey, man, especially man. Anacondas big enough to kill any giant, eyes gleaming in the night, coiled round the thickest of branches. The biggest one Garret had killed had been over thirty feet long. He'd shot it three times in the head and, with the help of two other men, it had taken him half an hour to uncoil it from the tree. Sly, evil creatures, but clever. Sometimes their baleful cries could be heard at night, snakes weirdly singing to one another, or trying to entice their prey, even imitating the cry of birds. Rattlesnakes didn't bother him so much; in length they seldom exceeded a yard and there was rattlesnake serum in the hospital. No, there was only one he truly feared, more deadly than any venomous rattler or cobra. This was the pit viper, a large, thick-bodied snake with a triangular shaped head which would strike at the hands of workers as they chopped at the jungle's undergrowth. A single bite was enough to bring about a rapid death, but it would keep striking, keep attacking, biting until its venom was exhausted. It was even known to hunt men down and chase after them if they tried to get away. It was always vicious, always wanting to attack. Ferradas crossed himself as he came to the end of his reverie. He took one last drag on his cigarette and then flicked it with practised ease into the river.

For the last time he cast his flashlight over the rippling water and then started back to the warehouse of corrugated iron. It was a dusty path he'd trodden almost every night for the last three years. Through the sheds and timber yard, across the rails which followed the loggers' road out beyond the compound.

36

The brick powerhouse and sawmill were next, the latter being a huge hangar of wood and glass, over three storeys high. After the hospital, the sawmill was the largest building in Carsonville. His flashlight travelled along the fresh planks, through the dusty basement windows to the sturdy benches, the half-sunken metal disks with their fiery claws.

Ferradas looked at his watch beneath one of the arc lights at the end of the sawmill. Above him was the metal chute on which the treated timber slid down during the day to be taken to the dock or to the workshops below. There was an hour to go until curfew. In two hours he'd be back in his bunkhouse. He shouldn't linger for too long. Nobody wanted to be caught out after midnight.

9

The night Miller arrived was warm and humid and his shirt stuck to his back as he followed Olsen, Carsonville's pastor, to the bungalow he'd been allocated. He thought he might have had time to get used to the climate, but then he'd hardly walked more than thirty paces in the tropical heat. After disembarking from the ocean liner in Brazil it had taken the paddle steamer six days to make its slow, winding journey from the port of Belem up the Amazon to Santarem. From the old slaving post it had taken another two days on a canvas-covered river boat before he'd finally arrived in Carsonville. Days spent in the hammock reading Lovecraft. For over a week he'd endured, first on the Amazon and then the Tapajòs, an unbroken, monotonous landscape: the brown river, the slender brush of green, the ominous grey sky; three interminable colours which had varied little from day to day.

The first sign of civilisation had been the white water tower which stood tall, like a giant crab spider, above the few trees left standing at the dock. On the water tank was the familiar oval design in which the red slanting letters spelt out the founder's surname. Strange to see it out here in the middle of the jungle. Stranger still to have sidewalks, telegraph poles, fire hydrants and street lamps. On stepping ashore the novelty of the project had lifted Miller's spirits. It was a monumental undertaking, given where it was, and no one could fail to be impressed with the man's determination. Generations of little men had nibbled like mice at the edges of the Amazon, until Carson had set his mind to the task of building his plantation.

Once he'd dropped off his battered suitcase and had agreed with the pastor on how homely it all was he was taken down to the canteen. Olsen was a genial guide, in his early fifties with a tonsure of silver hair, and it was easy to appreciate why he'd been given the job of greeting those arriving from the States. As soon as they'd finished eating their hamburgers the pastor insisted on them visiting the clubhouse for a nightcap. Miller thought it a rather sedate affair where no liquor was served, certainly not the kind of place you'd find a manager letting off steam. The two of them chatted idly over cream sodas and the pastor did his best to introduce the new agent to other people, including a British journalist who was writing an article for the *Indian Rubber Journal*. Miller was just about to leave when Olsen's wife arrived. She was a lissom woman, the same age or possibly a little older than Olsen, with copper-coloured hair and a slender face. Lucile shook the agent's hand firmly and sat opposite.

'You speak Portuguese?' she asked, the question, following the niceties of being introduced, sounding like the prologue to a reprimand. Her husband laid his fingers gently on her bare arm.

'I'm afraid I don't,' answered Miller good-humouredly. 'I got myself a dictionary before leaving, but that's about it.'

'Well, at least you've a dictionary, which is more than most take the trouble of getting. And I guess you'll just be talking to those from the States. Am I right?' She drew hurriedly on her cigarette.

'I intend to speak to as many as I can, and that includes the Brazilians, though with a translator if necessary.'

'I'm glad to hear it. Mighty glad to hear it, because they're

40

worth talking to, aren't they?' She turned to her husband, but didn't give him time to reply. 'You know, they say that after one year in the Amazon, the Americans have learnt enough Portuguese to say "Uma cerveja" and, after two years, enough to say "Duas cervejas". How long you staying for?'

'Six months.'

'Then if you can remember one word you've done well. You know how much they pay them?'

'Forty cents a day to work in the fields, which I believe is about double the normal rate for that line of work.'

'You've done your homework. I'm impressed. But then it isn't the pay which is the problem, is it?'

'Don't tell me it's the hospital,' said Miller dryly, 'or the talk of demons roaming round in the jungle.'

'No, it's neither of those, though nobody likes taking the goddamn tablets.'

'Lucile,' said Olsen softly, 'don't use—'

'No, what they bitterly resent are the whistles, the badges, the time-clocks, the curfew. You know the cost of the badge they have to wear is deducted from their first pay cheque? Not a good start, is it?'

'Lucile, Mr Miller has only just arrived. I think it's a little early to be trying to solve the labour issue for him, don't you?'

'On the contrary,' said Miller, 'if we're stirring resentment then that's something which needs to be looked into.' He smiled warmly, which seemed to surprise her.

'You'll have to forgive Lucile,' said Olsen, 'her biggest concern is the way we're treating the peons.'

'No, that's not true. I'm as much concerned about Detroit children digging through garbage cans for food less than ten miles from Mr Carson's estate as I am about what we're doing here.'

'And I share your concern,' said Olsen. 'I sincerely do, but I really don't think now's the time.'

'How about those from Michigan living here?' asked Miller. 'You have any sympathy for them?'

'Of course I do. They're miserable, they hate the weather, the insects, their wives and family. Or if they don't hate them, they feel guilty for having dragged them down here. That's why there are so many suicides.' She squeezed her husband's hand. 'Though you do your best, don't you, honey?'

10

Ferradas had enjoyed his last cigarette for the night sitting on his favourite bench in the well-tended park. It had become his habit to sit there, have a smoke and chart the moon's progress for several minutes from the water tower to the last tree before the pier. The moon that night was full, a creamy yellow disk floating in the blackness. A lone cloud had leisurely rolled like tumbleweed beneath it, shifting in colour and for a moment making the moon look as if it was smouldering in the heat.

He sat there for a while longer than he'd intended before wandering along one of the paths which meandered through the ferns and flowers. Every so often he would stop and raise his flashlight to admire a tangerine or guava tree. The park was heavy with scent and Ferradas loved it dearly. When he finally emerged from his piece of paradise he crossed the empty street and called into the hospital for his usual cup of coffee. When he'd first started he'd been told by Dr Masterson not to worry about checking on the bunkhouse behind the hospital, which he understood to be an empty makeshift ward, and so once he'd finished his coffee he headed towards the row of stores which lined the square. The bakery, butcher's, barber shop, ice cream parlour and shoe store all had their blinds down, but the door of the general store was wide open. Ferradas was always the last customer to call and his candy bar had already been placed on the counter by the owner, an old Chinese coolie by the name of Tang. In simple Portuguese they'd swapped their life stories several times over the last couple of years. Both men had worked on the railroads in the north, though Tang had managed to save enough to buy his first store in Santarem, while the Brazilian had simply drifted south.

Yet Ferradas was nothing if not conscientious and whereas others charged with checking the outskirts of town wouldn't have bothered, the black watchman was a familiar sight at night in the modest little neighbourhood at the top of the plantation. He started towards the small clapboard bungalows which stood in neat rows on top of the hill.

A hundred yards ahead of him was Miller. With the steady glow of the street lights it was an easy walk back to his bungalow, though the agent didn't remember the jungle being so close to the road. Out of the dark wall of vegetation came a low, drawn-out groan. The noise, which sounded like the distant roar of a boat's engine, startled Miller. He lifted his eyes towards the tree line. The leaves shimmered in the tangerine light of the last lamp. Animal noises, and most probably one of those howler monkeys Olsen had mentioned. He walked a little faster towards his bungalow, which was the last but one at the end of the American compound. The dwelling beyond was empty and he was glad of the buffer between him and the jungle.

Towards the end of Cherry Drive Miller shuddered; not out of a fear for what might be lurking beyond the visible trunks, but because of something in the air, a chill or a shift of wind. Then, as he approached his door, he had the unmistakeable feeling that somebody or something was watching him from one of the windows in the empty bungalow. The warning came to his mind sharply and unexpectedly, just as the yowl of some other creature rolled pitifully through the humid night. He felt eyes staring at him as he advanced, but resisted the

44

childish impulse to pause or turn round. Olsen had told him the place was empty, but still the feeling persisted. He stared back at the window, but it was impossible to see inside. Stepping over the dahlias, he cut across the small patch of lawn. The ground was soft underfoot, and for a couple of yards it felt as though the earth's skin was slipping beneath his shoes. Under the cover of the stoop he quickly pulled back the screen and unlocked the door, the key having been in his hand since he'd left the sidewalk. He hurriedly felt for the electric switch. Miller was not the type to be easily spooked, but, with the naked bulb illuminating the living room, he couldn't stop himself from glancing from his own window to the black screens of the vacant building.

11

The plantation's whistle pierced the dawn and roused men, women and children from their troubled slumber. Outside of the compound it stirred a cacophony of cries and howls in the waking forest. Six times a day, from the top of the water tower, it signalled one man's will, his grasp of time, the mechanical tyranny of his clock: dawn, turn-to, lunch, end of lunch, the end of the working day, curfew. Time measured, like a commodity, to be bought and sold. Lives regularised and regimented by the factory whistle, a shrill, triumphant blast in the heart of the forest. The rubber tappers could hear it from seven miles away and had come to accept its dominion over man, fish and fowl.

Miller stepped out onto the path and glanced at the empty bungalow next door. In the daylight it didn't look any prettier. The garden was neglected and the paint on the sills had started to peel. The curtains were drawn behind the wire grille and spattered windows. He pictured the airless rooms inside, the dead insects littering the wooden floor in semi-darkness, desiccated in the heat, a heat growing throughout the day, slowly baking everything left within. He wasn't sure if it was the warmth of the night he'd endured or the malaria tablets he'd just taken, but he knew his thoughts were straying from the rational. With an effort he broke the window's spell and turned his back, then started down the hill to the clubhouse.

Behind him a tear-shaped rent between the sun-bleached curtains shifted less than an inch and a shadow softly closed as though the heavy fabric had folded over onto itself. The bungalow stood motionless. Occasionally a board might creak as the walls imperceptibly expanded. The timber frame was filling itself again with the jungle's heat, a humid breath it would hold deep inside itself until the sun had set and it was ready to exhale.

Forty yards or so in front of Miller a girl, with a handkerchief screwed tight around her fist, stepped over a mouldering picket fence and headed downhill, seemingly oblivious to the man behind her. Miller watched, as though hypnotised, the sway of her red polka-dot dress, the way the hem floated just above the back of her knees as she sauntered leisurely ahead. She was short and blonde and had the curves of a woman, yet the gait of someone younger. Her shoes slapped against the concrete slabs while her hips undulated rhythmically. As he passed by the bungalow from which she'd emerged his eyes ran over the overgrown garden and weather-beaten property. Several cobwebs festooned the clapboard walls, particularly where the grass licked the paint. By its appearance there'd been a half-hearted attempt to spruce up the porch, but otherwise the bungalow was sorely neglected. He looked again at the girl, out of curiosity as much as that age-old appreciation a man might have for a woman's figure. Hard to guess her age from behind, but she didn't sit easily amongst those he'd seen. The agent realised he was gaining on her, and that she must by now have been aware of him. Yet he didn't want to make her feel uncomfortable. The inhibitions of the city were still with him, and he couldn't bring himself to call out.

With the boldness of youth she glanced over her shoulder. The frown on her freckled face dissolved at the sight of Miller, as though she was relieved to see it was him following her and not somebody else. She didn't know it, but her normally hard-bitten features had momentarily softened into a look of what could easily have been mistaken for kindness. Miller was about to say something, having recognised her as the girl in the newsreel, when he saw the pastor in his white shirt and khaki shorts ascending the hill towards them. Olsen's face was pink from the climb and he was dabbing at his forehead with his handkerchief. He greeted the girl with a hearty 'Morning,' and lifted his panama an inch or two. Miller saw her nod in response, but nothing was said in reply.

'I thought I'd call for you,' the pastor was saying, 'but I see you're up.' The girl had just passed Olsen yet for some reason she briefly swivelled her head back again, the ghost of a smile on her face. 'Thought we'd have a proper breakfast at the clubhouse. Celebrate your arrival in style.' Olsen had slipped his sunglasses into his shirt pocket and was standing a yard or so in front of Miller. 'It's my treat. There's plenty of time to get familiar with the delights served up in the canteen. Mr Carson is very keen on wholesome food, but sometimes a man wants more than just oatmeal and brown rice.'

Miller smiled briefly at the pastor, but was too preoccupied with his own thoughts to take in what the man was saying.

'Good to see you're wearing your hat,' said Olsen, pointing at Miller's faded mariner's cap, 'though most tend to go for something with a wider brim, if you don't mind me saying. I'll take you to the general store. So many arrive ill-prepared for the rigours of jungle life. You like sailing?'

'I was in the Mercantile Marine before I went to college.'

'How fascinating,' the pastor replied, though his response lacked any real enthusiasm. 'You must have seen a lot of the world.'

'Not really. I was on a ship plying the Great Lakes, but I learnt a lot about men and women.'

'I imagine you did,' said Olsen, turning and ushering Miller ahead.

'You said yesterday the bungalow at the end was vacant, but I'm thinking it was once lived in?'

'Mr Pinion and his wife used to live there, but he moved to Juniper Drive. It's a pity, but we've a number of properties empty at the moment and it doesn't take long out here for them to start falling into disrepair. By the way, that was Mrs Halliday you were trailing.' He paused to gauge Miller's reaction. 'Looks young, doesn't she?'

'Little more than a child.'

'Well, don't be fooled by young Goldilocks. She's got quite a reputation, though whether deservedly so is something I couldn't say. Husband used to work up at the nursery, but a snake bit him when he was on a trip upriver.'

'He's dead?'

'No, not all of them die. When he got back he spent a week in the hospital. Estelle mourned like a coyote when it happened. Thought he must have died, the way she was carrying on. But he recovered. He's on light duties, which I guess suits him just as well. According to Mr Pinion, who's in charge of planting, he never was the model employee. Apparently he sleeps for most of the day.'

'And the girl?' asked Miller.

'She doesn't work, if that's what you mean. Keeps herself to herself. My Lucile's the nearest thing she has to a friend; one of the few wives who doesn't call her a hussy. Strange child, and best to keep away from her if you can.'

'I appreciate the warning, though I do intend to speak to everyone. Their reputation doesn't bother me.'

'Be careful when you do. Some say she's highly strung, and her pregnancy doesn't seem to have helped. Anyway, Dr Masterson's taking care of her now, what with the baby. You'll need to see him today. Just so he can give you the once-over. We're very lucky to have a physician like him here, and he's doing well treating the snake and insect bites. Before Masterson arrived we'd be burying two or three a week, excluding yellow fever and all that. Why, before Mr Leavis, and not counting Mrs Pinion's suicide, the last funeral must have been at least three months ago. No, things are getting better, that's for sure.'

12

Dr Masterson sat back behind his rosewood desk. His elbows rested on the arms of his leather chair; his fingers, the tips of which were lightly touching, formed a steeple in front of his pursed lips. His hands smelled of tobacco and formaldehyde, both of which he found equally comforting. He was relaxed, even when having to deal with such a delicate problem.

Estelle sat opposite the doctor. A piece of cotton thread was hanging from the sleeve of her scarlet dress and she wondered if she could bring her arm up to her mouth. Her front teeth tapped lightly against one another, but she hesitated. Such informality was his prerogative, not hers. He could do whatever he liked, but she was expected to behave. Above them a ceiling fan leisurely stirred the stale air. He continued to look at her. She was all too familiar with his languorous manner, though the meaning of such a word would have escaped her. Yet behind his unhurried approach and slow, deliberate way of talking was a sharp and agile mind. Estelle, poorly educated but far from dumb, recognised his ill-disguised notion of his own superiority and had recently started to wonder why he'd chosen to come to Carsonville. His framed certificates from Haiti and the Carson Hospital in Detroit meant little to her, but his smugness was easy to read and, in her world full of angry, desperate men, it had begun to trouble her. She stared at him unwaveringly, trying not to appear intimidated. He was handsome for a man in his forties, she'd grant him that: his dark hair was thick and his physique was still that of someone much younger. Masterson had yet to speak and Estelle's uneasiness was growing.

He lightly tapped his lips with his index fingers and met her gaze with a look of almost gentle reproach. Her pregnancy was an issue which needed to be resolved. 'You've decided to keep the child?'

Estelle couldn't hide her nervous smile. Walking to the hospital she'd set herself questions, and this was one she'd rightly anticipated. 'I'm not giving it up for adoption, if that's what you mean.'

'Insides felt like they were dissolving,' said Masterson, reading from his last notes, 'but no clots of blood falling from between your thighs.' He looked up at her. 'For your own safety and that of the unborn child, you will have to be admitted here, you understand?'

'When?'

'Today, or tomorrow. You'll have a room of your own on the top floor where you won't be disturbed.'

'And Sam?'

'He'll have to return to the ward.'

'You're gonna put him in the ward out back? Some are saying it ain't nothing but a crummy bunkhouse.' She could tell he was trying not to let his annoyance show, that much was clear, and not just with what she'd steeled herself to say. She'd been drinking and it was something he'd put a stop to as soon as she entered the hospital.

'He'll be looked after, and perhaps once you've given birth you'll be reunited with him, at least temporarily.'

'You expect him to last that long?'

'It's possible. We just need to take good care of him, that's all. Ever since the incident with the agent I've been thinking it's time we took Sam back.' She could see he was trying hard not to chastise her again, but he just couldn't resist. 'You know you shouldn't have spoken to anyone, and what you did was just plain stupid.'

'You agreed to me having Sam. And I told you before, I thought you'd sent him.' She was becoming defensive, but didn't want to argue.

'Well, we can't afford another mistake like that, not with the new agent already here.'

'But I wouldn't—'

Masterson lifted his hand. He didn't want to hear her excuses. It was enough for her to appreciate that he was still unhappy about what had happened. 'Can we expect you today or tomorrow?'

Estelle sighed. 'Tomorrow morning.'

'Then Halliday will return to the ward tonight after he's finished his shift.'

'If Sam's going to be here . . . under your care . . .' She struggled to find the right words. 'Is there any chance of my heading—'

'You want to leave, is that it?' Masterson tutted. 'You know how far you are from any other decent hospital?'

'I just thought it might be safer away from here.'

'Why do you say that?'

Estelle dropped her eyes. She couldn't answer him truthfully without him getting mad.

'No, it's out of the question. You and Sam are here for a reason. I mean, who else would have you?' He glanced back at his notes. 'You're now in the middle of your second trimester. The sooner we get you into a ward the better. Women out here always think they're the first, but you're not.'

Estelle nodded. It was all as she'd predicted. 'Is there anything I should be scared of?'

'If you behave, and do as I tell you, then nothing other than

53

a little bit of insomnia and leg cramps. That's about it at this stage.'

While he was talking she noticed his gaze was sliding down her shoulders. It was a look he'd given her before, and in the past she'd been flattered, but since she'd done the terrible thing her feelings had changed. She'd seen a different side to him, one which had frightened her. 'So we're done?'

'We are, if you're satisfied.' Masterson stayed in his chair as Estelle stood up. On her way to the door she turned round as though to say goodbye, but his head was down. He had her papers spread out on his desk and was adding to her notes. Only as she slipped out of the office did he lift his eyes to snatch a final glimpse of her figure.

13

The two men stood next to one another, leaning on a wooden fence separating the cemetery from the dusty road to the quay. It was a large grassy plot near the river, larger than they had initially intended as it had taken over most of what had first been planted as an orchard. For Miller the many rows of wooden crucifixes were a sobering sight, one the pastor thought he should see before he took him round the plantation.

'The Amazon's a charnel house and that's the way you have to see it.' Olsen had his sunglasses back on and was chewing on a stalk of grass, deftly moving it from one side of his mouth to the other. 'They buried nearly two hundred in the first couple of years. One of them Mr Sullivan's own child.'

'Sullivan's been in charge from the start?'

'More or less. Comes to the service with his family every Sunday. Never saw Mr Leavis, though I guess he only had that one opportunity.'

'I doubt I'll be able to make it,' said Miller, glancing at Olsen. 'At least not this week.'

'You're not a religious man?'

'Superstitious maybe, but not rightly religious. Though I appreciate how a faith can give a man strength, particularly in a place full of deadly snakes and spiders.' A toucan landed in one of the few remaining mango trees. 'Colourful birds, tropical fruit; picture-book illustration for a child, and therefore easy to be deceived is what you're saying.' Olsen didn't comment. 'How many did you say are buried here?'

'In total we now have fifty-six Americans and about three hundred Brazilians, or at least those we found. Some workers in the field just disappeared. They had trouble at first, burying them, I mean. The ground can become waterlogged and then a big cat or some other creature was digging up the bodies which were floating up. Whole place was a mess, graves turned over, corpses either uncovered or disappearing. We had a sharp-shooter called Garret stay up at nights, but whatever had been disturbing the dead was never caught.'

'What about the coffins? A big cat couldn't get inside, could it?'

'Not everybody is given a coffin. A sack is what the labourers get, tropical tramps, Garret calls them. South from the sugar plantations, north from the cocoa. Swarmed into camp at first, but now not even Roeder can supply us with natives any more.'

'Roeder?'

'An old Belgian with a bad reputation. We used to get natives from him. Not slaves, you understand. They passed a law against that, though this was the last country in the Americas to do so.'

'From what I was told in Southfield it's hard to know what constitutes a slave down here. But what should be clear to everyone is that Carson Industries can't be using any, or dealing with those who have profited from their sale.'

'Well, I wouldn't worry about Roeder. Seeds for the nursery is about all we buy from him these days.' Olsen lifted his finger and pointed to a far corner. 'What's left of Leavis is buried over there, but he got a coffin. I made sure it was a decent burial. You want to go over? The ground's pretty sodden after the rain, but if you want to . . .'

To Olsen's relief Miller shook his head. 'Where was he found?'

'Somewhere in the jungle. I couldn't say exactly. You should talk to Ferradas, he was the last to see him alive.'

'And Ferradas is?'

'One of Garret's men. Patrols the plantation.'

'Where would I find him?'

Olsen looked at his watch. 'He works late, but I shouldn't think he'd still be in his bunk, or the canteen. He might be up at the nursery with Pinion. Takes an interest in what they're growing. You'll never meet no finer coloured fellow. We'll take a walk up there if you like, or we could carry on down to the dock.'

Miller looked back up the hill. Above them a heavy brown cloud from a dirty-looking smokestack was lazily drifting across the blue sky. 'That the powerhouse?'

'Looks like they're burning the waste wood, generating electricity.'

'And where's Riverside?'

'Up on the ridge to the left, hidden behind those trees. The managers tend to live there.' Olsen plucked the stalk from his mouth. 'Fewer mosquitoes, and some say the air's not quite as humid.'

'And your house is on Riverside?'

'It is.'

'Church and state,' muttered Miller. 'Must be handy for the rich to have their father confessor nearby.'

'I don't know about that,' said Olsen. 'Cherry Drive is pretty swell. Houses there are better than on Juniper.'

'You ever hear anyone refer to that part of the compound as the Fruit Farm?'

'It's all fruit and berries beyond Union Street.'

'But there's more to it than that, isn't there?'

'Perhaps a couple of incidents, nothing more. Most people don't mean anything by it.'

Miller nodded as though he was satisfied. He leaned away from the wooden fence and straightened up. 'This way to the nursery?' he asked, gesturing with his head.

'It is,' confirmed Olsen.

'You think it might have been a snake?'

'A snake that what?'

'Had something to do with Leavis's death?'

'It's possible.'

'What kind of snake was it that bit Halliday?'

'Couldn't tell you, other than it wasn't a viper. If it had been he would have been dead within minutes. They brought him back from Roeder's place. Luckily Dr Masterson was with him.'

14

Dr Masterson sat in his laboratory with the blinds drawn against the morning sun and stared at the naked, emaciated body of the tattooed stevedore who stood before him. The man's disappearance had caused little consternation; a Paraguayan in charge of a few peons down at the dock wasn't going to be sorely missed by anyone. Masterson rested his elbows on the laboratory bench behind him while his tattooed subject remained motionless. He wasn't the first to have been sent to the doctor, but an early specimen nevertheless. The illness, if that is what it was, had reached its tertiary stage and would inevitably end with his physical collapse in a week or so. But what of that? Man, as a species, wasn't that impressive and certainly the subject he'd asked to be brought to him was a particularly poor exhibit. Men die as dogs die, or was all that about to change? Masterson viewed the man as being caught in a living death, trapped by something which was just beyond his grasp.

He'd seen a similar thing in Haiti: corpses walking, compliant to every order. Yet there they'd never lasted more than a month or two. And once the word got out that the dead were being resurrected then superstition had quickly taken hold. He'd witnessed the beheading and burning of several patients, the mob threatening anyone brave or foolish enough to try and interfere.

It was on the island that he'd lost what little sensitivity he had to suffering. There was no place for superstition or sympathy in his world; both were symptoms of a malaise that had gripped the human race for much too long. Most men were too afraid, too weak or too soft to deal with such a situation rationally. They cherished themselves far above their actual worth to risk anything and, unlike the poor specimen which stood before him, they could only be trusted to act purely out of self-interest.

'In many ways,' said Masterson, 'you've improved with age.' The balding man, his eyes half shut against what little light crept beneath the blinds, made no acknowledgement of having been addressed. 'I believe you'd rather dedicate yourself to the advancement of the human race than chase a piece of skirt or swing by the nearest bar. Correct me if I'm wrong.' Masterson extended his right hand and picked up a scalpel from the metal tray which lay on the bench. 'I mean, this modern obsession with sex is just one symptom of man's decline, wouldn't you agree?' He slid off his stool and, taking it with him, walked over to the tattooed man. 'In the cities it's everywhere: billboards, magazines, comic strips, detective novels. Blonde girls like Estelle, gyrating lasciviously everywhere you look, turning men into monkeys.' He sat looking at the man's groin. 'I mean, if those in power can't be trusted to implement censorship because they no longer have the courage necessary then it's down to men like me to act.' With his foot he moved the bucket of ice an inch or two along the floor then gently cupped the man's scrotum. Masterson deplored the stupefying effect sex had on a person. 'Official curbs are crumbling, sensuality is invading everything.' His voice was quieter as he concentrated. The puritanical and the mechanical made perfect sense. The bestial part needed to be eroded, destroyed. The possibility of reproduction was one he had to explore, even though the man's scrotal sack was probably too cold a cradle for living seed.

15

A hundred yards or so beyond the end of Juniper Drive stood a low brick building with a large stoop which extended out over several long tables. There were terracotta pots of various sizes on each table and a good scattering of dark soil. Past the nursery and abutting the jungle was a ploughed field over which ran several gravel paths. Pinion, the botanist with dark curly hair, looked up from the nearest table at the sound of Olsen's voice. His cheeks were ruddy and his nose was broad and blistered. He wiped his hand on his shirt and then greeted the two men with a firm handshake.

When Miller asked him if Ferradas was nearby, Pinion told him that he hadn't seen him that morning, but thought he might be over in the fields to the west.

'Is he likely to be there all day?' asked Miller.

'Should be. We're planting a hundred an acre over there; left to nature it'd be a paltry two or three.'

'And here?' asked Miller.

'This is where it all started, though I don't mind telling you they got a few things wrong.'

'From what I've heard you had trouble clearing the jungle, that it didn't start until the rainy season and in the end you had to resort to kerosene to burn everything.'

'Nothing to do with me,' said Pinion, 'but you're right. For the first year after they'd cleared it wasn't worth putting anything in, but in the west we're starting over again.'

'And it's going well over there?'

'Yes, it is. With the right discipline a man can plant over a hundred rubber trees in a day, same regimentation, same logic they're using in the factories in Michigan. Putting them closer together gives you an economy of time, both the planting and the harvesting. You know, in the fields to the west we already have almost a thousand acres planted.'

'I'm impressed,' said Miller. He was familiar with Carson's philosophy and the time and motion studies he'd ordered in his tyre and munitions factories. 'Though last year you produced less than two hundred tons of latex, when the target was three thousand.'

'Like I said, they had some trouble in the past, including leaf blight, white fly, various caterpillars. And we're all learning on the job, but I just know we're going to meet next year's target. In fact, if we can get more men tapping rubber trees then we might even exceed it.'

'There's talk back in Southfield of getting experts down here, that those in charge at the moment aren't really experienced enough to look after a plantation this size.' It wasn't Miller's intention to make anybody anxious, but he preferred plain speaking when he had the opportunity.

'Well, I think that'd be a mistake, and a costly one too. It takes a while to understand a place like this, and to become a proper botanist, but that's what I feel I am now, and it'd be foolish to start changing things. We need more labour, but no more chiefs.' Pinion wiped his brow with the back of his hand. 'Why don't I show you round? I'll take you through what we're doing then you can see the progress we're making.'

'OK,' said Miller. 'I guess a short tour of the place would be worthwhile.'

Pinion smiled as though grateful for the opportunity and

his enthusiasm for the plants seemed genuine enough. Beneath the shade of the stoop there were seedlings, several different rubber hybrids, but all indigenous. '*Hevea brasiliensis* is the proper name for the plant, and what we're doing here is bud grafting, trying to find a pest-resistant stock to save on all that expensive fumigation. Once they're strong enough we put them out into this field. This is where we test their sturdiness, their ability to grow.' They followed Pinion out of the shade and, for a few yards, along one of the gravel paths. Miller tilted his cap forward to shield his eyes against the sun's dazzling brightness. The field, which was striped with thin ridges of dark earth, was hemmed in by forest. Only the first line of trees was visible, rippling in the heat. Behind their twisted trunks there was an olive darkness, an ominous maze of shadow and loss.

In the middle of the field, about three hundred yards from the men, were two natives in shorts and faded shirts. They had some sort of flat barrow beside them and were busy planting seedlings. 'They always work in pairs now.'

'Why's that?' asked Miller.

'Snakes, mostly. Working alone we just seemed to lose so many men. It's the same with tapping the rubber. No one goes out into the field . . .'

As Pinion was talking Miller noticed the ragged shape of a girl behind the two Brazilians. She was half hidden by the shimmering trunk of a magnolia tree, but was staring at them from across the clearing. Her face was pale and a cream sash appeared to be tied around her waist, but the rest of her was lost in the forest's shade. Should she be playing on the edge of the forest? Not that she was moving. He couldn't quite see her eyes, scoured out by a shadow that floated across her face, but he knew the girl was looking back at him. He squinted, but couldn't make out her expression, the nothingness adding to her strangeness. When Pinion had finished, Miller pointed to the girl, but as they looked towards the tree she seemed to merge with the blossom, as though by taking a step or two to the left she'd regained her invisibility.

'Was she an Indian?' asked Pinion.

'I can't see anyone,' said Olsen. 'You sure it was a girl?'

'Yeah,' replied Miller. He lifted his cap and rubbed his forehead with the back of his hand. 'A white girl in a pink dress.' He was sweating.

There was the impulse to go over to the magnolia tree, but Pinion's hand fell lightly on his arm. 'I can't let you go over there. Snakes tend to bask on the edge of the field.'

'Besides,' said Olsen, 'the children are all in school.'

Suddenly Miller didn't feel so well. The heat was such he felt his head was smouldering. Lifting his eyes he saw clouds like paper streamers floating above the swaying treetops, the sun beating down. The sky was bleached by the heat and the land continued to shimmer as though shallow frying.

'Let's get back under the shade,' said Pinion, taking Miller's arm.

'You got to adjust to it,' Olsen was saying softly. 'Midday is the worst time to be out. What you need is a proper panama hat. I told him that down at the general store.'

At first Miller resisted the gentle pressure. He wanted to remain on the path, gazing at the magnolia tree. He had the feeling she was still out there, her eyes fixed on his. There was something in her solitary appearance that pulled at him, siren-like. It strangely unnerved him to picture her; a sadness seemed to lurk out there, so entrenched it felt almost sinister. One of the tree's branches seemed to buckle slightly, though he couldn't say what it meant. He hesitated, waiting for the branch to stop swaying. Pinion spoke to him again, firmer than before. Whatever it was it was gone. He tried to look away. 'I could have sworn there was a girl out there.'

Olsen shook his head. 'The sway of the blossom, a monkey playing in a tree.' Miller had turned to look at him. 'I wouldn't worry about it. This place can play tricks on the mind.' They were leading him back to the stoop, Olsen speaking close to his ear, his hands grasping his arm. 'Why, when I was on the river I remember swearing blind that there was a tent on the beach. Made the pilot swing his boat towards it. Turned out to be nothing more than a boulder.'

'Are you taking the malaria tablets?' asked Pinion. 'Hallucinations aren't uncommon. Something my wife suffered from all the time.'

'I'm taking them, as prescribed.' They were sitting him down. Pinion was pouring him a glass of water from his flask. Smooth lozenges of ice tumbling quietly.

'You've never had any trouble before?'

'No. There was the war, but nothing as queer. Did Leavis?'

'I didn't hear anything if he did,' said Pinion, putting the glass into his hand. 'Did you?' he asked Olsen.

The pastor shook his head. 'How are you feeling? You went white as a sheet out there.'

'Better, thanks.' He'd felt fleetingly lightheaded, but it was already passing. The glass was cold in his hand and he watched the ice melting. There was no need for them to fuss over him.

'Of course I never spoke to the fellow,' Pinion was saying.

'Have you read any of his reports?' asked Olsen, bringing out his packet of cigarettes from his shirt pocket and offering them round.

'Only the one he cabled just after he'd arrived,' said Miller. He allowed Olsen to light his cigarette while Pinion pocketed his. 'I need to see if he left anything behind.'

'When you're feeling ready we'll head off and I'll walk with you to the municipal hall. Sullivan's secretary is your best bet if you think he might have left something.'

'Then come back and we'll talk some more,' said Pinion, 'perhaps when it's a little cooler. Talk about how we can keep our labour force, how we can get all the tappers we need.'

'That's right,' added Olsen. 'Just like Leavis would have done.'

16

Masterson sat at his desk in his office, the slow ticking of the ceiling fan accompanying the scratch of his pen. When last in New York he had met with three doctors and a professor of archaic lore and letters. The professor, a solemn, bespectacled Romanian, had given him the address of a certain Dr Ernest Skertel in Berlin. Skertel was an expert on coma patients, those who were trapped, as it were, within a living death. He was said to have considered not only the medical implications of such a stultifying state, but also the possibility of demonic possession.

In his first letter to Skertel, Masterson had introduced himself as a man of science as well as one familiar with certain primitive beliefs. The response he received, written in perfect English, was encouraging. The German doctor completely understood the opposition which could arise when science and superstition appeared to intersect. This, according to Skertel, was increasingly liable to happen as men like Masterson uncovered secrets in what he referred to as 'God's own crucible'. Scientific knowledge was expanding and it was inevitable that one day it would challenge traditional moral values. What he proposed was a synthesis of science and the black arts. He referred to the existence of demons hiding out in sparsely populated regions of the globe, and to the slavish nature of the undead which, when harnessed, could create a miraculous world. The wording was a little too fanciful for a doctor from Detroit, but otherwise there was an understanding which prompted him to write again.

This time he wanted to give the German doctor a clearer picture of what they'd discovered and how he intended to exploit the situation. He'd written a couple of paragraphs and he was satisfied with its cordial tone. Masterson praised Skertel on his English as well as the richness of the German language, the doctor having included unfamiliar words which, when dwelt upon, seemed to be perfectly apt. How like the Germans, thought Masterson, to have a word for such creatures. There was, of course, the word zombie, which he'd first heard in Haiti, but since he'd seen *White Zombie* it seemed such a tawdry word for the condition he'd uncovered.

The start of his second paragraph reintroduced what Skertel had classified as the *untermenschen*, or subhuman. Masterson had in his letter identified those suffering from photophobia to a certain extent as twilight creatures, neither dead nor alive. He knew Skertel would appreciate his desire to catalogue every detail and the unsentimental approach he was taking. As a young man the German had fought the British in East Africa and his experience had shaped his attitude towards both the living and the dead. 'One cannot,' Skertel had written, 'give up the world to those one despises, those who are weaker or burn not as brightly. We must control them and corral them. The perfect worker is a machine part.' It was uncanny how remarkably similar his outlook was to the American's. Masterson glanced again at the German's letter and began to nod in agreement. 'What the modern world needs is a machine-like man; honest, reliable, one who never seizes up or breaks down, one always willing to do the master's bidding, never fomenting dissent, never missing a day through sickness. Idle thoughts, creativity, eccentricity, such things have no value within manufacturing and must be abolished if the workers are to be dependable and unswerving in their allegiance.' Skertel's twilight creatures would strive only to meet their master's expectations, and order was what he craved, an established order as dependent upon breeding as it would be upon the re-education of others.

The German was curious about the reanimation of the *untermenschen* and their transformation into willing subjects. In his mind this was the only way to protect those destined for high office against the petty and degrading aspirations of fools and swindlers. 'Democracy,' Skertel went on, 'has unleashed the debauched and dim-witted cravings of the stinking slums and the world is in danger of losing what moral order it once had. Politicians posture in order to placate the congenital degenerates. You shout with moral and righteous indignation, but this is how the world is being run. Listen to the voice in your head. You know I'm right. Democracy has served to give them the illusion of choice, one of many distractions to keep them from realising they are only fit to serve their betters, but they are banding together and will drag us all down if we don't control them. Our wives will become whores, our sons will become brutes like them. They will join the vast dissatisfied, rebellious herd of men and women who cannot ever be trusted.'

Skertel, like Masterson, was a disciple of the evolutionary school of anthropology. Why shouldn't the slum-dwellers become twilight creatures, docile and dependable workers for the assembly lines of today, the machines of tomorrow? In certain passages Skertel sounded like an atheist, but Masterson liked to think that this was God's work, that they were finally to have dominion over the living dead. Unless it was the devil who was responsible for the transformation which he had witnessed, and somehow they had made a Faustian pact.

And Masterson wanted to find out how willing Halliday was to obey an order which went against his instinct. Once it was given would his mind be deaf to argument or persuasion, or would there be something left of his conscience? Perhaps, in the future, the brightest amongst them would be able to travel alone, to carry out an order given weeks before . . . why, they might even be able to assassinate someone, sink a battleship, bring down an aeroplane. Without compassion, or a conscience, they could kill thousands without any hesitation. They would be the workers and weapons of a new world order. They wouldn't require sleep, or food, or nourishment of any source. He felt the hairs on the back of his neck standing on end. And unlike the cowards he treated every day, you couldn't frighten the dead.

17

Sullivan's black Zephyr was parked outside the three-storey building. Out of curiosity Miller glanced in as he passed by. There was a grey raincoat on the red leather of the passenger seat, but nothing else, nothing to give him an indication of the type of man who ran the place. He mounted the stone steps of the municipal hall and asked at the counter for Sullivan's secretary. He was asked to sit down on one of the benches, while the woman dialled the plantation manager's office.

After five minutes Sullivan's secretary appeared. Mrs Shriver was a short, dark-haired woman in her early thirties. There was a tanned fleshiness about her, and her tight-fitting blouse appeared to have been chosen to accentuate her ample bosom. She listened attentively to Miller's request, her head tilted slightly to the side, then she retreated back behind the counter.

Another five minutes and she reappeared, though the smile she'd left him with had vanished. 'I'm afraid Mr Leavis's paperwork and personal belongings have all been shipped back to Southfield.' She shrugged apologetically. 'Your paths must have crossed somewhere along the East Coast.'

'When were they sent?'

'Oh, about a fortnight ago. We kept them here for a while,

but I wasn't told about your arrival until just last week. I guess the cable didn't make it to the right desk.'

Miller knew that it would take at least another week for the papers to arrive in Southfield. 'Did anyone investigate his death?'

'Walter Garret looked into it, but he had little to go on, other than Ferradas being the last to see him alive.'

'Do you know how he died?'

'There's a whole host of hows and maybes when it comes to death out here.' Her smile was back on her face but it was strained. She seemed to have been momentarily flustered by his question. 'I mean, it could have been anything. Lord knows what kind of critters you'll find outside of the compound. If you fancy playing the Texas Ranger, why don't you speak to Garret?'

'He's some sort of sheriff?'

Mrs Shriver nodded, her dark ringlets shaking. 'You could call him that. He's in charge of sanitation, which means clearing up all kinds of mess.' That didn't sound right, and Miller saw it in her expression. 'He was a sergeant in the army, and now works as a sharpshooter,' she explained. 'He shoots the wild boars that eat the seeds, and if any animal wanders into the compound Garret or one of his men deals with it.'

'But I'm right in thinking he doesn't know who or what it was killed Leavis?'

'Just because he hasn't found whatever killed your friend, doesn't mean he doesn't have any idea.' There was no smile now. She hesitated. Her eyes left his face for a second. 'Listen, Mr Miller, you've only just arrived. It's hard out here, hard enough to get through a day, let alone avoiding the horrors that lurk outside of the plantation. If you want to take this further, speak to Garret. He'll put you straight.'

18

At the tender age of seventeen, Estelle was already a connoisseur in degenerates: bigoted drunks, heroin addicts and the sexually depraved. She'd once courted their looking. And in response she'd been sly yet graceful, slothful yet able to move on her feet with a fleetness that had taken some men by surprise. Clean-limbed and weary of cheap chivalry, the girl had seen it all, done it all. They saw her as a demi-virgin and she let them believe it, played the filthy girl, even played the innocent child if it got her what she wanted. Most times, though, she'd been left for dead, until Sam Halliday had come along. In the early days he'd shown her a degree of tenderness which she'd never experienced before. Nothing but a bellyful of sin and death until he'd rescued her from herself. Yes, she'd been warned against him, had heard about the girl who'd teased his friends and then hadn't played along. The rag soaked in chloroform before they'd ganged her proper. For two days they were at it, even selling tickets on the last night to young bucks they'd normally have lynched for laying just so much as a finger on a white girl. In the past he'd go on telling these stories until he was too drunk to talk or to give her what she wanted. But he'd chosen her, and for that small mercy she tried to be grateful.

It was dark in the bedroom, just the silhouette of Sam standing at the end of her bed, or what was left of him. How helpless he looked in the ugliness of his sleep. If anything was to happen she needed a drink. She needed to forget, to pretend he was still with her, though whatever was left wasn't going back to no Texan prison farm. He'd made her promise him that much. This had been their getaway, his lying low. Running from the law and it ended up like this. And he'd shown her the revolver, taught her how to use it. And hadn't she shown the agent who he was dealing with? Hadn't she warned him? Even now she felt the cachaça rising in her throat with rage. Chrissake, he should have known she had a temper.

Masterson had warned her not to tell a living soul, but the drink had softened her way of thinking. Yet the trigger had been too easy to pull; easier than tying a shoe. Her mind suddenly flipped and she went all weak remembering that she'd actually shot him. In her head she started to scream, and it was like laughing, only it felt horrible and she was afraid she'd never stop. She lifted her glass and tried to drown the sobbing which had taken hold. The alcohol seemed to stiffen her back. She was trying to guess what Sam would have said, anything to keep her from thinking about how they had dragged his body away. It's my fault he's dead. I didn't mean to kill him. I killed him. There it started, all over again. Automatically, she made the sign of the cross.

'And all the convictions of the uninformed.' That was still rattling round in her brain, the teacher trying to belittle her in front of the class. If it wasn't her poor attendance, it was the things she said. The dried-up spinster deserved the slap she gave her. Papa was proud. But what if the teacher had meant something by it? This was what, without Halliday, she was trying to figure out. Up until a month ago it had always been his voice in her head, though she knew darn well what the other men said about her, knew what the women said about her too, which was worse. 'She's kind of nuts – got a nuts look in her eye. Spreads her thighs as easily as butter. Goes out walking at night.' She heard the voices. They didn't always speak in a language she could understand, but the sentiment was always easy to interpret. Angry, bitter, jealous voices. Why, even the scrubwomen looked at her as though she was just a piece of dirt.

Estelle, with her lubricating lips, undulating hips. Yet there was someone who didn't know her, someone who'd caught her eye. It wasn't an infatuation, just an idle curiosity. She didn't regard the new agent with anything akin to love – and yet love feeds on the unknown. In her mind's eye she sat silently watching him: posture, hands, face, noncommittal. She conjured up a meeting as she was wont to do. Her imagination was the undoing of her; her imagination was going to be her salvation.

It was dusk in her head as she climbed the steps into the general store. She became a breathless, shy girl; knowing there was nothing more destructive or more deadly. She paused to get her breath then entered with a degree of composure she thought she'd lost forever.

He was in there with two empty bottles. 'You got a couple of cold ones I can trade you for?' he asked the owner. Voice as dark and as deep as a cello.

'Sure. But it'll cost you a dime to trade.'

He heard the fly screen open and close behind him, but he chose not to turn round. Estelle stepped up to the counter. As she did so she glanced at him, took him in, and looked away. His unshaven face shocked her a little. She didn't stare at him, but she felt his eyes on her.

'How do you do,' he said.

'How do you do,' said Estelle, out loud. It would have been 'Hi' to anyone else, in any other situation. But where to take it? She didn't want to overplay it, not yet. She wasn't cheap, not in her dreams.

When he'd gone the owner, who felt sorry for her, would

75

tell her what she already knew. 'He new agent.' The new agent from Southfield. To make amends for her stupid mistake.

'He doesn't look much like an agent. Not like that other queer fellow. He looks more like a bughouser than an agent.'

'Well, he good agent. Never ask for credit.' Estelle smiled. She had Tang down to a tee.

19

Miller found Garret sitting alone in the clubhouse. He recognised him from the descriptions he'd been given: lean cowboy, Stetson resting on the table, face like a witchdoctor's rattle. Rather than walking straight up to him, Miller wandered over to the counter and ordered himself a soda. He studied the man's reflection in the mirror above the hatch. In the gloomy firelight glow of the seven-watt bulbs Garret sat there nursing his Coca-Cola, his long legs stretched out in front. Few tables were occupied and for a Saturday night the place seemed awfully quiet. In the background there was music being piped from some South American station, but rather than lifting the mood it added to the melancholy feel of the place.

Beneath heavy brows the eyes of the man in charge of sanitation followed Miller as he crossed the floor towards him.

'You're Mr Garret?'

He didn't answer at first, just kept his eyes fixed unswervingly on the face above him.

'I'm Vernon Miller, the sociological agent sent to replace Leavis.'

'You want to know what happened to him?' He spoke with less of a drawl than Miller expected.

'That, and where I might find Ferradas.'

Garret snorted. He was either amused or offended. 'You're asking the jungle janitor what I think?'

'I was told you're the nearest thing to a sheriff round here,' replied Miller calmly.

Garret tapped the leg of a chair with his boot by way of an invitation to sit. 'There's only one place he's liable to be on a Saturday evening. And that goes for just about every bachelor.'

- 'But I'm thinking you're a bachelor, yet you're here. It's not for the drink, is it?'

Garret's eyes narrowed. There was something dynamic and mean about them, which didn't fit the nonchalant manner he appeared to be cultivating. It wasn't quite a mocking look, thought Miller, more an expression of impatience mixed with contempt. 'My shift's in what,' he looked at his watch, 'less than half an hour. No chance of me going anywhere else. Soon I'll be out there, keeping you all safe in your cots.'

'I thought Ferradas was on tonight?'

'You thought wrong. He swapped shifts with someone else this morning. Besides, there's more than one shift at night.'

'So why isn't he here?'

'His kind ain't allowed. It's only white folk in the clubhouse.'

'Unless you're serving or cooking out back?'

'You know what I mean. Those are the rules. Besides, they don't serve anything stronger than soda here. Black or white, it ain't the place you come to party.'

'Then where do you go to drink?'

'You mean no one's told you?'

'I wouldn't be asking if they had.'

Garret looked like he didn't know whether to trust him. Some men put the company and its rules above all else. No such thing as brotherly feeling, no concession to the jungle or the type of man who might work in such a place.

'This isn't for any report,' Miller reassured him.

'You like a drink?'

'Is there anyone who's been at sea who doesn't?'

78

'Mercantile?'

'That's right. Sailed on the Lakes and then served in France.'

'Whereabouts in France?'

'Marne, Belleau Wood.' Miller let the names sink in. 'I read you were decorated with the Croix de Guerre. Started as a sniper, promoted in the field to sergeant. That's quite a record you've got.'

The unyielding look on Garret's face didn't change, but the agent knew he was flattered. As though satisfied with the agent's credentials, he produced a silver hip flask from under the table. He deftly poured a colourless shot into Miller's glass before topping up his own. 'Why don't we toast the boys at sea?' Their glasses clinked and the sanitation manager watched Miller above the rim of his glass. 'You like it?'

Miller's head shuddered. 'Kicks like an angry mule, I'll say that. But it's certainly not the worst I've had. It's cachaça, isn't it?'

'That's right. Know what the natives call it? *Bafo-de-tigre*, the tiger's breath. You want another?'

'Sure, why not?'

'You know, you don't look or act like an agent,' said Garret, half filling Miller's glass. 'You're too . . .' he wanted to say easy-going, but it just didn't seem right. 'You like being an agent?'

'I like finding out what makes men tick. Hearing the dreams they cherish or the argument they want to have with their maker. You know, once you get beyond their initial reserve, most people like answering questions about themselves. It's only when they've something to hide that the job becomes difficult.'

'Nothing to hide here,' said Garret, relaxing back into his chair. 'Ferradas will be at one of the whorehouses along the river. It's the same most Saturday nights. The company managed to get rid of some of them. Bought up strips of land just to tear down the shacks, but they spring up in hidden groves, or just further down the river.'

'And the married men?'

'With their wives at home. Some of the older ones come in later, sit together in silence looking bored with one another, but most just stay at home. No wife likes to see her man go off drinking on a Saturday night. You married?'

'Was once. Went to France and then had the audacity to return.'

Garret laughed derisively and his head briefly rolled backwards. He hadn't liked Leavis, though they'd hardly exchanged more than a few words, but Miller was different.

'And you've been out here since the start?'

'Just about,' answered Garret. 'I saw the snapping turtle giving you the tour earlier.'

'You mean Olsen? Yes, he showed me round. Seems a nice enough fellow.'

'He sure knows how to preach, I'll say that for him. If you don't believe in hell, all you need is to hear him speak about it. He really believes in it, the way people used to believe in it way back when. All you have to do is see his face, his voice on a Sunday when he says the word.' Garret paused, as though lost in reflection. 'You know he showed Leavis round before he disappeared?'

'What do you think might have happened to him?'

'Could have been just about anything. Jaguar or perhaps a python. You get a lot of snakes along the bank.' Garret leaned forward. 'Body may even have been in the river. Piranhas could have started it, then a caiman drags out what's left. Some people just go crazy out here. He could have just wandered off.'

'You think we'll ever know?'

'I doubt it. Seemed queer to me, anyhow. No offence, but he dressed like a man who took it up the ass. Just the way they're bred, I guess, though if it was up to me I'd string up every one of them.' Garret saw Miller's face harden. 'Want another drink?' he asked, nodding at his empty glass.

Miller shook his head. It was his job to listen, though the things they came out with were sometimes hard to stomach.

20

The girl, stumbling into a clearing, is suddenly illuminated by a shaft of moonlight. When it hits her bowed head she stops abruptly and then, after a moment, seems to uncoil. She straightens her back, an effort which gives her the appearance of a performing dog, and totters on what remains of her shoes. Her head is then thrown back, her dark hair, knotted and unkempt, falling away from her grubby velvet dress like tarred lengths of fraying cord. Patches of bluish-grey scalp, no bigger than a dime, shine in several places, though most are half-hidden beneath dark strands held by the clumps which are still attached. Her nose is in the air as though trying to pick up a scent. Around her the jungle has fallen quiet. She is an abomination and every creature above the insect world has retreated from the menacing aura of death and decay which stalks her sorry corpse.

She pirouettes amongst the dead leaves, an ugly parody of the balletic movement taught to her in Manaus. Her pink velvet chest swells a little as she sucks the air through nostrils half-clogged with clotted blood and mucus. The girl revolves more than a dozen times in the dark, her eyes closed, feet shuffling. When her spinning starts to slow she wobbles a little like a wooden top coming to rest. Her shoulders become hunched again and her head falls forward. The noise of the leaves being stirred fades into a soft whisper then disappears. The girl stands motionless, silent. Her eyelids part. Grey pupils expand invisibly in their sunken sockets. She draws the jungle into her, the shadows, the scent of night tinged with the sweat of a man. He is ahead of her. She can just hear the fall of his boots along the path. Snap, snap go her teeth. Sharp daggers of tainted ivory.

21

Ferradas had been warned the agent was looking for him. Not that it bothered the Brazilian. He'd decided he didn't know what had happened to Leavis. Easier that way. Didn't want to get anyone into trouble, didn't want to lose what he had, didn't want to be without a crib he could call his own. The moon lit the path which ran alongside the river and he followed it unswervingly. He wasn't yet too afraid of the jungle to walk alone, though he didn't feel quite as brave as he did when he was a youngster.

As a boy he'd run away from the sugar plantation on which he'd been born. By taking his chances in the swamp he'd been able to avoid the master's hounds, hiding in the branches of a tree during the day, at dusk making his way through the tepid water. Wasn't anything scary about the night back then, though the cave was something else. He'd stumbled across it in the jungle, its mouth larger than any cave he had ever seen. It was as if it was waiting to swallow the earth. He'd slept at its entrance during the night and when it was light explored as far back as he dared. Within a hundred yards it became too dark to see anything. And yet he'd felt the warm wind gently rising from the bowels of the earth, had sensed the threat of death.

Indians had found him feverish just inside its mouth and nursed him back to health. He embraced their way of life; anything was better than being a slave, being woken in the night by a sadistic master. He fervently desired to please and impressed the elders with his willingness to learn. He participated in every rite of passage deemed necessary for him to become a hunter, though he never liked returning to the cave or the ruins of the Jesuit mission nearby. Even when caught in the thrill of the chase, his feet would falter at the sight of the high limestone outcrop and its jungle canopy. The elders understood why and the young hunters would never press him to follow.

From the Jacona he'd learnt how to track the panther and to fish for the manatee, how to charm birds and monkeys out of the trees. One elder had taught him about the medicinal plants in the forest, how each snake bite required a different cure, and where each spider was liable to be found. He stayed with the tribe for three years, and would have remained for longer if his young wife hadn't died in childbirth. He knew the customs of the tribe as well as any warrior, but he couldn't let them cook and eat her flesh without putting up a fight. A week after he'd buried what was left of her he decided it was time to leave and continued south, drifting from railroads to cocoa plantations. How he came to be at the river bank when the first ship weighed anchor nobody other than Ferradas knew.

When Carsonville was being built he'd given them advice, telling the Portuguese architect where it flooded during the rainy season, and where the snakes burrowed into the earth. At first they'd left his shack undisturbed in the forest, and he watched the building of the place and shook his head. It was an opportunity to improve his home, with a zinc roof and the occasional piece of furniture, but their talk made no sense to him. Not until they bulldozed his shack, and gave him a number and a cot in the bunkhouse, did he finally understand. He grieved for a while, but then three square meals a day and the company of other men made up for a lot. There was safety in numbers and something was stirring in the jungle, something dark and malevolent.

He'd told them as much, but they'd ignored him. He was old. They'd called him a witch doctor, a dabbler in swamp magic, when they saw him wearing one of his monkey-tooth necklaces, but they didn't see his wisdom. He knew Carsonville was doomed to fail long before anyone else working on the plantation had the courage to admit it.

It wasn't far to the bunkhouse now and he'd be back before the curfew. He could hear something splashing in the water: a fish or something slightly larger. It didn't bother him too much, so long as he had the flashlight firmly in his hand.

22

When Ferradas wasn't patrolling the American compound it fell to Cecilio, a nineteen-year-old who'd left his young wife and their child in Santarem in the hope of making a better life for himself. Cecilio had no intention of following Ferradas' routine, of walking to the top of Cherry Drive and making his way back down Maple. Instead, the young night watchman went up Juniper and headed for the nursery. He always paused just beyond the last bungalow and waved his flashlight over the building. If nothing appeared he would wander across the field until he was twenty yards away from the dense wall of foliage.

Earlier in the evening Garret had told him to keep an eye out for a girl who'd been seen wandering round on the outskirts of the settlement. The American wanted her brought in alive; a skinny girl, no more than thirteen. Cecilio thought she must have come from one of the *cidades fantasmas* and was probably trying to find her way back. Funny how the tribes had been drawn to the ghost towns along the river. The nearest one, Carabas, had been abandoned shortly after the rubber boom had collapsed. In twenty years the once prosperous town had become a refuge for a tribe which had no understanding of how to maintain anything. Semi-ruinous houses stood in silent streets; vines and creepers were slowly reclaiming every inch of land which had been paved or built upon.

If she wasn't from Carabas then she'd be one of Roeder's from the abandoned mission. His mother had once told him that wild dogs, large grey brutes like wolves, haunted the place and at sunset legions of bats emerged from the crumbling church. During the day the tribe served Roeder and worked a small plantation of cane, but after dusk they would barricade themselves inside, living in perpetual fear of what lay in the cave just beyond the mission's crumbling walls. If she was an Indian from Carabas then she stood a chance of making it back, but if she had escaped from Roeder then there was nowhere else for her to go. If he saw her he'd take her to Garret, though he assumed it was Masterson who wanted her brought in alive.

Between him and the vast expanse of the jungle were now just grasses, weeds and a few dead branches. Behind him lay the ploughed field and the nursery. He was armed with an old Smith & Wesson and at this point his right hand always rested lightly on its pearl-grey handle. If he was ever to see a panther then it would be here, its eyes gleaming back at him. Last week he'd seen a jaguar, during the day, drinking down by the river, but the pelt of a black panther was worth more than any jaguar's. A panther's ferocity and strength made it more feared than any other cat. The vines and leaves glistened as though sweating in the yellow moonlight, but there were shreds of shadow which stubbornly remained in darkness. In the treetops something was moving, swinging from one branch to the next. Nothing more than a monkey, yet it took his eyes and the flashlight away from what lay ahead for the briefest of moments.

That was all it took for the creature to emerge from the jungle. In one second it wasn't there, in the next it was. It was the sudden dry rustling of leaves which alerted Cecilio to the fact that something was closing in, moving almost too rapidly for him to register its speed. He barely had time to look down, let alone bring the flashlight to bear or draw his revolver. It didn't take much to knock him to the ground, his legs having more or less given way after the glimpse he was given had swamped his mind with fear and revulsion.

In amongst the tall grass Cecilio struggled briefly against his fate. He managed to get a hand between his damp chest and the soft, slender neck of the creature and, with a strength which was soon to desert him, was able momentarily to push the thing back, lifting it an inch or two, sufficient to catch the stench of death emanating from its gaping mouth. Its face was distorted by a fixed grin of hideous intensity, but in the shadows which twisted above him he only managed to see the teeth, yellowing, ferocious teeth in blackened gums, snapping dementedly in front of his eyes.

23

Garret stood soaking up the morning's heat like a lizard. He was overseeing the removal of suitcases and wooden boxes from a house on Maple Drive, watching with half-closed eyes two labourers throwing everything out on the mottled lawn. Miller was looking for Ferradas. He wasn't in his bunkhouse and he'd failed to show up for work. 'It ain't like him to miss a shift,' said Garret, 'but don't you worry. I'll ask around.'

'You don't think he's wandered off?'

Garret frowned. 'Ferradas ain't dumb. He'll be somewhere.' The sanitation manager leaned towards Miller. 'We've a couple of young widows on the compound. Old mule like Ferradas might well be the kinda comfort a woman is aching for.'

'You think he's playing hooky?'

'Call it what you want. He's playin' summat, that's for sure.'

Miller smiled. It wasn't sincere, but Garret wasn't going to be satisfied unless the agent showed some sort of appreciation.

'See this here,' said Garret, his hand hovering over three scuffed suitcases. 'All that's left of one man's life. His widow's next door. Dabbin' her pretty eyes and waiting for us to finish clearing out their stuff. She'll be taking the boat back to Santarem, back to Michigan. A damn shame she's leaving. Legs like a racehorse and pair of bubbies I get one on just by thinking about. If she wasn't so raw, I'd tell you to go and talk to her. Let her tell you what she thinks of this here venture in the jungle.'

'What happened to her husband?'

'Some sort of fever. Happens so quickly. Two or three days and then . . . Hey, is that it?' He'd suddenly raised his voice and was addressing the two peons who were squatting down under the shade of the veranda. He turned again to Miller. 'I'm going to borrow Sullivan's Zephyr. At least she can ride out in style. You going anywhere?'

Miller brought out his notebook. 'Sam Halliday. I heard he was bitten by a snake a while back so he's on light duties now. Got his address as Cherry Drive.'

'You won't find him there. He's back in the hospital. A real pity, what with his young wife being pregnant. I'll walk you down if you like, though you're unlikely to get much out of him.'

'That's all right. I've still got some calls to do round here. I'll leave the hospital till tomorrow.'

'Might not be with us by then, but I suppose that'll be one less report to file. Who's next on your list?'

Miller flipped over a page in his notebook. 'Curtis Bell. In charge of accounting.'

24

Curtis and Leonor Bell lived with their three small children in one of the white and green Cape Cod bungalows on the edge of the American compound. They'd been there from the start and promotion had come easily, Bell's predecessor having drowned on the Tapajòs while bringing the wages back from Santarem. Officially it was said that his boat was tipped over by a storm that came out of nowhere, though rumour had it that it was a native attack, co-ordinated by white men bent on stealing the payroll.

The couple sat in their Sunday best in front of Miller. Bobby, Neil and Susan were playing outside and their squeals could be heard from the living room. Like all American families they had a maid, but she was away. It was something Leonor fretted over, in that she didn't like the children playing outside unsupervised. Bell had loosened his tie, yet otherwise he'd made few concessions to the heat. His dark, slicked-back hair and pencil moustache shone like patent leather and in his fat hand he held a large cigar, as was his custom after the service. He brought the cigar box over to Miller and made a show of his silver cigar-cutter which was clipped to his keychain.

'It's like living in a steam bath,' Leonor repeated. 'You know, those Detroit architects couldn't imagine a land without snow.'

Miller knew something about her from having spoken to Olsen and his wife. He knew that she made short little pants in the sewing circle for the children of the Indians and she had a pet monkey called Chico, which was also out on the lawn at the front. She was heavy like her husband, but her hair was fair, parted in the middle and left to fall not unbecomingly to her tanned shoulders, where it curled at the ends.

Bell held his dark crimson tie to one side and dusted cigar ash from his cream shirt. 'Other fellows think of me as an old blow hard, a grouchy son of a gun, but what kind of a darn fool thought of constructing these houses with metal roofs lined with asbestos?'

'I was told they were designed to repel the sun's rays,' said Miller.

'They do nothing of the sort. In fact they keep the heat in. By nightfall it's a galvanised oven – hotter than the gates of hell. You lie awake sweating for the first half of the night and then, when you finally stop tossing and turning, you undergo a fierce siege of heat-provoked nightmares. You know Sullivan wanted thatch? Makes perfect sense, but they wouldn't allow it, not for the houses of foremen, anyhow.'

'Have you been to the American pool?' asked Leonor.

'I haven't yet, ma'am.'

'Of course they say you get more bugs with the thatch, but hell,' continued Bell, 'these screens just keep the goddamn bugs in.'

'Language,' said his wife.

'Sorry, but it just defies logic. Are you taking the quinine pills?'

'Yes,' answered Miller.

'Any side effects?'

'Not that I'm aware of.'

'Not even a girl dancing on the edge of the forest?' asked Bell, trying to keep a straight face.

'She looked real to me, and I swear I felt her staring back, though I know it could have been the heat.'

'Hey, we all see them from time to time, secret is you mustn't take anything out here too seriously. Otherwise you start to get paranoid. Pinion's wife, for example, started imagining all sorts of things. Did they tell you back at Southfield that you'd have dope every day? If the malaria don't get you the nightmares from those pills will if you're not careful, ain't that right?' He glanced at his wife. 'You had it bad to begin with, didn't you?'

'Yeah, pretty bad,' Leonor admitted.

'Saw all kinds of weird things,' continued Bell, seemingly oblivious to his wife's discomfort. 'Demons in the shadows, children climbing out of graves, dead men hiding in the jungle.'

'Curtis,' said his wife firmly, 'I'm sure our guest has questions he needs to ask us.'

'Well, as I explained to your husband, it's just a short sociological survey.' Miller took out his pen and notebook from his jacket. 'Though housing is certainly something I can raise.'

'You do that,' said Bell, punctuating his words with a stab of his cigar.

'And if the tablets are causing problems, then again I can have someone notify the chemists back at the Carson Hospital, though I imagine Dr Masterson has already put in a report.'

'He will have done,' said Leonor. 'He's a good man.'

'However, it's morale and the number of employees we're losing that bothers Southfield. I know fewer are dying out in the fields, but we don't seem to be able to retain sufficient workers.'

'Well,' said Bell, 'I think the two things are linked – morale and how many we're retaining. Of course now we ain't just taking any tropical tramp or renegade.'

'They say in Granite Mountain he ain't employing no coloured folk,' said Leonor. 'But then people say a lot of things.'

'Don't really matter down here,' Bell said. 'As long as they're healthy, honest and dependable, that's all that really matters.

No, if they were to improve morale then I think things would get better.'

'And how might the company do just that?' asked Miller.

'Well, it's obvious, isn't it? Rubber production needs to increase. I'm sure you're not unaware of the fact. I mean, Southfield wouldn't have sent you all the way down here if things were swell, especially with what happened to the other guy.'

'You've spoken to Garret about what happened?' asked Leonor.

'Yes, I have.'

'Well, he's the expert on these things. Unexplained deaths, deadly snakes and spiders – and jazz. Do you like jazz?'

'Why do you ask?'

'Garret has one of the best collections,' declared Bell, 'probably *the* best collection of jazz records for a hundred miles or more. Blues as well, though Lord knows what they're saying. Probably best not to know.' He paused as though recollecting something amusing. 'The man will never see forty again, yet he whistles at all the girls as if he was twenty-two. One of the few sanitation men who ain't cracked like a coconut. I mean, take Ferradas . . .'

'Ferradas ain't worth talking to,' said Leonor. 'A ready enough smile, but what was all that hoodoo voodoo about?' She shook her head, her wide lips curled as though sucking a lemon.

'You know what happened last night, don't you?' asked Bell, but he didn't give Miller a chance to answer. 'One of Garret's men was found dead this morning.'

'We heard the news this morning,' Leonor cut in. 'Torn apart down by the river.'

'Ferradas found what was left of the boy. Seems whatever it was must have dragged him halfway across the plantation.'

'That's the danger when you're out there at night on your own,' added Leonor. 'But at least he discovered him before he was really messed up, unlike your friend.' She smiled apologetically.

'Could have been a snake that brought him down,' said Bell. 'You should ask Garret about them vipers. They're evil creatures, just tan stockings of pure spite. Ten times worse than any *puta* you're ever likely to meet.'

'I need to speak to Ferradas.'

Bell frowned. 'Whatever he tells you ain't gonna be much help. He's pretty shook up, and if you believe half of what he says, he's seen some pretty awful things. Used to live with some tribe, though personally I can't imagine him outside the canteen or in one of them whorehouses along the river.'

'All right, honey,' said Leonor, her voice firm enough to sound a warning. 'I think it's time we gathered up the kids, don't you?' She turned towards Miller. 'We're having lunch at the clubhouse, so we really need to be getting ready.'

'Perhaps I can come and ask you a few more questions over the next week or so?'

'Maybe next Sunday afternoon,' said Bell. 'The maid will be back by then and we might be able to rustle you up some supper or something.'

25

The canteen was filled with Americans and Brazilians, moving in slow indecision before brightly lit counters of food. A man, carrying his straw hat in the crook of his elbow, lifted a doughnut from beneath a smeared glass bowl while one of the few women hesitated over a tomato and pepper salad. Below the hamburgers, sliced ham and corn muffins the tiled floor was covered in dust from the road outside.

Miller stood towards the end of the line, picking up a dessert. He fanned himself with his blue cap and slid his tray along with his other hand. There was something like a Scandinavian firmness to his perspiring face, which didn't go unnoticed by one of the young nurses. He'd chosen meat loaf, string beans, mashed potato, chocolate ice cream. He grabbed a coffee and handed over his lunch ticket, then left the line and made his way towards the far side of the canteen.

Miller sat alone by choice, his tray squarely on the table, the used ashtray precisely in the middle. He looked up when a tray was set down heavily next to his. The old man was wearing ragged overalls washed almost white. Black forehead creased and shining, tired brown eyes, the whites a curdled yellow. On his grainy neck, just beneath his bony jaw, was a square piece of fresh bandage taped to his neck. 'You look for me?' he asked, his dry voice crawling out from the back of his throat.

'Ferradas?'

The man nodded reluctantly as though it was likely to get him into trouble.

'You want to sit down?'

This time he shook his head.

'You were the last to see Leavis alive?'

Ferradas looked at him and at first didn't say anything. He was playing dumb, pretending he didn't understand. That was the best way. Miller was conscious of the watchman's hands resting on the table, a rosebud of pink curled between thumb and finger. Ugly scratches on the pitted back, like thorns or ragged nails. The agent repeated his question. He made it sound like an accusation, something the Brazilian had to acknowledge.

'Yeah, I saw him.'

'Can you tell me what happened?'

Ferradas shrugged.

'Well, where did you last see him?'

'Cherry Drive.'

'Was he heading to a particular house?'

There was that unwillingness again.

'Listen,' said Miller, 'if you know anything which might—'

'Go,' interrupted Ferradas, though the word was softly spoken. 'Fucking go.' It was gently said, but what surprised Miller was the effort he put into the word *fucking*. Teeth right down over his lower lip, forcing the initial *f* out so that it flew. 'Fucking,' he cried, 'fucking leave. This ain't no place—'

'I'm sorry?' said Miller, now on his feet.

Ferradas looked embarrassed, even scared. 'Halliday,' he whispered. Nothing more than a whisper but enough to sap his strength, to make him silently cuss himself for talking out of turn. He shook himself free of Miller's gaze and looked round to see if anyone else had heard.

'Hey,' cried Garret. 'You know you shouldn't be over this side of the canteen?'

The watchman sank into himself and would have bolted if Miller hadn't quickly grabbed his sleeve. 'It's all right, he's just answering a few questions, that's all.'

Garret sat himself down facing the agent. 'And has he answered them all to your satisfaction?'

Miller glanced back up at Ferradas. He was leaning away from the table, almost cowering like a dog that expects a beating.

'You answered his questions just like I told you to?' asked Garret impatiently.

'Yeah, sir.'

'OK, then you go back over to your side.' Garret turned to face Miller. 'I wouldn't go paying much attention to what any of them say, though trouble always seems to be snapping at his heels. Guess you heard what he found last night?'

'Is this the boy who was killed?'

'Yeah, that's right.'

'Seems to be happening a lot recently.'

'Must be a puma, or some other big cat. Probably the same one as killed the other agent. Found what was left of him on a path along the river, out towards one of them whorehouses.' Garret started to eat. 'That reminds me,' he said, his mouth chewing, 'anyone told you yet about the Island of Innocence?'

'I can't say they have.'

Garret smiled, or at least came as close as he could to smiling. 'Nobody told you yet?' He shook his head in disbelief. 'Best place to find a real nice piece of ass, and on its own island too. Help you forget all your troubles. Drink rum without ever having to look over your shoulder, finest Portuguese wines if you can afford them. Dames are all clean and the best you'll find outside of Manaus.'

'You ever been married, Garret?'

'Was once.' He glanced up from his plate. 'You got somebody back home?'

'Not any more. She moved down to Florida.'

'This your wife you're talking about?'

'That's right. Dolores. A woman who always wanted new things.'

'That the worst thing about her?'

'No,' replied Miller, 'she used to lie to me, and you know, the funny thing was I wanted to believe her lies.'

'Olsen says when you lie to yourself, that's when the devil starts to work his way into your soul. And when you believe everyone lying 'bout everything, that's when the devil's won.'

'Well, you won't find me disagreeing with that.'

26

'I'd like to visit one of your patients,' said Miller, 'name of Sam Halliday.'

A nurse with bleached hair and a pinched face glanced up from the typewriter she'd been pecking at. 'You a friend?'

'Not really. I'm with the Sociological Department from Southfield. I just need to speak to Mr Halliday.'

'Visiting hours this afternoon are four till six. If you'd like to come back then I'll let you know if Mr Halliday wishes to speak with you.'

'I'd like to see him now, miss. It's a matter I'm authorised to deal with.'

'Well, I don't know if he's well enough to speak to you.'

'Then who would know?'

'Dr Masterson.'

'And where can I find him?' Miller's frustration had begun to creep into his voice.

'I'll get one of the orderlies to ask him.'

'I'd rather see him myself if that's possible.'

'Then I'll ask them to ask him if he can spare you a minute. If you'd like to take a seat, Mr Miller. And by the way, I believe you were asked to see Dr Masterson.' There was a pause. Olsen had reminded him, but he'd somehow forgotten. 'If you'd like to take a seat we'll see what we can do.'

The agent walked away from the panelled reception desk, acknowledging with a nod the presence of a rubber tapper who sat cradling his limp arm. The man blinked through his damp lashes and murmured something in reply. An orderly appeared and beckoned to the Brazilian to get up and follow him. They disappeared behind the swinging doors which led to the wards. Miller sat and waited for another five minutes and then rose quietly to his feet. He expected the nurse to look up but she was too busy typing out the notes, one corner of a blue carbon sheet rising between the papers.

By the time he'd pushed a door open she could only cry out in annoyance. Rather than turn into the busy corridor, Miller bounded up the staircase and turned sharply. From the floor below he heard the doors swinging open. She called again, an indignant voice which filled the stone stairwell. He waited. No one came to her aid. The doors swung back on their hinges and Miller peeped over the concrete balustrade. A sign told him he was on the floor for the Lincoln Ward. He was gripped by curiosity, by the conviction that he was better off making his own way. He wanted to find Halliday, but he also wanted to explore. Was there another ward, could he find Dr Masterson? He sprinted up the next two flights of steps. Double doors greeted him and he peered through the mottled glass. It all seemed quiet. He pushed tentatively on one of the brass plates. Not a sound. He slipped through. It was a long and narrow corridor, the dark linoleum lit by several bulbs suspended in tin shades.

He was trespassing, yet felt compelled to walk the length of it. The first room on the left was an empty ward: twenty beds and mattresses, but no sign of any of them having been slept in. He brushed a finger over the top of a dusty cabinet, took in the view of the park. There was nothing untoward about this, he reasoned; they obviously expected the population of Carsonville to grow and had planned accordingly. He went out, passed a locked door which didn't have a sign on, then stopped at the far end. Through an open door he could see into a laboratory. He glanced back to where he'd entered the corridor. It was nothing more than curiosity which drew him inside. He didn't expect to find any answers, but he was drawn nevertheless.

The laboratory was dark, oppressively warm and smelt of formaldehyde. Shelves covered the far wall. In the dim light he could just make out large clear jars in which floated all manner of peculiar specimens. He went inside to investigate. There were strange, deformed foetuses; three were monkey-like in appearance with black protruding eyes and broad, almost muscular shoulders. In one jar a large hand was suspended. At first glance there didn't appear to be anything unusual about it, other than its size, but then Miller saw what looked like claws sprouting from its knuckles. Like the hand, they were pale in colour and tapered to a point an inch or so beyond the fingertip. He tried to see it as a paw, but there was something too human about it to make any sense.

Miller stepped back from the jars and looked around the laboratory. Diagrams relating to human anatomy adorned the other walls, along with strangely coloured charts of the surrounding landscape. The windows were draped in thick purple gauze. In one dark corner something sat huddled on a battered old chair. At first he thought it was a monstrous broken doll, but then realised it was a young girl, slumped forward, her dark hair streaming over her face. It was the girl he'd seen at the edge of the forest. She was wearing the same pink dress, though beneath her chin and across her narrow shoulders were ugly brown marks as though she'd been sprayed by mud. The lace was torn and horribly stained at the neck and cuffs, and one piece was trailing across her thin hand like a viper. Around her slender waist was the yellowing sash. She sat with her chin on her flat chest, her large, lifeless eyes staring down at her tattered shoes. He tentatively brushed aside her sooty locks. Her brow was a greyish-white, her temples hollow. Her unwavering eyes continued to look down at her feet. Was she alive? Miller clicked his fingers in front of her nose. There was no response. He glanced at her shoes, at the leather soles which, having worn through at the balls of her feet, exposed both her frayed stockings and blackened skin. Miller put his ear an inch or two from her mouth and listened. There was nothing at first, then, perhaps, the slightest ingestion of air. Imperceptibly her lips began to open. Her left hand, unseen by Miller, began to lift from her thigh, the fingers spreading in readiness. The trailing piece of lace slid from her bony knuckles. He was so entranced by the girl that he was only dimly aware of the door clicking shut behind him. Only the girl responded to the sound. With the same slow, invisible movements, the hand began to descend, the mouth to relax.

'I see you're admiring Violeta,' said Masterson.

The doctor's voice, so close behind him, startled Miller, yet for some reason he fought the impulse to turn his gaze away from her. 'Is she asleep?'

'It's a catatonic state, but one I can control.'

'Her dress is—'

'Her parents were rather old-fashioned. Violeta,' snapped Masterson, 'stand!'

The girl slid almost horizontally from the chair and raised herself up. She stood there, grotesque and obscene in her short, shabby dress.

'She's obedient in this state. Doesn't hesitate to perform any task, no matter how irksome or unnatural. A dissolution of spirit is how I'd describe it.'

'How long will this last?' asked Miller while scrutinising the thin girl who swayed slightly on her feet. Her illness was there on her skin which was blanched as though it had never seen the sun, and in her eyes: a silvery blue, the faintest he'd ever seen.

106

'It's a condition we don't fully understand. It could last for another hour or another week. She's been like this since she was brought to me.'

'When was that?'

'Last night. One of the sanitation men found her wandering outside.'

'She belongs here?'

'She does, though her parents are dead. I should really have shipped her back to Michigan, but then this happened.'

'How did it happen?'

'An insect bite, perhaps. Or a snake. They seem to be the most logical explanation.'

'Are there others like this?'

'We've had one or two cases. Sadly they died before we were able to cure them.'

Miller lifted a finger to her cheek and put it against her skin. Her pale flesh was chilled to the bone and reminded him of nothing more than a cut of raw pork. She didn't respond to his touch, but continued to stare ahead. He studied her eyes, clouded by a dryness which failed to reflect even the smallest glimmer of light.

'I'd rather you didn't touch her. The flesh bruises very easily.'

'She isn't blinking,' said Miller.

'She doesn't do anything without being instructed. Drops give her eyes a lucidity, but she doesn't appear to be in any discomfort. Blink, Violeta.' It took a couple of seconds, but the girl did as she was told.

'Her parents . . .?'

'Both dead, as I've said. Some sort of fever. I'm acting, Mr Miller, as her guardian. I can assure you she'll be well looked after.'

'Then why isn't she cleaned up?'

'Refuses to take her dress off. Turns into a wildcat when you try.'

107

'I thought you said she doesn't do anything without being told?'

'And that's right. Up to a point. I guess she's just bashful, but don't you worry, we'll get her out of it.'

'And when did her parents die?'

'Before you arrived. A few months ago.'

'Shouldn't she be in one of the wards?'

'There are still a few tests I need to carry out, and light seems to have an adverse effect on the child, particularly on her eyes. Hence the heavy drapes over the window. It's easier to keep her here for now.'

'And Southfield knows about this illness?'

The doctor hesitated. 'Until I've fully diagnosed her condition I feel it would be premature to inform them. I wouldn't want to unduly alarm anyone. Anyway,' Masterson opened the door behind him, 'you're not here to discuss Violeta. I assume you want to know about the general health of Carsonville's workers. Shall we go into my office?'

'What about . . .?'

'Violeta, sit.'

Without turning the girl fell backwards. Her skinny backside caught the lip of the seat, but not enough to remain on the chair. She toppled forward and would have fallen had Miller not caught her arm. The girl swung towards him, her head rolling back. He glanced down into her eyes. They appeared lifeless and yet they seemed to gaze briefly into his own. Her mouth had fallen open, a small dark void on her blanched face. He heard Masterson tutting in the background. There was hardly anything in Miller's grasp, little more than skin and bone. With one hand he lifted her with ease back onto the chair.

Masterson locked the laboratory door and they descended the tiled steps together. The doctor talked about having far fewer patients to deal with since the curfew had been introduced. For the labourers it meant less time at the whorehouse,

108

less time to get drunk. Outside at night there was always the possibility of being attacked, like the poor boy last night.

It was cooler in his office, the ceiling fan stirring the humid air sufficiently to give both men relief after the stifling heat of the laboratory. Miller asked Masterson about Halliday. Yes, he'd been admitted to the hospital, but he'd died just within the last hour. 'It was fever,' he answered when pressed, 'the snake bite having crippled his immunity. No one likes to admit he's been outwitted, but there are things in the forest we don't understand. It wasn't malaria, but not dissimilar. Would you like to see his corpse?'

'Not especially. I assume you've completed a death certificate.'

'Of course. You'll find nothing wrong with our paperwork.'

'I know he was married, but I don't have any record of his having a wife?'

Masterson paused before answering. 'A wife,' he repeated absently. 'Yes, he was married. I can't vouch for the records at the municipal hall, but here we document everything. I can assure you of that. Why, is she in trouble or something?'

'No, it's just I'd like to talk to her, that's all.'

'That won't be possible. You see, she left here just this morning. An unhappy woman, quite the quarrelling bird. Never happy on the plantation, and by all accounts made her husband's life a misery.'

'She left before he died?'

Masterson paused again. 'Sounds strange doesn't it; kind of callous for her to do that, but that's what she did. I guess she knew her husband wasn't going to pull through. Perhaps I should have listened to her.' He shook his head ruefully, wondering how this would play out, if he could keep her hidden from Miller. It was an audacious lie, but a challenge he wasn't entirely unprepared for. In some ways he thought it would make up for the unfortunate discovery of the girl. 'We get a lot of wives who can't cope. Or that's the excuse their husbands give. You'd be surprised how many gutless men we get sent down here, men who shrink back in terror at the sight of a bug, men who'd rather be crawling round Detroit begging for a crust than working for an honest dollar.'

Miller nodded as though he sympathised with the doctor. 'And you've been here since the hospital was built?'

'Not quite, but I've no wish to be anywhere else.' He felt he had the situation in hand now, and talked easily as they descended the stairs back to the entrance hall. 'For most men nothing more exciting than a yawn ever happens here, but for the inquisitive doctor the Amazon offers up a whole host of possibilities. Spellbound is the man who seriously considers its enormity, its poisonous nature. Take the narcotic effect of a bite which paralyses the spine, or *beriberi galopante*, which can carry off its victim in less than twenty minutes. Why, Halliday's peculiar fever has yet even to be classified.'

27

A nurse had shown Estelle to her own room on the top floor of the hospital. Masterson had been too busy to see her for more than a minute or two, but he'd promised her he would visit that evening to make sure she'd settled in. There was a view of the park and she had her own bathroom just across the corridor. She was to be waited on hand and foot and the idea appealed to the girl who'd never really been looked after by anyone. On her way to the hospital she'd called in at the little library. First customer of the day and the old woman had seemed surprised by her appearance so early in the morning. Estelle wasn't much for books, but given the length of her confinement she thought she'd give them a try. She sat back on the bed and, having put aside *Ethan Frome*, she picked up the photograph of Sam she'd found beneath her tan stockings. In the picture he sported a thin Clark Gable moustache. He was handsome, though even then she knew he was going to be trouble. He'd never explained to her how he'd managed to serve only half of his sentence at the prison farm, but she had a pretty good idea. At least they'd both escaped Cement City. He said he'd write to her and he had done. Always keen to keep the simplest of promises, though bigger ones were harder.

After his release he'd got the job as a filing clerk in one of

Carson's factories in Detroit. Quick as a flash, but he had contacts, that's what he was always saying. At sixteen she hadn't worried, but now she was a year older, a year wiser, and some things just didn't tally. She hadn't thought it worth worrying about when they'd been together. She'd been comforted by the fact that he'd actually learnt something on the prison farm, enough at least to have been out in the field. Why he'd become increasingly nervous before he was bitten, she couldn't say for certain, though she'd guessed he was in trouble again. Estelle didn't like to think of him as having squealed in the can, but she knew what kind of circles he'd been mixing in. Back in Cement City the Ellison boy was always used as a warning: strike a deal with the cops and they'd hunt you down, and after they'd had their fun you'd end up beneath one of them highways. He was anxious about that, determined to get as far away as he could. Yet always looking over his shoulder, afraid they'd send someone after him to teach him a lesson.

How then was she to know he was just a company agent? Sam wasn't in any state to tell her anything or defend himself. And Masterson had warned her to keep his recovery quiet, drummed it into her that only a handful of people knew about what had happened. She hadn't wanted to let either of them down, couldn't afford to lose the doctor's kindness, not with so many nasty folk around, so many rotten hearts.

And there'd been a nastiness about the agent who'd come a-calling, a self-satisfied cleverness which it was only right and proper for her to have taken offence to. The little fancy man had deceived her and she'd always found being tricked hard to handle, especially when she'd been made to feel stupid. If he'd flirted with her it might have been different, but he was queer. Even making eyes at Sam. A stubby queer with his trumped-up cleverness. And Estelle didn't like them, just as she didn't like anyone whose skin was darker than her own. She didn't know why, other than she'd had it drummed into her that they were one step below in the pecking order, the one thing the men she'd grown up with had had the luxury of despising. If he'd been black she wouldn't have let him in. How dim she'd been to think that someone like him would have been sent to help her, to listen to her.

None of them, except Masterson, had ever had a good word for her, not even after the accident. The bite on his ankle hadn't looked much, but the doctor had said it was enough to kill a man. She remembered how his hands grew cold despite the heat, how he cursed his sorry life. He'd said some horrible things, but she'd done what she thought he would have wanted. Foolish to think he'd ever be grateful, that he ever really loved her as a woman. He'd taken her innocence and naivety and used them against her, tricked her into believing it was more than just physical.

Estelle cast the photograph aside, her mood having soured. She stood up and looked at herself in the mirror inside her wardrobe. Twisting her shoulders, she managed to fasten the back of her frock with a safety pin. There was no need for her to dress at all, but she wanted, while she still could, to look her best for Masterson when he called by. Below her eyes there were dark semi-circular hollows. That was Sam's fault. Worrying about him and what she'd done. She knew he was in the bunkhouse at the back of the hospital, but she hadn't been to visit. Besides, she didn't think she was even allowed to. The nurse had told her she'd have to stay in the hospital, not even to venture out to the canteen. Still, maybe she ought to try and visit him. They couldn't keep her cooped up, day in, day out, not if she didn't want to stay inside. A little lipstick and a little powder, maybe even a walk in the park. Just so long as she didn't talk to the new agent. So long as she played along he'd look after her and Halliday. It was a concession she'd agreed to, but she wasn't sure she was inclined to keep it. Estelle tilted her head coquettishly, the cropped blonde hair touching one shoulder. Miller was his name, he'd told her that

113

much. A tight-lipped smile spread over her face. Maybe Masterson was jealous after all. And that was perfectly understandable.

Earlier, from her window, she'd caught sight of the new agent heading towards the hospital. It was one of those glimpses a girl like Estelle could read a lot into if she was so disposed. He was tall and handsome, though she saw he carried that tiredness which struck the new arrival. She'd seen it in the way he'd sauntered across the road. Alone in her room she'd watched him with the unabashed casualness of one practised in the art of observing men who took her fancy. One thing she'd initially liked about Sam was his height, but he'd started stooping. They all did, once it had taken hold. She cast upon the new agent the ability to conjure familiarity out of thin air, a shining, spell-like ability which made those who crossed his path nod courteously.

Suppose, thought Estelle, that what had happened to Sam was a hideous nightmare, induced while under an anaesthetic, or that Sam wasn't real at all. Suppose she should wake up confused in the night, speaking thickly, not really quite sure of her surroundings, the nurse bending over her and a voice saying 'that wasn't so bad, was it?' On waking she would look around at the room she was in and the prim nurse would be there to reassure her, to say everyone has strange dreams under ether.

28

It was a humid night, and the heat seemed to have brought with it a stillness that quelled insect and mammal alike. Miller didn't like the quiet. He wasn't used to living in a house. An apartment was his natural habitat, the muffled noises of others, the rattle of pipes, the passing automobile. He found it hard to settle, lying alone in a clapboard house in the middle of the Amazon, his thoughts caught up in the Halliday girl's departure and cowed by the silence which enveloped him. On the ship and the tramp steamer there'd always been the throb of an engine. For the first few nights after his arrival he'd been too tired to register the change, but now an invisible void surrounded him. He tried to ignore it, but there was something oppressive, something cavernous about the silence. Occasionally it was broken by a distant cry from the forest, loud enough to slide in through the screen. He recognised the howler monkey for what it was, but there were other sounds, the yawl of a big cat or the elongated screech of a bird. He lay awake for almost an hour, thinking about the Hallidays and Leavis and what might have happened.

It was the noise of something nearby which woke him from his hard-won slumber. The sound had entered his consciousness, but eluded him now he was awake. He waited, expecting to hear it again. He was listening hard. Trying to stifle his own breathing in order to catch what it was. He couldn't even be certain if it had come from the forest or somewhere in the compound.

Then he heard the brushing of leaves just below the open window. It sounded like a dog padding about beneath the screen. It continued to investigate the grass, treading backwards and forwards. Miller slapped his hand against the wall above his head. The noise stopped, but he figured it hadn't run off. He slapped the wall again. Nothing. He waited. Perhaps it had slunk away. He thought of Garret and his men and whether or not one of them was still around. The thin swish of grass or leaves started again. This time Miller threw aside the cotton sheet and climbed out of bed. The sound of his feet on the floor brought about a reaction, in that it must have frozen. He put his face against the screen, the mesh cool against his cheek. He couldn't see anything below, other than the long grass beside the bungalow. 'Scram!' Miller yelled, smacking the window-frame as he did so. Something long and low shot out across the lawn. It was too fast and too dark for him to make out what it was, but that didn't matter. 'Go on,' he cried, but before he could say 'beat it!' the creature had veered round and darted to the right of the house. Miller was perplexed. Why hadn't it gone straight ahead, crossed the gravel road, lost itself in the forest? What had scared it enough to send it hurtling back?

He peered into the darkness, half-hoping to glimpse a big cat or a large snake. Instead he saw the pale outline of something almost shimmering in the blackness. It was standing still and Miller again had the distinct feeling he was being stared at. Was it the faint outline of a dress? He rubbed his eyes. Was he seeing things? If only it was a few yards closer to the house, then he could be certain.

Stealing from the window, he flicked the light switch in the bedroom. He peered again into the night. The light illuminated the lawn, but everything else was cast in shadow. Without hesitating, other than to switch on another light, he went to the front door. He leapt down from the porch and half circled the house until he was beneath the window. Standing there in nothing but his shorts, encircled by light, he softly called her name. He walked to the edge of the lawn, the damp grass sliding beneath his feet, and tried again. Tree trunks and twisted vines grew out of the gloom, but there was no sign of anything else. He was about to head back to the bungalow when there was the snap of a twig somewhere in the dark. 'Anybody there?' called Miller. He waited patiently, but didn't expect a response. 'And answer came there none,' he said to himself. The whine of a mosquito next to his ear reminded him of where he was. He wasn't going to go into the forest. He was going back to bed. There were no phantom shapes in the dark, just a tired man who needed to get some shut-eye.

He went back inside and closed the door. As he checked that it was locked he noticed a faint odour had followed him into the narrow hall. It was somewhere between rotten wood and putrefying meat. Miller lifted first one foot and then the other. His wrinkled soles glistened, but were clean. He straightened up. The smell had receded. In the bedroom he didn't notice it at all, only it didn't feel quite as stifling as it had been when he'd first climbed into bed. He pulled the sheet over him, more out of custom than necessity, and soon fell asleep. There were no more sounds to disturb his slumber, and yet he didn't sleep well. The ashen face of the girl he'd seen in the laboratory haunted his dreams. Although unconscious, he had the strange notion that she was there in the room, standing at the end of the bed, watching him as he slept, studying his face. And there was the smell, more pungent than before, a smell of mould and decay. It was the stench and the suspicion which disturbed him. He never caught sight of her, and yet in his mind Violeta was there, as still as a statue, not even breathing.

29

Miller had seen plenty of dirty postcards in France (Juno sitting in a snowy cemetery, a young maid bathing while a French soldier peers round a patterned screen), yet he wasn't the type to revel in obscenity. He'd an appetite for women, but without the warmth of a body or the firmness of a thigh to caress he couldn't understand the compulsion merely to look at a piece of coloured card. Garret, however, had spoken to him about the Island of Innocence and had increased his curiosity with words of rough poetry. A week's wages, but they were beautiful, they were clean; sophisticated, broad-minded dames with an etiquette that made it a holy service. 'You don't pay,' said Garret, twisting round to see Miller's face, 'it's a donation to Mary Magdalene's church of blameless love. See, it ain't like a hookshop on land or sea. She makes the girls take table-manner lessons. Those whorehouses along the river are full of dead-beats, worn-out mulattos, evil-looking gypsies. On the Island of Innocence you have the prettiest things, finest-looking cinnamon-coloured skin a man is ever likely to see. And the customers, nothing but managers, foremen, salesmen in linen suits. Nothing but the best on both sides.'

The boy, who was guiding the wooden canoe with his paddle, steered it round the last bend. It was a warm evening and a mist rose from the water as if the river was gently steaming. The setting sun cast ashen shadows across their bow and Miller could hear the faint sound of a piano's melodic notes.

'You ever thought about giving the place a pitch on the wireless?'

Garret, who was sitting in front of Miller, shook his head. 'I guess I get kinda carried away sometimes, but this is one helluva place.'

'I'm thinking I'm not the first you've taken here?'

'I've taken a few of the others, but there's a need for them to be more discreet. Like you, I don't have to worry about hurting anyone. I can say what I like, praise what I like. I know some folk call me a greaseball, that I'm dirty, loud and mean, but I ain't no hypocrite when it comes to women, nor places I like.'

'I appreciate that,' said Miller. Seldom had he found an employee of the company willing to talk as openly as Garret.

On the island ahead several tropical palms stood like silent sentinels, their leaves stroking the tiled roof which was littered with dead foliage. Two rose bushes had been planted on either side of the stoop's wooden steps, though neither had taken in the sodden earth. The bordello, as Garret preferred to call it, was run by Madame Triffaux, a tall woman in her sixties with bleached hair and lips painted an ochre red. Her partner was a short, fat Italian in his fifties called Papallardo. He sat on the stoop looking out over the river and welcomed the boats as they docked at his jetty. Beside his native tongue, he spoke sufficient English, French, German and Portuguese to gauge the circumstances of each visitor.

The Island of Innocence was not for your local labourer. There were other brothels along the banks of the river which provided cheaper entertainment, and Papallardo would, on occasion, instruct those he deemed undesirable to search for their bawdy amusement elsewhere. And while Papallardo had his revolver to counter any argument, and a machete was kept

120

beneath the piano, no other weapons were allowed on the island. By reputation, it was known as a civilised brothel and those who were permitted to land respected its rules and genteel manners. The drawing room, like the narrow corridor, was kept in semi-darkness, but with its upright piano, pot plants and a mahogany table it was little different to those found in bourgeois homes at the turn of the century, albeit with half-undressed daughters of various shades.

Miller followed Garret up the steps and into the drawing room. On a velvet couch, the back of which was covered by a length of floral chintz, knelt three young women in stockings and satin underwear. Their shiny backsides were presented to the men and they were talking to Madame Triffaux, who sat at the table behind them with two other girls, both of whom were polishing glasses. On the piano stool was a black albino. He continued to play and, unlike the others, failed to look up or turn around. The atmosphere was heavy with rum and cheap perfume, though the dampness was there like an undertow. Over the years it had seeped into the chaise longue, the thick embroidered curtains, the fabric of every piece of furniture and clothing.

'Well,' said Madame, rising to her feet, 'if it isn't my favourite soldier home from *la guerre*. And you have a friend with you.' She rested her hands on her thickening hips and stood hieratic in her green cotton dress. Her face was manly, but she had soft, doe-like eyes. As was customary, she took a moment to look Miller up and down, to judge his worth and appetite. '*Bonsoir, Monsieur.*' He was passable; enough to make what her girls endured no worse than meaningless. There was a hunger in his blue eyes, but there was also a reticence, an appreciation of being her guest. 'A drink, for our two American friends. Champagne?'

'Every time you ask the same thing,' said Garret, 'and what do I say?'

Madame laughed as she always did when a man tried to

amuse her. 'Why, a glass of *vin rouge*, and the same for your handsome companion?'

'Why not?' said Miller. 'Haven't tasted wine for almost twenty years.' Garret made some comment about the agent having served in France, which seemed to impress Madame. Miller was looking at the three girls on the couch who were now whispering between themselves. One of the girls at the table produced a bottle from somewhere and was uncorking it. The other went over to the chaise longue. She sat upon it with her silken knees pulled up to her chin, a strip of taut pink satin visible between her thighs. Her brown hair was tied in bunches and she held an old Pierrot doll to her chest.

'*Mon enfant*,' said Madame as she noticed Miller's gaze linger for a second on the freckled face of the green-eyed girl on the chaise longue. 'You like Belen?'

'I like all women,' replied Miller, 'but that doesn't mean I want to sleep with any of them.'

'But Belen isn't like all women, isn't that right?' Madame looked to Garret, who was cradling his glass beside the table.

'Now let's not hurry anything along here,' he said, wearing a smile of detached anticipation. 'We're in no hurry tonight.'

On Belen's lips was a bloodless grin and even in the dim light Miller could see there was a chalky whiteness about her skin. The girl remained tightly crouched on the chaise longue, her cream negligee reaching only to her waist, leaving her thighs exposed. There was the flash of pink again between her pale legs. They must spurn the sun's rays and powder their skin. Madame and Garret were chatting, genially abusing the people they both knew.

Miller sipped his wine and reflected on the sight which played before his eyes. He wasn't immune to what he saw and yet there was something iniquitous about it all. Here he stood fully clothed while they sported in their underwear. It had been a while since he'd slept with a woman, yet, after the most fleeting of thoughts, the idea of taking advantage of the situation was too troubling to contemplate. Within a few minutes he'd realised he'd seen enough, but couldn't leave without Garret. He drained his glass and put it back on the table. A young woman with dark plaits asked if he'd like another. Her eyes stared into his own, implored him to take what he could from her. She asked him again if he'd like another glass and against his better judgement he nodded.

Garret raised his hand to her buttocks as she slid past. Miller saw him caress them, feeling the firmness of her flesh through her satin drawers. She ignored his attention, and when she returned with Miller's glass she smiled up at the agent as though he might appreciate her conduct. 'You like a girl who behaves like a lady?' she asked. 'A girl who is obedient?' Her accent sounded Italian, but Miller wasn't sure. Again, she looked unwaveringly into his eyes.

'I've no interest in sleeping with anyone tonight.'

'That's not what I asked. Would you like to play with me? I'll be good if you want me to be.'

'Answer's the same, I'm afraid.'

'What is your name?'

'Vernon.'

'Vernon,' she said, as though she'd never heard the name before. 'Why don't I just call you Johnny, like every other American that comes here to play?' She appeared to be amused, but Miller didn't smile and the girl's performance faltered. 'Vernon? This is your real name?'

'It is.' He turned to see Garret being led through the door next to the pianist.

Madame rolled back towards her chair and sat in it heavily. 'You like Livia?' she asked, gesturing to the woman who was still looking at him.

'Is that your real name, Livia?'

'It's been my name for as long as I care to remember.'

'You like Livia?' repeated Madame.

'She's swell,' Miller replied, 'but I won't be partaking.'

'Then you should sit down and wait for your friend. He won't be long.' Smiling to herself, she pulled out a chair from beneath the table, but Miller remained standing. He asked the woman next to him where she was from.

'From Sicily. I'm Papallardo's niece.' She gave a little laugh, both of them knowing she'd used the word loosely. Miller encouraged her to go on and she told him she'd lived in Manaus from the age of twelve, that her parents had died of yellow fever, and how Papallardo had been there to take care of her. As she was talking, an old man Miller didn't recognise returned to the drawing room. He had white hair and his shoulders were narrow and stooped. Seeing Miller there he nodded politely, but didn't speak. Madame rose from her chair and they spoke quietly in German to one another. There was the offer of a drink, but the man declined and quickly settled his account.

While the old man said his goodbyes Miller idly watched the door to the bedrooms. The albino continued to play upon the piano and Livia asked him about Michigan, a conversation she'd no doubt had with several other men in the last week or so. Madame left her table and went through to the back. Miller looked at his watch. There was no sign of anyone returning to the drawing room. As he finished his second glass of wine, Madame reappeared. Trailing behind her was a dark-haired girl, chalky-white in appearance and looking not much older than thirteen. She was wearing a pink velvet dress tattered around the hem and with a cream sash tied around its waist. With a hand upon her shoulder, Madame gently guided the unseeing child until she was perched in the shadows at Belen's pale feet.

Miller instantly recognised her as Violeta, the girl he'd seen at the edge of the forest and in Masterson's laboratory. Madame saw him staring, but she didn't proffer an introduction. 'What's she doing here?' he asked.

Madame smiled, a thin smile that wrapped itself round her

124

masculine face. 'She has always been here, monsieur. And she is much older than she looks. A favourite with those who wish for something different, to play again the games they played in the schoolyard.'

Miller shook his head. 'I saw her with Masterson.'

'That wasn't Masterson.'

'No, at the hospital. She was his patient.'

Madame looked puzzled. 'Perhaps she was being examined. Why don't you have a drink on the house? A glass of Burgundy? A strong wine for men who need to be fortified against the horrors of the jungle. Who need the courage to indulge in pleasure. Not that you are weak, Monsieur Miller.' He didn't like her tone and he resisted when she tried to take his arm and gently turn him back towards the table. There Violeta sat, staring into space, her hands limp across her lap. Livia slipped her arm round his. He felt the warmth of her hip through the satin of her drawers, her bare shoulder resting against his shirt.

'No, it wasn't like that. It wasn't just an examination. She's sick.'

Madame shrugged while Miller pulled himself away from Livia and went over to the chaise longue. He knelt down in front of the girl. The two women followed him. 'You want to know about Violeta? Why, she is very biddable,' said Madame. 'It's a trick of hers, her obedience, her submissiveness. She gives men the illusion they are in control, invincible.'

'Something's wrong with her. Masterson told me himself.'

'No, monsieur. She is play-acting and will continue to do so until you are gone. Isn't that right, Livia?'

'Yes,' said Livia, though her answer wasn't quick enough to fool anyone. 'It's an act some . . . find attractive. Carmela is just the same.' With her head she gestured towards a thin girl who had stayed kneeling on the couch. At the sound of her name she appeared to stiffen but otherwise remained motionless.

There was something equally unnerving about the girl on

the couch, yet Miller turned his attention back to Violeta. She paid no heed to him or the two women who had gathered around her. He took hold of her cold, clammy hand. Her eyes were misted over. 'She's blind?'

'Almost,' replied Madame. 'She's an orphan. Out there she wouldn't last very long. Here she is looked after.'

Her skin was powdered, her cheeks rouged. But the white dusting was smudged around her neck. Her skin was bruised; black and grey marks had started to appear, around her neck, her wrists, across her shins. 'She's been beaten.'

'No, monsieur. She's delicate. That's all.'

Her faded pink dress was stained and there was a broken strap on her shoe, and beneath the scent of rosewater and violets there was something rotten, something putrid. He lifted her hand to his face. It was there on her skin, a skin that was laced with tiny scars.

'You want to take her home?' It was Garret behind him. 'We can wrap her up if you like.' It was a joke, yet his smile faded when he saw Miller's face. 'What's the matter? Has something happened to the girl?'

'She needs to be back in the hospital.'

'Was she in the hospital?' Garret asked Madame.

'She saw Dr Masterson last week. He will visit her here.'

'The girl's sick,' interrupted Miller. He placed his hand on her powdered brow but couldn't discern anything. He studied her eyes. Whites like curdled milk, pupils like sunken grey nickels.

'She should come back with us.'

'She doesn't look right, I'll give you that,' said Garret.

'We take care of her. Do not worry, Monsieur Garret. We will have the doctor visit her tomorrow.'

'This isn't any place for a child, no matter how swell you think it is.' Miller had given up trying to hide his impatience.

'Hold on. You say the Doc's coming tomorrow?'

'He is,' Madame answered, 'though we look after her.'

126

'Stand up,' said Miller. The girl wasn't looking at him, but she heard well enough. The agent watched as she slid her backside almost to the floor and then somehow straightened her spine. It was snake-like how she elevated her body from a nearly impossible angle.

'You not take her away,' warned Madame. 'Rosario.'

The pianist lifted his fingers from the keys. He didn't turn round, but Miller knew he was listening, waiting for her next command.

'How about we talk to Masterson when we get back? Just to make sure this is all above board. How about that?' No one was listening to Garret. The albino still sat on his piano stool, facing the panelled wall.

'Can she speak?' asked Miller. 'Can she tell us how she's feeling?'

'She's mute,' answered Madame. 'Violeta, smile for the gentlemen, smile if you're happy.'

The girl remained motionless for a second or two, then her mouth started to stretch. It was not a smile she gave them, but a grimace, a grotesque contortion of the mouth which made her appearance all the more disturbing.

30

The journey back to Carsonville began in silence, just the sound of the oar dipping into the water. It was harder to paddle back upstream and the boy was soon sweating against the current. Miller was glad to be outside. The moon shone brightly, the river a ribbon of silver running between the silent trunks of ancient trees. He'd found the whorehouse hot and oppressive, yet didn't like leaving Violeta behind. What puzzled him the most was how she'd escaped from Masterson's laboratory.

A flash of mottled silver leapt out of the river just in front of the canoe. 'Piranha on its tail,' said Garret. 'Fingers in the boat. And don't even think of pissing over the side either.'

Miller didn't say anything, just stared at the back of the man's Stetson.

'You OK, sailor?'

'Just thinking about the girl.'

'Listen, if I'd had my revolver it might have been different, but this is outside of our jurisdiction. No need to worry, though, Madame will look after her. It don't pay to have a dying whore on your hands. Besides, you should see some of the girls Roeder supplies to some of the whorehouses. She certainly ain't the youngest.'

'We should see Masterson when we get back. Tell him where we found one of his patients.'

'It'll be too late for that. We'll see him together in the morning. Make sure her story ain't just a pile of horseshit. You want a drink?' Garret was holding his flask above his head.

'No, thanks.' Miller thought for a moment. 'Didn't this Roeder used to find natives for the plantation?'

'That's right, though you couldn't depend upon them out in the field. And if you were ever inclined to raise your voice at them they'd fall on you like a ton of tomcats.'

The river began to narrow, the banks closing in to within ten yards on either side. Above them stretched a canopy of branches. At dusk it had been a pleasant part of the journey: butterflies fluttering above the canoe, the golden light seeping through the foliage. Then it seemed the native had only to steer downstream, as though nature itself was colluding with man and craft.

'You know, you should have slept with one of the girls. Almost rude not to. I mean, I don't want to argue with you, but I thought going to a bordello, particularly one as fancy as Madame Triffaux's, entailed a certain obligation.'

The boy was digging hard into the water as though he shared Miller's unease, his desire to get back to the plantation. There was something darker than the night about the forest, something unsettling about the invisible interior. Few of the moon's rays penetrated the verdant ceiling. 'River runs deep,' said Garret, as though showing he was prepared to change the subject if only to get a response. 'In some places it goes down at least a hundred foot.' His voice had softened and Miller wondered if he too was affected by this stretch of the Tapajòs. A small bat zigzagged over them.

Behind the canoe something splashed into the water. Garret's head swivelled round. 'You get huge otters along here. If we're lucky we might see one. Boy, you got a light?'

His answer was slurred, as if he'd been drinking. 'No, I know way.' There was something else in Portuguese which neither of them understood. The boy sounds anxious, thought Miller, but he's trying to reassure us. The speed of the paddling increased.

'This is what you get when you pay bottom price,' said Garret. 'If we had a light you'd see their burrows.'

'And caimans?'

'You don't get many along this stretch of the river. Too many boats passing through.'

'How big do they get?'

'Big as alligators. Black ones bigger than any you'd see in Florida. And faster too.'

'They ever chase canoes?'

'It'd be unusual, but not unheard of. More likely to be attacked if you were swimming in it. Why, I remember when I first arrived a maid was bathing in the river. She had her arm bitten off by a caiman and bled to death. Nothing Masterson could do. You know what the nearest tribe call the Tapajòs?' Garret paused but didn't expect an answer. 'They call it the River of Evil.'

'Why's that?' asked Miller, though he wondered if this was the right time to be asking. They were still enclosed by branches and vines and the tunnel of vegetation had more or less plunged them into total darkness.

'Same reason I'd call any stretch of water out here evil: caimans, stingrays lurking on the sandy bottom, electric eels, piranhas, snakes. Why, above our heads are probably all kinds of poisonous snakes and insects, spiders as big as dinner plates. You ever hear of the candiru?'

Suddenly the canoe lurched to the right, tipping slightly as it swerved off-course. The boy muttered to himself but was able to steady the craft within a second or two. 'A submerged branch, nothing more,' said Garret. Nevertheless he glanced back again as though to confirm what they all wanted to believe. He told the boy to be careful. There was no need to hurry. Taking a dip wasn't going to be the end of them, but he certainly didn't want to get his best shirt and pants wet. 'The candiru,' Garret began again, 'grows to about two inches long and looks for—'

The second collision was a more dramatic affair. This wasn't a branch. Something was trying to overturn their canoe, and had almost succeeded. A thick, gnarled tail lashed through the water, splashing the men on board. Miller gripped the sides of the wooden craft and tried, as the other two did, to compensate for the sudden tilting of the hull. The boy yelled out.

'Caiman!' cried Garret. 'Keep it steady.' He didn't have his revolver, but suddenly produced a bone-handled knife from somewhere. 'It's likely to come again. Just be ready.'

Miller scanned the river as best he could, wet fingers clinging to the rough sides. They had another fifty yards or so before they were out from under the canopy. They'd stand a better chance of seeing their adversary in the moonlight. Ripples started to disappear. The river, though never smooth, appeared at least to settle back into what it had been. Yet the boy hadn't stopped paddling. There was an increased urgency about it, each stroke aggressively hitting the water, pushing them forward, a stabbing motion across the undulating surface.

A moonbeam slid alongside the canoe. It caught Miller's eye. In a second he saw the murky bottom of the river: silted with jagged diamonds of black and grey. In a second he saw what it truly was. As its back broke the surface, Miller turned to see its gaping jaws flying at the paddle. In the murky darkness he saw its row of jagged teeth, its flapping mouth flung over the arm of the boy. He heard, more than saw, the snapping bite, the crunching of teeth tearing through flesh and bone. With its full weight it hit the river, dragging the paddle, stripping the boy's forearm of flesh, locking its jaws over his hand. Miller grabbed his waist as the boy shrieked in agony. Sinews snapped, bones were ripped from sockets, the canoe's side dipped beneath the water's inky edge. The river poured into the hull until the boy fell back into the wooden craft and it miraculously righted itself. One arm was shredded beneath the elbow, his hand no doubt still grasping the paddle as it sank with the caiman. Miller called to him but he was unconscious.

'Is he dead?' cried Garret.

'I don't think so.'

'Soon will be. You've got to drag him over the side.'

'What are you saying?' They spoke hurriedly to one another while the canoe turned in the current and began drifting back the way they'd paddled. 'We have to try and save him.'

'Throw him out,' repeated Garret.

Miller's hand ran across the boy's chest. He could feel the heart beating. His fingers found his shoulder, travelled down to where the forearm should have been. Blood was spurting out from just beneath the elbow. He could try and staunch it with his shirt, but how much blood had he lost already?

'It'll be back if we don't throw him out.'

Miller heard Garret turn on his knees, blood and water sloshing round as he inched towards him. The canoe bumped against something. It was the gentlest of knocks. They'd drifted up against the bank. 'You can't just drag him out,' said Miller.

'Can't I?' said Garret. He had his foot in the muddy water and was reaching for the boy. 'He ain't gonna make it back, and nor are we if we don't get rid of the blood.'

Miller watched as shadows danced in front of him. He had one hand on the boy's sodden chest as though to protect him.

'All kinds of critters sniffing his blood. We got to get him out.' Garret had hold of the boy's legs and had begun to pull. 'If you don't let go, it'll be me that pays the price.'

'Get back in the boat.'

'I ain't getting back into no coffin. Now quit arguing for Christ's sake and let go.'

There wasn't anything Miller could do but lift his hand. He

felt the smooth features of the boy's face passing beneath his wet palm as his body was dragged from the canoe. There was the squelch of feet wrenching through the mud. Garret was feeling his way along the bank, sliding his hands over sludge-covered trunks. In the river little eddies began to form as though something was making its way back towards the surface. There was the faintest of ripples just to the left. Miller was listening hard. In the forest a branch or vine was being shaken, dry leaves rustling in the dark. Was it Garret? Should he have followed him onto the bank? An insect brushed against his cheek. Nearby there was a sound: a short, dull clenching, like a heavy rag being thrown over something which yielded with each landing. It came twice in quick succession. The canoe rocked against the tree-lined shore, roots like giant fingers knocking at its side.

In the water something was being dragged away.

'Miller?' came an urgent whisper.

'Here.'

The same squelching sound, hurrying towards him. Garret's hand fell against the bow of the canoe. He shoved it away from the bank and then tumbled inside. There was the soft clatter of wood against wood. 'We can use it to keep us away from the banks,' said Garret, dipping the twisted branch into the river as though keen to demonstrate.

'Jesus,' said Miller, 'wasn't there at least a chance we could have saved him?'

'Not with what's out there.' Garret was using the branch to push them away from the muddy shallows. 'If we keep away from the banks we might make it.'

The canoe began to drift downriver, the branch inching them out into the middle.

'We're heading back to the whorehouse?'

'We've no choice. We can't make any headway against the current. Here,' said Garret. 'Take my knife. Just in case. If we make it back we can borrow their boat.' The canoe slowly continued to drift. Once they were out of the narrow passage Garret found it easier to keep the craft away from the bank. Neither spoke for a while, both reflecting on what they each thought was the right course of action. In the end it was Garret who couldn't stand the silence. 'I guess if you were pissed at me before, you're doubly pissed now.'

'I just think we might have saved the boy, that's all. If you hadn't jumped into the river we could have all climbed ashore.'

'And then what? One of us fends off the caiman, while the other wrestles with a puma? I'm sorry, but this is the jungle and we're just meat to every other living thing out here. One thing you have to—' Garret broke off. They could both hear it. In the distance there was the throbbing sound of an engine. They drifted for another minute before they were sure it was heading upriver.

When they saw a triangle of golden light shining from its bow they cried out with relief. 'Thank God,' said Garret. He began yelling at the covered launch, Miller did likewise. They couldn't see anyone on board, but the noise of the engine collapsed into a low hum as it gently drifted towards them.

31

The Syrian trader who'd rescued them beached the canoe at the edge of the clearing for the harbour and then headed his craft towards the small wooden jetty. Above them a solitary light shone from a window in the customs house. 'He won't come out unless he has to,' said Garret above the sound of the engine. 'Usual procedure is for him to log such accidents. I'll go and speak to him. You should head straight back to your bunk. It's past curfew.'

'Shouldn't we see Masterson?'

'It's too late for that. No one's gonna stir for a dead Indian and a runaway orphan. You head back. I'll call on you in the morning.'

'You don't want me to stay?'

'No, I'll handle this. You go, and then we'll see Masterson tomorrow.'

'OK.' Miller was too tired to protest, a weariness exacerbated by the thought of Violeta and the God-awful death of the boy. He'd seen men die out in France, screaming for their mother, but never a boy savaged by something so wild and primeval. He shook his head to dislodge the gruesome attack. He was beat and just wanted his cot, yearned for the oblivion which he hoped sleep would bring him.

The walk to Miller's bungalow was uphill, but although his legs ached he was glad to be stretching them on dry land. Tomorrow he'd go with Garret to see Masterson. They'd get to the bottom of what Violeta was doing in a whorehouse rather than in the hospital where she belonged. And what about the boy, where were his parents? They'd need to be told. Would the company compensate them for their loss, would Garret even want the company to know where they'd been?

As he left the road from the dock and turned up Union Street he saw a man standing at the edge of the sidewalk. He appeared to be staring at a clump of trees. Miller thought he'd whip round at the sound of him walking along the paved road, but he continued to stand where he was, his eyes looking straight ahead. The last thing Miller wanted was a conversation, but the man's fixed stance was too unusual to pass by without comment. 'Hey,' cried Miller. There was no response. 'You all right, buddy?'

He slowed his pace as he came closer. Was the man too focused on something in the vegetation to even acknowledge his question? His back was lit by the moon, so it was hard for Miller to see the man's face. 'Are you OK?' he asked, glancing at where the man was gazing, though there was nothing to be seen. Miller rested his hand on the fellow's arm. He was short and slender and his stature reminded him of Leavis, yet his shoulders were hunched as if he was cold. 'Hey,' he said again, squeezing the man's shirt sleeve and feeling little more than bone. 'Leavis?' the word crept out. The man turned to face him, and in the moonlight he saw the haggard features of someone who hadn't had a square meal in days. His cheeks were too hollow and his lips were too tightly drawn across his teeth to be the agent, and yet there was something familiar about the face. Miller looked into his eyes. The irises were there, unlike Violeta's, but it was impossible to tell their colour, or that of his hair, clumps of which appeared to be matted together. From Main Street

138

he heard a piercing whistle and immediately the man turned and started walking down the hill. His stride was clumsy, his feet dragging as though drunk. Leavis didn't walk like that. His grace, his purposefulness was missing. And yet Miller felt he had to follow him.

On the road down to the dock he saw a dozen men standing perfectly still. One stood apart and turned sharply at the sound of their approach. 'You found him,' he said to Miller. 'Where was he?'

'Up near the clubhouse. Just staring at a bunch of trees. You know who he—'

'Who the hell are you?' came the sharp response. 'You shouldn't be out here, mister.'

Miller couldn't tell whether it was his voice or his face which the man had taken offence to, but he decided to let it ride. 'I know,' he said, almost apologetically, 'but we had an accident on the river. Indian boy attacked by a caiman. But there's something wrong with this fellow.'

'That's not your problem. You just turn round and head back to your house.' The man took a few steps towards him and Miller saw one hand resting on his holster.

'Is his name Leavis?' The agent gestured to the one he'd found.

'That's none of your concern.'

Miller heard footsteps behind him and turned round. Whoever it was held a flashlight and pointed it straight at Miller's face. 'Say,' came the disembodied voice, 'what in damnation do you think you're doing out here at night? You want to end up in the cell?'

'We had an accident—'

'You sure did. Is that blood?' The flashlight was on Miller's shirt.

'It was a caiman. It took the boy whose canoe—'

'He found him by the clubhouse. Wants to know if his name is Leavis.'

'Who's wanting to know?' The flashlight was back on his face. 'What kind of a punk wanders round after curfew?'

'You don't understand,' said Miller. 'I was with Garret and we had an accident. A boy was killed—'

'Indian boy?'

'Yes, he—'

'Listen, Mr . . .'

'Miller, I'm the sociological agent from Southfield. I replaced Leavis.'

'Well, that obviously ain't Leavis, now is it, Mr Miller?'

'There's something—'

'You're new here, so this is just a warning. You get back to your house for your own safety.' The man with the flashlight seemed to be softening.

'What's wrong with those men?'

'They're patients,' said the one nearest to him, 'that's all.'

The beam of the flashlight pointed Miller's way up the road. 'You gotta go now. And we won't say any more about you breaking the curfew.'

'But I just thought—'

'No time for thinking. You just move along.'

'Speak to Masterson in the morning, if you need to,' said the one behind the light, 'but we got to get these men back to their ward. You'll be interfering with our work if you don't disappear.'

Miller held up both hands in a placatory gesture. 'All right,' he said, 'you win. I'll speak to Masterson.' As he started back up the hill he racked his mind for some sort of disease or illness which only permitted exercise in the middle of the night. He was tempted to turn round but he knew that at least one of the orderlies would be watching him. It made sense to go back to the bungalow and have a shower, try and forget about what he'd seen on the river. And Violeta? What he'd just witnessed must have had something to do with her. He glanced over his shoulder. The troop had moved off, shuffling out of the shadows but bowed as though by the weight of the moon. It was foolish to try and follow them, but he'd done many foolish things in his time.

He skipped across the sidewalk and ducked down. Doubling back across the front lawns, Miller made his way to the stoop of the last house. He could see them heading down Main Street, a cloud of silver dust kicking at their heels as they trudged down towards the dock. There was one orderly at the back, with the other leading the group. From somewhere at the front an order was barked and they slowly wheeled right.

Running from one tree to the next, Miller kept out of the moonlight. The streetlamps must have been switched off at the start of the curfew and so it wasn't too difficult to avoid being seen. The men had the look of convicts about them, though there were no chains. How many in the quiet, damp heat of their beds knew anything about what was passing? He certainly didn't know what he'd gain from trailing them, but there was something sinister about what was happening. Staying fifty yards or so behind the slow-moving troop he followed them into the square. There was an eerie stillness to the heart of Carsonville. By day it was a triumph, but at night it looked as if it was clinging onto a world that wanted to shake it off its back. Even the park seemed poised to leap beyond the railings as soon as he took his eyes away.

For a moment he thought they were being slow-marched straight into the hospital, but they picked their way round as though heading back out to the fields. Seeing them disappearing behind the hospital, Miller cut, with some trepidation, across to the park. He took the first gravelled path to the right and ran as best he could under the overhanging leaves. Once he was out and facing the hospital he took the sidewalk to the back of the building. There was no sight or sound of them. He peered round, his cheek pressed against the rough edge of the brick. At the back was what looked like a bunkhouse, half hidden by trees but lit midway by a feeble light coming through a square of glass in one of the hospital's fire doors. Behind the bunkhouse the forest had been partially cleared and in the tall grass lay several iron girders. Miller spied a chicken-path which appeared to lead to the far end of the bunkhouse. This was the way they must have come, and yet there was no light to indicate anyone was inside. Miller stepped onto the dirt path. At the near end of the bunkhouse he could just make out a concrete tank for washing clothes, though it was half veiled by undergrowth and vines. Miller picked his way towards the grey rectangular shape and tried not to think of how many snakes might be lying hidden or coiled round the branches which hung merely yards from his face.

As he cautiously approached the bunkhouse he began to smell something stagnant being carried on the warm air. He thought at first it must be coming from an open drain, but as he inched forward he realised it was emanating from the wooden cladding of the building. Above was a grimy window. It was ajar, opening inward, with the wire screen nailed roughly to the outer frame.

He was trying to see in when the door at the far end was flung open. Miller pressed himself against the bunkhouse. If he just kept still he thought he might avoid being seen. He watched as two men emerged from the shadows and descended the wooden steps. They began walking towards him. If they went through the back door into the hospital there was a chance he wouldn't be discovered. He held his breath as they stopped midway. The jangling of keys broke the silence. Their faces, hard and brutish, were lit by the light of the stairwell inside. Both wore the collarless white shirt of an orderly. The one holding the flashlight was putting the key into the lock when Miller felt something tentatively touch his hand. It was a gentle stroke, nothing more at first, then a second, followed by a third. The slight weight of something being carried on soft bristles clambered onto his knuckles. It paused briefly, fanned across his hand, before one thin leg followed by another started to insinuate itself between his wrist and his damp sleeve. Had it stopped there Miller could have remained still, but he felt it lifting the cuff as though looking to drag its silken carapace into its cotton cave. He shook his hand vigorously. A shudder of revulsion ripped through his body and whatever it was fell from his wrist.

The sudden movement and swish of grass as he stepped away caught the attention of the two orderlies. In the light which spilled from the open door Miller saw first alarm and then annoyance on their faces. A hand was at a holster and then the flashlight blinded him for the second time that night.

'Didn't we tell you to stay away?' It was the voice of the one shining the beam into his face, a Southern drawl, whining rather than angry, but all the more menacing because of it. 'You want to be locked up with them, is that it?'

Miller stepped back onto the path and shielded his eyes against the light. 'What's wrong with them?'

'Ain't none of your business.'

'You never answered me before.'

'We don't have to.'

'You were warned. I warned him.' It was the other one; threatening violence.

The flashlight was moving closer. He could hear one of the orderlies on the path, the other cutting through the grass beside the bunkhouse. 'As an agent sent from Southfield I demand to know what it is—'

He didn't see the fist flying towards his chin until it was too late. It was an ugly punch which scraped his face as it flew up. Half blinded by the flashlight, he couldn't even say which one had hit him. Miller staggered back, determined not to fall. The taste of blood was on his lips.

There was an unseen scuffle and the beam buckled in the air. The Southerner was angry, swearing at the other, but Miller wasn't listening. The light hit his eyes again. He was willing to launch himself at them, but he saw a hand spread out to keep him away. 'You goddamn punks,' he was shouting. 'If you want a fight . . .'

'Shit,' said the Southerner, 'he's bleeding.'

'You shouldn't have done that,' said the other.

In the bunkhouse there was a sluggish drumming of feet.

'God, it's his nose. It's dripping everywhere.'

The clapboard beside him started to groan as though being pressed by the weight of many men. With one eye half open he squinted up at the screen above him. There was a wrinkled forehead packed hard against it, the top of it shining with a strange luminosity. Like Miller, the man had his eyes screwed up against the light, his face twisted towards the darkness. It was only a glimpse, but his jaw was slack as though sucking the air through his mouth. Behind him was a low, guttural, almost inhuman murmuring.

'Get him out of here, for Christ's sake.' The agent felt a hand at his elbow, guiding him back down the path, away from the bunkhouse. He was frogmarched four or five yards, and was about to put up a struggle when he saw a figure at the end of the path.

'Is that you, Miller?' It was Garret calling to him. 'What the hell are you doing down there?'

'I'm real sorry,' the voice beside him was saying, 'but I did warn him. Will you take him?'

Miller wrestled his arm free but continued towards Garret. 'You know either of these damn hoods?' he asked.

There was no answer to his question, just another rebuke to swallow. 'Thought I saw you sneaking out from the park, but I wasn't sure. Thought you had more sense.'

'They're not going to get away with this.'

'It's past curfew. If anyone's in trouble it's going to be you, you know that, don't you? No reason for you to be wandering about.'

'I don't care what—'

'That's the ward for those who've been quarantined. That's

all it is.' Garret had his arm around Miller, leading him away from the bunkhouse. 'They must have thought you were up to no good.'

'I want to see Masterson. I want to know what's going on. There are too many here disappearing, too many dying, too many taking off without even a by-your-leave, and I want an explanation.' Miller was bruised and tired and wasn't feeling exactly sane.

'That can all wait till the morning. It has to wait till then. Like we agreed, remember? Now, let's get that nose cleaned up. You want someone to take a look at it?'

'Yeah, I want to see a doctor.'

32

It wasn't unusual for Masterson to be working late in his laboratory. He preferred the relative coolness of the night and the fact that he was unlikely to be disturbed. Eleanor had grown used to his returning to the hospital after dinner. She didn't like it, but had learnt that complaining only upset the hour or so spent at the table or quietly reading in the same room. Perhaps she'd foolishly thought that coming to Carsonville would have given them more time together. Truth was, she saw less of him now than she had when he'd first started working at the Carson Hospital back in Detroit. It had gotten so bad he knew that sometimes she wished she could just turn the clock right back and start all over again.

For his part, Masterson tried not to dwell on his marriage. At the back of his mind he knew he neglected Eleanor, but if she understood what he was trying to do then surely she'd be more sympathetic, more supportive. He walked meditatively around the operating trolley he'd wheeled into the centre of his laboratory. At least she had the sewing circle and the dog he'd given her last Christmas: a black-haired mongrel with large, bat-like ears. The leather straps on the trolley creaked as the arms and legs pulled and kicked helplessly against them. She'd named him Boson and he was now less worried about

147

her long walks around the plantation. He held the scalpel just above the elbow. Yet she insisted on letting him off the lead, despite his constant warnings that if she did it was only a matter of time before he was bitten by something. The incision made the subject flinch slightly, as though a piano wire was pulling at the muscle, then the forearm slackened as he cut through the tendon. A brown, noxious sludge trickled from the gaping wound. Even behind his mask he could smell it, that God-awful stench that sometimes seemed to follow him back home. He wondered if Eleanor ever smelt it on him. If she did, she never said anything.

Masterson stood back from the gurney and looked down at the naked girl lying in front of him. Her skin had once been the colour of cinnamon, but not any more, not for the last week or so. He'd watched it grow pale, that bluish tinge surfacing in a matter of days. She'd been left strapped to the gurney since she'd been brought to him. The thought that he'd need more female subjects depressed him. Not that Masterson had any qualms about experimenting on girls, it was just they were harder to come by. It would require another trip up the river to Roeder. The depraved Belgian was as hard-nosed as Masterson towards the natives and thus could always be relied upon to supply him with what he wanted. He pinched the girl's breast, which was no more than an upturned saucer; the nipple half an inch, the thickness of a cigarette stub. The skin was becoming loose, the flesh slackening, and, despite his pinching it, remained an ashy-white. He'd tried the mercury-quartz lamp but the ultra-violet light had had no effect, other than to annoy her. Around the wrists and ankles the skin had practically worn away with her constant twitching, yet she'd remained mute. Not a squeal or a whimper. He'd tried, as he had with the others, to make her speak.

His eyes travelled up her blanched thighs. There was just the slightest growth covering the pudenda. He brushed his hand lightly over her mound and as he suspected the curls

148

came away with his fingers. The thought of blowing the wiry hairs from her sunken midriff crossed his mind, but it was too intimate an act. Peculiar, to baulk at such a simple thing when he'd just severed every tendon in her left forearm. Masterson stepped round to her head and shaded her eyes with the palm of his hand. If hair be wires, black wires grew upon her head. Her eyelids slowly parted. Her features were quite delicate for a native, an almost slender nose, the elegant chin of a child. Behind the few lashes which clung to her lids the girl seemed to stare at Masterson's palm. There too, on the top of her scalp, the hair was being shed.

Looking at her she was probably just about old enough to reproduce, but that experiment had been taken care of with Violeta and the other girl Roeder had delivered straight to the whorehouse. He smiled contemptuously at the thought of the name he'd given her: Violeta. How easy it was to dupe the agent, how ultra-quick he'd been coming up with it. In the blink of an eye, and it suited her too. The fact that she responded to it made him think it must have been similar to her own name, though he had no idea where she'd come from, or how long she'd been wandering out in the jungle. Her old-fashioned dress made him think it was possible she'd been surviving in the wild for much longer than any of the men who'd been brought to him in the past few months. And if there was to be a breeding programme then Violeta could be the first. He could see nothing wrong in trying to get them to breed, though for him to participate in such an experiment would have been too undignified. Besides, there was Eleanor, and he'd sworn to himself that he'd never betray his wife again.

If only he could find a way to harness some of that native fecundity. He glanced once more at the girl's pretty face. Her eyes, which would remain open while his hand shaded them from the light, were like oysters. The brown irises were now almost invisible, the way a light scattering of snow will cover a muddy field. Roeder had once told him about an Indian stud farm on Rio Madre de Dios. A rubber baron at the turn of the century, concerned about the loss of his labourers through illness and accidents in the field, decided he needed to take a hand and began to breed them like cattle. Six hundred Indian women living on the farm beside the river, giving him all the slave labour he needed to tap rubber. Masterson licked his dry lips in admiration. The thought excited him. He needed to think big. If he couldn't conquer life, perhaps he could conquer death. Perhaps now wasn't the time to be prissy or sentimental. From the window overlooking the bunkhouse at the back came the sound of raised voices, but Masterson had other things on his mind.

33

'I don't see you much in the canteen or the clubhouse?' said Garret, standing in the bungalow's small kitchen. 'That was one of Leavis's mistakes. Never really made himself known to the men. Maybe if they'd known you, no one would have thrown a punch.'

Miller ran a finger lightly over the side of his nose. Outside the first whistle of the morning had blown and from the nearby forest the birds were screeching in one almighty cacophony of noise. 'You want a coffee?' the agent asked.

'Not for me. I've already had breakfast. They do a fine one in the clubhouse: orange juice, cornflakes, fried eggs, enchiladas, flapjacks. You take your pills with your coffee?'

'That's right.' He showed him the two yellow anti-malarial pills in the palm of his hand.

'You know,' said Garret, 'a lot happened last night, but I can't stop thinking about the boy. Maybe I should have done more to try and save him.'

'Perhaps,' replied Miller. He was conscious of Garret watching his reaction.

'Sullivan ain't gonna like the fact we were attacked. Nor the fact we were coming back from where we'd been.' His eyes hadn't strayed from Miller's face. 'But I guess we've gotta report what happened. Wouldn't be right if we tried to keep it quiet.'

'And we need to see Masterson.'

'Yes, we do,' answered Garret. 'That girl was a pure dope-head, wasn't she?'

'Something like that.'

'And that guy was wrong to punch you, but you shouldn't have been sneaking round after midnight.' Garret looked at Miller as though he expected him to say something. 'You went straight back after seeing Dr Barnes?'

'Yes. Though the fellow I saw out on the road looked a lot like Leavis.'

'How could it be Leavis? We buried what was left of him, and before you ask I was sure it was him. Clothes were his, hair was his. Wasn't much else to go on, but enough to identify the man in anybody's book.' Garret paused. 'You said he was thin with a stumbling walk, rounded shoulders. Not the Leavis I saw. It must have been someone else who fell ill, was put in quarantine. They must have put them on pills or something. There's a few of them taken out at night, I know that. Masterson cares for them.'

'Like he cared for the girl?'

Garret snorted, though what passed for a laugh betrayed a certain edginess. 'Well, that's something you can discuss with him as soon as you've finished your coffee, though I hear you've already spoken to him about Halliday.'

'I just wanted to speak to him and his wife. Just routine, that's all. But it seems I was too late.'

'Kind of callous leaving him to die, though she would have had all sorts buzzing round her now. Nice lookin' girl, whole-some yet sly looking. Come-to-bed eyes and one of them asses just crying out to be turned into a pillow. You ever catch sight of her?'

Miller was about to answer when he noticed Garret was waiting for his reply with what he recognised as a false nonchalance, his

152

finger running up and down the edge of the sink as though anything he said was of little consequence. 'No, I didn't,' Miller lied.

Garret, for his part, said that was a pity.

The nurse at the desk was the same bird-like woman he'd met before. In her cold-blooded greeting she curtly acknowledged Miller by name, but saved any warmth she had for Garret.

'Dr Masterson around, Rosie?'

'He is. You'll find him on the Lincoln Ward. Go right on through. Is Mr Miller accompanying you?'

'He is. That's not a problem, is it?'

'No. Just make sure he doesn't get lost.'

Garret nodded with something close to a grin and led the way. 'Rosie's got a real nice house along Riverside. Parties they throw are quite something, I can tell you. Sort of free and easy.'

'I thought the houses on Riverside were just for the bosses?'

'That's right,' said Garret. 'Her husband's in charge of clearing the land. You should see them when they get to work with their chains and tractors. When they're finished it looks like a battlefield, all craters and stumps.' Garret went on talking about what they were doing to increase the size of the plantation, but Miller wasn't really listening. He was starting to become increasingly wary of those around him. It was partly to do with Leavis's disappearance, but on top of that, the events of last night had made him seriously wonder exactly what was going on.

They found Masterson at the far end of the ward. He briefly acknowledged their presence with a nod, busy as he was attending to a Brazilian who was stripped down to his shorts. The wretched man was lying on his back with his sweaty limbs splayed across the bed sheet. He'd been bitten by a spider and his left calf, which was dark purple in colour, had swollen to twice its normal size. 'It'll spread,' said Masterson. 'He'll die

153

limb by limb. Most we can do is to make him comfortable. I've given him morphine, which will take the pain away.' The doctor took his eyes from the dying patient. 'Now what can I do for you two gentlemen?'

'I found Violeta in a whorehouse last night,' said Miller. 'I don't know if you're aware she'd escaped?'

Masterson acted confused, his head slightly tilted to one side. 'A whorehouse?'

'Island of Innocence,' said Garret.

The doctor shook his head. He suddenly appeared to be conscious of the men in the ward, several of whom were quite obviously listening to the conversation. 'Well, you got me there,' he said, his voice more apologetic than his expression. 'Say, why don't we go up to my office and discuss the matter?'

'Fine by me,' said Miller.

Masterson asked the nurse to draw the curtain round the peon's bedside then followed the other two between the iron beds.

In his office the two men were gestured to sit down while Masterson went behind his desk. 'You know, I've just received a delivery of Cuban cigars.' He opened the small wooden box in front of him. 'Mr Garret, I assume you'd like one? Mr Miller?'

'I'm fine.'

'Take one anyway.' He nudged the box towards him. 'There's nothing better than a rum and a nice fat cigar at the end of the day. If nothing else, it helps keep the mosquitoes away.'

'We're here to find out how Violeta ended up at a whorehouse and why one of your orderlies felt it necessary to punch me last night, and why patients were being marched round in the middle of the night.'

'That's a whole lot of questions you got there, Mr Miller, though I believe you saw Dr Barnes early this morning and he apologised for what happened and also explained why no one should be wandering round the isolation ward. I certainly don't

want your health, or theirs for that matter, put in jeopardy.'
Miller was about to respond but Masterson went on. 'As for
Violeta, I'm glad you found her, though I am horrified to hear
that she was in some whorehouse. I won't ask how you
happened to be there,' at this point the doctor glanced across
at the sanitation manager, 'but at least we know where she is.'

'You said yourself she wouldn't do anything unless told to.'

'It's not the first time she's disappeared, I have to admit.'

'How's that possible?'

'Well, she must have just walked out, unless you're insinuating something I wouldn't like even to consider. I accept my
diagnosis was wrong, has been wrong. But she's older than
she looks and her state is a highly unusual one. Papallardo's
a notorious procurer of women. He must have found her
somewhere wandering round the plantation and taken her back
to the island with him. Come to think of it, we had one of his
girls in here. Nasty rash on her thighs. Must have been the
same day Violeta disappeared. Garret, you'll have to go and
get her.'

'It's what we wanted to do last night, but they were reluctant
to say goodbye to her.'

'Take a couple of men. It shouldn't require too much
persuasion.'

'And what about Papallardo?' asked Miller.

'What about him? You want me to bring him in for questioning?' laughed Masterson.

'Well, isn't he guilty of kidnapping? I mean, that's what
you're insinuating, isn't it?'

'Look,' said Masterson, as though it pained him to speak,
'I didn't want to say this, but Violeta has a history, before she
became ill. I'd rather not talk about her parents, but let's just
say this isn't the first time she's been turning tricks.'

'A history?' Miller repeated. It was becoming harder for him
to believe Masterson was telling the truth; the way he smoothed
his oiled hair as he spoke, the pitch of his voice. Miller knew

he'd already shown more interest in the girl than was warranted and yet he couldn't let it drop. Perhaps it was the thought of his own daughter, or the idea that Masterson was trying to hide something far more sinister. 'I'd like to see her records. I'd like to see her parents' records. You said her father died from a fever?'

'Now hold on,' said Masterson. There was an ill-disguised look of annoyance on his face. 'Isn't this going just a little bit beyond what's necessary?'

'As a sociological agent I can ask to see any records I deem it fit and proper to examine. What did you say Violeta's surname is?'

'I didn't.'

'Dr Masterson ain't gonna let her escape again,' said Garret, though his words were cut across.

'I'd also like to see your records for births, deaths and burials for the last two years.'

Masterson was shaking his head as though the request merely amused him. 'You certain you have the authority?'

'I can telegram Southfield if that makes it any easier for you.'

'That won't be necessary. But I would like to know why you feel obliged to burden yourself with something Leavis never gave any consideration to.'

'If he hadn't disappeared you'd be dealing with him and he'd be asking you the same questions. He would certainly have wanted to know why a Mrs Halliday was here and yet in Southfield she doesn't even exist.'

'Well, I'm sure there's a simple explanation behind that. Now if you say you have the authority then that's good enough for me. Why don't you come back tomorrow morning? We can have all the paperwork ready for you by then. And we have a registrar in the hospital who can help you sift through it, though what you hope to gain from it I have no idea.'

'Why not this afternoon?'

'The registrar isn't in today.' Masterson paused briefly. 'She's been unwell, but she should be back tomorrow. I would give you a key, but I think Mrs Wilde is the only one entrusted with it. Of course we could try and find a janitor . . .'

'I suggest you do just that.' Miller didn't hold out much hope of getting to see the records before tomorrow morning, but he was nevertheless prepared to press the issue. 'And Violeta's surname?'

'Why, I've clean forgotten,' said Masterson with the suggestion of a smile. 'No, I do recall. It was Smith.'

'Then I'll return this afternoon to see what records you have concerning the Smiths. In the meantime I'd like to see your isolation ward.'

'I imagine there's nothing I can say to deter you from seeing those in quarantine? I thought not. Garret, would you be so kind as to take Mr Miller back down to reception? Then I think you should go and bring Violeta back, don't you? Before she gets herself in any more trouble.' Masterson looked across at Miller. 'An orderly will take you over to the ward, and I'll ask a nurse to see if we can find you that key.'

'You got something of the gunslinger about you, that's for sure,' said Garret as they descended the stairs. 'I thought he was mighty civil, all things considered.'

'You'll go and speak to someone about the Indian, won't you?'

'Of course I will. They'll want to know whose canoe it is beached near the jetty.' They stopped for a moment at the bottom of the stairwell. 'Listen,' said Garret softly, 'it doesn't do to rile too many people. I think a quiet word with Sullivan will put matters straight, but just be careful not to get on the wrong side of Masterson.'

'I appreciate the warning, but you make sure you bring Violeta back.'

'I'll put things right, don't you worry.'

They went through the double doors into the hospital's entrance hall. At the reception desk Miller was told that Masterson had rung down and a nurse had gone to fetch an orderly to escort him over to the ward.

After several minutes an old man appeared in a grubby collarless shirt. His unshaven face was flushed and his brow was glistening with sweat. He introduced himself as Finkleman and made it clear to Miller that this business was an unwelcome imposition. In his hand he carried two large cotton pads from which dangled rubber straps.

'You'll need one of these,' he said, pushing open a door. 'It stinks in there, and nothing shifts the smell.' In the stairwell he handed a pad to the agent while his mottled fingers found the right key. 'We don't normally allow anyone into the ward, but I guess you must have a good reason.'

They crossed by way of the dirt path from the back of the hospital to the wooden steps of the bunkhouse. The door was latched open and there was the smell of bleach mixed with something of the stench he remembered from the night before. 'You best put it on now.'

Miller did as he was told and followed Finkleman inside. The gloom briefly retreated a few inches as the yellowing curtains lifted slightly in the breeze. The agent struggled at first to make out the patients, covered as they were by thin cotton sheets. There were six wooden beds at the far end of the bunkhouse, otherwise the place was empty. He saw one patient standing perfectly still in a corner beside his bed. The man was wearing grey pyjamas which hung loosely around his emaciated frame. His chin was on his chest, just as Violeta's had been.

'Is this all there is?'

A frown crossed Finkleman's brow. 'It's the ward,' he said.

'I saw more of them last night. Where are the others?'

'Ain't no others in isolation.'

Miller grunted in frustration and stepped into the bunkhouse.

Finkleman tried to restrain him, but he shook him off. He walked over to the nearest bed. What looked like the head of a cadaver rested on a clean pillow. Even in the dimness of the makeshift ward the skin looked ghostly pale. There were bald patches on the scalp. It was impossible to say how old the man was, but whatever had put him in the ward had certainly robbed him of what youth he might have had. Miller bent a little closer and saw that the man's eyes were half open and staring at the ceiling. There was nothing to indicate that he was alive. Miller went over to the next bed. The same translucent skin, the same stillness.

The pad stretched across his mouth and nose was growing damp with sweat. He glanced back at the door where Finkleman stood watching him. Where were the others? Last night there had been at least a dozen. There were questions which needed answering. Where was the one who looked like Leavis? He wiped his brow with the back of his hand and found himself staring at the patient who was out of bed. Miller took a few steps towards him, slipped his fingers inside the rubber band and lifted the pad away. There was a muffled warning behind him which he ignored. The warm smell of putrid meat made him feel nauseous.

'Lift your head,' he said to the skeletal figure. There was a moment's hesitation before the man did as he was asked. 'Can you speak?'

There was no answer.

'Where are the others?'

Nothing.

Was it the face he'd seen forced against the screen? The stench was quickly becoming too much to stomach. He pressed the pad back over his nose and mouth and briskly returned to the door.

34

After knocking she'd walked respectfully into his office, thinking she could be the kind of woman who knows how to keep quiet. She sat docilely in the chair in front of the desk, her hands resting over her belly, her eyes submissively lowered.

'Estelle,' said Masterson, her name sounding like a half a sigh. 'Didn't the nurse tell you I'd come and visit?'

'She did, but I've hardly seen you since I arrived. And I just want to know . . . 'bout Sam . . . 'bout the agent.'

'Sam's dead,' said Masterson. 'That's what I told him. And if he finds you then you've just to say you returned from Santarem.'

'I don't mind if he questions me. He won't get nothing.'

'Chances are he won't have the opportunity to talk to you, but if he does you need to be ready to answer his questions.' Masterson wasn't blind to the fact she'd made an effort to make herself attractive. Her lips were painted and there was the smell of perfume. The polka-dot dress she wore was obviously her favourite, though it was becoming increasingly tight around her breasts and rounded belly. 'Mrs Halliday, I have a lot of work to get through, and for your own safety I think it best if you went back to—'

The ringing of the telephone on his desk made her jump.

Masterson gestured for her to leave, but she was stubborn. There were questions she wanted to ask, still things she wanted to know in exchange for her co-operation. Obstinately, she sat there watching him.

'Yes,' Masterson said into the mouthpiece. He looked across, conveying his annoyance at her still being there. 'If he comes back don't let him out of the entrance hall. Of course I want to be told if he appears again.' Another pause. 'Because we can't have the same thing happening here.' He looked pointedly at Estelle. 'Look, I can't talk now. You'll have to see to it.' He replaced the receiver. 'Mrs Halliday, you need to return to your room.'

'You know I ain't Mrs Halliday. All I want to know is if I can see him.'

'He's being cared for, but you won't be able to visit. He's too far gone for that.'

'You said he might be cured.'

'I can't recall making any promises. Besides, you wanted him back. You begged me to do what I could given—'

'Didn't have to beg that hard,' Estelle interrupted. It was a cheap shot, but it was worth reminding him.

'Given,' he tried to start over again, but couldn't. 'In your care his condition worsened dramatically. I shouldn't have agreed to it, but I did. Lord only knows what will happen to him over the next few weeks.'

'If he dies you ain't having this baby.' It was a gamble, but she was guessing that's why he wanted her there in the ward, why he tolerated her.

'Listen, Estelle. You don't mind me calling you Estelle, do you?'

Her mouth twitched. 'Time was when you seemed to prefer it to Mrs Halliday.'

Masterson shook his head wearily. 'All I'm trying to do is to protect you. It's better for you that you don't speak to that agent, better for the both of us not to dwell on the mistakes we've made. You and Sam both knew the risks involved in coming down here. We gave the pair of you a safe place to hide. You're still safe. Now Sam annoyed a lot of people back home; if they can't take out their feeling of betrayal on him, they might well decide to punish the next best thing. You understand?'

'I ain't afraid of going back.'

'I understand that, but we need to look after you. And Sam wouldn't want you to leave, now would he? I mean, how would it look? You wouldn't want folk here to think you'd run away.'

'But that's what you're telling them, isn't it?'

'The people around you know the truth. That's all that matters.'

Estelle shook her head as though clearing her mind. 'Why did Mrs Pinion hang herself?'

'That's something I can't answer.'

'Her husband wasn't involved in no racket, was he?'

'How do you mean?'

'He wasn't on the run? I mean, Sammy thought he was and then Sam got bitten and—'

'Estelle, you don't really think anybody else is hiding down here, do you? I mean, why would we give anyone else sanctuary? In Sam's case, after he got out of prison, he needed a place where he wouldn't be looking over his shoulder, and he found a friend who was able to help. I was told because, well, because I understand. Those farm prisons are brutal places and it's easy, at a tender age, to fall in with the wrong crowd.'

Estelle listened to Masterson and pretended to be reassured, but his oily words weren't enough to quell the doubt which had lingered ever since Sam had been bitten at Roeder's place. No, despite what she'd said, she was looking forward to speaking to Miller.

35

The canteen was starting to fill though Miller found an empty table where he could sit on his own. He looked round as he put down his tray. Faces were becoming familiar: Ferradas sitting with two labourers in dirty overalls, Olsen with his wife and a man he didn't recognise. The couple beckoned him to join them, but he chose to remain where he was. He watched Ferradas eating, knowing the Brazilian was conscious of being looked at. The thought of going up to him and asking him why he'd mentioned Halliday crossed his mind, but he was unlikely to elaborate, at least not publicly. Besides, wasn't Halliday dead? If he'd been connected in any way with Leavis's disappearance then Miller was never going to hear his side of the story, or his young wife's.

No one joined the agent at his table and it was just as well that, after his wife had left him, he'd grown to prefer his own company. He'd picked his fight with small-town America long ago and as a consequence he'd tried to fence off his everyday opinions. Yet it wasn't until a year after his marriage had ended that he'd truly set himself apart. By then he'd learnt to drink in moderation, to recognise the bestial appetite that lurked a hair's-breadth beneath the skin for what it was and to keep his dreams to himself. And yet he'd be lying if he didn't admit that he'd been living a grey half-life, biding his time and thinking, perhaps more than was good for him, about Dolores and their daughter.

Maybe he should just keep his nose clean. Do his six months without stirring up any more trouble, without upsetting anyone or trying to uncover things which were really none of his business. And yet he was never one to hide behind the protective armour of common sense or, after Dolores, to allow any kind of deceit to remain concealed, at least until he was able to ascertain why they were lying.

It was the same nurse on the front desk. The same irritable attitude. She'd no idea what Miller was talking about. There were, of course, medical records, but these were confidential. She'd need permission from Dr Masterson before she could let him see them. And Dr Masterson had been called away. An injury somewhere out in the field. She had no idea when he'd be returning.

'But there's a registrar I can talk to?'

'There is, but she isn't here and won't be coming back till tomorrow.'

'Well, do you have anything on a Miss Violeta Smith?'

'Violeta . . .' The woman looked at him as though she'd never heard of the name before.

'She was here a few days ago,' prompted Miller.

'I don't know anybody by that name. I think you should return this evening, or perhaps tomorrow morning. Dr Masterson should be back by then.'

'But you must have a record of her being admitted.'

'Not necessarily. If she's Dr Masterson's patient then he sometimes takes care of his own.'

'Is there another doctor I can see?'

'There's Dr Barnes, but he's busy right now. I recommend you come back and see Dr Masterson. He's in charge and I know he'd want you to speak to him before you go questioning anybody else.'

36

Miller had no choice but to telegram Southfield. He composed the cable in his head as he walked along the sidewalk to the municipal hall: *Hospital uncooperative. Dr Masterson yet to release records. Please confirm authority to review all paperwork.* That would be enough to shake them up. He wasn't going to be messed around. There was a brief exchange in the lobby about whether he was authorised to send a telegram to Southfield. It threatened to become heated, but his annoyance was such that he was soon given directions to the wireless office on the third floor.

In the corridor he was greeted by a thin, angular man in his thirties called Shriver. It was obvious to Miller that the desk had rung ahead. Shriver's handshake wasn't firm and there was a wariness about the wireless operator that kept Miller on edge. He ushered him through into his office, which was a narrow space with one wall given over to electrical equipment. The door to the fire escape was wide open, yet the room was still crackling with heat. 'I just got to sort something out, then I'll be with you.'

'You paying extra for the view?' said Miller as he stepped out onto the iron balcony. It was the first time he was able to appreciate the enormity of the plantation, screened as it was from the town by what he realised now were merely thin strips of forest. Apart from the scale of the thing, what struck him was how little appeared to be thriving in the sun-baked earth in contrast to the dazzling green corridors which had been left or were yet to be cleared. Surveying the landscape, Miller realised that they must be coming close to the last shake of the dice. If what they were clearing to the west of the town failed, then that'd be the end of Carsonville. Logging would go some way to offset the running costs, but this wasn't why they were here. He glanced directly below. To the right was the bunkhouse he'd seen last night. It looked even more forlorn amongst the rampant vegetation. 'What's down there?' he asked, as though he didn't know.

'That bunkhouse is part of the hospital. Though what they use it for I've no idea.' Shriver came to stand by the agent's side. 'This gives us access to the roof,' he continued, twice slapping the ladder above in quick succession. 'We've three aerials on top, you might have seen them from the sidewalk. You want to take a look?'

'Maybe another time. I need to telegram Southfield. You can do that, can't you?'

'Sure can, though we only broadcast during certain hours. We send a whole batch of cables and save on time and the cost of intermittently transmitting. Though we're always open to receive.'

'When you sending the next batch?'

'In just under an hour. You write it down and I'll put it with the rest.'

Shriver went back inside. He pushed a pad and pen to the edge of the small desk jutting out from the equipment. 'You want to write it down here?'

There was no other way but to telegram Southfield, yet his determination almost faltered. It was foolish to think he was being disloyal or ungrateful to anyone. Miller had to take the extreme course – if only to observe himself doing it. He had

168

a suspicion the message was hardly likely to be sent, but he wanted to know the repercussions of such an action. Ironically, it was the thought that it wouldn't be sent which spurred him to commit his words to paper. There was something strange going on, perhaps even sinister. He had to let them know about the irregularities he'd uncovered, the hunch he had that there were more men unaccounted for.

Shriver took the sheet from Miller but didn't look at it. He'd do that when he was out of the office.

'Much obliged,' said Miller. 'I'll no doubt be seeing you again.'

'Any time,' replied Shriver, making a show of putting it on the spike.

37

Until dusk descended she would stand at the window watching the palm trees' long shadows move all the way down the park. Dusk was the shadow-gatherers' time: the hour for those who have neither rest nor sleep. Some shadows gathered like memories, others like unborn children with pale and secretive eyes. Estelle knew when the shadows waited to come by, knew how lost they felt, how unwanted they were feeling.

On her bed she shaped her hands in a slow fantasy, like a drugged hula dancer. Her fingers flowed like separate things before her eyes, weaving half-forgotten fairy tales. 'What big blue eyes you have,' she said aloud, twisting her lips into a loose and sensual line. She laughed derisively till the forgotten fairy of her mind replied, 'All the better to see you with.' She was always pleased to hear such words come so easily to her mind, as if spoken by another: some happier, some used-to-be or never-was Estelle.

The air hung wearily round her narrow shoulders. Restless at night, she threw aside the well-thumbed movie magazine and swung her slender legs off the crumpled sheets. The linoleum floor was warm beneath her bare feet. She padded quietly back to the window and pulled aside the curtain. Her reflection was there in the glass, illuminated by the lamp on the bedside cabinet. The room was insufferably warm, despite the window being ajar. She stood for a moment, her hands cupped around her face, nose pressed to the glass. There was the moon, the park, the trees lining the river, the white dome of the water tower. Silver grey in the moonlight. She revelled in the stillness of the scene. Estelle had no business leaving the hospital, Dr Masterson had made that clear to her, yet at night she had taken to wandering the corridors. During the day she was frequently confronted by nurses and orderlies who shepherded her back to her room. Few remained awake during the night, and fewer still were vigilant.

She briefly listened at her door before quietly opening it. With one hand held protectively across her belly, she crept lightly down the corridor. At the stairwell she stopped. In front of her were the laboratory and an empty ward. There was little chance of being seen up here, but last night all the doors were locked. No, tonight she'd take a bigger risk. Silently she descended the stairs, pausing only when she'd reached the ground floor. Nothing was any different from the night before, other than the door to the records office was ajar. Someone was working late, but that hardly bothered Estelle. In the stairwell she tried the back door, though she guessed it was locked. She paused for a moment to stare, as was her custom, at the bunkhouse. She'd never seen it lit, which didn't surprise her. She went over to the double doors which opened into the entrance hall. On tiptoes she could see above the pane of frosted glass, saw Finkleman sitting, his balding head nestled in his arms which were slumped across the reception desk. She gently pushed open one of the doors and slid into the hall. There was no sign of the orderly waking but still she tiptoed as best she could across the floor. Before she knew it she was out of the hospital and beneath the starry sky.

Thrilled by her success, she glided down the steps and walked purposefully towards the park, just wanting some distance from the place before she put the other part of her plan into

172

action. She stopped at the park entrance. She wasn't going to walk through it. It was too dark, too shadowy. Her feet were covered in the dust which blew over the road. She leant against the railings and brushed off the grit. It would have been foolish to go back for her slippers. Outside she felt wide awake; she was playing hooky and revelled in her mischievousness. Sam had always been so careful about obeying the curfew, as though pumas and panthers had it in for him. Funny to think he was just behind the hospital. Wouldn't he be surprised to see her? No, he wouldn't show any emotion. Foolish to think he could still feel as she felt. It was shameful to think it was only the sex she missed, but that was about it. His language she could do without: jumping her bones, splitting her peach and putting a hole in her. Vulgar, dirty words which perhaps had had some effect at first, but back then she wasn't even seventeen. She'd visit him for old times' sake. A daughterly duty, nothing more. If he'd already started his shift she'd wait. In the empty ward she'd maybe rub one out if the fancy took her.

Estelle recrossed the road. She'd go round the back. She'd seen the wooden building from the outside before. Built like the barracks the peons had, but labelled a ward by Masterson. From the corner of the hospital she could see the lights were still all out. Ferns and long grasses bowed across the chicken walk and brushed against her bare arms. She trod as lightly as she could, the dirt path rough beneath her feet, and rubbed her forearms for fear of insects. The drab curtains were closed. What kind of a ramshackled ward was it they were keeping him in? There were three wooden steps up to the bunkhouse door; damp, creaking wood; then there was a padlock across the bolted door. Estelle leaned in and saw it wasn't locked. Someone hadn't troubled themselves to snap it shut, but had left it swinging. She lifted it out of its ring and pulled aside the latch. She listened, and then tried the handle. The door was open. She pushed it a little and the darkness seemed to drift out. The smell of death and decay almost made her retch.

Estelle cupped her hand over her mouth and nose, determined not to be defeated by the terrible stench. There was not a sound within. Holding her breath, she put her head inside. It was impossible to see anything at first, and she felt reluctant to step over the threshold. But she wanted to see Sam for herself, to make sure that he was being properly looked after. He'd always done his best for her, and she at least owed him a visit. Trying not to breathe, she ventured with one hand outstretched, to the nearest rag of a curtain. She lifted the greasy corner and a splinter of moonlight lit the dirty floor. There were no beds, no orderly, nothing. The place was bare, yet she'd seen Dr Masterson escort Sam into the ward.

Something stirred in a corner of the empty bunkhouse. Estelle heard it before she saw it. A slight hissing sound, as though velvet was being slowly rubbed against one of the wooden walls. There was a shadow, darker than the space through which it floated. She tried to keep the filthy curtain lifted but it slipped through her fingers as she took a step backwards. The spectre was lost in the descending blackness. Estelle had found the doorframe. She stretched her trembling hand out. Where was the switch? A floorboard softly sighed. She took another step backwards and as she did so her fingers brushed over a cord hanging from the ceiling. 'Sam,' she whispered. 'Is that you? You're scaring me.' Another board creaked, closer this time. Ten yards away, no more.

Estelle pulled on the switch. A solid clunk above her head and the urgent heavy hum was there, showering the room with electric light. It was caught directly beneath the bare bulb. A skeletal shock of pink, aflame with wiry black hair. With a childish wail it half collapsed to its knees, its thin white hands gripping its wasted face, covering its eyes. For a second or two it had no momentum, but then it began to fall forward, staggering rather than running towards Estelle. There was something in its reaction to the light, its drunken gait as it blindly lurched ahead, which terrified the young woman. Estelle didn't want the sick, evil-looking girl coming anywhere near her. Flinging the cord away, as though banishing what was reeling crookedly in her direction, she deftly moved onto the wooden step and slammed the door.

Another howl of demented torment reverberated inside. For a brief moment she thought of holding the handle, keeping her trapped. Yet she couldn't face the struggle which would ensue: madness, she knew, gave lunatics a deviant strength. Then she remembered the padlock. With one hand she lifted it from the ring. Thud and buckle went the bunkhouse wall, punched by a body colliding. She pressed the latch home, held the padlock ready to thread through when the walls buckled for a second time, so close to the door that she felt the reverberations through her knuckles, through her fingers slick with sweat, fingers which felt the warm metal sliding earthward. Instinctively she moved her foot out of the way and heard the padlock hit the wooden step before it rebounded out of sight into the grass. Faced with no choice but to run, Estelle quickly descended to the path, almost tripping as her feet touched the ground. With damp hands clutching her belly through her nightdress, she lumbered as quickly as she could away from the door. Thudding, crunching: a moth throwing itself against the light. Trapped inside was a girl who had once dreamed of ball gowns, Arabian stud-farms and beaus. She crumpled in her blood frenzy, pulled her dress from around her knees, and was up again. Estelle heard the heavy clatter of the door being thrown open and scampered in terror, no care taken over how hard she turned on her bare soles. Violeta, still reeling from the light, stumbled down the stairs and collapsed momentarily in the thick grass. On all fours she sniffed the air, caught the scent of her quarry, slid back to her feet.

38

Flush-faced and panting, Estelle staggered into the hospital. Finkleman lifted his creased face from the desk. 'Halt,' he managed to cry. But she wasn't stopping. At the stairwell she paused at the sight of the door to the bunkhouse. She knew it was locked and was momentarily drawn to it, to the rippled pane of glass above the handle. Nothing but the framing of a dull black and the snowflake shimmer of the light behind her head. Estelle glanced over her shoulder; Finkleman had stepped from behind his desk and now stood with his hands on his hips looking at her. She wasn't afraid of him, of his admonishment. It was the sound of something scratching on the other side of the door which made her jump. Slap went the glassy hand. Slap. Slapping as though taunting her, slapping the glass in front of her face. Estelle didn't hesitate for another second, but skedaddled up the stairs as fast as her veined and aching legs could carry her.

Finkleman didn't see the hand at the window. He was more concerned about whether he should ring Dr Masterson, or let the incident go. He'd been told to ring him if anything untoward happened. The orderly scratched his pate and followed the woman as far as the stairwell. She must have run back to her room. He'd leave it. Mrs Halliday had returned from wherever she'd been and he'd probably just get himself in trouble for not having noticed her escaping. He was going back to his desk when he saw a scrap of pink floating through the darkness in front of the hospital. Peculiar to see anything after curfew, let alone what he took to be a child. Was this what Mrs Halliday was running away from? Certainly wasn't no big cat. He stepped towards the entrance. It was a short dress, a child's dress, running into the park.

It was a cloudless night and a cool breeze shuffled the leaves. Finkleman, worried for the girl's safety, buttoned up his jacket and descended the hospital steps. He hollered with his hand cupped over his mouth. 'Hey,' he called. 'I saw you. Come out.' He walked over to the entrance to the park. The smell of the magnolias on the soft wind caressed his face, refreshed his senses. He should have brought a flashlight, though the waning moon illuminated the trees and bushes well enough for his tired eyes to see. He passed beneath the wrought-iron entrance entwined with firecracker vines which had shed their tiny orange petals on the path below.

He called out again. Shadows from the palm trees danced in front of him. The garden was eerily quiet. In the middle, set upon a circular brick plinth, was an engraved map of the world on a flattened hemisphere of polished bronze. Finkleman glanced at it as he passed and in his mind briefly linked his life and its passage to the lines drawn across its face. His life was almost at an end; he would never return to Munich and the Englischer Garten, never hear again his tongue as he spoke it or the oom-pah of the Oktoberfest. The only dream he now harboured was to see out his final days in a cheap apartment in Manaus. A small apartment with, if he could afford it, a balcony overlooking the river beach where he could watch the families sunbathing on the sand. He'd almost forgotten why he was out there when, as he came towards the end of the garden, he heard something from behind one of the wooden benches. It was a soft, lilting voice. The words were blurred, ill-formed, yet the tune was there. In his head he could hear it clearly. '*Guten abend, gute nacht, mit rosen bedacht . . .*' It was a child's lullaby. The unseen tongue dribbled out the melody. The smeared lyrics were there: '*Guten abend, gute nacht, von englein bewacht . . .*'

It gave him goosebumps to hear it now. It had been one of his wife's favourite tunes. 'That can't be you, Nesta,' he uttered in German. 'Is it you?' The voice wasn't hers, but it belonged to a child. There, he saw her, through the wooden rails of the bench.

As Finkleman approached, she rose to her feet. He gestured for her to come out, to mind the rose bushes for fear that the thorns would scratch her pale flesh. Her black eyes were fixed on him with a disturbing steadiness. He took hold of her wrist and with that Violeta leaned towards him.

39

On the third floor Estelle lay on her bed crying, overwhelmed by the horror which surrounded her, the incessant nightmares which made a mockery of sleep. By murdering Leavis she'd sullied herself, only to be betrayed by those with whom she thought her act of violence might have gained her acceptance. It hadn't. Instead it had brought shame and sleepless nights, but it had helped her to see things more clearly, to understand what she meant to Masterson. Whatever had flung itself at her was proof of how little he cared. 'First they tell you lies,' she whimpered, looking down at her belly, 'and you believe them. They make you believe them. Then they give you a little of what you were promised. Just a little, enough to keep you thinking you're in it together, that they want to help. Then you find out that you've been tricked. Just like everyone else.' It was a lesson she wanted her unborn to understand. She'd tried to please him, but he'd recoiled from her willingness to be like him, as if they were better than her. They were no better. They were worse. It was their fault she'd done what she'd done. It wasn't in her nature. She wanted to come clean. There was a vast, heartbreaking ache inside her, a poignant longing to tell someone. 'I've often wanted to be left alone,' said Estelle untruthfully, trying contrarily to reconcile herself to her confinement, to give herself a crumb of comfort. But it was no use. Miller was solider, rosier, clearer-eyed. When she saw him she'd tell him, tell him straight. 'There's a bunkhouse, just a little way behind the hospital. No one goes in or out of it during the day, but there are creatures locked inside, they're dead like Sam.'

'Sam?'

'He was my . . .' No, there was no need to lie about Sam. She never would have married him. 'They're working a shift. Don't ever work in the daytime. Only at night.'

'How do you know?' He was grateful, baffled, impressed by her knowledge, taken in by her beauty.

'I've seen them, just after curfew. But it ain't just them that come out at night. They hobble, amble. Like they're all drugged or manacled together. But there are others that fly at you, that want to . . .' The thought of what might have happened made her shudder. 'You have to take me away. We've got to get away.' It was a conversation she played out in her mind. Her imagination, her scene. Miller sat there, listening to her, at the end feeling nothing but sympathy. No, that wasn't right; sympathy and old-fashioned desire, not a slippery lust but an ability to see her as she once was, as she would become again once the baby had been born.

40

The wind picked up in the early hours and the screen of the empty bungalow next door started banging. Miller tried to ignore it, but it soon became unbearable; creak, bang then silence, repeated nearly rhythmically, making him realise he had no choice but to go out and deal with the damn thing.

He felt around for the lamp on the bedside table. He checked his watch – just gone three a.m. – then picked up the flashlight he'd bought that afternoon from the hardware shop. 'You no go out after curfew,' the storekeeper had said. 'You no make mischief.' The man wasn't smiling and it wouldn't have surprised Miller if the whole compound knew about the night before. The thought of the curfew made him pause briefly, but surely shutting a screen door wasn't going to get him into any more trouble?

The night sky was blanketed with thick clouds, yet by keeping the beam to the ground he saw well enough to skip smartly over the lawn outside his bungalow. The grass was tall in the neighbouring garden and, thinking anything might be hiding in there, he took the path to the entrance before climbing the wooden steps to the porch. Someone had forgotten to latch the screen. It was easy to solve. He barely had to think about it, and was about to walk away when he saw that the wooden door was ajar by an inch or so. 'What the . . .' he said quietly to himself as he placed a hand on it. Curious as to whether or not anything was inside, he gently pushed. The door swung slowly open. For some reason he hesitated before lifting the beam. 'Anyone there?' he cried.

Nothing, except the wind stirring the house, making the boards sigh. He put a foot inside. From the narrow hall he couldn't see a stick of furniture. The layout was the same as his: just a one-bedroom bungalow with a kitchen, bathroom and living room which doubled as a place to eat. He walked past the kitchen and into the living room. It was warm and dusty and had that heavy, fetid smell of decay. There was a large dark stain on the floor. He was curious as to what might have caused it yet he carefully avoided putting his foot on the tarnished boards. Whatever it was, it had stripped the varnish from the wood. He tiptoed carefully into the bedroom. Like the rest of the house, it was decorated with thick cobwebs and dust. Over the windows were draped heavy curtains. There was a gap between them. He knew the window looked onto the side of his house. Nothing more than curiosity led him to it, just to see what kind of view it had of his place. He peered with one eye between the embroidered fabric, switching the flashlight off as he leaned towards it. It took a while for his eye to adjust to the dark outside.

At first there was just a darker mass where the bungalow was and the grey blackness of the sky, then something seemed to float between him and the building. It was an amorphous shape at first, hanging between here and there, yet as it advanced rapidly towards the window he quickly discerned what it was: a thin, angular, triangular silhouette, a hideously disjointed shape that was suddenly running towards him. Screen hammered against window; moon-like palms and thin, translucent fingers. Miller recoiled, but not before he'd seen her face: the narrow face of a girl in agony; a crumpled paper-thin picture of a tormented child pasted to a shuddering skull.

He held the flashlight in both hands, fumbled to switch it on; a finger momentarily glowed a pinkish red. He looked up at the curtains. Dust floated through the light. There was no sound except for his breathing; fast, shallow breaths. Then a click, beyond the bedroom. The sound of a door being closed. He stepped forward and shone the light down the narrow corridor. Something darted into the kitchen, a blur of pink dispersing into darkness. He could hear her murmuring to herself, a low, swelling growl as though she was chewing on her words before spitting them out.

He thought of closing the door on her, getting someone to come and take her back to the hospital, but knew he couldn't lock her in; he had to face her, to reason with her. There was desperation in her voice, a rising pitch which threatened to finish in an agonising scream. Tightly gripping the flashlight in one hand, he pushed the kitchen door open. As the light filled the room the scream broke loose, a hissing, rattling shriek reverberating in its wooden box. The girl shrank back, tried to climb over the cooker, threw herself within a foot of the greasy ceiling; all skinny arms and thighs and swinging locks of matted hair. Miller kept the beam fixed on her, not from a desire to torment her, but to prove himself right. It was the light she was trying to escape from. Like a wild animal she scrambled this way and that, until she could take it no longer. She flung herself at Miller just as the flashlight dipped beneath her scrawny waist. This was something he hadn't expected and he had no time to raise a defensive arm or to swerve away from her flying, flailing limbs. She sent him reeling and his head was thrown back hard against the plastered wall.

41

It was just before dawn when Finkleman was found by a labourer working with the sanitation squad. He was lying on his front a few yards away from a bench. He'd fallen head first into the flowers, and though a light rain had washed the leaves clean above his head, the earth was dark beneath the shiny seat of his pants and the worn-through soles of his shoes. At first the peon thought Finkleman must have collapsed and, after hesitating momentarily, he grasped the damp collar of the old man's jacket and lifted him from the bush. He lowered the orderly gently onto his back. On what remained of his head there was no longer a face. Where his flesh and eyes should have been there was only blackened bone and dirt.

The partly devoured corpse was hurriedly removed from the park and taken to the hospital's morgue. When Masterson saw the body he didn't need Garret to tell him it was hardly likely to have been a big cat. With the girl having disappeared from the bunkhouse he started to wonder if she was to blame. Could she become a different creature during the night? Yet the others were docile, vacant corpses, animated when instructed to move, but unthinking, stinking carcasses of decaying flesh. Somehow they'd been granted a stay of execution, and he was putting them to good use before they fell to pieces. Yet if the girl who'd appeared out of nowhere had survived for longer than a few months then perhaps she was feeding on the only thing which would sustain her. Strange, though, that it was only the face which had been attacked. Perhaps she'd been disturbed by something. If she hadn't she might have devoured more of the old man. Early on he'd tried to feed the undead with no success, but what if it was human flesh they were given?

Masterson shifted his gaze from the cadaver to the orderly who stood at a respectful distance on the other side of the trolley. 'The man went missing just before dawn?'

'Yes, doctor,' he answered promptly. 'An hour before dawn. I waited for him to return. Then telephoned.'

'You did the right thing.' Masterson brushed down his lab coat. The dead German was a non-entity, just another piece of jetsam washed up on Carsonville's shore. 'I'll have Dr Barnes sign the death certificate. There's no need for him to see the corpse. Tell him that the bite marks are in keeping with those of a large predator, probably a big cat.'

188

42

The first whistle blew and Miller felt a hand cradling his head, his own hand, unconsciously seeking out the bruise from where he'd fallen, fallen as she'd pounced, her vacant eyes rushing into his, burrowing into his mind. She'd pressed her blood-stained face against his own until he was swamped with the greyness of her sight, the stench of her putrefying flesh. Yet he recalled the tenderness of the lover's embrace as he fell backwards, the hand softly clasping his neck. He'd been knocked cold and she'd fled into the forest. He remembered wandering out there, finding no sign of her. He'd called out, convinced that her eyes were upon him, that somewhere hidden in the shadows she was watching him. With his flashlight he'd stripped the jungle of its darkness, but she was too cunning to let herself be revealed.

Outside of his bedroom the birds and monkeys were filling the air with noise; to Miller it now sounded like they were boasting of their survival, rejoicing in the sunlight. He lay there listening, trying to make sense of it all. When dusk fell they screeched hysterically, but at the crack of dawn there was gaiety. The brightness of the February morning filled him with a strange sadness, until the second whistle blew and an involuntary shudder, part annoyance, part apprehension, rose between his shoulder blades.

When he approached the nurse at the reception desk he was ready to be unreasonable. However, to his astonishment she greeted him cordially and told him that Mrs Wilde, the registrar, was waiting for him on the first floor.

'I'd also like to see Dr Masterson,' said Miller. 'I assume he's in his office?'

'I'm afraid today's his morning off.'

'Well, perhaps you'd be kind enough to pass on a message?' He paused momentarily while she reached for a pad and pen. 'Just tell him I found the girl, Violeta, wandering round in the middle of the night. I'm going to speak to Mr Sullivan about it, but I just thought he ought to know.'

Miller didn't wait for her to finish writing out the note but headed towards the stairwell. He paused on the first floor, tempted to continue up to Masterson's office and the laboratory above. Wondering whether he could trust anyone in the hospital, he was about to ascend the stairs when a nurse appeared with a breakfast tray. 'Can I help you?' she called down.

'I'm looking for Dr Masterson.'

'I'm afraid he's not here,' she replied, descending the stairs, 'and besides, the floors above are off limits unless you have an appointment.'

'You don't happen to know about a young girl he's treating, do you?'

Her face seemed to lose a little of its colour. The tray she was holding, with its grapefruit rind and dirty glass, encroached an inch or two towards his chest. 'I'm not at liberty to discuss patients with anyone other than the doctor or a member of their family, you must appreciate that.'

'Oh, I do understand, and I've been told several times already. It's just that a young patient of his is on the loose again and I thought he should know.'

'I think he's aware of that, Mr Miller. Now would you like me to escort you to the records office? That is where you're meant to be, isn't it?'

Miller concealed his surprise that she knew who he was. 'I'm sure I can find my own way, but I appreciate the offer. It's such a large hospital one can so easily get lost.'

The door at the end of the corridor was open and in the cramped, windowless room he found a woman surrounded by wooden shelves on which were stacked countless manila folders. There was a small desk just to the side of the door with a chrome lamp sitting on top and a chair neatly tucked beneath it. Mrs Wilde, a thin, stooping woman in her late forties, smiled serenely and proffered her hand. 'I've already pulled out one folder, but if you'd like to see others you only have to ask.'

The agent thanked her and glanced at the folder. There were three names on it: James, Dorothy and Violeta Smith.

'I'd also like to see where you record your deaths and the death certificates.'

'We have a ledger for deaths,' she replied, bending at the knees and retrieving a green, leather-bound volume, 'but you'll find each certificate is stored in the appropriate folder.'

'And the cause of death?'

'Will be included on the certificate and in the ledger.' Having put the volume on the desk, Mrs Wilde stood with her hands behind her and leaned back against the wooden shelves.

'And you'll be here the whole time?'

'Dr Masterson asked me to stay with you, in case you needed anything.'

'Well, that's very considerate of the doctor. And you make sure you tell him as much when you next see him.' Without sitting, he picked up the file which had been left on the desk and carefully lifted out a handful of documents. He found, as he knew he would, two death certificates for James and Dorothy Smith. There was also enough paperwork to prove the existence of both the parents and their daughter. Miller sank into the chair and started to check the papers carefully. He pulled out a file at random in order to compare its contents with the Smith file. On the desk were soon papers of all shapes and sizes, papers in longhand or in print, papers white or yellowed with age, all with elaborate signatures and official stamps. He scrutinised every detail, cross referenced every death that interested him. Everything appeared to be in order, but then Masterson had had plenty of time to make sure there were no mistakes.

43

He'd been sitting in the office for over an hour poring over the medical records of the Smiths, the Hallidays and several other families when his eye was caught by two black box files. 'What do you keep up there?' he asked, gesturing to the shelf above.

'Just hospital receipts. Are you authorised to examine those?'

If the registrar hadn't posed the question he wouldn't have lifted them down onto the desk. 'Be assured, anything that takes my fancy will be examined.' He wasn't expecting to find any financial irregularities but he thought he may as well take a look. There were invoices for drugs shipped from Belem, each one rubber stamped with *paid* and a date scribbled below, receipts for mattresses and linen and soap flakes. While shuffling them into piles, Miller spied two notes written on pages torn from an exercise book. The handwriting was barely legible, each signed by the same individual. 'I see you've had dealings with a Mr Roeder in the past,' Miller called over his shoulder. 'You couldn't tell me what it is he's supplying the hospital with?'

'Maybe it's medicinal herbs.'

'At what, sixty and thirty dollars a pop? That's a lot of herbs.'

She was standing over him now, as though trying to scrutinise the papers he held in his hand. 'Maybe,' she answered, though her tone wasn't convincing. 'Some of the plants round here are quite rare. Listen, are you going to be much longer?'

'Oh, at least another hour,' he lied.

'Well, I'm going to get myself a coffee. Would you like one?'

'Sure, why not.' Miller sat back and stretched. Was she genuinely wanting a break or was she trying to avoid his questions, at least until she'd spoken to someone? Either way it didn't bother him. In the second box file he found another receipt from Roeder, the earliest one, dated just over a year ago and with Masterson's name at the top. Every three months Roeder seemed to be selling something. He tried to make out what was written. 'For Services Rendered,' seemed to fit. Miller heard footsteps behind him and at first thought she must have changed her mind. Yet the tread on the linoleum was softer. He didn't turn his head until they'd stopped outside the office. Instead of the scrawny Mrs Wilde, there stood Estelle in a tight dress. 'Mrs Halliday?' he exclaimed.

Flattered but equally unnerved, she felt herself blushing. 'You're Miller, the new agent?'

'I thought you'd gone back to the States?' He'd risen from his chair, glad to see her in more ways than one.

Estelle glanced back down the corridor. 'They warned me you'd be here, but you mustn't tell anyone you saw me.'

'Why not?'

'They don't want me talking to you, not after what happened.'

'You mean with Leavis?'

The look she gave him was more afraid than guilty. 'That's not why I'm here,' she replied imperiously, her nerves twisting her feelings all out of shape. 'I want you to know they killed Sam, that it's dangerous and I want you to get me out of here.'

'Now hold on. What happened to Leavis?'

'Same as Sam. They did it. We gotta get out.'

'Who's they?' Miller had a hand on her forearm; her flesh

was soft and warm to the touch. She didn't flinch but rather gravitated towards him. 'Did they kill Leavis?'

'They did it.' She couldn't bring herself to utter his name, terrified of what Masterson would do if he found out she'd openly accused him. 'You have to take me away. I'm begging you.' What courage she'd had waiting on the stairs had evaporated. 'She'll be back, I know she will.' Again Estelle glanced down the corridor to the double doors. She was terrified of being caught, of being seen; the betrayal she'd endured and the awful thing she'd done were hurting her more than she could say. There was a lump in her throat, a feeling that it was all welling up inside her. 'You gotta get me out of here before something bad happens.'

Miller could see she was close to tears. 'Where have you been hiding?'

'The top floor, next to his laboratory. They got me cooped up in there. You gotta get me out.' She tried to pull her wrist away, but Miller held it firmly. 'I can't be seen here. You ain't someone I should talk to.'

'Is Masterson involved, is it Roeder?'

Her knees seemed to buckle at the names, her body sinking an inch or two in front of his eyes. 'Don't tell Masterson you know about him!' she cried. 'Don't say anything.'

The sound of one of the doors swishing open brought a whimper to her lips. Instinctively, Estelle tried to inch behind Miller.

'Hey,' called Mrs Wilde. 'You're not supposed to be out of your room, young lady.' The cups trembled in their saucers. Estelle, the back of a hand pressed against her cheek as though she could hide her face, slid past and scurried down the corridor. 'You don't want to listen to her,' the registrar was saying as the girl fled back to her room. 'She's our mad woman in the attic, every hospital's got one. Ought to be sedated, the way she carries on.'

'I was told Mrs Halliday had left Carsonville.'

'That's what happened, but when you're pregnant you don't always think straight. Got as far as Santarem and turned round.'

'You know, I think I'm finished here.' Miller began to follow Estelle, but as soon as he'd gone through the doors he heard Masterson calling to him from below. 'You all done?'

'Just about.' He mounted a step or two.

'Now hold on. No one's at liberty to go up there without my permission.'

Miller wasn't quite ready to challenge the doctor's authority, and so waited impatiently, trying to decide whether or not to confront him with what Estelle had been saying.

'Everything in order, I hope?'

'No doubt as you'd want it to be.'

'Damn nuisance about Violeta,' Masterson climbed the last step and turned to face the agent. 'Plum jumped out of the launch on the way back here.'

'Really?' Miller tried hard to hide his incredulity.

'And I hear you saw her last night.' Masterson pulled out his handkerchief and wiped his brow. 'Can I ask you whereabouts?'

'At the end of Cherry Drive. In the empty bungalow.'

'I'll send Garret over there right away. You know, I feel awfully bad about poor Violeta and what she's been through. Once she's been caught we'll take better care of her, I can assure you.'

Miller hesitated. But couldn't resist mentioning it. 'And I understand Mrs Halliday's returned.'

'Now how do you know that?' To Miller's surprise, a faint smile played across Masterson's lips, as though his adversary was proving to be a better match than he'd anticipated.

'You're going to tell me she just decided to return?' asked Miller.

'That's right. From Santarem.'

'Just like that?'

'Just like that. Pregnant women can do funny things. Unpredictable.'

'Funny, Mrs Wilde said just about the same thing.'

'No doubt you'd like to see Mrs Halliday.'

'Yes, I would.'

'Then you will. Straight after you've seen Mr Sullivan. You know, the big chief's awfully keen to see you. Saw him just now and he told me to send you straight over. Tell you what, I'll telephone to let him know you're on your way.'

44

It was noon and Miller was seated squarely facing Sullivan. He was a tall, sinewy Virginian who spoke slowly in a low monotone. A cigarette was dangling in the manager's right hand, while the fingers of his left were spread out over the arm rest. It was a show Sullivan was putting on. He was in an ugly mood, that much was being telegraphed. The only sounds were the clackety-clack of Mrs Shriver's typewriter from the outside office and the whir of the ceiling fan above their heads. Sullivan was staring at him, like a lean prize-fighter weighing up his opponent from the other side of the ring. Miller stole his eyes away from his gaze, not because he felt intimidated, but because he refused to play any silly games. He'd let him have his say about the telegram and then he'd tell him about Violeta and ask him about Roeder and his dealings with Masterson. Miller wasn't going to say anything about Estelle, at least not until he'd spoken to her again.

On Sullivan's large mahogany desk was a stone idol, similar to something the Incas might have shaped. It was about eight inches tall with an elongated head and folded arms. There was an inscription of some sort, carved across the sandstone body.

'Why did you ask Shriver to send that telegram?'

'It was a complaint I felt I had to send.' There was menace

in the statue's face. Its eyes were narrow, its lips were curled. Whoever had carved it had given it the mouth of a snarling dog. Miller looked up at Sullivan. He wasn't half as threatening as the idol.

'Why didn't you come to me?' Sullivan was asking.

'Why didn't you send it?'

The manager shook his head at the agent's impudence. 'If I'd let Shriver send the thing it wouldn't just have reflected badly on Masterson, it would also have reflected badly on you, perhaps even on the whole goddamn operation. You must understand that any lack of harmony or hint of impropriety can rattle those back home. Particularly with what happened to the last agent.'

Miller wasn't surprised he was right about the telegram. The events of that morning had convinced him that there were few, if any, employees on the plantation he could trust.

'Thankfully Shriver brought it straight to me,' continued Sullivan. 'And I don't know where you're getting some of the ideas you've been sharing, but you got to be careful. I mean, the malaria tablets can play tricks on the mind. They can get you seeing all kinds of weird things. You've spoken to Masterson, haven't you?'

'Yes, and I can assure you I'm doing my best to cling to rational arguments.'

'And you've been through the hospital's records.'

'After some delay I was allowed access.'

'You know, it's the ingratitude which gets me,' sighed Sullivan. 'We had no trouble with Leavis. It was terrible what happened to him, but I must say he was a proper gentleman, appreciative of how accommodating we were. I mean, haven't you been well looked after since your arrival?'

Miller acknowledged that he had, though it did little if anything to alleviate the look of suffering on Sullivan's long face.

'Do you appreciate, for instance, how hard everyone here has been working?'

'Why, it's obvious—'

'No, I don't think you do. And you know, we're doing a lot of good out here. We're here to modernise, to help Brazil become a successful nation, and yes, to make sure we have the rubber we require for the automobile industry. You understand that, don't you?'

'Of course.'

'You should have seen this place when we first arrived, seen the squalor with your own eyes, listened to the wild tales they had to tell, all sorts of superstitions and diabolical beliefs. Tribes killing twins, burying their children alive to spare them the shame of being enslaved. Burying them alive thinking they'd come back as demons and taunt the Spanish.'

Miller knew it was a matter of letting him blow, of allowing him to finish the performance he'd no doubt rehearsed. Just listen and learn, he repeated silently to himself.

'If we're to make the right impression on these people, then we've got to behave ourselves, to lead by example. Now I know you went to a whorehouse with the sanitation manager and I've already spoken to him about how disappointed I am. I've also been told that you were out after curfew.'

'That was because of the attack by the caiman.'

'An attack in which an Indian boy lost his life. A boy rowing two drunks back from an island the very name of which is an insult to any right-minded American. Am I right?'

'Many of your managers—'

'Don't talk to me about my managers.' Sullivan stubbed out his cigarette as though he was crushing the man in front of him. 'You know, I'm tempted to send in a little report of my own. Tell those at Southfield just how impressed I've been by your professional conduct.'

The threat didn't alarm Miller. He knew his cue well enough and it was time to give Sullivan what he wanted in order to move the conversation forward. 'I'm sorry,' he said, 'if I caused any offence with the cable I intended to send.'

The manager nodded. He was glad Miller appreciated why he was in his office. There was a pause. Sullivan was readying himself for a change in approach. 'This is good work we're doing, hard work. You have to live out here to appreciate it. See the jungle for what it is. Coming from Southfield it's hard to appreciate what has to be done, how hard it is to succeed against a psychotic mother nature.' Again he paused. 'They're not putting pressure on you, are they, those in Southfield?' Sullivan's manner was now almost avuncular. 'They didn't send you here simply to find fault, did they? You can tell me.'

Miller hesitated. 'No, they did not. But there are some peculiar things going on around here.' His eyes fixed on Sullivan's and he expected him to ask 'Like what?' but instead the manager just shrugged his shoulders.

'Like I said, go easy on those malaria tablets.' Sullivan suddenly seemed to want to bring the meeting to an end. 'Well,' he concluded, his hand wiping an imaginary speck of dust from the desk, 'let's draw a line under this. In future, I think it best if you come to me with any message you want to give to the folks back home. Agreed?'

'All right,' said Miller, knowing he wouldn't be able to get any message out without the manager's approval. 'But I just need some clarification about a couple of things before I go.'

Sullivan made a show of lifting his wrist and glancing at his watch.

'There's a girl called Violeta Smith who's a patient of Dr Masterson's. We did find her—'

'I know, he's been keeping me informed. It's dreadful what's happened to her and I know she should never have been able to leave the hospital like she did. I understand Garret's looking for her now and I appreciate your concern. Anything else?'

The rapidity of his interruption, and the fact that Masterson had already spoken to Sullivan about the matter, stalled Miller briefly. Yet the agent recognised a primed response when he heard one. There was obviously nothing to be gained from labouring the point or questioning him about the night shift he'd come across. But he wasn't finished yet.

'One other thing I keep hearing is the name Roeder.' He studied Sullivan's face as he said the name, but there was little there to read. 'What is it he supplies Carsonville with?'

'Rubber seeds.'

'And Masterson?'

'Nothing, as far as I know.'

'I understand he lives in the grounds of an abandoned Jesuit mission, not far up the river. That he used to supply natives to work on the plantation, but they proved to be too unreliable.'

'That's right.' For the first time Sullivan appeared to be losing some of his self-assurance.

'These natives came freely? I mean, we're not talking slaves, are we?'

'Certainly not.'

'And you wouldn't object if I took a trip upriver to his place?'

Sullivan hesitated before answering. 'By all means. It's not a place I'd recommend to anyone, though having said that it'd give you a chance to get to know the area. And Pinion's always keen to collect more seeds. You know Pinion, don't you?'

'Yes, I do.'

'I guess accompanying him will help you get some perspective. How about after lunch? Trip like that doesn't usually take more than an afternoon.'

'I'm interviewing patients in the hospital.'

'They'll all still be there when you get back.' Sullivan smiled. 'Take a couple of days. I tell you what, I'll contact Southfield, tell them you've entered into the spirit of the thing, that I've been impressed by your sense of adventure.'

'It'll have to be tomorrow morning, and I'd like Garret to accompany me.'

'Well, OK,' said Sullivan, 'I'll see what I can do. Though

I have to admit, I'm curious to know why you want to see Roeder's place.'

'Well, as you said, to gain some perspective. It'll also give me a chance to appreciate what this place was like before we transformed it into Carsonville. I mean, as you've made clear, this is such a beacon of industry and progress it's hard for someone like me to imagine how dark and malevolent the jungle must have been before our arrival.'

Sullivan nodded as though satisfied that Miller was sincere. 'And if Bell tags along then you'll have to pay a visit to the cave just beyond the mission. That statue you were admiring earlier is something Bell brought back from the last venture. The abandoned mission is the nearest thing we have to a lost city, though I don't mind admitting it gives me the creeps. No doubt Roeder will tell you all about it. He's a charismatic fellow, according to Masterson, though some carry on like he was the devil himself.'

45

Through the morning mist a frustrated Miller could see the silhouettes of four men waiting beside the covered launch; their cigarettes rising and falling, intermittent pinpricks of smouldering light. Miller had returned to the hospital after seeing Sullivan, but Masterson had given Estelle a mild sedative. He'd been allowed to see her, but she'd said very little which made any sense. She needed rest, Masterson had explained. Mrs Wilde had told him about their little chat and something must have upset her. After his boat trip he should look in on her again. She'd like that, though he must understand she'd been through a lot. Miller thought of waiting for her to come round, of visiting her that morning, and hated the thought of being outwitted. But then if Roeder and Masterson were involved in something underhand he figured the quickest way to gather evidence was by going out into the jungle. If the 'they' meant the doctor was responsible, amongst others, for Leavis's murder then it would take more than Estelle's word to build a case against him. Why Leavis might have been killed was still beyond him, but he was now convinced it had something to do with Masterson.

'Like Frisco, ain't it?' said Garret, flicking his cigarette stub into the river and taking a step towards him. 'All fog and a chill breeze blowin'. Just the smell of boiled lobster and we'd be there. Ever been to Frisco?'

'No, never got that far,' answered Miller tersely. 'How many are coming with us?'

'Six if you count Alvarez,' replied Garret, gesturing to a man whose head was hidden by the launch's cover. 'Six and a half if you include his boy. And that's plenty. We'll draw less attention to ourselves this way. Any bigger and the Indians will think the troops are moving against them.'

'You think it's going to be dangerous?'

'Not in *Joana*, with the engine she's got. I've yet to be attacked with poisoned arrows, but it happens if you stray too far. Round here things are pretty quiet and any Indians we see are likely to be tame. Roeder's can be quarrelsome, but then we got old Ferradas here. He can speak some of the lingo.'

'Well, I'm glad to hear it.' Miller shook Ferradas' hand, which took the watchman by surprise, then Bell's and Pinion's.

'Come on,' said Garret, 'we'd better get on board if we're going.'

Alvarez Cabral was the captain of the launch, a short, freckled Brazilian who wore a frayed shirt and a pair of faded slacks cut off above the knee. His silver crucifix swung across his whiskered chest as he took the rifles, hammocks and burlap bags from the four Americans and stowed them under the benches which ran along both sides. The tarpaulin cover was held aloft by a sturdy wooden frame and Miller, the tallest amongst them, had to stoop a little to avoid dragging his head along it.

Once he'd manoeuvred the launch away from the jetty, Alvarez beckoned the boy to come and sit beside him, then allowed the craft to drift out into the middle of the sluggish-flowing river. With the men all seated he pushed the throttle forward and the diesel engine spluttered in protest. Then, after a moment's hesitation, the craft began to roar through the muddy water. Miller watched as Carsonville receded from view. Within twenty yards of the jetty the jungle had begun to reclaim its shoreline with trees, ferns, vines all conspiring to hide what man had made. He glimpsed the boy's canoe resting on the sandy bank. Still haunted by the attack, Miller glanced across at Garret, but he was staring fixedly ahead.

For most of the journey *Joana* scudded noisily along the river, a damp breeze flowing between the men. Occasionally pockets of dense mist would appear and the engine's noise would fall. Then a phrase or two would be spoken, an observation, a question. It seemed to Miller there was something dog-like about the way Bell held his head, his round face tilted up as though sniffing the air, his dark hair lifted by the breeze. He caught the agent looking at him and nodded in a friendly manner. Pinion just seemed to be gazing at the bow, while Ferradas was curled up with his eyes closed. Miller was glad Ferradas was on board. When the time was right he'd like to have a quiet word with the watchman. The agent's eyes moved along the bench. He still didn't know what to make of Garret. Sure, he belonged in a two-fisted mining town rather than a place where you couldn't sneeze without permission, but at least he was candid in his views.

Miller switched sides and sat next to Bell. He leaned a little towards the Texan's ear, cupping his hand to protect his words from the noise of the engine. 'I hear you've been out here before.'

Bell shuffled round on the bench. 'Sure have. And glad to be going again, though Roeder ain't the sort of fellow you want to spend much time with.'

Miller nodded yet looked as if he expected more. It was an old trick, and most people were either glad to have someone giving them their full attention or felt too uncomfortable to stay quiet for long.

'We should be there by midday,' said Bell. 'I've been told you can walk it in just over a day on one of the old trails, but I wouldn't want to cut through the jungle.'

'Why not?'

'Snakes, spiders. Usual reasons.'

'Sullivan tells me you like your archaeology.'

'That's right. Rumour has it that the mission was built on some sort of ancient site. Roeder doesn't like people exploring the cave behind it, but I've got a hunch there's more to be discovered in there. You've heard the stories about Roeder?'

It wasn't quite a nod, but enough to satisfy Bell. 'And doesn't the cave also have something of a sinister reputation?'

'It's more to do with the area outside.' Bell leaned forward. 'You heard of the Peruvian Amazon Company?'

'Can't say I have.'

'It was a powerful company. Doesn't exist any more, but it came as far east as here. A land grab, colonising, bringing with them their rubber tappers. They met Indians – savages, they called them. There was a minor incident, no doubt provoked by the company. In response the Peruvians decided to round up as many as they could. It went on for years, with many of those captured being taken to the cave's entrance. There the men were castrated and then beheaded, or crucified upside down on the trees that stand at the edge of the clearing. They tied whole families together with vines, poured gasoline on their heads and set them alight.'

'This was when?'

'Late 1870s.'

'Before Roeder arrived?'

'Sometime before, though he's of a similar stock if you believe only half of the stories they tell about him. To rape a girl, slit her throat and then feed her to his dogs is the sort of thing he'd do without batting an eyelid.'

46

It was Olsen who'd first told Miller the story about the Belgian who lived twenty miles upriver. No one could say how old Roeder was or exactly how long he'd lived out in the jungle, his reputation having been established by long-forgotten men. For several years he had held a lucrative position with a rubber firm which, in the 1880s, had owned vast swathes of land along the Madeira River. As a young man Willem Roeder was reputed to have been handsome: tall, blond and burnished by the sun. His smile was angelic and in Manaus it was not uncommon for the pampered daughters of the wealthy to dwell for a line or two on the Belgian's appearance in letters to their cousins in Lisbon and Munich. What wasn't so widely celebrated was the pleasure he gained from the suffering of others. Only by degrees did it become known, spreading first among those who plied their trade along the Madeira and then through the gentlemen's clubs and bordellos of Manaus. Talk of Roeder drifted like cigar smoke over the rosewood table and the velvet chaise longue, and it was soon agreed even by the rubber barons responsible for the slaying of count-less Indians that his callousness went beyond any other man's and was more like the eternal indifference to suffering of the infernal jungle. It was something lodged deep inside him, as though he had, in his early years, decided that he would cultivate his unnatural passion for cruelty, just as other men nurture a talent for painting.

Like most overseers, he had no qualms about killing, yet he seemed to relish every opportunity. For the flimsiest of reasons he would have the wrists and ankles of a native bound together. Half flogged to death, the native would then be thrown in the river to drown or be eaten by piranhas. With an axe he'd once calmly butchered two peons who were discovered sleeping when they should have been tapping rubber. Towards the end of his career his bloodlust started to overcome any inhibitions he might have had earlier and he began to shoot natives with his rifle from the veranda of his house for the fun of watching their final contortions. Yet the large plantation he oversaw remained profitable and his antics were tolerated. No doubt, had he not returned to Manaus one fateful March, he would have continued to manage the plantation successfully until he had married a younger daughter of one of the wealthy inhabitants of the city, or at least until the market for Brazilian rubber collapsed.

However, around the turn of the century came Roeder's change of fortune. It was the week of the carnival and he'd been invited to celebrate the end of Lent with Señor Nascimento's family at their mansion, an ornate affair of pale peach and cream on the outskirts of the city. He wasn't a stranger to the rubber baron's hospitality, having twice before swapped his squalid room at the Hotel Leopold for a thick mattress and heavy cotton sheets. His window, made of clear French glass, overlooked the cobbled stable yard with its ornate fountain of Italian marble, and it was from this window that he was thought to have first admired Nascimento's daughter. A cloudburst had caught Larissa reading in a hammock a black maid had strung up for her between two orange trees in a far corner of the garden. Choosing not to take shelter in the rococo summerhouse, she made for the portico of glass and iron which stood beneath the window of her father's overseer. By the time she'd reached the manicured lawn her fuchsia dress was clinging to her lithe body. Roeder was seen at his window, watching the girl as she ran back to the mansion.

At dinner Larissa sat between her German governess and her mother. She said little at the table and appeared to be distracted, absent-mindedly twisting her dark curls around a finger until quietly told to desist by her mother. Two other overseers had been invited to celebrate the end of Lent and Roeder spoke enough Portuguese to make himself an agreeable guest. Course followed course, all served on gilded plates, and the champagne flowed freely, drunk, as Nascimento boasted, from glasses of the finest Baccarat crystal.

After the women had retired from the table, the host suggested a carriage ride down to the river. His 'modest' banquet had left him feeling bloated and he had decided that they all needed a little gentle exercise at a discreet establishment which occupied the first floor of the customs house. Bouchard and Arana readily agreed, but unlike the other two, Roeder had no appetite for the corseted and powdered softness of Paris and Buenos Aires. Instead he retired to his room. Roeder, or *Diabo Loiro* as he soon became known, was neither extravagant nor patient. Rather than court or even attempt to seduce the fourteen-year-old daughter, he entered her bedroom a little after eleven and, by all accounts, raped her. Whether she had encouraged his amorous attentions was, until the family left Manaus, a matter of quiet debate amongst the wagging tongues of widows, but the discovery of his visit – the maid having heard what she at first described as a soft squealing – led to Roeder fleeing the house before her father returned. According to the family, Larissa, against her will but being threatened either by a dagger or a revolver, was forced to assist Roeder in his escape and disappeared with him.

The story went unreported in the Manaus newspapers and the *polícia* were never informed. However, Nascimento lost no time in putting a price on Roeder's head and the harbour was watched day and night for the first month or so, the theory being that he would try and make his way back to Brussels. Other men were sent upriver: first to the plantation, and then further into the Amazon. The discovery in May of Larissa's dead body on the steps of the church in Carabas focused the search on the Rio Tapajòs and the town of Santarem. His daughter, Nascimento declared, had at least in death escaped Roeder's clutches and for that he thanked God. For another month the search continued and it is agreed by those most familiar with the story that, had Nascimento not died that winter of yellow fever in what was to become the nearest ghost town to Carsonville, Roeder would not have lived beyond his twenties. As it was, with the death of the father, the mother and her young son returned to Lisbon and the search for the Belgian lost the urgency it had once had.

For several years it was thought Roeder must have either perished in the jungle or succeeded in making his way back to Europe. Yet stories started to circulate that he'd ventured into a blank spot on the map with little more than a machete and a compass. Such tales were dismissed by most and interest in Roeder had all but disappeared when it was reported by the captain of a gunboat that he'd been spotted living along the Rio Tapajòs. For a month or so, before the price of Brazilian rubber started to fall dramatically, he once again became the talk of salons and clubs, and with each telling he became the blacker devil as the sins of their fathers were piled at his feet. At the height of his infamy he was even accused of having dug up Larissa's corpse, the earth above her grave in Carabas having been disturbed only weeks after she'd been buried. An old acquaintance of Nascimento's spoke of organising a posse to bring him back to Manaus, but it was curiosity alone which fanned the brief flame of interest, and this proved insufficient as a motive for anyone to pay men to go looking for him.

Word, however, crept out of the jungle about his whereabouts and soon traders started to visit Roeder. He was said to pay for his tinned meat and flour with diamonds, saved from his days as an overseer. He also had at least one Winchester and a small army of natives to guard his camp.

Garret described him to Miller as a tall yet threadbare sack of skin and bone, an old man in ragged jodhpur-like trousers, but with hypnotic eyes, milky blue with age, but still shining with diabolical radiance. Roeder, it was said, relieved the boredom of living in the jungle by having a harem of four young and pretty natives. How he ruled his camp was a matter of dark conjecture. The Belgian was known to be accompanied by two large hounds, mangy brutes which snarled and barked at everyone except for their master. When Garret had first visited him with Masterson they'd paced menacingly around the two men until the Belgian had shouted at them in his gruff voice and they had come to heel.

47

'And what do they say about Roeder now?' asked Miller.

'That he's mad,' replied Garret, who'd come to sit beside him. 'That, having been the most vicious and evil of overseers, he continues to lead a life of unbelievable cruelty.'

'You don't meet a man like Roeder, you guard against him,' warned Bell. 'If you believe the stories then there's nothing he isn't guilty of: the breaking of every promise, theft, torture, murder, incest, defiance of the gods. He's become the great corrupter. He attracts the weak and exhausted to him and makes all men ill. If Manaus means the mother of gods, a mother to all those rubber barons, then Roeder was her fallen angel.'

'There's nothing I'd like better than to have an excuse to nail his hide to the wall,' said Garret. 'Trouble is, I've been told he's too useful a neighbour to be got rid of.'

'When did you last see him?' asked Miller, flicking his cigarette butt over the side.

'Must have been November. Pinion and I gave him a bottle of whisky and we picked up a sack of seeds. Didn't leave on particularly good terms, but I know he appreciates our visiting him. Even the most sadistic son of a bitch can't stop himself yearning for company, and so long as Carson Industries keep

215

paying him in dollars and cents he ain't going to give us any trouble.'

After travelling for most of the morning the vegetation started to change considerably. Squat, bleached trees began to appear along the river and in places banks of mud and sand broke the water's surface. Alvarez slowed the launch, the noise of the engine falling as they stared warily out at an increasingly hostile environment. Miller had listened to the stories Garret told of natives attacking boats, how in the past white men had been taken and tortured, at least those who hadn't been killed by a poisoned dart or flying spear.

There were no birds singing or monkeys playing in the bare branches along the shore. It was as if thick velvet curtains of various shades of green had been pulled back to reveal the forest's denuded white carcass. The water had thickened into a silt-like morass and the launch seemed barely able to drag itself forward. Garret told them to keep their eyes peeled. This was a dangerous part of the river. Miller lifted his Winchester from the bench and even Ferradas sat up to take in the lifeless forest. In the distance they could see vast ridges of rock rising above the branches that seemed to scratch at the sombre sky. Dark clouds appeared to be drifting purposefully towards the launch as though racing to greet them.

'It's somewhere here,' muttered Garret as the river began to meander through rocks and mounds of dull brown sand. 'It twists hideously about,' he continued as though charged to give a commentary above the noise of the engine. 'There's no point going any farther.' He pointed directly ahead, where the bank of the river rose up in front of them. 'There,' he said. 'Head towards the shore.'

Alvarez sought confirmation while Miller stared at where Garret was pointing. There did seem to be a break in the trees, an earthy escarpment. Alvarez, muttering what sounded like a prayer under his breath, slowly steered the launch in the direction of the muddy shore. It was an eerie, silent land they were gliding towards, a land where the trees were skeletal and twisted, stripped of bark and leaves. There was a stark greyness about it, a monochrome forest of silence and shadows. Beyond the approaching muddy bank there was nothing that was green, just a matted deadness of trampled earth and rotting grass. 'Fire ants,' said Ferradas. 'Strip everything, bark, leaves, flesh.'

With a sudden churning of the propeller, Alvarez manoeuvred the launch closer to the shore of sludge and debris and there it was: Roeder's wooden jetty half hidden by a fallen tree. If Garret hadn't been certain of its existence they could easily have sailed by. On the far side toucans and macaws began to squawk a warning above the noise of the dying engine as the craft's momentum took them alongside the bank. With the launch's waves the landing stage twisted sluggishly. What looked like the upturned belly of a dead caiman rose and fell, trapped inside the bone-white branches which stretched out into the river.

The boy scrambled ashore and a rope was quickly thrown to him from the stern. There was a smell to the land: an earthy, humid stench, the strength of which made it almost noxious.

'Looks like we're going to get wet,' said Garret as he stepped onto the rickety wooden platform. 'But at least it ain't far. A couple of hours at most.' Alvarez and the boy were staying behind to guard the launch, the idea being that the Americans and Ferradas would spend the night at Roeder's, if he was in the mood to entertain visitors.

As the men clambered off the jetty and up the bank, flying insects, drawn to the invisible ripples of sweat and heat, danced around their faces. Tiny specks and bloated flies zigzagged in a whining frenzy; tasting, feeding. Once they'd shouldered their packs, Garret led the way, his machete swinging by his side. At first nothing impeded their progress, though their pace was slower than Pinion would have liked. Though he knew he couldn't outrun the flies and mosquitoes, the botanist stuck doggedly to Garret's heels, his head bowed and his hands

217

waving ineffectually. Miller came next, his cap pulled low over his brow, his rifle hanging by its leather strap from his shoulder. Bell and Ferradas followed the others, the Brazilian's Winchester slung across a hunched shoulder.

Within two hundred yards or so the jungle started to reappear. At first a few ferns and vines crossed their path, then a wall of vegetation suddenly reared up in front of them. Garret began to hack at the leaves overhanging the well-worn trail. Few words were spoken and what passed between them was uttered in whispers as though they were afraid of drawing attention to themselves. They walked in single file, the damp, stifling heat taking its toll. Sweat dripped into their eyes and there were times when it was hard to see anything. It was after noon yet little light seeped into the forest. The black clouds which they'd seen from the river had obscured the sun and induced strange chatterings and whoopings from the hidden branches above.

Miller glanced uneasily into the gloom of the near-nocturnal forest and began to wonder whether or not his own zealous quest to uncover the truth was actually worth the effort it entailed. Raindrops started to fall – big, fat drops that at first brought relief to the men, broiled as they were by the heat and humidity, yet the rain's welcome was short lived. It fell thick and fast, drilling into shirts, hammering against leaves, saturating the ground. Pools quickly formed on the path ahead and their boots squelched through the mud that was already inches deep. Instinct told them to seek shelter and yet they pressed on. Garret hardly faltered, though even his wide-brimmed Stetson didn't stop him from repeatedly wiping his eyes with the back of a hand. Rain was ricocheting all around, yet he was doing his best to keep moving. Peering through the cascading water Miller saw mud sliding like a thick carpet down from a ridge in the forest onto the path they were on. Garret was hacking incessantly, while the rest walked with bowed heads behind him, watching their boots sinking into the shifting floor of the forest.

When the rain finally eased the insects began to re-emerge and Pinion started cursing, just a little louder than he had before. He wasn't only soaked to the skin, but now plagued by mosquitoes and biting gnats. For most of the afternoon they continued to carve their way through the forest, yet eventually the vegetation began to recede, leaving just a green, living canopy of vines and leaves curled over the path. The machete was still needed, though by occasionally bending a little their progress was almost unimpeded. Sweat was dripping off every man. 'Roeder can't be more than half a mile from here,' said Garret, trying to reassure the others. Then he called to Bell, who was several yards behind, peering into the undergrowth. 'Isn't this what you wanted to see?'

'What is it?' cried Miller.

'Looks like a wall,' said Bell.

Miller bent forward and his eyes followed where Garret was pointing. A dozen or so yards from the path there was something running parallel: a greyish-green line, half-buried under ferns and vines. There could be no mistaking the mossy wall, though what was visible was no more than a few yards in length.

'Buried under forest, I shouldn't wonder.' Bell straightened his back. 'Pinion, do you have your camera?'

The botanist took it out of his haversack but refused to leave the path. In the end it was Bell who waded into the jungle. It was curiosity which drove the Texan. For some reason he wanted to touch the wall, to see that it was real. Beneath the dark green canopy and looping vines the jungle seemed to hiss with insects and the rustling of leaves. He knelt down and used his pocket knife to scrape away part of the moss. 'This doesn't belong to the mission,' he shouted to the others, 'this is something much older.' He'd studied pictures of Aztec and Inca carvings and these didn't look dissimilar. But what surprised him was the look of pure evil on the angular faces that stared back. How long had the wall been there, and where was the

219

rest of it? To the right he saw that a root had scattered blocks of masonry. He stood up. Along the undulating ground a line seemed to coalesce before his eyes. The wall was there, but buried under earth, roots, ferns and grass.

As they continued other pieces of masonry were discovered close to the path: blocks of moss-covered stone, mainly, but occasionally what looked to be a carving of some sort. One appeared to have the shape of a winged demon, though it was throttled by vines and lay in a dark corner of the jungle. Soon, through gaps in the foliage, they spied a high stone wall. As they drew closer they were able to distinguish an arched gateway. It was hard to discern what lay beyond the wall, or how far it stretched, though it appeared to run on indefinitely, or at least until it was lost in the trees and ferns that gathered on either side. The wall was the colour of the jungle, and thick vines embraced its pitted surface. Some large blocks had fallen from its crown, but otherwise it seemed untroubled by the passing of time.

'Don't get too excited,' said Garret, 'it ain't nothing but the entrance to the mission.'

Yet Miller was filled with awe and trepidation at the sight of the stone archway. 'Should one of us go first?'

'You don't think it's safe?' asked Pinion.

'If you wanna see Roeder,' said Garret, 'then we head through. His settlement lies inside these walls.'

'OK,' replied Miller. He lifted the rifle's strap from his shoulder and grasped the wooden stock in one hand, weighing it carefully. Without another word, the five of them headed for the archway.

220

48

Since Francisco de Orellana first navigated the Amazon in 1541 the story of an abandoned city had always been a subject of wild speculation amongst those who were ardent for riches and glory. Yet the lost city was part of a bigger myth, from stories of a silent colossus stalking the land at night to a creeping death crawling from a cave. The tribes near Carsonville, whenever questioned about the Jesuit mission, had always spoken of it having been built on something much larger. It had once been a place haunted by demons, half-glimpsed fiends that left their prey in gnawed dismemberment. Miller had heard such stories since his arrival. They were told by people at drinks parties and occasionally repeated by bored wives bent on entertaining the young men from Michigan who were too polite or too flattered to stop them in their tracks. 'Not long ago,' he'd been told, 'when Carsonville was first being built, a party set out in search of a lost city which was rumoured to be out west. Only one man was ever found, raving beside the Tapajòs and gnawing on what looked like a human thigh-bone.' It was a familiar story and one he'd never found any evidence to support; a tale, perhaps, which Roeder had spread himself in order to keep people away.

There had been expeditions before; Bell knew about those,

was familiar with the story of Fawcett and his search for the city of Z. Like Miller, he'd read Fawcett's account of his journey up the Amazon; knew the explorer had disappeared ten years ago with his son and his son's best friend. 'It's bad country, all right,' said those who'd never travelled further than the plantation, 'populated by bloodthirsty savages and wild colonies of fugitive slaves.'

The tales he'd been told now haunted Miller as he passed through the archway with its half-hidden carvings of sinister-looking creatures. The five men followed the paved thoroughfare which ran through the mission. It was a wide avenue running towards a low red-brick building and the hills beyond. On either side were what must have once been gardens but had turned over the years into shallow lagoons where inexplicable mounds, along with blocks of masonry and broken stone, were just visible above the tall grass and rushes. Stunted trees, cruelly twisted as though by some giant's hand, dotted the eerie landscape. Beyond the stagnant water, and sheltered by the mission's circular wall, were what appeared to be stone houses, set as though in terraces.

'If Roeder lives here, then where is he?' asked Miller.

Garret gestured towards the red-brick building covered with a dark thatch. 'His house is at the far end, down by what's left of the church. It's hidden by the orchard, but he'll know we're here.'

A gentle rippling noise made them turn to the shallow lagoon on their right. It was ten yards from the wide path and was obscured by tall rushes and clouds of hovering insects. What Miller had first thought were smooth rocks started to slide through the weeds. They began to rise from the water with a snakelike grace. Instinctively the men started to retreat. Dark heads and shoulders emerged: Indians, their backs smeared with mud, crouching half-hidden amongst the reeds. There were twenty or so rising to their feet, shaking themselves like dogs; survivors of an ancient civilisation hiding amongst the

222

ruins of the mission, wading quietly through the shallow water towards the Americans. The figures were so silent and furtive that Miller felt as if he was being confronted by a tribe that made a habit of hiding, of men afraid not of them, but of something perhaps far more sinister.

'Don't be alarmed,' said Garret, holding his machete tightly in his sweaty palm, 'it's just a welcoming party, that's all.' Miller and Ferradas grasped their rifles in readiness, their eyes fixed on the Indians as they emerged from the lagoon. Several carried long spears; others held blowpipes or bows, the strings stretched taut.

'You know this tribe?' asked Miller.

'They're Korubo,' answered Ferradas. 'They're evil.'

'Now don't raise them rifles. It'd be suicide to fire. Just everybody stay calm.' Garret moved a yard or two closer to the lagoon. 'We're here to see Roeder,' he cried, his voice a little higher. On all sides the Indians were starting to surround them: faces patterned with jagged blue lines; jet-black hair tied behind their heads. They approached in silence, stopping at three or four yards' distance. One raised his spear and gently laid its serrated edge against Miller's shirt. The American remained motionless. Another stepped forward. He was naked, save for a thin strip of leather round his waist and a monkey-tooth necklace which glittered in the low-slung sun. He stared into Miller's eyes. On his breath was the jungle: raw, wet and bloody.

'Don't move an inch,' cautioned Garret. 'They're Roeder's men. His warriors.'

'Then where the hell is he?' muttered Miller while holding the Indian's gaze and trying to read his thoughts. There was a firmness beneath the painted forehead, a look of resolute determination, but not – he was convinced – a bloodlust such as Garret had once described; a glum-looking resolve, but no murderous intent. The Indian glanced down at the Winchester and Miller thought he understood, yet he hesitated to make a

223

gift of the rifle. Another lifted Garret's arm and ran his thumb along the machete's edge.

One young warrior lifted his blowpipe and pointed it at Pinion. The botanist cursed the Indian under his breath, though his voice trembled. The blowpipe fell a little and slowly swung a couple of inches to the left. It was now pointing at where Bell's shirt was clinging taut across his stomach. This time the Indian didn't hesitate but quickly filled his painted cheeks with air and pressed his lips to it. His head jerked forward, his hair and pendulous earlobes swinging as he blew. Bell cried out and clutched his side, his fingers kneading the shirt into his flesh. There was nothing there, no poisonous dart, no scarlet feather half-lost in the folds. There was laughter from the Indians who'd been watching and the warrior who'd pretended to shoot his dart was smiling and nodding at his friends.

'What kind of a dumb-ass game are you playing?' cried Garret. 'We ain't here to be messed about with.' He was anxiously trying to see over their heads. 'Where's Roeder?' As though in answer five more Indians stepped forward and began to lift the packs from their shoulders. 'OK, you can look,' said Garret, 'but you can't take anything.' A broad-shouldered native casually rested his spear against the sanitation manager and squatted down amongst them. He began to search through each pack, twisting his head slightly as he spoke to those standing behind him. The men watched as he started to collect the flashlights they'd brought with them. 'No, you can't have those.' Garret gripped the man's bare shoulder and rocked him back on his heels.

Miller expected the man to fall on his bare buttocks, but with an agility which surprised them all the Indian sprang to his feet. Thrusting his head forward, he brought his nose, with its solitary quill suspended through his nostrils, to within an inch or two of Garret's face.

'Why don't you just back off a little?' Garret said.

In response came a few words which none of them understood,

224

though Pinion glanced expectantly at Ferradas. The Indian jabbed with his finger at the building which lay ahead. He spoke again, angrily this time, and as much to the Indians who were gathered around as to the Americans who stood in fear for their lives.

'Look,' said Garret, firmly pushing the native back. 'We're just—'

No one saw where the dart came from. One moment his neck was unmarked, the next a purple plume had blossomed above his grubby collar. There was no sound attached to it, no whistling or swoosh of air, though everyone heard the little cough Garret gave as he clutched at the dart embedded in his flesh. He staggered forward a step or two then fell to his knees.

'Jesus,' cried Miller, while from someone in the crowd there came a cruel whooping. Bell was suddenly licking his lips, stuttering the three or four native words he knew, and Pinion was cursing behind him, a mix of terror and frustration rather than the fury Miller was feeling. The Indian in front of Miller showed no flicker of understanding. His painted face filled with annoyance, he grabbed the agent's arm with one hand. Two natives were shouldering their way through to Garret, who'd collapsed on the paving. One of them lifted his cheek from the slab and briefly studied his face. He grunted in disappointment or dismay then let the head drop with a sickening thud back to the stone slab. Garret groaned but didn't move. They took hold of his feet and started to drag him out of what had quickly become a swaying, heated body of men.

Without thinking, Miller wrestled himself free and took hold of Garret's shirt: one hand clutching his collar, the other grasping the rifle, trying to decide if he'd be better off firing into the bare flesh around him than endeavouring to keep hold. The agent's heart was beating fast. He couldn't lift his head to see what the others were doing. There were grunts and the shuffling of feet, but none of it gave him a sense of what was happening. He didn't want to risk his life, and yet he didn't know if there was a chance of saving Garret. He couldn't let go of him without knowing, without trying to keep him alive. Hands were shoving and pulling, trying to loosen his grip on the rifle and the hold he had on Garret's shirt. It was a tug-of-war he was bound to lose and he was desperately calling to the others for help. One of Ferradas' muddy boots inched into sight. There was a deafening shot. It wasn't Miller, though the thought he'd somehow pulled the trigger was there. No, the Brazilian had fired into the sky. And then came a high, urgent screaming from somewhere; an angry voice outside of the melee. A child's voice, but with an anger and authority which had an instantaneous effect on those who surrounded the four strangers left standing.

Bare feet stepped away; others fell to their knees and cowered. Some turned their heads as though the real danger lay not with the rifle, or the approaching child, but further afield: in the forest or beyond the church. The men who'd come forward to take Garret quickly scuttled on all fours back to the blackened shore of the lagoon.

Ferradas pointed his rifle at the sky and hands shot up as though imploring him not to fire again. Fear was now written on several of the painted faces, though why they were alarmed didn't make any sense. They pressed their weapons against the ground as though wary of inciting any further quarrel. The furious, rasping voice of the child broke the near-silence, and all eyes were now turned towards her: a naked girl of no more than twelve with the same black bowl-shaped hair as the men, most of whom now lay prostrate before her. She continued to harangue them and cautiously they started to get back to their feet. Her impatience was clear, but nothing else. Bell had his hands clasped in front of him as though in prayer, while the other three stood mutely watching. The girl seemed merely to be shooing the Indians away and yet they readily obeyed; not vanishing in amongst the reeds, but hurriedly walking to the stone archway as though banished from the mission.

'How do you figure that?' asked Pinion, but no one was paying him any heed.

Miller was kneeling beside Garret. He'd gently lifted his head from the dusty slab and was carefully extracting the dart. 'God knows what was on the tip of this.'

'How is he?' asked Bell, wiping the back of his neck with a handkerchief.

'He's still alive, though God knows how long he'll last,' answered Miller. Garret was staring up into the sky, his eyes flickering, his breathing shallow. Ferradas was kneeling by the agent's side. He'd picked up the dart and was sniffing the point.

'Why are they leaving?' asked Pinion, his manner agitated, even aggressive now that the Indians had walked away. He turned back to the girl who stood patiently waiting. 'Are they afraid of her, or afraid of being shot full of lead? If you'd shot earlier maybe this wouldn't have happened.' He waved a finger over Garret. 'Damn, this shouldn't have happened.'

'You can't fathom the way their minds work,' said Bell, attempting to calm Pinion down. 'Just be thankful they saw sense.'

'This not poison,' said Ferradas. He brought the dart up to his face again and dabbed at the shaft with the tip of his tongue. 'This *imobilizar . . . paralisar*, not kill.'

'You mean he's going to live?' asked Miller.

Ferradas shrugged. 'Maybe.'

'Well, let's pray he does,' declared Pinion. 'What the hell did they want him for anyway?' He glanced at Ferradas, but didn't expect an answer. 'And why in God's name isn't Roeder here to sort this out?'

On the paved way ahead the girl stared quizzically back at Miller, her head tilted to one side. Without a word she beckoned him to follow her. Then she spun round and trotted away, the pattering of her bare feet on the paved stones lost within a few yards beneath the buzzing of insects and the distant, plaintive cries of birds disturbed by the gunshot.

49

The men walked silently through the cool shade of the mango and guava trees, Miller and Ferradas dragging Garret between them. Birds chirruped above and the branches rattled as a tame monkey followed their slow progress from tree to tree. Nothing else stirred, yet they knew they were being watched. Warily they stepped out into the open. A hundred yards in front was Roeder's wooden cabin with its large stoop and pitched roof. From a black-iron flue wisps of blue smoke rose up into the dying afternoon. There was an eerie stillness to the scene, the girl having disappeared before they'd entered the orchard. An ombu tree of primordial girth grew beside the cabin on the left, its canopy of branches covered in what looked like Spanish moss, while to the right were six mud huts and the ruins of the half-thatched church.

Miller and Ferradas laid the unconscious Garret down in the grass before approaching the stoop. Shading their eyes against the setting sun, they saw the tattered jodhpurs of a man watching them from a rocking chair set half in and half out of his doorway. Across his lap was a rifle, but above his waist he was lost in the darkness. Pinion called out to him in English, and then in Portuguese. In response the man slowly placed the butt of his rifle on the boards and rose leisurely to his feet. As he did so, two large dogs sauntered out from behind him.

Miller strained his eyes to see the man's face. It was Roeder: menacingly half invisible, a tall, thin man, no more than a shadow and yet one which seemed, even hidden as his eyes were, to express a malevolent watchfulness.

They halted just short of the steps to the cabin, the scent of mango still heavy in the air. A small group of young natives, their naked skin reflecting every degree of dark and fair, gathered round in front of the cabin. The tallest girl held a mattock, three boys held machetes. Roeder stood at the edge of his stoop, the barrel of his rifle resting on the wooden balustrade, one hand tight on the trigger. It only needed to slide a couple of inches to the right to be pointing at Miller who, for comfort more than anything else, cupped his hand beneath the wooden stock of his rifle which remained hanging from his shoulder. Beneath Roeder's feet they could see the black and buttery skin of a jaguar. Pinion called out to him again, followed by Ferradas. It had been three months since his last visit, but Pinion was confident the Belgian would remember him.

Standing beside Roeder was the girl they'd met on the path. He squeezed her thin waist and she went into a jelly-wriggle of silent laughter. He leaned forward, his scalp descending out of the darkness: pitted and speckled and threaded with yellow. Roeder whispered something to her and she mimed pushing his head away. He gripped her thin arm until her mischievous expression turned into something less assured. She managed to shake herself free and ran through the doorway behind her. The Belgian stood up straight and lifted the rifle from the wooden railing. The light caught the reflection of his round-rimmed glasses as he took a step forward. His unshaven face was thin, his cheeks hollow. His handsomeness had been twisted with age, yet there was still a cruel nobility in the set of his mouth. 'One of you is wounded.' His *w* was a flattened *v*; the Flemish burgher with a thousand years of gothic solemnity.

'We were attacked,' protested Pinion. 'Your men surrounded us, blocked our path. Garret was hit by a dart. He needs . . .'

Roeder, with his rifle and his two mastiffs, stepped down from the stoop. There was something striking about the way he held himself erect. He wagged a finger at Pinion as though he didn't want to hear him whining. His dogs left his side and went over to Garret, who lay as pale as a ghost in the long grass. 'You're the same height as me, or at least as tall as I used to be.' Roeder stood in front of Miller. 'Same hair.'

'I'm Vernon Miller, sociological agent with Carson Industries, and my first concern—'

'Pleasure before any worries you might have, Mr Miller.' He turned to the botanist. 'You bring me gin, dollars?'

'No gin, but rum.' Pinion beckoned Ferradas forward and the Brazilian produced an unlabelled bottle from his burlap bag. Pinion made a show of giving it to Roeder, while Bell continued to wipe his brow with a grubby handkerchief.

'Is this—'

'We need to get Garret in a bed or a hammock,' interrupted Miller. 'We can't leave him lying in the grass. And your dogs shouldn't be sniffing round him.'

Roeder frowned at the blond American, but clicked his fingers. With slavering jaws the hounds retreated a foot or two from the body they'd been nuzzling indecently and returned to their master's side. 'Take him to the church. You sleep there. Your name?'

'Pinion, Tom Pinion. We've met before, I—'

'Masterson's friend?'

'That's right.'

Roeder nodded, as though satisfied. 'Why don't you stay behind for a minute?' He looked at Miller. 'And you can take your sick friend to the church.'

'I'll need to speak to you, Mr Roeder,' said Miller. 'I need to know what it is you're selling, or what you've provided the plantation with in the past.'

'We're hoping to buy more seeds,' said Pinion.

'Seeds,' repeated Roeder innocently enough, though to Miller's ear there was an ill-disguised touch of levity in his response.

'Is that all you're supplying?'

The Belgian glanced back at the botanist before answering. It was no more than a brief look, but enough for Miller to make up his mind. 'Seeds, I assume, is all you require.'

50

The thatched roof of what had once been the Jesuit church was covered with vines and creepers and several stones had fallen from just below the wooden rafters. Large, drab-coloured birds took flight as they approached, before returning to caw and swoop above their heads. There were steps worn smooth by the tread of feet leading to the entrance, which was decorated with carvings of strange two-legged serpents obscenely intertwined.

Inside there was another opening at the far end, to the right of the stone altar. Like the main entrance, there was no door, the wood having been taken long ago. Where the thatched roof had caved in a dull light seeped through and several bottles and empty cans glinted in the fading sunlight. Flies zigzagged continuously in the shaft which illuminated the detritus of what must have been a relatively recent expedition. 'Looks like we missed the party,' said Bell, trying to make light of the situation.

Miller grunted in response as he helped Ferradas settle the unconscious Garret on the stone floor. The agent took off his cap and ran a hand through his hair. He was about as low as he'd ever felt. Not only did he feel responsible for what had happened to Garret but what little Roeder had said hadn't given him much hope of uncovering anything. There were no manacled Indians, no pens where slaves were being held, no visible evidence of the sort his imagination had so willingly provided. With the sole of his boot he stroked a bottle into a roll. It jingled over the flagstones until its curving revolutions foundered in the pulpy remnants of some kind of yellow fruit. There was also Estelle. Masterson couldn't keep her under sedation for long, not in her condition, and the sooner he returned to her the better.

'Maybe we should head back to the launch. With Garret the way he is, I think he'd want us to get him to the hospital.'

'Are you serious?' said Bell. 'You don't want to be out in the jungle after dark, believe me.'

'But he could be dying.'

'He doesn't look dead to me. Sleeping peacefully, isn't that right?' Ferradas looked up at Bell but didn't say anything. 'Besides, I thought you had a few questions to ask Roeder. No, we have to stay till tomorrow, and if he invites you to join him for supper then you have to go. All I need is just some time in the morning to have another look inside the cave.'

'OK,' said Miller, albeit with some reluctance. 'But if he's no better in the morning then we should leave as soon as it's light.'

Bell shrugged in response.

'How many times have you been here?'

'Just once. I was with Garret and Masterson when they first visited Roeder.'

'Did anyone bring anything else back?'

'Not as far as I can recall, though trips here are never without incident. Last time Pinion visited, someone was bitten by a snake; happened before as well if I recall correctly.'

'But you don't know of anything he might be supplying Masterson with?'

'Medicinal herbs,' Bell suggested. 'There was talk of setting up an orphanage, but I don't know how serious Masterson was. Of course, you'd be better off asking him, or our patient.'

He moved his foot towards Garret. 'He's been up here more times than anyone else, though I don't know how he can stand spending more than one night. I mean, you only have to take a look around to see what kind of fun Roeder's had in the past. You haven't noticed those above your head yet?'

Miller looked to where Bell was pointing. Skulls, grinning in the shadows, had been wedged between the rafters and blocks of stone. 'One for every rafter,' said Bell, 'and set in something as hard as cement.' The collar bones were just visible and it occurred to Miller that there was space in the thick walls for the bodies to have been entombed, that perhaps they'd even been alive when it had happened. 'Did he do this?'

'Says he didn't. That it was like this when he found the place.'

'They were here before,' said Ferradas, pulling out Garret's hammock from his pack.

'And how would you know?' asked Bell.

'I was here a long time ago, before Roeder came.'

'Is that so?' said Miller. 'And what do you make of Roeder?'

'He's an evil man, but not as evil as the cave. Roeder's right to warn you to stay away.'

'It's just superstition,' said Bell. 'That's all it is.'

'And this cave has never been explored?' asked Miller. 'So practically anything could be hidden inside?'

'That's right,' Bell said. 'It's just beyond the mission, behind the church. One of the strangest things you'll see.'

'*Boca do Diabo*,' muttered Ferradas. 'The Mouth of the Devil. You shouldn't go there.'

'Ignore the old fellow,' said Bell, patting him on his stooped back. 'You should see it before it gets dark.'

'Why shouldn't we go there?' asked Miller.

'It is cursed. It is where evil lives.'

'Come on,' urged Bell. 'I'll show you where I found the stone statue. You'll stay here, won't you, boy, and look after Garret?' He paused by the altar. 'You coming?'

235

51

Miller followed him out into the crimson light of the fading sunset. Running from the back of the church was a wide and well-trodden path which led to another gaping hole in a wall of granite. Behind it stood the limestone escarpment they'd seen from outside the mission. The thick vegetation of the forest tumbled over the wall, vines and roots obscuring its rugged contours, and it was only when they were up close that Miller saw that it had not been formed by man, but by nature, a giant gateway shaped by a primeval river that had disappeared long ago. As they passed beneath the arch, he touched the smooth stone. The black rock had been eroded by years of water flowing through and yet at the base it was almost too polished to be the work of nature. To the height of a man it was clear of leaves and branches, and Miller couldn't stop himself from surmising that countless bodies had rubbed against it.

'Kind of takes your breath away,' said Bell as they stepped beyond the archway and gazed upon a clearing of scorched earth from which strange sandstone pillars sprouted like elongated hourglasses. Above them the jungle had grown a canopy of green over the barren space below. In the forest they had come across impenetrable walls of vines and brush, but here it felt that the vegetation was almost ashamed to show its face.

In the dark green light the pillars looked too perfect to be natural, and yet what other explanation was there than that this patch of land was one of those freaks of nature?

'It's like the work of a drunken artist,' Miller said wonderingly, 'or a giant aviary.' There was warm sand beneath their boots and the earth undulated as though it had been turned over many times. Sickly-looking trees curtained the clearing, yet seemed somehow to bow away from it as if invisible shoulders had pressed themselves against each twisted trunk. Nature held back, forced to scurry above and beyond the sandy plain. It was only after their eyes had adjusted to the dimness of the place that Miller saw the cave. It was to the right of the wall and almost hidden in shadow. It was a huge, monstrous void, disguised almost by its size and lack of foliage. Only a dozen or so leafless vines trembled over the uppermost rim, hanging no more than a couple of yards across the darkness as though unwilling to trespass any further. The mysterious opening filled the limestone as if the rock was shaped merely to frame the colossal entrance. Its vast size drew the men towards it.

'How far have you been inside?' asked Miller, who'd wandered up to the cave's entrance.

'Only a hundred yards. It was Masterson who pulled me out, first time I was told Roeder doesn't like anyone going inside.' The air was heavy with moisture and an earthy scent of dampness and decay. Pools of insipid water stood just inside. Behind them dusk was turning rapidly into darkness and it was impossible to see anything in the cave, let alone how far it continued.

Miller was taken by an unspoken notion, an apprehensive sense of standing between two worlds, on the threshold of somewhere they didn't belong. A warm, gentle breeze played over their faces. From some dark, hidden region it carried a faint, malign odour, and yet it almost drew them further forward. Filled with a strange unease, he instinctively disliked the place.

'Perhaps we should head back,' said Bell, who was already retreating from the cave's mouth. Miller was about to turn away when he thought he saw a faint glow coming from somewhere inside. A firefly, perhaps, lost in a shadowland of pre-existence.

52

Ferradas was lying in his hammock which he'd strung up in a corner by the main entrance. He was struggling to read a detective magazine Miller had given him. At the mention of Roeder he looked up, but didn't say anything. He was comfortable and dry and had his flashlight and rifle nearby. He'd tried to warn them about the place, but they hadn't listened to him. He looked up at the three men standing just inside the doorway. They were talking in low voices, staring at Roeder's cabin.

'Roeder says if anything happens to Garret we'll have to burn the body. Not to bury it, burn it.'

'Why's he saying that?' asked Miller. 'Nobody's dying.'

'Superstition,' said Bell. 'They're full of it round here.'

'But Garret's not going to die.'

'Demons breathe life back into it. That's what he's been saying.' Pinion had been with Roeder for almost an hour and was now giving Miller and Bell his account of what had been said. He'd already told them that Roeder wanted to see the agent, that he'd invited him over there for supper. Nobody else was to accompany Miller, something over which Pinion and Bell feigned indifference or relief.

'You think there's any sort of reward still on his head?' asked Bell.

'Hush,' whispered Pinion. 'Talk like that will get us all killed. Death is what the forest deals in, that's what he said. According to him this place is cursed.'

'If it's so dangerous why's he still here?' asked Miller.

'It's where all runaways hide. They would have killed him if he'd stayed in Manaus. Only fools stray this far into the jungle.'

'Did he say that?' asked Bell. 'Is that what he thinks we are?'

Pinion wearily shook his head. 'No, he didn't say that.'

'If no one's hunting him, why doesn't he go back?' persisted Miller.

'No reason, though he says here he can do whatever he likes. There are no consequences. This is where he says he'll die. Where all fugitives die, where all demons are drawn to death.'

'When you go over there you could ask him why he has so many concubines,' said Bell.

'Why, are you jealous?' asked Pinion.

'And why so many acts of cruelty.'

'And we're all above reproach, I suppose?' Pinion's voice was rising in annoyance. 'Bell, you've no idea what living in a hell like this can do to a man.'

'There's only one hell on earth I've ever seen,' said Miller, 'and that's a battlefield, a man-made hell of the first degree.' He shook his head. 'If the stories are true, this fellow's nothing but a sadist; one who's committed every sin, whored his way across Brazil, and was rightly damned for turning daughters into little more than panting whores.'

'That mean you won't have supper with him?' asked Bell. 'Or are you obliged to dine with the devil?'

'Just can it!' Pinion glanced at Miller. 'You're being honoured, afforded a great privilege, there's no way you can refuse.'

53

'Your English is good, I'll give you that,' Miller said as he sat down at the table which had been brought out onto the stoop. A silver candelabrum had been placed in the middle and the crystal glasses, wine bottle and cutlery flickered in the candlelight. The table was set for three, but only Miller and Roeder were seated.

'My mother was from England,' explained the host, whose lean face was now clean-shaven. 'She was a governess who had an affair with my father when we lived in Brussels, all rather predictable but true. I assume you'd like wine with your supper.' He didn't wait for a reply put poured the agent a generous glass. 'One of my last bottles of Fitou, but worthy of the occasion.'

'The other place is set for . . .?'

'It's for Larissa. She'll be joining us shortly, or at least her successor will. No doubt you've heard the story of how I came to be living here, a version I presume incomplete and twisted, but a tale worth telling nevertheless.'

'Your reputation precedes you, that much is true.' Miller took a sip from his glass as Roeder did the same.

'You've heard about Larissa, then? How I raped her then forced her to leave her home?'

'That's more or less what I've been told.'

'Perhaps then you will not believe me when I tell you that

she came willingly, that when we were discovered we fled together.'

'It's possible, I guess, but it would be peculiar.'

'Peculiar?' repeater Roeder as though mildly affronted. 'In Brazil it is not uncommon for a girl of fourteen to elope with a man in his twenties, and I know that even in your country the author of *The Raven* married his thirteen-year-old cousin when he was almost thirty, so perhaps it is not so strange, not so peculiar.'

'But wasn't she the daughter of a wealthy rubber baron?'

'Is that what troubles you the most?'

'No, it's just that—'

'I see you don't believe me. You still think, as my reputation clouds every opinion, that I must have kidnapped her.'

'All I know is that you have a harem of young girls at your beck and call and Indians who attack with little provocation. And if you didn't kidnap her, then I say you still took advantage of her innocence. You were the adult, she was just a child.'

Roeder took off his round-rim glasses and slowly began to polish them on his handkerchief. He looked up at Miller with his milky-blue eyes. 'What you don't know is that I brought her here. This is where we came when her father was pursuing me. In some ways you're right. She was just a child and I was then foolish enough to think that a girl who'd been pampered all her life could survive in the jungle, that I could protect her from anything. You have to understand that she'd humiliated herself for me, willingly humiliated herself. Do you know how that makes you feel?'

'I can't imagine, nor would I want to.'

'It makes you feel like a god. I believed I was her god. All her piety, breeding, grace, bent to my will. I could do anything with her. But then – and how the gods do mock us – she became ill; bitten as we slept in the church. Fearing that she would die, I sent her downriver in a canoe with two of my most trusted men. I could not appear in Santarem myself for fear of being arrested, but they had a letter and money for the hospital in the town.' Roeder paused to pour more wine into Miller's glass. 'Neither Indian ever returned and it wasn't until the following winter that I heard Larissa had been buried in Carabas.'

'Why are you telling me all this?'

'Because it's like looking in a mirror when I look at you, and who can resist confiding in oneself, getting the record straight as it were, before what we're doing starts to become, even for ourselves, something impossible to fathom?'

At that point the door to his cabin creaked open and out stepped the girl who'd led them to the orchard. Rather than displaying her lithe, naked body, she was now wearing an outmoded, ill-fitting dress of lemon-yellow taffeta. Her black hair had been tied back, her face powdered and lips rouged. The burlesque appearance of the child disturbed Miller profoundly, yet it was the realisation that this was indeed Larissa's successor which troubled him the most.

Roeder, observing the agent's reaction, put down his glass of wine. For a brief moment he appeared almost shamefaced, but then his features seemed to harden as though his debauched nature, which had grown over the years, had regained the upper hand. 'You're perhaps wondering how many there have been?' He waited, but Miller didn't speak. 'I think we're some-where in the twenties. A few are better able to play the role they are given and therefore last for one or two years.'

Miller realised he was being used in some sort of sordid revival. What Roeder was describing, taking pains to recreate, the smell of her perfume . . . 'Your dealings with Masterson . . .' It was no good. He'd listened with as much civility as he could muster, and was trying to accomplish what he'd set out to achieve, but words were failing him. He lifted his glass and drank. He'd come to appreciate, sitting across from the two of them, that there was something far more indecent than a naked girl.

'Listen,' said Roeder, 'let me try and put you at your ease. You want to know if I have supplied slaves or orphans to the plantation.' He smiled and also, with the discreet raising of a hand, appeared to signal to someone over Miller's shoulder. 'Now do I look like a man who would have any qualms about giving men such as Masterson, Garret or Pinion what they desire?'

'You've sold slaves to the plantation? Is that what you're saying?'

'I'm not saying anything of the sort. And you'll find no evidence here. I just want to put aside why you're here and have a civilised dinner, for—'

'Is this what passes in the jungle for a civilised dinner? This whole thing is for you and her—'

'—for her to be privy to a more cultured conversation. You've read Mark Twain, I take it?'

'Can she even speak English?'

'A little, though her Flemish is better. Please, Mr Miller, don't think of leaving, or losing your temper. The Indian responsible for this afternoon's accident has been punished, but I wouldn't want the same thing to happen to anybody else.'

'Are you threatening me?'

'I'm warning you, that's all. The last time Garret was here he took advantage of my – how shall I put it? – hospitality. One of my foolish warriors thought he'd take the matter into his own hands.' Roeder paused, and focused beyond the stoop. 'Ah, I do believe supper is on its way.'

Miller glanced behind. From out of the gloom stepped two natives, their ears pierced with macaw feathers, carrying three china plates and a silver gravy boat.

54

It was night. A silent realm of inky black. At the cave's entrance things were shuffling out into the world. From their taloned feet lines appeared in the damp sand, unseen patterns made and unmade, crossed and recrossed by the shambling gait of other creatures. There was a whispering amongst them, the rare excitement of a scent, and the whiff of death on the breeze. Soon the barren patch of land which stood between the cave, the forest and the archway was crowded with strange, crooked shapes. Misshapen limbs, encrusted with bark-like skin, swung with simian grace or pushed nervously against their neighbours, fingers and claws running through fur or becoming entwined in matted hair. As the crowd swelled those at the outer rim started to trample through the jungle. The rustle of dead leaves, the yielding of sand and low, expressive growls. Others poured through the archway and crawled, scampered or shuffled their way towards the church where three men were sleeping. The demoniacal creatures circled round it, sniffed at the ashes which had long since cooled, danced at either end, but had yet to cross the threshold. Several climbed the walls with reptilian ease and stared through the broken thatch at the men below. At the openings they swayed backwards and forwards, their hips sliding obscenely through the air, grotesque mockeries of the men who lay asleep.

First one and then another entered the building. They slithered on what passed for feet. Others lumbered over to the four shadowy figures cocooned in their hammocks. With a stealth long practised they lifted the mosquito net from around Garret. Fingers slid beneath his corpse. The other men stirred in their sleep. Foul, fetid bodies shifted through the darkness. The rank air stirred unconscious minds, pricked an instinctive fear.

Miller, not knowing at first whether he was awake or still dreaming, stared into the blackness. There was a hush, a near-silent shifting of flesh on stone. He couldn't place the fading sound. It was gone, slipping from his consciousness as he tried to make sense of the malign stench. There was nothing to be seen, no variation in the blackness which surrounded him, no rectangle of changeable nothingness at either entrance.

And then he felt it. Across his cheek there came the slow, rolling warmth of a breath which tumbled slowly through the humid night. There was no sound, no intake of air or soft tremor in exhalation. Just the rhythmic caressing of his cheek, and stars which, through the ragged roof, floated in and out of view. He lay there, cocooned in his netting. Was it Ferradas or one of the others standing over his hammock? Or perhaps an Indian who'd returned to murder them all? And yet it was too quiet to be human. He focused on his own breathing; briefly held his breath to see if he could catch just a whisper of something. Nothing, other than the sluggish flutter of fetid air across his face. Should he call out and show himself to be awake, or get out of the hammock and attempt to grapple with what he now assumed was some intruder? He decided to dismount on the other side of the hammock, away from whoever or whatever it was that stood over him. It couldn't be done silently, but at least it would give him an opportunity to escape.

Half expecting a hand to clamp down on his shoulder, he

rolled to his right, his feet sliding across the cold stone. It was an ungainly descent but it had an immediate effect. Bell suddenly cried out from inside his netting. There was the sound of suppressed laughter, a soft, malevolent snorting that rippled through the chamber. There was more than one of them. Miller stood coiled and ready for the first to lay his hand upon him, and yet nothing happened. The strange, unearthly gurgling died down.

'Is that you?' called Bell, his disembodied voice tiptoeing anxiously through the darkness.

Miller didn't want to give his whereabouts away. Neither did Ferradas.

'Answer me!' cried Bell, desperate to know that he wasn't alone.

Miller knew somebody was behind him; warm air squeezed between them. The smell was overpowering, yet it didn't linger. It passed by. There was the sound of movement, a soft shuffling of bare feet.

Bell had fallen silent. Miller listened. They were leaving. The hammock he clasped in his hand was given a little tug. Just enough to alarm him once more, a departing tease. He heard someone climbing out of their own hammock.

They'd gone.

The blackness clicked yellow and everything shimmered for a second. Ferradas swung the flashlight through the infected air. The floor was covered in muddy prints as though a circus had marched round the sleeping men. Garret's hammock hung limply from the wooden rafters. He'd been taken. 'Pinion's gone as well,' cried Bell.

'Not Pinion,' said Ferradas. 'He's with Roeder. But Garret's gone.' He pointed to the open doorway beside the altar. Miller, carrying his rifle, followed the Brazilian. They stopped on the first step. Bell stood behind them, the beam of his flashlight interweaving with Ferradas'.

Outside the stunted trees reared up like colossal hands and

shadows raced through the long grass. The beams faltered at the end of the path and yet they could see the black gaping hole in the wall. In the revolving night Miller thought he saw something passing through the archway, a crooked and misshapen back which dropped out of sight. Where the stone steps were greened over with weeds and moss there was sand and wet, clayish prints. 'We should go after them,' said Miller, leaning into Bell, who'd let the beam drop to the floor.

'And get us all killed,' cried the Texan. 'You saw what weapons they had. You step outside and you'll be dead within five yards. We wait till dawn.'

'You think they were Indians?'

'Just takes one of them hiding in the grasses. You saw what they did to Garret.'

Ferradas shook his head. 'It wasn't Indians.'

'Now what does that mean? You saw how they wanted him,' Bell insisted.

'But he's sick,' protested Miller. 'If we don't do anything he's not going to survive.'

'He's already dead,' declared Ferradas. 'That's why they took him, the demons from the cave.'

'That's crazy talk,' said Miller. 'I mean, he could be out there crying out for help. You said yourself he was going to be all right.'

The three of them continued to stare into the blackness, the moths fluttering through the beams, but not one of them stepped out of the doorway.

'He wouldn't survive anyhow,' replied Bell. 'You go chasing after him alone and there'll be one less returning to Carsonville. Those are Roeder's men, you understand? God knows why they wanted Garret, but we ain't in a position to stop them.'

'Ferradas, you coming?'

The watchman stared back at the agent. 'Evil is out there. Safer here in the church.'

'If they've taken him there ain't nothing we can do till it gets light,' said Bell. 'It'll be dawn in a couple of hours.'

'We could go see Roeder,' suggested Miller. 'Get him to chase 'em down.'

Bell snorted with derision. 'You want to get us all killed. And who's to say there's not an Indian lying in wait just outside the entrance?'

'But if Pinion's over there?'

'Then that's where he belongs.'

55

Miller watched as the sky began to slowly lighten. A shallow, milky greyness was spreading through the tangle of branches and vines which clung to the top of the blackened wall. He'd barely slept. When lying in the hammock, possessed by a wakeful concentration, he'd recalled the wild tales Garret had told him and had become convinced that beyond the archway there lurked a malign force lying in wait. The sun was shining yet a quiet dread seemed to hover about the strangely domed hills. He called to the other two. There was no reason to delay their pursuit any longer. Ferradas took some persuading, but eventually they cajoled him into coming. It was agreed that they wouldn't disturb Roeder as he'd most likely prevent them from going near the cave.

When they left the church Ferradas involuntarily shivered in the sunlight. 'There's no hope of finding him,' he told the other two. 'He's gone far from here.' He spoke quietly and without fear of contradiction. His uneasiness was shared by the other two and yet the agent couldn't walk away without searching for Garret.

The undulating ground in the clearing looked as if it had been churned over by a thousand feet. Miller and Ferradas, gripping their rifles, trudged along the roughly hewn wall. Bell was holding Garret's machete in one hand and his flashlight in the other. It was an eerie landscape of inexplicable dunes and in places it even felt as if an undertow was pulling at their legs. It wasn't quicksand they were crossing and yet towards the forest wall the earth became increasingly moist. Ferns and grasses, corroded as though singed by some unearthly fire, lay between the trees and the lifeless sands. At the edge Bell waved his flashlight over the gnarled and hideously shaped trunks. The vegetation remained sparse for several yards, yet beyond the wilted grasses, sagging ferns and vines there was the green darkness of the jungle. Shadows in the distance slid from emerald leaves yet otherwise all was still. No bird or insect flitted through the tangles of vines and creepers. No sign of anything other than the sullen jungle.

Reluctantly, they turned towards the cave, the only other place where Garret could have been taken. 'Ever seen a picture of the Carlsbad Cavern?' Bell asked, keen to keep it light, his nerves under control. 'It looks something like it. But I reckon this is bigger.' His head was tilted back. 'Six storeys, maybe seven. Impossible to say how fragile the ceiling is, yet it appears solid enough. Been standing for at least a few thousand years.'

Miller and Bell stepped across the threshold, which was marked by a slight discolouration in the damp sand. Daylight illuminated the first thirty yards or so, but then abruptly dissolved, lost in the vastness of the chamber. Bell swept the flashlight from side to side, yet its beam shone into nothing but blackness.

'You sure you want to go in?' asked Ferradas.

'We have to,' replied Miller. 'At least until we start to lose sight of the entrance.'

'Garret,' called Bell, though it was hardly a shout. There was no conviction in the cry, no belief in him still being alive; it was tempered more by fear than anything else. They stood and listened. There was the distant sound of water dripping onto rock. Flanked by Ferradas and Bell, the latter doing his best to hold the flashlight steady, Miller walked into the cave. For a minute or two there was nothing other than the darkness ahead and the sound of their boots shifting through the sand. Then something loomed out ahead. At first it appeared as no more than a shadow, a square of darkness that grew in height as they approached. It remained stationary and passed from grey to silver-brown. 'This is about as far as I got the last time I came in here,' said Bell. The monolith in front of them stood eight feet high and was carved with deeply engraved characters, an alphabet none of them recognised.

'What do you make of it?' asked Miller.

Bell shook his head. 'I've no idea. It isn't local, it's not native. It looks more like hieroglyphics than anything else.' Following Bell's lead they circled the monolith. Miller noticed subtle changes to the engravings. On one of the four roughly equal sides there appeared to be fire-breathing bulls and hydra-headed serpents, the latter more in keeping with what he'd seen in photographs of Inca temples. Each image had an element of menace about it and the agent found himself looking over his shoulder. The entrance was still there, though now no taller than the monolith which stood before him. 'You think it was once a stalagmite?'

'Hard to say,' said Bell, who was kneeling down and feeling round in the damp sand. 'But I think it was placed here.'

'Must have taken some shifting,' said Miller. They were reliant on the flashlight and so when the beam suddenly moved away from the carved rock, Miller and Ferradas followed its path through the darkness. 'Thought I heard something,' Bell explained.

'Like what?' asked the agent, lifting his rifle to his shoulder and pointing the barrel towards where the torch was pointing.

'Something slithering over there.'

'Not going further,' said Ferradas.

'What's that?'

Miller could just see what Bell meant. Somewhere at the end of the beam's reach there was a dip in the floor of the cave, a depression in the middle of which there floated a dark pool of nothingness.

'Looks like a shaft,' said Miller. 'You want to take a look?'

'There were gold mines around here once,' replied Bell. 'Dug deep into the hills.' He began walking towards it, Ferradas reluctantly following the flashlight, afraid now to break away on his own.

They were within ten yards of the shaft when the side of the cave started to emerge out of the darkness. The discovery of the monolith and its strange engravings had baffled Miller, but what they looked upon now took his breath away. There was the same strange alphabet, shifting and changing but running in vertical lines. Each letter was as tall as a man and spanned the ceiling above them. In alternate columns were strange mythical creatures. Each carving was unique, though some seemed to follow a pattern. There were various winged serpents, warped and bloated bison, obscene and demented-looking demons with several limbs. Some were embellished with a giant phallus, others had a monstrous vagina. On one lascivious-looking creature it stretched up to her bulbous neck, giving her the hideous appearance of a strutting Venus flytrap.

'This is some find,' Bell marvelled. 'If only we could read what it said.'

'I think the pictures are enough to tell us this ain't Coney Island.'

'It's not Inca or Aztec. It's incredible. No wonder Roeder wants to keep this all to himself. Why, he's probably been exploring every day. I mean, who knows what he's been finding?' Bell turned to Miller. 'Think you can take a picture?'

'No flash. It wouldn't work.'

'Still, you could try. With the flashlight maybe—'

'But we still need to find Garret. That's why we're here.'

'You're right,' said Bell, while motioning for Ferradas to get

Pinion's camera out of his rucksack. The Texan called again into the darkness. The word rebounded on the wall and echoed through the cave. 'Nothing,' he declared. 'Here, take this and the flashlight.'

With Ferradas holding the flashlight, Miller took a picture of the Texan beside the wall.

'Take another, just in case, then we'll have a look down the well and turn back. There's no point in us going any further. I mean, I would if there was any sign of him, but we gotta get back.' Bell took back the flashlight and stepped tentatively towards the hole. 'Just a last look.' The other two followed a yard or two behind. It was strange how the sand disappeared. It looked like a sinkhole, large enough to swallow an automobile. Standing a couple of yards away, Miller could see that it wasn't a mining shaft. Beneath the sand there was gravel and stone. It went vertically down into the earth. Bell took a nickel from his pocket and flipped it into the gaping hole. He vainly waited for it to make a noise.

'Can you turn off the flashlight for a second?' said Miller. Ferradas protested, but Bell did as he was asked and they were plunged into a blackness deeper than one could imagine and yet, as their eyes adjusted, a faint lambent glow seemed to float up from the shaft.

'You see that, don't you?' said Bell.

'I had a hunch,' said Miller, 'but I couldn't explain it.'

'Feel that?' asked Bell anxiously. He flicked the flashlight back on.

'What?' Miller replied.

'Felt like something brushed between us.'

'Must have been a draught,' Miller said dismissively. 'What I want to know is what's down there. Maybe it's some sort of lava.'

Ferradas turned round. 'You see the entrance?'

'We went over to the right, been descending ever since. There must be an outcrop or something in the way.' To reassure them,

257

Miller took a few paces back the way they'd come. As the other two came towards him he continued to retrace their steps.

'Where is it?' asked Bell, his voice rising as his unease mounted.

'We just need to keep going, that's all. It must be straight ahead.' Nothing could block such an entrance, thought Miller, it had to be there. They must have just turned in their approach to the shaft.

'This way?' asked Ferradas.

'Those are our footprints, aren't they?'

'If they are, then we were being followed.' Bell shone the light down at their boots. There was a muddle of prints in the soft sand. 'Look to the right.' He shone the beam over to where Ferradas must have been walking. Following along the fragile ridges above the compressed sand was a furrowed impression, as though someone had been dragging a heavy sack. Yet the smooth furrow hadn't wiped everything away. At the edges were what looked like claw marks, three sharp indentations pinched into the damp sand.

'Oh, *meu Deus*,' muttered Ferradas.

'Thought I heard something,' Bell was saying, 'and there it is. There's the proof.' He swept the flashlight through the darkness. They strained their eyes, yet all they saw were golden dust motes suspended in the air. 'Perhaps they were dragging Garret.'

'We go,' cried Ferradas, holding the butt of his rifle against his shoulder as though he expected to be attacked at any moment. '*Rápida*.' They hastily continued to follow the rough depressions, the ploughed sand weaving in and out. Then their tracks started to disappear. First one, then the other. Miller tried to hide the rising panic he was feeling. The monolith couldn't be more than a hundred yards away. Ferradas suddenly stumbled over something: Garret's boots, tossed aside. They immediately realised that they'd been tricked; led off course by someone or something wanting them to remain lost.

'You sure they're Garret's?' asked Bell, though he didn't need an answer. 'Then these weren't our tracks.' How long had they been following the false trail? How could the Indians have seen their way in the dark? Where had they led them to? Without warning the others, Ferradas fired his rifle.

'Jesus!' cried Bell. 'Calm down or you'll get us all killed.'

'There,' pointed the Brazilian. 'A face.'

'Get down,' ordered Miller. 'Kill the light!' The other two followed his lead and fell to their knees. Blackness enveloped them. There wasn't a sound. They remained crouched, listening, trying to figure out what was going on. 'You sure you saw something?' whispered Miller.

'A face, maybe a shadow.' Like the agent, he spoke quietly, afraid of being heard.

'Why'd they try and get us lost?'

'Try?' hissed Bell. 'You don't think we are?'

Their voices were climbing above a whisper, yet nothing else was happening. With their eyes staring into the void, colourful specks floated across their vision. 'Did you hear a ricochet?' asked Miller, 'because I didn't. Maybe we can find the walls by firing and listening out.'

'Shouldn't we save our bullets?'

'I can spare a couple, and so can Ferradas. Besides, if they wanted to kill us then we'd all be dead by now. If I shoot the way we've just come, we should hear it strike against the stone.' Miller felt for the other two. He rose up and balanced his elbow on one knee, bringing the rifle up to his shoulder. He was about to fire when he heard a faint hum. A distant ripple of sound, a soft wave gently rolling inexorably towards them. Even though it was some way off there was an angry edge to it. Something floated across his fingers. A light flutter of small wings. Rather than pull the trigger he shook his hand. The irksome hum was getting louder, rising to a furious drone.

'What the . . .' began Bell before cursing. Miller too felt the tight, white-hot pinch of a sting at the back of his neck. A

259

click and the flashlight momentarily blinded him. Then he saw Ferradas staggering to his feet, cursing in Portuguese with his arms flailing. It was as though what he was seeing had become unstitched: dots of darkness diving and zipping between them. Stinging insects from God knows where, a cloud of hornets descending on the men. A grey wave pulsated round the Brazilian, retreated in yellow from his swipe then flew at him again. Bell was also on his feet. He'd dropped the flashlight and was hunched over, running like a man caught in a storm. Miller was stung again, this time on the hand, then on the cheek. He fought the impulse to run and threw himself down, rolled over on the ground then pressed his face into the sand. With his palms under his chin, he held the edges of his cap by his fingertips. At first he wasn't spared any attention, and yet there was so little flesh exposed he thought if he could just stick it out, they wouldn't trouble him as much. It was a gamble and he had no idea if it was any better than trying to outrun them. Where his damp shirt wasn't caked in sand he felt them lancing through his flesh. He wriggled as best he could into the shifting ground. There were at least two on his neck, picking their spot. His ears were barely covered by his cap, and one managed to pierce the skin beneath a lobe. Through the navy cotton the angry buzzing was a muffled drone. The same sharp, searing pain at the nape. He could smell the moist earth. It was tight against his damp face, filling his nostrils. At first he could feel the feet of Ferradas stamping nearby, but then the reverberations faded.

In all he must have been under attack for no more than a minute, yet it was a time intensified, drawn out like no other minute he'd experienced since his days in France. When the buzzing finally faded he was in no hurry to move from his makeshift crater. He lay there for another couple of minutes, just raising his head slightly in order to draw a proper breath. He couldn't count the number of times he'd been stung but thought it'd been no more than fourteen or fifteen. In his mind

260

he tried to isolate each pulsating flame but just couldn't quite manage it. How had the others fared?

He lifted his face, this time until he could see beyond the ridge of his sandy crater. The flashlight's beam was half hidden, having been thrown to the ground, but the yellow light was trickling across the sand. He half expected to see a dozen hornets crawling over the undulating landscape, yet there was no sign of the swarm. He gingerly rose to his knees and brushed himself down. He was careful not to make too much sound, not to move too rapidly, as though the slightest noise or tremor could bring them back. Three of his fingers were swollen just above the knuckle and he kept his hands as flat as he could. He needed to take stock of what had happened to the other two. Wincing with pain, he picked up his rifle and then climbed to his feet. He swayed a little and felt as though he was going to be sick. What venom there was in his bloodstream was making him nauseous and unsteady. His heart was beating rapidly. Bent low, he stumbled clumsily towards the light. His neck was erupting, a blistering pain searing through skin and flesh. Every movement lacerated it afresh. He knelt down beside the flashlight. Holding it awkwardly between his thumb and his palm, he quietly shuffled round on his knees. At first he kept the beam low, being wary of drawing them back.

'Hey,' he cried. It wasn't a shout; he didn't want it to be louder than was necessary. No one answered, but then there was no humming either. Miller lifted the flashlight and cried out again, then he hollered, fear of an Indian attack having been overtaken by the disappearance of Bell and Ferradas. He shouted again. Was it an echo he heard in response? He cried out for the fifth time and this time there was no mistaking it. Someone was yelling back.

Miller kept calling as he dragged his feet through the sand. There was only the one voice replying and it was hard to make out what was being said. A sting to the lips, or perhaps even the tongue? At least he was alive. He found Ferradas lying

261

foetus-like in the sand, his slender frame making him instantly recognisable. From a distance he didn't look too bad, but as the agent approached, the idea that Bell might not have survived started to worry him. Ferradas was in a bad way. He was whimpering and shivering like a dog but lifted his face at the sound of Miller's footsteps. One side was bloated beyond all recognition. There was hardly any mouth visible and one eyelid was so swollen he couldn't see anything out of it. Yet he reacted to the light as it fell upon him and tried to speak. His words dribbled out, incomprehensible. How much effort it had taken him to open his mouth was impossible to say. His poisoned cheek, ballooned to the point of bursting, shimmered while saliva bubbled over his contorted lips. The only thing he could communicate, through a childish whine, was the intense pain he was in. Miller touched him lightly on his shoulder. Ferradas flinched, giving a strange, pitiful yelp, and the agent took his hand away. 'You need to get up. We need to get you out of here.'

The Brazilian had given up trying to speak, but there was an almost imperceptible shake of the head.

'I can't leave you here. If you won't get up I'll try and lift you.' Again, Ferradas shuddered at the thought of having to move. Was he going to die? Perhaps he wanted to die. Miller knew sometimes the shock was too much for the body to cope with, but how much venom did it take? The agent waited, trying to comfort Ferradas by telling him he was going to be OK. While he spoke he shone the flashlight up and down the man lying on the floor. More than twenty hornets were squashed against his shirt and trousers. There were two half-smeared across his unshaven chin. Between his thumb and forefinger Miller carefully peeled them away. He held one up against the light. He'd never seen such giant hornets before. He didn't like holding it and yet there was some deep, instinctive desire to know his enemy, to study its short, fat body, its yellow armour-plated head and enormous jaws.

As he stared at it, Ferradas started to shuffle his way to his knees. Miller could see the tears running over his inflamed cheeks. He was groaning pitifully but had more determination about him than Miller would ever have given any man credit for. 'That's it, you can do it.'

Ferradas was on his feet now. His back was bent, but he was inching forward, lightly guided by Miller. The agent had no idea which direction they were heading in, but it didn't matter too much. If there was some fight left in the Brazilian then it wasn't time to quit. The agent continued to swing the flashlight ahead of them, searching for Bell. Their progress was slow, but at least they were heading somewhere. If there was a suggestion of an incline Miller would follow it, calling softly into the darkness. Sometimes they'd be gradually climbing only to find it was a large dune they'd ascended. From the edge of one such, Miller spied an array of sawed and split bones scattered in the sand. He said nothing to Ferradas about them but gently steered him away. Occasionally he'd switch the flashlight off, the darkness conjuring a cry even after he'd warned Ferradas he was about to do it. There was no sign of Bell, no sign of the entrance. Nothing but a blackness that seemed to penetrate the mind.

When he was eventually confronted by a wall of the cave, his first sluggish thought was that they'd gone round in a circle. Yet it only took a few seconds to appreciate there was something different about the damp, reddish stone. Instead of being engraved with huge letters and fantastical images, it was pockmarked with black rectangles which, as they made their slow way towards it, grew into unlit portals. Miller tried to explain the find to Ferradas, suggesting that their way out might lie at one end of what lay ahead.

It was a bizarre discovery, a catacomb of chambers deep underground. Miller was certain it was unique, that nowhere else on Earth was there such a strange and eerie place. He wished there was someone else there to witness it, to tell him it wasn't a figment of his imagination. By the time they'd reached one of the entrances, Miller had given up trying to figure out why they were there or what they were for. He helped Ferradas gently down into the sand and told him he wouldn't go far, that he just wanted to see if there was another way out. The watchman tried to protest, but he made no sense. Miller knew he was too tired, too tormented by the countless stings he had suffered, to go anywhere.

56

Miller, bending a little, stepped through one of the entrances. What he saw as the flashlight danced around the cavernous hall made him shrink inside himself. It was the precision as much as anything, the order which had been imposed. There were thirty altar-stones, each one the length and breadth of a tomb, standing in regimented rows. Warily, he walked amongst them, running his hand over the smooth black stones. At first the depressions in the surface meant nothing to him, but then, as the uniformity of each became undeniable, he realised to his horror what they must have once cradled. There had lain the head, the shoulders, buttocks, heels. The contours appeared to have been shaped by no chisel, but were more likely the result of countless bodies being placed there, wearing away the polished slab through repetition over many centuries. But that wasn't the only disturbing discovery. In the centre of the hall was a shaft, similar to the one they'd discovered in the sand outside. Around its circular rim were curious little fragments of bone, splinters from skulls, jawbones, ribs. Several teeth glinted in his beam as it revolved round the edge of the sinister well. Placing his feet as carefully as he could, and with one hand resting lightly on the corner of an altar-stone, he peered down into the abyss. Warm air caressed his face, though it carried with it a bitter smell. He blinked several times. How far it descended into the earth was difficult to determine. When he lifted the flashlight away he could see a soft glow at the bottom. It was no bigger than a star in the night sky, and like a star it seemed to shine with a fiery luminescence. He tilted his head slightly, the twisting of skin making him wince. Was it the rushing of the air rising, or was there a faint confusion of sound coming from the abyss? There was no way of knowing; foolish to think he could hear the shrieking and roaring of anything from so far below.

Conscious of his need to hurry, he stepped back from the shaft. On the far wall were nine archways cut into the solid rock. Above each one there was a bas-relief of a serpent's head and at either end of the hall were roughly hewn stairwells. Having spied a gallery above him, he was tempted to climb to the next floor but knew he couldn't stray too far from Ferradas. Instead, he crossed the hall and looked through the nearest arch, catching the pattering sound of running water. He paused at the threshold with an unnerving sense that he was being observed, but this wasn't what had caused him to cease his hurried exploration. It was the decorations in the passage beyond the arch which the flashlight had thrown into stark relief. For as far as the eye could see, the perverse ingenuity of those who had carved the edifice from the rock was abundantly clear. Near at hand was an image of a winged demon and a man kneeling beneath him. Somehow the stone had been channelled so that the water emerged from the demon's giant phallus, to disappear between the man's lips. Beside it several demons were raping a woman, their seed washing over her, overflowing from her every orifice and then channelling below into the mouths of women and children. Centipedes tunnelled through limbs; spiders as large as dinner plates emerged from between their naked thighs. The carvings were obscene, grotesque in their exact execution, and yet to his shame Miller found himself transfixed by the perverse inventiveness of each macabre scene. He gazed at one after another, until the feeling of revulsion, for them and for his own fascination, became too much to bear.

He had no idea how far the hellish passage continued, yet he'd seen enough to appreciate that the area was honeycombed with chambers and repulsive carvings. Miller was about to leave when in the corner of his eye he thought he saw something flit through the darkness. It was perhaps nothing more than a swirling shadow, and yet the idea that it wasn't just a flicker of light and dark haunted him. Again, he felt he was being watched, that from some murky gap in the wall malevolent eyes followed his every movement. In the humid air there lurked a note of tense and evil expectancy. From somewhere beyond the beam of his flashlight, in the dark, interminable corridor, he thought he heard a faint half-musical sound accompanied by a distant chanting. Was it the trickling of water, or were words being whispered? Curious though he was about the source of the melodic murmurings, he quickly turned and retreated back into the vast hall, moving swiftly to the opening through which he'd entered. The flashlight was beginning to lose some of its brightness, and he was starting to feel increasingly vulnerable.

When he heard the sound of bare feet behind him he prayed it was the venom playing tricks with his mind. Or was it Bell? He was confused, but brave enough to turn round. There was nobody there. Could the Texan have made it this far? Had he been hiding in one of the chambers? 'Is that you, Bell?' he called. Over his shoulder he heard Ferradas give a muffled answer. 'Bell!' he called again. There was no answer, yet he could hear it: an ominous chanting and confusion of voices. The noise was getting closer. It was coming from the archway he'd been through. Shadows started to revolve above his head, ugly silhouettes sliding over the jagged wall. He was convinced he wasn't alone in the hall. Everything he saw was unspeakably menacing and yet none of it had any substance. A foul, malignant stench started to drift through the air. Convinced that a terrible and invisible evil was stirring, he hurriedly made his way out of the hall.

Ferradas, relieved to know that Miller was next to him, allowed himself to be roughly lifted to his feet with barely a whimper. They stumbled through the sand, the Brazilian not knowing where they were heading or why he was being urgently told to press ahead. Miller was following the cave wall. He had no idea if he was going in the right direction. He figured he had an even chance of getting out alive, but anywhere was better than the place he'd just been. He didn't believe in ghosts, and yet either it was haunted or he couldn't think straight any more. Occasionally, despite his better judgement, he would glance to his left. The wall was perforated with subterranean tunnels and narrow passages, yet gradually the number of entrances and casements started to diminish. He wasn't sure of anything, but he swore to Ferradas that they were climbing, heading back to the surface. 'You just need to keep moving,' he was saying in between breaths. 'We can't stay here.'

When he saw pinpricks of orange light dancing ahead of him, he didn't know if he should feel relieved or cursed. Was this another trick to torment him? For a hundred yards or so they continued to walk towards them, but then Miller told Ferradas he should rest, that they needed to lie down. With a faint groan the watchman did as he was told. The agent watched the lights as they approached, then lifted the rifle from his shoulder and lay down next to Ferradas. He switched off the flashlight and waited patiently for whatever it was that was coming slowly towards them. In the pitch-blackness the lights appeared to falter, to hesitate before continuing on their path. 'You need to be quiet,' whispered Miller. 'There's something coming. I need to see what it is.' He held the rifle as tightly as his swollen fingers would allow. He wasn't going to fire until he could ascertain exactly what it was he was dealing with. The darkness enveloped them, protected them. The lights

268

were descending, they flickered now not like stars, but flames. Five burning torches held aloft. Figures started to appear out of the gloom. It was hard to see their features at first, but then Miller recognised them: natives from yesterday, he counted fourteen of them. Those not carrying torches held weapons: arrows ready to fly, spears to be thrown.

They came forward in silence, nine of them walking in a crab-like, crouching manner as though ready to defend themselves from an impending attack. Their path was taking them to the left of where Miller was lying. With any luck they wouldn't see them. The Indians had to be responsible for laying the false trail; it was the only logical explanation. But what had logic to do with what he'd seen and heard in the hall behind him? Was there a malevolent force within the cave or was he losing his mind? The idea that they'd come to rescue the Americans seemed preposterous, and yet it was a hope he couldn't deny. Had they taken Garret? Or rescued Bell? Too many questions were blurring his ability to think. He was awfully weary of not knowing where he was, what he was up against. As he watched their progress, he felt almost glad to be facing fellow men rather than the fiends and phantoms which had recently inhabited his thoughts. Perhaps he could forge an alliance. Ferradas needed help, needed to escape. He too was suffering. His nerves were on edge, his mind polluted by what he'd seen.

He was about to switch on the flashlight when the large and crooked outline of a heavy man suddenly appeared in front of the Indians. He was stumbling towards them, his hands groping towards the flickering light of the torches held aloft. It was Bell. He was hunched over, limping, and, although he was more than a hundred yards or so away, they could hear the strange guttural sounds he was making. Startled by the misshapen figure emerging out of the darkness, some lifted their spears, others fell to their knees and pulled back their bow-strings. Miller, with the vague notion of protecting Bell if they attacked, raised the rifle to his shoulder. A wary stillness momentarily descended. Even the laboured breathing of Ferradas became shallow as though he sensed the tension around him. Bell was calling to them, trying to communicate his distress, his need for compassion. Two spear carriers were creeping forward, flanking the American. One Indian, crouched low, was trotting towards him. Bell raised his hands to show that he wasn't armed, that he was throwing himself on their mercy. The Indian in front of him walked erect and when Bell reached out then tumbled forward, the native grabbed him and stopped him from falling. The cry the Texan gave was an agonising jumble of relief and physical pain. For a second the Indian held him steady, then with one almost balletic movement he spun Bell round so he was facing away from him. A hand came up to the American's neck and was drawn quickly across. From the distance they were at Miller couldn't see the blood as it jetted onto the damp sand, but, as Bell sunk to his knees, it was obvious what had just happened. His finger caressed the trigger. Revenge pounded in his head as Bell toppled forward. The shadowy figure was within range. It was a clear shot. Perhaps he'd even get to kill another before they all fell to the ground. But what then? Did he have bullets for them all? With Ferradas the way he was, they couldn't outrun them.

The natives were gathering round Bell. In the blazing torch-light Miller could just make out the colourful feathers tied to their arms, the look of triumph on their painted faces. Two of them were bent over the dead American, talking animatedly as they turned the body over. The impulse was there again: to pick one off, to punish them for murdering Bell, yet even as he watched in horror as two Indians began performing what looked like short sawing motions over the corpse, he knew it would be suicide to shoot.

'Ferradas, you need to crawl,' whispered Miller. The Brazilian, at the sound of their voices, had been silently weeping. 'You need to keep low and follow me. We've got to get out, but we can't make a noise.' The Indians had brought death, but they'd also given Miller a possible way out. Their best chance of escape now lay in heading in the direction from which they'd appeared.

57

The journey back into the open, when recollected, was a fractured affair: the smell of smoke from the burning torches, the sweat dripping from his face, Ferradas trying to stifle his whimpering, a grey lightness and then, as they cautiously crept forward, a blinding brightness followed by the blistering heat of the sun's rays.

Miller knew there was no time to delay. One side of Ferradas' face was a livid mess of welts, with one eye shuttered behind a shiny purple weal. His lips were hideously bruised, a swollen lampooning of a mouth.

'Can you see OK?'

Ferradas winced as he nodded while Miller told him of his plan to grab what they could from what they'd left behind and then, if it was safe, to cut through the mission and head back to the launch. If they saw Pinion then all well and good, but he wasn't going to risk being seen if it meant they ended up like Garret and Bell.

Warily they walked through the archway and along the path to the church. Miller tenderly clasped the rifle. His dizziness had nearly left him, yet hands, neck and limbs still felt as though they'd been seared by the sun. He delicately wiped his sweaty brow with the back of his unsteady hand and squinted at the ruins of the church. The place appeared to be deserted and the near continuous screeching and yawing of the forest had fallen into little more than the occasional cry. Shading his eyes he looked at his watch. It was after two and the afternoon heat seemed to have lulled all living creatures into a stupor.

Cautiously they entered the church. Their hammocks were as they'd left them, though their rucksacks had been emptied. Strewn across the floor were small tins, Bell's dog-eared copy of *The Lost World*, broken kola-nut biscuits. Miller's penknife had been taken, but he managed to find a tube of ointment for insect bites and Garret's flask.

He lifted the flask to Ferradas' chin, gently placed the rim of it against his cracked lips and slowly poured the water into his mouth. It pooled beneath the Brazilian's tongue before he had the courage to swallow. Miller took the flask away and drained what was left. He hastily smeared the yellow ointment over the back of his throbbing hands and neck and then lifted his fingers to Ferradas' face. With a few deft strokes he lightly spread it over his eyelids, cheek and lips. Then, grabbing a small box of cartridges, he stuffed it and several other items he thought might come in handy into one of the rucksacks. The thought of Mrs Bell and a keepsake flitted through his mind, but he had no time for sentimentality. If he seemed callous it was because he knew their ordeal was far from over. He slung the pack over one shoulder, squirming slightly as it rubbed across stings he'd almost forgotten, and walked over to the entrance that looked out across the mission. Taking care not to be seen, and holding the rifle close to his chest, he searched for signs of movement in the orchard.

Nothing appeared to be stirring. Whispering to Ferradas to stay close, Miller descended the steps and walked briskly to the nearest tree. When the watchman joined him, he moved on to the next. He'd thought of going up to Roeder's cabin and trying to see if Pinion was there, but it was too dangerous. The dogs would start barking and the whole place was bound to erupt. Better, thought Miller, to get down to the launch and wait for him there.

Taking every care not to be seen, they made their way through the orchard and out along the wide pathway which skirted the lagoon. Miller tried not to stray too far from Ferradas, though along the shore it was hard to keep from running. Once out of the mission they walked to the river at a less hurried pace, though they still made the journey in less time than it had taken them the day before. Miller couldn't stop himself from wondering what kind of retribution Sullivan would deliver once he'd been told about what had happened. Men had died around him during the war, but never before had he witnessed such a cold-blooded murder as Bell's.

As the vegetation started to thin he began to allow himself to think that they had made it. Greater then the disappointment when, spying the jetty through the bare branches of the dead forest, there was no launch in sight. Miller cried out in anguish. His last hope was that perhaps Alvarez had anchored out in the river. He clambered down to the wooden jetty, telling Ferradas to stay on the bank. His eyes scanned the rippling water, but there was no sign of the launch. 'It's gone,' he called over his shoulder. 'God knows what's happened, but it's gone.'

58

Pinion, the only American on the *Joana*, was stretched out under the tarpaulin on one of the narrow wooden benches. Moving with the current, they were making good progress. There'd be no need to spend the night at anchor or make camp on one of the banks. No, they'd continue downriver and be back in Carsonville in an hour or so. The sun was sinking, but there was a rudimentary headlamp attached to the bow of the launch. Pinion, who'd been slipping in and out of sleep all afternoon, lifted his head as Alvarez ordered the boy to the bow as a lookout. As the light faded, Alvarez reduced *Joana's* speed and the noise of the engine dropped accordingly. Between Pinion and Garret it had been agreed that if anything was to happen to Miller then they were to deliver to Masterson what he'd requested. The botanist was sorry to have left Bell behind, but with the disappearance of Garret he was in no mood to delay his return.

The sounds of the forest now floated over them, strange whoops and twitters rising above the mechanical growl of the motor and the incessant high-pitched ticking and humming of insects. They rounded a long bend in the river and, as what little sunlight was left disappeared, the noises from ashore faded. There, to the left of the launch, was a desolate spot, similar to the one where they'd landed. Pinion glanced across at the four children, who seemed to be staring at the warped branches which loomed like skeletal fingers out of the gloom. He studied the muddy bank and tried to peer into the darkness. There was no sign of any movement. Nothing alive, only the queerest suspicion that they were being watched, that somewhere out there under the cover of dusk, in amongst the forbidding gaps, was a sinister creature who had stopped near the shore to watch their passing. The children started to stir. A bare foot slid silently onto the wooden deck. Gracefully, a young boy shifted his weight and lifted his torso. His toy spear rolled onto the deck while he rose in one flowing movement until he was standing, his eyes unblinking. Just beyond the shoreline Pinion, for one brief moment, thought he spotted something pink standing stock-still, almost out of sight in the shadows – a bird, a flower? Silently it seemed to gaze upon the launch, the foamy ripples at the bow. At the stern Alvarez rested one hand on the small wheel while the rippling wake slid quietly behind into the darkness.

In the distance there was the rumble of thunder and soon raindrops started to beat against the tarpaulin above their heads. One of the girls turned her head and fixed her eyes on Pinion. The American watched her warily. They were some ten yards apart and yet he sensed an invisible threat in the girl's gaze. What Masterson wanted with these silent, passive kids was anybody's guess, but they sure gave him the creeps. The rain hammered down. He could feel it spraying onto his shirt. Suddenly, a thin, childish wail broke out behind the launch, somewhere near the shore.

59

It had been Ferradas' idea to retrace their steps for a hundred yards or so and then plunge into the forest. Ferradas had laboured to speak, then gestured for Miller to follow him. There was a path which ran not far from the river, an old rubber tapper's trail. Each syllable he spoke was ill-formed as though the words themselves were too heavy to pronounce. They would come after them. Roeder's hounds would pick up their scent. He knew of a path which would take them to the outskirts of the plantation, away from Roeder and his Indians.

'Here,' said Ferradas. The word was slurred, but Miller understood. After the sparse vegetation by the shore the overhanging trees seemed unnaturally large, the undergrowth thick and almost feverish. It was already late afternoon. To Miller there didn't appear to be any path, yet Ferradas was forging ahead, quietly pushing back ferns and leaves. What choice had he but to follow? Above their heads creatures screeched hysterically and bugs rained down upon them. They marched under a nocturnal green, their shirts clinging to their backs, their sweat inflaming each sting.

At dusk the wild chattering, cawing and howling rose to a crescendo as shafts of golden light appeared briefly on the trunks of ancient trees and then, as the darkness descended, the cacophony fell almost silent. Black and amber eyes watched as the two men continued tramping through the forest, Ferradas holding the flashlight, its dying beam little more than worthless.

Miller began to wish he'd untied the hammocks. He wanted desperately to rest, but with some kind of indefatigable determination Ferradas kept going. To lie down on the forest floor was suicide; worms eating into your flesh, big cats a-prowling. Occasionally slivers of silver moonlight illuminated their path; otherwise the Brazilian was beginning to feel his way through the jungle. Miller held onto his shirt tail for fear of losing him. After a while the noise of the pair of them crashing through the jungle was the only sound that could be heard. The trail was there beneath their feet, but since it had first been carved out nature had never stopped plotting to take it back. Vines and creepers fell across their path and in places the grass had grown to waist height. Miller kept expecting Ferradas to call a rest, or to pause, the sight of a snake or the suspicion of a puma forcing them to crouch low. But he never did. He just kept on ploughing ahead.

Miller's mind started to drift. He was staggering behind Ferradas and yet it was as if he was dreaming. The church floated through his thoughts. Occasionally, the Indian congregation would part and a woman, naked from the waist up, would emerge either with a beaker in her hand or with a large leaf from which she would scoop a yellowish ointment. With long, cool fingers she smeared it over his eyelids, cheeks and hands. A girl gently lifted Miller's blond hair as though admiring its fineness while a woman, possibly her mother, having carefully stripped him of his shirt, saw to his back, neck and fingers. Others stood around, speaking to him as though he understood their strange rustling utterances. His limbs were heavy, his eyelids closed.

Ferradas suddenly stopped; Miller collided into his back and both squirmed as if they'd been stung afresh. There was the smell of woodsmoke and baked earth. Peering from behind, Miller saw the vast expanse of smouldering earth which had made the watchman hesitate. It was a strange, apocalyptic sight, made all the more nightmarish by his lack of sleep. In the middle of the charred earth stood the machinery used to clear the land: tractors and stump pullers, seemingly abandoned. Ferradas, having muttered some sort of oath, began walking between the charred logs, the draught caused by his passing momentarily fanning a fiery orange blossoming of embers. The drifting smoke made their eyes water and it was only when they were over halfway across that they noticed what looked like the shape of a figure standing at the far side. It wasn't moving, just staring into the jungle, and they detoured towards it. Miller's hands were slippery with sweat, but he clutched his rifle as tightly as he could.

Ferradas, lifting the flashlight to the face, was the first to recognise Garret. As if unaware of the two men who stood either side of him, his eyes remained fixed on the scorched and ash-covered leaves at the edge of the clearing. Miller put a hand on his shoulder and the man turned his head. There was no look of recognition, his pupils dilating as though he was finding it hard to focus.

'My God!' exclaimed Miller. 'I thought they'd killed you.' He felt his forehead. If anything, it was cool, but certainly there was no fever. 'Are you OK?' he asked, the relief at having discovered him now overcome with apprehension.

Garret's head twitched as though he understood the question, yet his face remained expressionless. 'We'll get you to a doctor. Take you to Masterson.' A second twitch, a familiar name. Like Violeta, he wasn't blinking. It was the same condition, the same unseeing stare, the same veiled memory which had set him on the path back to Carsonville. Dumb and yet no doubt susceptible to suggestion. Around his wrist was tied a scrap of bark-cloth, the sort worn by the Indian women over their pubic region.

'He's dead,' said Ferradas, the words ghosting between his swollen lips.

Miller wanted to dismiss the Brazilian's opinion as mere superstition, and yet he knew he was telling the truth. This was what Leavis must have uncovered, what must have been the cause of his death, if indeed he was dead. 'You can follow us,' he said to Garret and, as they left the smouldering clearing, the walking corpse fell in behind and the rain began to fall.

60

'Happened last night,' said the nurse. 'Second time this week there's been a body found in the park.' She held the breakfast tray out to Estelle, but the young woman was already climbing out of bed. 'I'll just put it here,' continued the nurse, pulling the sheets straight with one hand. She took the glass of orange juice and went and stood beside Estelle. 'You need to take these before I leave.' In her palm were two pink tablets.

Estelle took them from her and lifted the glass twice without saying a word. Her smile was phoney but it seemed to satisfy the nurse. 'You know who it was?' she asked with a forced nonchalance. All Masterson had told her was that Miller had gone upriver to visit Roeder.

'They won't say, of course, but one of the orderlies thinks it's somebody who worked up at the nursery.'

There was no dismay, only relief.

'Most likely a panther, I guess, this far from the river.'

Estelle nodded as though she accepted the lie. They both stood at the rain-streaked window and watched the commotion down in the park. The ragged, blood-stained body was being hastily wrapped in a blanket and carried out of sight.

'Hard to feel safe, what with Finkleman and now this. I said to Larry, we really ought to be thinking of leaving. There are folk falling sick and it doesn't look good. I mean, when you have kids, something like this upsets you all the more. At least no child from Michigan's been attacked.'

Estelle looked at her quizzically. 'From Michigan?' she said, as though she'd never heard the word before.

'I mean, the guilt the parent would be feeling having brought the poor child down here. But then I guess this was one of ours.' She pointed at the park.

The nurse was a mother and yet she spoke like Sam, a voice Estelle hadn't heard for so long it was hard to remember what it sounded like. But the words were Sam's, the sentiment: ours and theirs. Maybe she was changing, maybe she was feeling the vulnerability all mothers feel. Hard for her not to think of the dead man's mother. She placed her hand over her belly and rubbed it slowly in a gentle, circular motion.

The nurse had gone, and Estelle was about to leave the window when she saw three men being escorted through the rain by a labourer with a machete up Union Street. One walked with the slow, stiff gait of Sam, but she knew it wasn't him. One had snowy white hair, the other, with a rifle slung over his shoulder, wore a navy cap.

61

At the hospital Ferradas was given a bed in one of the wards and Garret was escorted to a room on the ground floor. Miller insisted on speaking to Masterson and refused to leave the entrance hall until he was found. He remained standing while he waited, afraid that if he sat down he would fall asleep.

When the doctor appeared he approached the agent as though glad to see him. 'Ah,' he cried, 'you've come back. But you're soaking and you've been stung. Now Dr Barnes has just told me—'

'I don't care what you've been told. I just want to know what the hell is going on. And why we were abandoned. Pinion's here, isn't he?'

'Yes, he is.' It wasn't a lie, though the fact that what was left of him now lay underneath their feet in the morgue wasn't information Masterson felt he needed to share. 'But why he left you behind is something you'd have to ask him. As for Garret, I haven't seen him yet but—'

'Garret, Violeta . . .'

'I imagine it's the same fever, one which leaves them with hardly any heartbeat. Their breathing is so shallow it leaves little if any trace on a glass.'

'. . . and Roeder.'

It was obvious the agent was exhausted. 'They seem to survive,'

Masterson continued, 'at least for a few weeks, on nothing. Then they begin to waste away and, not unlike leprosy, the body disintegrates.' He was gently steering Miller out of the entrance hall and down the corridor. 'You know, you really should get some rest. We can give you a bed here if you like.' He paused outside a door.

Miller shook his head. His eyelids were drooping. He couldn't accuse Masterson openly, not yet, not when he was feeling so tired that he could hardly formulate his thoughts. 'I've got to see Sullivan. Tell him what's happened. Speak to Estelle. You can't stop me. She's still here, isn't she?'

'Of course she is. And I'll speak to Sullivan. I'll ring him from my office. Once you've rested I'll send her down. How about that?'

'I wouldn't go back there without at least a dozen men. They need to be punished . . . what they did to Bell . . .'

'I'll tell him. Here's the room,' he said softly, opening the door. 'I believe you're next to Garret.' It was hard to keep his eyes open. Masterson guided him to the chair. 'Let me take that from you.' He started to lift the rifle from Miller's shoulder. Impulsively a hand clutched at the strap. 'It's all right,' said Masterson soothingly. 'A nurse will have the bed made up in a few minutes, then she'll help you get out of those dirty things. We can give you some pyjamas.' Masterson's voice was coaxing him gently towards staying. 'Wouldn't be a bad idea to have a look at those stings, either. Probably best if we get some liniment on them. Wouldn't want them to get infected. What do you say?'

'Where's Pinion? I need to see him. I should be getting—'

'We can get you some breakfast. I'll send someone to get you some clean clothes. What do you say to the prettiest nurse I can find? And then we'll talk later. When you've had a well-earned rest.'

62

Masterson put down the receiver having spoken to Sullivan. The manager only had the haziest idea about what was going on but was seriously disturbed about the number of recent attacks and talk of a fever sweeping the plantation. What frightened him most of all, however, was the number of Americans who'd left Carsonville in the last twenty-four hours. They'd taken boats, launches and even a cattle barge and fled downriver to Santarem. Masterson had told him what he wanted to hear, reassuring him without thinking too much about what he was saying.

Sullivan knew about the discovery of Pinion's corpse, but Masterson hadn't mentioned the four young specimens he was supposed to be delivering to the laboratory. Neither had he dwelt upon Garret's condition or the fact that Bell was not with them. The manager had enough to worry about and Masterson, rolling his unlit cigar from one side of his mouth to the other, couldn't help pitying him for having agreed to fight a battle it was impossible to win. But that was the way Carson wanted things: a manager too busy trying to prop up a failing venture to take too much interest in the real work that was being done. The rubber plantation would never succeed, not in the way Sullivan wanted it to. He was having to resort to tapping rubber outside of the plantation, sending men out into the jungle. He'd been given a task which it was impossible to accomplish. Yet there was an illusion to maintain, and the last thing anybody wanted was it to fold completely.

Extra labour had been brought in, and with Garret's help Masterson had been surreptitiously recruiting from the Eastham Prison Farm in Texas. Halliday and several others had believed that it had all been orchestrated by a bent warden, that they were being given a new identity and a safe haven because a criminal gang had recognised their potential. Thinking that they'd been smuggled into Carsonville, they'd wanted to lie low, not cause trouble or bring attention to themselves. Who better, other than the natives Roeder supplied, than a convict on the run to disappear without any fuss being made?

Estelle had complicated matters by turning up with Halliday, and if she hadn't become pregnant he wouldn't have tolerated her for so long. Of course he assumed it was his. Yet Estelle had surprised him more than once, though he understood it was fear that made her do the things she did. He'd always controlled people by threatening them with what they were most afraid of, and he'd warned her that if anyone else found out about her so-called husband she'd find herself in a juvenile prison for aiding and abetting a convicted criminal on the run. Fear had compelled her to shoot Leavis, admittedly a fear he'd miscalculated, and that had led to their being sent an agent who couldn't be trusted. Miller didn't have the unquestioning loyalty the company thrived on, which kept others blinkered to the truth. He was cynical, better at criticising than understanding the pressures they were under. Perhaps that's why he was an agent they valued. Masterson knew this, because he had already done his digging, already contacted his friends in Southfield to see if they could find fault with Miller. That he'd returned from Roeder's was a big disappointment. Why Garret, Bell and Pinion, but not Miller? Now he would have to take responsibility and make sure that the agent was dealt with appropriately.

63

Miller slept beyond lunch and into the late afternoon. It was a deep, insentient sleep; the kind that seems to pass in seconds. Just as dusk was beginning to fall a nurse brought him his dinner on a tray. She roused him gently. There was another person standing in the room: Olsen. Miller leaned forward stiffly and the nurse plumped up a pillow for his back. He ached all over and his head was fuzzy yet he greeted the pastor, who apologised for not having brought Lucile with him. She was busy packing and had stayed at home. Olsen sat down, his dog-eared copy of the Bible resting on his knee, and urged the agent to eat what he could.

The food didn't taste of anything and at first what Olsen was saying was just so much background noise. Talk of the incessant rain and the coming storm. It was only when he started to speak about Garret that Miller began to listen.

'It was at the end of the war when they started to see such symptoms, though recently they've been growing in number.'

'Who's they?' muttered Miller.

'The nuns at the convent just beyond Roeder's place. In my opinion it's not contagious, yet how the illness is contracted is a mystery. In the thatched roof of one of their huts they found a huge apazauca spider, a sort of black tarantula so large a plate could scarcely cover it. There is a theory that they're being bitten by a spider and live on in a comatose state.'

'It's possibly an insect bite,' said Miller. 'Though Ferradas thinks it's something beyond the realm of the physical.'

'Well, that's just it. That's what others are saying, that this living death could have a supernatural element to it.' There was an urgency now with which Olsen spoke. 'You know, something Sister Agnes once said has always been at the back of my mind. She was in charge of the convent when the armistice was signed. She said to me, half jokingly, that the fighting in Europe had to stop because hell was full. It was one of those remarks which aren't to be taken seriously, but it stuck. And when you think of all the atrocities that have been committed over the last fifty years then perhaps it's not such a ludicrous idea. Perhaps hell doesn't have room for any more sinners; perhaps demons are spilling out of it as we speak.'

'We were at the cave . . . I saw things and I had this feeling, that there was something evil lurking in the cave. One moment we're simply trying to find a way out, the next we're being attacked . . . Ferradas and I are lucky to have survived.' Miller paused. He hadn't really stopped to dwell on the loss of Bell. He was too numb to do so, too hardened by what had happened to grieve. 'And have you seen Pinion?'

'I haven't, though I know the *Joana* made it back to the jetty last night.'

'I'd certainly like to see him, tell him to his face what I think of him. You know, he may as well have left us all for dead back at Roeder's.' Miller half expected Olsen to jump to Pinion's defence, but the pastor just sat there gently shaking his head. 'Have you ever been to the cave?'

'Garret once offered to take me, but I couldn't stomach the idea. By all accounts Roeder's beyond redemption. You know some think he's guarding the gates of hell?' It was Olsen's turn to pause, to weigh up Miller's reaction. 'Bell once told me they have inscriptions, pictures of the fire-breathing bulls. They have the same carvings in Greece, the same stories about demons hiding in the mountains.'

'Demons?' asked Miller.

'They believed demons would come out of the cave at night and steal corpses. That they were able to breathe life back into some, those who have sinned, but still have sins inside them, sins they have yet to commit.'

'Roeder said something similar. There was talk of dismembering . . . Bell in the cave. I saw them hacking at his limbs.'

'Why, that's what they're said to do.' Olsen leaned forward; glad to hear the confirmation he'd just received. 'That was to protect him, to chop up the body or set fire to it. That's how they stop the demons breathing life back into it.'

'You think that's right?'

'I do,' said Olsen. 'There's no cure for people like Garret. They're beyond the power of prayer and they're not to be trusted.'

'What do you mean?'

'I've seen people like him before. The doctors won't admit it, but I know. They say the heartbeat is weak.' Olsen tutted, as though insulted by the very idea. 'There's no heartbeat, no breathing. The Jesuits knew about the cave, what it truly is. Their manuscripts are kept at the church in Santarem. Sister Agnes translated a passage for me. Here.' Olsen opened the Bible he'd brought with him and pulled out a sheet of paper. 'You read,' he said, pointing to the sentences he'd underlined in blue ink.

'The dead shall wander eternally, gaining neither peace nor damnation, but everlasting oblivion. Redemption shall not be theirs, nor their name recalled on judgement day. Sin upon sin committing, they shall roam the earth, cast out of the light and cursed by all living things. Awoken from their slumber, only the flesh of the righteous will satisfy their hunger.'

64

Outside the rain continued to fall through the growing darkness. It had been the wettest February anyone sent from Michigan could remember, a month of almost incessant rain. And now the storm was saturating the earth and the cemetery was half flooded. The river was so high that had a grave been dug to bury the dead it would have pooled water at a depth of two feet or less. All through summer it had been rising steadily, spreading silently and soaking the ground, drowning grass and flowers.

Down by the Tapajòs bones floated on the surface and muslin sacks of flesh started to appear like islands. The mired and warped corners of coffins poked through the stagnant water while creatures hiding in the shadows sniffed the air in delight. Some of the sacks were torn, some discarded. A four-foot coffin had split and the grey boards bobbed like toy boats on the swelling pool. Bare feet squelched in the maggot-ridden mud. Eyes snapped open like a doll's; dull, unseeing eyes that had fallen back into their sockets. Nostrils had widened and the few strands of hair which were left were thin and scummy. The sharp wing-like juts of shoulder blades were visible beneath a shift. The water lapped at ankles, pooled round wooden crosses, receded to reveal a gnarled root or a patch of blackened grass. One by one they shrank away, sidled through the water and disappeared like wraiths into the forest.

65

Once the nurse had reassured him that Estelle was on her way, Miller drifted back to sleep. He dreamt that he was in the jungle again, stumbling through the dense foliage, the light fading. Suddenly he was in a familiar clearing, staring into the devil's mouth, standing before the gates of hell. From there it became a jumble of images: the ugly stone idol on Sullivan's desk, natives emerging from their thatched huts, descending to the chambers underground. Deformed men with burning torches parading on unknown errands, shuffling past windows where lights and twisted faces unaccountably appeared and disappeared. What was stirring was an ancient nightmare, an unholy foulness spreading out from the shadowy entrance of the cave, claiming dominion over the night. The Indians were being overwhelmed. There was a smell like thunder, the flash of lightning. The noise straddled the conscious and the unconscious world, thrusting Miller from his nightmare. He awoke in a cold sweat of terror, the bed gently rocking as though he'd been wrestling with an invisible assailant.

At first he feared he was back in the cave, but then, as his awakening senses took in the pillow and the soft, unfamiliar bed, he remembered the hospital. Rain was lashing against the window and thunder continued to crack through the night. It was sheet lightning, the room momentarily leaping with a watery whiteness. He was safe inside and yet he sensed the presence of someone else. A silent, unspoken threat seemed to hang in the air. Miller turned his head. Standing beside his bed in the dullest light was the silhouette of a man. His head wasn't lowered and yet Miller had the feeling that he was staring down at him. He wasn't sure at first who it was, though the silhouette wasn't unfamiliar. Rather than confront the man immediately, Miller lay looking at him. Did the figure looming over him think he was still asleep? He lay there watching him for a couple of minutes. The man did nothing but stand there. When a pulse of lightning leapt between the curtains, illuminating the face and chest with a horizontal bar of brilliance, his suspicion was confirmed: Garret; at attention, hands clenched and hanging by his sides.

Miller climbed out of bed, his limbs still sore. 'You gave me a start.' He tried the bedside lamp, but it was dead; not surprising with the storm outside. In the inky blackness he stood in front of his nocturnal visitor. Miller's eyes were adjusting to the darkness. Like him, Garret was wearing the pyjamas Masterson had given them. There was no change in his posture, no stepping back when Miller brought his own face to within an inch of the ashen features of his night watcher. 'Feeling any better?' he asked, knowing that he was unlikely to get a response. There was a smell coming from Garret; a trace of tainted meat. His lips were slightly parted. Another flash of radiance. His pupils already appeared to be frosted over. Was that the tip of his tongue, glinting like an insect's carapace? Miller refused to dwell on what it might have been. The accompanying thunder rolled out as he took Garret by the shoulders and tried to turn him back towards the door. Initially, Garret resisted; a smouldering frustration or anger at being taken hold of seemed to emanate from his rigid flesh. 'Let's get you back to bed,' the agent urged softly. Slowly Garret's head turned to look at him. His eyes were wide open.

Another shove and he finally relented, picking up his feet and allowing himself to be guided back to his room.

His door was ajar and Garret wearily did as he was told. Miller tried the switch, but with no luck. He heard the man climbing onto the bed. The agent was about to close the door when Garret gave out a low, rattling groan which ended with a dry clacking of his tongue. Was he trying to speak? Miller took a step towards him and felt something hard beneath his foot. Picking it up he realised it was a crucifix. Garret's head was on the pillow, turned towards him. There was no breath to carry his words, just the flaccid movement of his mouth. Miller carefully placed the crucifix on the bedside table. As he did so he bent his ear towards Garret's mouth. Suddenly the man's fist swung out and collided with the agent's face. As the flailing hand fell it knocked the cross back onto the stone floor. He wasn't hurt, but Garret had caught him by surprise. 'Jesus, buddy,' said Miller, not hiding his annoyance. He lifted the dangling arm and placed it, with a little more pressure than was necessary, against the man's side.

Garret was still struggling to speak and a slurred, static sound reverberated around his palate. As the last syllable disintegrated his arm sprang violently from his side again. This time he grasped what he was after, his bony fingers digging deep into Miller's forearm. With a strength no sick man should have had, he pulled the agent towards him. His head was off the pillow, his neck straining as he brought his mouth up to Miller's face. There was no breath, just a stale, sulphurous smell. Miller tried to draw away, but Garret's grip was firm. Shadows shifted beneath the agent: lips were curled back, teeth pulled apart then whipping down, biting with a brittle grind. Something fell from his mouth to the floor. Miller tried to shake himself loose but couldn't. Garret was drawing himself up in the same snake-like way he'd seen Violeta slither from her seat. He was twisting towards Miller, his other hand gripping his throat, fingers pressing into his windpipe; the harsh cracking of teeth, Garret's mouth inching closer to Miller's neck. He tried to shove him away, but when he gripped his shoulder Garret lunged at his hand like a rabid dog, just missing his wrist. Another flash of lightning and Miller saw his chance. With his other hand he smashed his fist down into the snapping face which had turned momentarily towards the pillow.

Just as abruptly as the attack had begun it ended. The patient slumped down onto the bed, his arms falling limply by his side. There was the flicker of a light. The pattering of shoes in the corridor. A young nurse appeared carrying a kerosene lantern.

'Are you OK?' she asked, a look of concern on her tired face.

'Yeah, I'm OK,' Miller replied, rubbing his knuckles. Garret had sunk back into whatever trance he'd been in, though his head was lolling off the mattress and the fingers of one hand were trailing on the floor.

'Why's he hanging out of bed?' she asked. 'His door was locked. I saw Masterson lock it myself.'

'He just attacked me.'

'Surely not?' The nurse put down her lantern and began straightening Garret out. 'I mean, in his condition.' She saw on his bottom lip a thick, inky substance and turned to Miller. 'Did you hit him?'

'I did what I had to do. He was trying to kill me.'

'Why would he try to kill you? He doesn't even have the strength . . .' The nurse lifted the lantern and held it over Garret's face. A dull thud came from beneath the floor. 'It's too dark for blood.' Something caught her eye on the floor beside the bed.

'Listen,' said Miller, 'he's not—'

'Oh my Lord!' the nurse cried. She shuddered in disgust as she threw whatever it was she'd picked up onto the sheets. It looked like a piece of dark gristle. 'He's lost half his tongue.'

Miller shook his head. He thought he'd seen something fall

298

but couldn't quite believe Garret had bitten through his own tongue without so much as a whimper.

A second and a third thudding drifted up while the nurse tried to prise apart Garret's lips. 'Where is that infernal racket coming from?' Miller asked.

'There isn't anything below here,' answered the nurse over her shoulder, 'other than the morgue.'

66

The rain was pattering on the river, drumming on the tarpaulin. Above the brown water tripped the soft splash of bare feet on wooden boards. In the covered launch two hammocks hung above the deck, cocooning their sleeping occupants in their cotton netting. The one near the bow rocked slightly as the boy turned, disturbed by a dream in which caimans, piranhas and eels churned the creaming river which was as dark as black coffee.

The dripping figure on the jetty stopped as though sensing the motion in the air. His head turned to the launch. The blood had only softened rather than dispelled the dry aching in his mouth and throat. Nothing for him endured. His limbs were tightening, contracting, his mind shrinking to a point where there was only the vaguest recollection of his ever being human. For a long time he'd known that he was dying, though not that he was already dead. He found succour where he could, though there was no appetite for fish or foul; just a raving thirst scraping inside his desiccated body. There'd been the dying glimmer of a notion and he'd chosen to flee from the others, had retraced his steps back to the dock. He had the sense of being wronged, of being robbed of life before his time. It was almost an act of revenge he was about to commit, the settling of a score for having been carried here by the river. His arrival hadn't quite faded from memory: incessant rain, tears of condensation, the shudder of a ship's engine.

The man at the stern coughed, causing his hammock to swing.

The figure standing on the boards raised his delicate chin and drew the air through his nose with such force it seemed to push his head back on its hinges. A scent he recognised. It was there in the mist, creeping up from the boat. Stealth was something he understood. In the thick gloom he began to tread furtively to the bow.

67

The young nurse carried the lantern to the stairwell, with Miller following behind. The noise was coming from the morgue in the basement. It was a thumping against wood. A dull, repetitious knocking, lacking urgency or even purpose other than to broadcast its frustration. 'Is there someone we can speak to, someone who can tell us what's going on?' After the cave he was wary, and the nurse shared his apprehension.

'I'm the only nurse on this floor, and Dr Barnes failed to turn up for his shift. But let me get you a flashlight before we go down there.' The nurse pushed open one of the double doors. In the entrance hall two Brazilians, with a rifle and a machete on a bench beside them, sat playing cards in the glow of their kerosene lantern. They looked up from their game as the nurse and Miller entered and watched as the woman went behind the reception desk. There was the sound of a drawer being opened and for a brief moment her face and auburn fringe was lit from below.

Behind her, through the glass, Miller thought he saw something running towards the park. It was only a fleeting image, a phantom-like figure flashing through the rain and the glass. Was Olsen right about there being demons roaming outside? He was trying to cling to the rational, but things were conspiring against him. The flashlight she gave him helped a little to stem his growing feeling of trepidation, though the thumping continued unabated. No crying out, no call for help, just the dull thud – thud – thud. Miller asked the peons if they too could hear the noise from the basement, but they looked up uncomprehendingly. 'They're simply here to guard the door,' said the nurse. 'That's what they're paid to do and I can't see them doing anything else, can you?'

'Why do you need guards?'

'There's been trouble in the park, and we don't have an orderly for the desk. Most people seem to be leaving because of the sickness.'

The banging started to increase in volume. 'We should really take a look down there,' said Miller, 'though you can stay here if you prefer.'

'No, I'll come with you. Word has it you're inclined to lose your way.'

Miller appreciated the sentiment with which it was said, and smiled back at the nurse. They left the men to their game of cards and returned to the stairwell. After descending a few steps Miller called out, 'What's with the racket?'

Another thump and then silence. Halfway down they could see the laundry door to the right, which was ajar, and to the left that of the morgue. 'You have the key?'

The nurse lifted a jangling bunch out of her pocket and held them suspended in front of her face. They stood outside the door. It was locked, as he'd anticipated. 'Is anybody in there?' Again his question was met with silence. The nurse looked up apprehensively at Miller. Was it simply his own nervousness which had made her uneasy? He gently pressed his ear against one of the wooden panels. It felt warm against his flesh. There was no noise on the other side, at least at first. Listening closely, Miller thought he heard a low tapping or grinding. From the corner of his eye something flickered on the wall in front of him.

'Who's down there?' It was Masterson's voice, the sound of his footsteps on the stairs. The beam of his flashlight danced in front of him. 'For God's sake don't unlock it!' he cried out, seeing the keys in the nurse's hand lifted towards the door.

'Why not?' demanded Miller. His voice challenged the doctor, disguising any relief he might have felt for having been stopped. 'Why not?' he repeated.

'You wouldn't want to let him out, believe me.'

'Who?'

Masterson beckoned the nurse away and she dutifully returned to the stairs. 'He needs to stay locked up until he's calmed down . . . a drunken orderly,' he added with a sigh, as though tired of lying. 'Jane, I understand you're the only one on the ground floor tonight?'

'Yes, doctor. I'm sorry, I didn't realise you were in. Mr Garret's—'

'Well, I suggest you return and don't stray down here again. Is that understood?'

She nodded, mumbled another apology and quickly ascended the stairs.

'Who's really in there?' asked Miller.

'I've told you. Of course, if you'd like to have a look I can let you in, though—'

'Though you're going to say it's not safe to go in.'

'Words to that effect,' said Masterson.

'Then I think it's time to discuss matters in your office, don't you?'

68

Masterson opened the varnished box of cigars on his desk and with a practised movement slid it two inches towards the agent. 'If you don't want one now, you can always smoke it later.'

Miller shook his head. 'I just want you to tell me what's happening. I mean, are you setting yourself up as some kind of necromancer? Is that what's been going on? Because it seems to me you're desperately trying to hide something.'

The lid tipped shut, the box deftly manoeuvred back out of the way of the flashlight. 'Nobody's trying to hide anything and there are no dark arts being practised in Carsonville, at least not to my knowledge. And all we have here are patients, as I've explained to you.'

'Then I need to see Sullivan and send a telegram. Tell Southfield what I think has been happening, because something's not right and I can see it in your eyes, no matter how hard you try to pretend everything's OK.'

'We've had some problems, it's true, but they will be resolved. And I'm afraid sending a telegram isn't going to be possible. It seems some spiders have been spinning webs from the wires to the ground. It causes the electrical equipment to short-circuit. Hence no lights either. It's a fire hazard in the making, but then everything comes with a risk out here.' Masterson rubbed a hand over his weary face. 'By all accounts you had a tough time. I checked on Ferradas earlier and he still doesn't look too clever, though he's more worried about—'

'When do I get to see Estelle? Why did Pinion abandon us? What dealings do you have with Roeder?'

'What a lot of questions you seem to have, and I must say I'm disappointed Mrs Halliday hasn't visited you yet. She usually finds it hard to keep herself away from men, harder still to stop herself from saying what they want to hear. And as for Pinion, you mustn't be too angry with him. He no doubt assumed you were a lost cause. So many die out in the jungle. You know, tomorrow we're sending men over to Roeder's just as you suggested. We can't let those savages get away with murder. Bell was a good family man. Seeing him butchered, Garret being the way he is . . . well, these things must have taken their toll on you.'

'Nothing I can't cope with.'

'I appreciate that, but I've been speaking to Sullivan and we're both agreed. I think it'd be best if you headed back.'

'You mean back to Detroit?'

Masterson nodded. 'Sullivan will give you a glowing testimonial, and you'll have time to recuperate. Southfield isn't going to let you go. I'll see to that.'

'But I'm no quitter, and the way I'm seeing things at the moment, you're just trying to get rid of me, trying to keep things hidden.'

'Like what? Our labour shortage?' Exasperation was starting to creep into Masterson's voice. 'That's still our major problem, isn't it, and why crucify yourself over something it'd take a genius to fix?' The doctor paused. 'You've had a stressful time and you've done your stint. Hell, you lasted longer than Leavis. I don't mean any disrespect, but it takes a certain sort to thrive out here, what with the heat and the bugs and the sickness, and not just of the body but the mind as well. Take the cave, for example, it can seriously mess with a man's way of thinking.'

'You ever been inside it?'

'Just the mouth. Roeder wouldn't let us go any further, but he gave me a shrunken head. Hard as rock and black as ebony.' He pointed with his fountain pen at a bookcase to the right of his shoulder. There, acting as a bookend, sat the head, no larger than an apple. 'It's the real thing. You have to be careful they don't sell you a shaven monkey. They look awfully similar, but the hair isn't as long. Why don't I give it to you as a souvenir? Something to show the folk back in Southfield?'

Miller shook his head. 'You don't believe in these demons?'

'Why should I? I'm a man of science. There's nothing here for you to worry about.'

'And if I do agree to leave, what happens when I return?'

'When you return you'll see a doctor and he'll find you fit for work. At the moment I believe you're ill. Some people find the Amazon saps their strength, takes away their ability to think straight. Don't go stirring up trouble, and you can continue with your life.'

'But there's something you're hiding, experiments taking place.'

'It's better if you leave. Believe me, you don't want to know any more than you already do.'

'And what happens to Estelle?'

'Mrs Halliday?' asked Masterson, failing to hide his surprise. 'Why do you ask?'

'I'm just concerned, that's all. Violeta, Halliday, they were experiments of yours, weren't they?'

'Violeta,' he repeated as though the name amused him. 'She has what Garret has, though perhaps there's something within the young that slows the whole degenerative process. Of course it's possible there's a stronger survival instinct, an appetite for life, as it were.' Masterson paused. Could Miller possibly appreciate what he was doing? Other than in his letters to Skertel he'd never shared his thoughts before. The temptation to expound his theories with someone whose credibility with the company could so easily be destroyed was too much to resist. 'Do you really want to know what's going on?'

'I wouldn't still be here if I didn't.'

Masterson sat back in his chair. 'All right. Before you leave, let me try and explain something. Our understanding of what it is to be mature, to be an obedient and productive member of society, is founded on the tacit notion that human development is linked to human passivity. Agreed?'

'OK, but you're going to have to give me more than that if you want me to leave.'

'Well then, would you agree that when we say we expect people to act in a mature manner, we simply want them to obey orders; that this is the age of conformity, of mass man, the extinction of individuality?'

Miller nodded, which in his mind wasn't the same as agreeing, but enough to encourage Masterson to go on.

'What we need, therefore, are human machines. If the brightest amongst us are to enjoy the freedom to pursue our thoughts and dreams, if mankind is to continue to excel, then we need to leave those with little intelligence or imagination behind. We need an underclass to serve, to become as one with the machine, the means of production.

'Now your concern for Estelle is touching. However, I believe it is motivated by a physical attraction.' Miller began to protest, but Masterson ignored him. 'She has a face and a figure, even when pregnant, which appeals to most men. Now I'm not accusing you of being dirty-minded. Where no free will exists, it is impossible for there to be either dirt or cleanliness. You're simply a victim of the sexual imperative. You can't control yourself or your thoughts. And you're not alone. Sex and fear rule people's lives. They suffer every humiliation, they obey every stupid order they're given, afraid to tell their masters what they truly think for fear of being thrown out. You're given a task not worthy of you and yet you complete it with hardly a grumble. Inside you may be screaming, but you do what's required. We

310

all do. Because we're all afraid, or too busy chasing a girl, or the bigger house in the better neighbourhood, or moving out of the city altogether. Because we've turned our cities into open sewers, clogged with crime and motor cars and—'

'The dead staring eyes of a million men?'

'Exactly.' Masterson smiled. 'What are the trolleys in the city but hearses for the living dead?' Perhaps Miller did have the intelligence to understand what he was trying to do. 'And how do most men behave? Like cattle, standing in the rain, bearing the discomfort of living with a bovine stoicism. Don't you see?' asked Masterson. 'By keeping the likes of Halliday alive I'm saving the dumb from the pain of living, of worrying about the next pay cheque, meeting the rent, getting caught cheating on their wife or their boss.'

'And what about you?' Miller demanded. 'Are you to join the living dead?'

'No,' replied Masterson firmly. 'Those who are resurrected are to serve the apotheosis, the fruition of man's evolution. We sacrificed human values for material gain a long time ago. Look at what the Belgians did in Africa, what the Japs are now doing in Manchuria. There will be another war, and before it comes we need to ratchet up production if we're going to win. I know you may not see it, but one day industry and labour will be as one. The last war wasn't just about the machinery of war, but it was also about the mechanisation of production: women in factories working on assembly lines, serving death more efficiently than they could cook hot dinners. Here, in the Amazon, we're bringing nature into line. No more labour unrest, no more divided loyalties. You see there's no moral dilemma in a dead man, just a willingness to serve.'

'To serve what? The devil? What you're talking about is a world without morality, a world where cowardice and greed have triumphed, where the dead serve the living.'

Masterson shook his head in disappointment. 'And is that so very different from what we have? I'm just improving efficiency, reliability. Of course how they are reanimated after death is something I've yet to discover, though it does seem to be happening more often, and not just outside Roeder's cave.'

'And what happens when they start to fall apart? What then?'

'We bury what we can.'

'And these reanimated corpses, do they still have souls, do they find peace?'

'Those who are undead have sinned, I think that's obvious.'

'How can you be so sure?'

'Haven't we all sinned?'

'But wouldn't the devil relish punishing the good as well as the bad?'

Masterson smiled resignedly. He saw that he wasn't going to convert the agent to his cause, but at least others did believe in what he was doing. 'It's important work, Mr Miller, and I hope you at least appreciate the reasoning behind it. Now, I think we should sort out what's going to happen tomorrow, don't you? A launch will take you back to Santarem in the morning and—'

'Hold on. I still haven't agreed to quit.'

'Oh, but you will.' He pulled open a desk drawer and withdrew an envelope. 'With more than enough to take you from Santarem to New York.' He placed it in front of Miller. Masterson wasn't foolish enough to expect a word of gratitude, but he was dismayed not to see any sign of appreciation. 'You know, we can't really afford to have another agent dying on us out here . . .'

'Which reminds me,' said Miller. 'How did Leavis die?'

Masterson paused for a second. 'Now that's a question I think you'd better off asking Estelle.'

69

When she finally saw him descending from the floor above, her heart fluttered. Estelle had almost convinced herself that she'd never see him again, and here he was, coming down the stairs alone.

She was smiling in a kind of sad delight. There was nothing to lose now, and the only pleasure she could derive from her sad plight was by telling Miller everything she knew. At first she hesitated to follow him. She covered her belly with her dressing gown, skin stretched to bursting. Matron, if she was still around, wouldn't be checking on her until just before breakfast. Masterson was the only one she worried about; his appearance would spoil everything. Estelle was trying to keep up with the light and yet cautious of being seen too soon.

His progress faltered when he heard her satin slippers shuffling down the stairs. He turned swiftly and for a moment looked perplexed. Then, to her relief, he gave her a weary smile and beckoned her to follow him to his room. In silence they walked down the corridor, Miller having lifted a finger to his lips. She'd make him her saviour and warmly shivered at what it might cost her.

Once inside his room the excitement made her chest heave, all swollen and heavy: a glimpse of cleavage sitting on the edge of his bed, her gown loose around her narrow shoulders. Miller pulled a curtain aside and glanced out of the window before settling in the chair. He lowered the beam of the flashlight so it wasn't shining directly at her.

She couldn't say anything at first, unsure how to conduct herself. To converse using words – rather than her body or a sly look – was a novelty to her. 'Didn't think I was ever going to see you again.'

'They said they had to sedate you, but that was just to keep you from talking.'

'Well, they can't stop me now. I didn't like the other one, but I know I can trust you.' Estelle faltered for a few seconds. She'd had all day to work out the repercussions of speaking out, but still she wasn't sure. 'It turns my stomach to cheese to dwell on it, but Sam ain't human no more.' There, he could take that in. That made sense. 'Or at least he looks human, but he's just a rotten corpse. I thought Masterson was going to look after him, but they got them working at night.' Suddenly there was a rushing desire to tell him what was happening. 'It ain't decent. It ain't right. He told me the dead are more Christian than we are. That a taste of purgatory's enough for them. Besides, they come back all child-like. It makes you yearn for them afresh.' She laughed until she began to scare herself.

Miller leaned forward. 'I know,' he said, and put a hand on her knee to steady her, to bring her back to herself.

'Ain't it awful hot in here?' she complained, the line even to her own ears sounding contrived.

'You want to tell me what happened?'

'Trouble is, I heard Masterson say, their brains turn to mush. He says even the simplest task becomes too much.' As she spoke, Estelle's fingers were constantly pulling through her blonde hair or readjusting her gown, mostly out of nervousness but not always for decency's sake.

'And what about Leavis? What do you know about him?'

'Who's Leavis?' she asked, quicker than she could think.

'The agent.'

'The other agent?' Estelle replied, unable to stop herself from sounding insulted or falsely accused.

'The agent before me. The one you'd said *they* murdered.'

Estelle, her hands trembling slightly, began to slip her gown from her shoulders. Beneath it was her negligee, worn so thin it was practically transparent. 'How should I know?'

'You said yourself that they murdered him, and Masterson tells me you know something about it.'

'Oh, did he?' She suddenly shook her head as though she had trouble seeing clearly. Her skin was flushed. 'You can't believe what he says.' She lifted the gown which lay crumpled around her waist and pulled out a man's handkerchief from one of its pockets. 'When I first spoke to you I wanted you to follow me . . . I wanted . . .' She dabbed at her brow and neck, the cotton tight within her fist. 'How old do you think I am?'

'I've no idea,' said Miller, though he'd given it some thought.

'I'm seventeen and I got nobody. Nobody's looking out for me and Sam ain't any use. I thought he might get better, but there's nothing left of him inside.' There was a pleading, yearning look to her face. 'I don't want to die like him in this stinking hellhole. You need to take me away. I shouldn't be here.' The spectrum of love for Estelle began with the sexual and never had much to do with the spiritual. She couldn't talk for effect, but she knew how tight her negligee was across her breasts, how high it had climbed across her thighs.

Miller was trying hard to ignore what she seemed to be offering. 'It's difficult when you're alone and I know how tough it can be.' He paused. Estelle sensed he was stirred by the sight of her, that he was struggling to keep his thoughts in order. 'My daughter's just started telling me the same thing. She's about the same age and I haven't seen her since she was little more than a baby.' Miller paused again. By mentioning his daughter he was trying to keep her at bay. She knew that. He didn't have to shift away. 'Listen, you need to tell me what happened to Leavis.'

Estelle sighed and her chin sunk a little. She didn't want to lie to him, but if he was forcing her to say something then she had to. She looked up at him, her eyes beseeching him to take her as she was and not for what she'd done. She could tell he knew when people lied and understood that they lied when they were scared – and she was more scared of not gaining Miller's protection than anything else. 'Sam shot him. I begged him not to, but he did.'

'Why?'

'Because he tried to take advantage of me.' Her voice had begun to waver.

'How do you mean?'

'He tried to . . .' Estelle bit her lip. It was the beginning of another desperate lie, a suggestion as to why any man would shoot another in her world. But she couldn't carry it through. 'He got angry and shot him,' she added awkwardly. It was the last thing she wanted to say; she didn't want the lie to be any bigger than it already was.

Miller knew she was on the edge of being damned in her own mind. Halliday didn't shoot Leavis. What must have happened was all too clear. If it wasn't for her saving grace of being unable to finish one of her lies he would have hated her. As it was, he understood her better than anyone else could, he even sympathised with her a little. There she sat, with her legs parted a little too carelessly, on the verge of tears, and yet almost smiling with gratitude at his silence.

70

The two Brazilians put their cards down and stood up as Masterson entered the entrance hall. He didn't acknowledge them, but went directly to the double doors where the rain was rat-pattering against the glass. Things had started to get out of hand the night before and he'd just endured the worst day of his life. The fact that Pinion was dead was regrettable, but the disappearance of the four children, along with Violeta still being at large, troubled him a great deal more. Added to that, the experiment of feeding one of the undead human flesh had led to a revolt within the pack which had ended with an attack upon one of the orderlies. In the ensuing chaos three of the undead had vanished. It had been a mistake to try such an experiment without proper supervision and he could only hope that those remaining would, by tomorrow, have calmed down sufficiently to begin their shift work again; though of course that also depended on having enough orderlies to take them out.

As he waited for one of the peons to unlock the door he checked his watch. Just before midnight. Eleanor would be asleep by now, the dog lying beside the bed. She didn't always remember to lock the door and this worried him. He idly wondered if things would have been different if they'd had children.

317

Outside there was still the demonic murmuring of thunder, but the torrential rain had gone. In its place was a light drizzle, which ensured he kept one hand holding his mackintosh tightly around the neck. The power appeared to be out all over the plantation, but he had his flashlight and, to calm Eleanor's nerves, he carried a Colt semi-automatic. Unlike Sullivan, Masterson preferred to walk to and from Riverside, where he assumed his wife had stayed in the house for most of the day. Of course he'd heard the rumours that evening that some Americans were banding together in the canteen and clubhouse, while others had remained in their homes, preferring their chances away from the commotion generated by those crowded together. It was an overreaction, similar to the one which had preceded the rioting three years ago, and yet it was perfectly predictable. The living and the undead weren't that dissimilar in behaviour. If he could just pack Miller off tomorrow morning, then they could get down to the business of sorting out this mess. The last thing he wanted was Carson finding out that he'd briefly lost control. At least Skertel had the right idea, though he was afraid the German might be stealing a march on him. He'd come up with the notion of gassing people and thus preserving their appearance. It was a neat solution and one he'd discuss with Roeder when the time was right.

The path he took led him past the park and down towards the quay. Everything was quiet, but that wasn't unusual at this time of night. It was only the lack of street lighting which made it feel a little disconcerting. Of course, if things got really out of hand he knew Shriver would call for the hydroplane. There were plans in place after the riot to evacuate all Americans if anything untoward happened.

From behind one of the stores there suddenly came a cry which rose to a loud ululation. Masterson's first thought was that it must be some kind of wild creature, yet it unnerved him enough for him to take his hand from his neck and lightly pat the mackintosh just above the hip, where he felt for the

318

reassuring outline of the pocket semi-automatic. There shouldn't have been anyone out after the curfew, but he wasn't going to investigate the noise. He was too tired for a start and, as far as he was aware, the working party had been taken out to the edge of the plantation to clear more of the forest.

The road down to Riverside skirted left behind the row of stores and, like most roads, it had a sidewalk. In the last couple of weeks the vegetation which flanked it had encroached unchecked, and consequently he now walked in the middle of the road. His house was no more than five hundred yards from the stores, though between it and the centre of Carsonville the forest had been left virtually untouched, forming a corridor of pine and spruce. As the road wound uphill, Masterson had the feeling he was being spied on, that there was someone hiding in amongst the trees. Whether he heard anything behind him he couldn't say, yet at the same time he was spooked by the idea that he was being followed. In answer to the thought, there came a shuffling of branches to his right. He swung the beam of the flashlight to where the leaves were shaking and quickly began to unbutton his mackintosh round his waist. Glancing behind, he saw several dark shapes emerging from the forest, stepping out onto the road and turning ponderously towards him. The nearest was just ten yards in front, caught in the flashlight, its head of lank hair bowed. The sight of its dirty, mud-splattered overalls momentarily reassured Masterson. Yet when he looked back over his shoulder he saw that not all of them were dressed the same. One was a naked boy, an Indian of about twelve or thirteen, and, apart from the bluish patina to his skin, he looked remarkably alive. Another was wearing what looked like the remnants of a cotton shift, though the sex was impossible to tell, its head being as bruised and as black as a forgotten mango. He played his flashlight over the withered cords of its neck, the shrivelled hands lifted as though in prayer. The smell of rotten flesh was closing in on him, thick enough to make him want to gag.

319

'Stay back,' he croaked, his mouth dry. He tried again, but they kept coming. There was the danger that they would congregate round him. Bullets, he knew, were useless. Only dismemberment could stop them, and even then limbs were inclined to writhe for several hours. He held the automatic out in front of him. 'Stop where you are!' he cried, acutely aware of the note of desperation in his voice. He'd given them a direct order and while it seemed to have some effect on those in overalls, the others kept coming. The Indian boy, on the outside of the procession, even seemed to have a swagger to his walk, a rolling of the hips, a nimbleness of movement which the others lacked. It was the Indian he fired at first. The bullet took off one of his ears, but otherwise had no effect, no flinching in agony or screaming in pain. Masterson trembled with the responsibility he felt to be his. He fired five more times, but while each bullet blew a hole in his target the only other result was a physical recoil, as though a sudden gust of wind had shoved hard against its chest. Masterson found himself backing away.

He could cut through the forest behind him and make it to his house that way. The undead were slow and stupid, and he could easily outmanoeuvre them. Before he'd made up his mind to flee, he found himself turning sharply and looking for the best way through the trees. He was anxious now to get back to Eleanor, to make sure she was OK.

In the forest snakes glided noiselessly away through the slick grass, while above his head the interlacing lianas danced in the beam. He heard the yowl of what sounded like a rutting cat as he fought his way through the vegetation. It was somewhere behind him on the road. He knew there was a path in amongst the trees; Bell's children had made their own short cut to school, though they were always being told never to go in amongst the trees. He felt for one moment as though he was inside the giant ribcage of some primeval creature.

Moths as large as his hands floated through the flashlight's beam. The whine of a mosquito in his ear and then a second yowl, closer than the first. Vines and creepers impeded every other stride. There was the urge to run, to escape from anything which had been brave enough to pursue him, but he couldn't take flight for fear of tripping. A spider, as large as his fist, scuttled slantways from the centre of its web and away from the flashlight's erratic swing. The silken threads were still vibrating when Masterson ducked. On he cantered, stumbling one way and then the other, his shoulders brushing leaves and branches. Webs shimmered, idle monkeys peered down into the darkness, birds squawked in alarm. Along the path the vibrations grew, alerting every creature to his approach. Sweat stung his eyes, clouded his sight. He was bending, leaping, gasping for breath. He wiped his brow, tried not to blink. He wanted to see beyond the flashlight, to glimpse the curve of the tarmacadamed road.

Somehow his beam had missed the figure which stood stock-still on the path in front of him until he was merely a yard or two from colliding with it. It wasn't there, then it reared forward in all its ghastly, rotting solidity. The light ran up its short length before he had time to think about what it was. He caught the battered shoes first, the black leather uppers now a poor casing of stippled brown through which the laddered socks had blended in colour. The putrefying thighs and calves beneath the olive shorts were hanging as though the flesh was melting in the warmth, trapped in skin which was mercifully covered in dirt. The emaciated arms rose as though wanting to protect the frail body from the careering white frame which was falling towards it. All that he saw startled Masterson: the hunched, dishevelled body, the unnatural stillness of the boy's posture, yet it was the face which tripped him into terror. It didn't belong to Violeta, but it had the same grey, unseeing eyes that smarted as the light traversed them. Not blinking, nor seeing. Its mouth was open and its mottled teeth were snapping, piranha-like, biting the air.

Masterson thought for a second that he'd managed to brake in time, the fear of colliding and shattering the fragile frame almost equal to the revulsion he felt, yet the ground was sodden, the path covered with leaves. He didn't crash into it but, as his foot conquered his momentum, a thin hand shot out and grabbed his coat. He felt the nails digging into his flesh, yet even with its fingers around his forearm he thought he could escape. He never foresaw, until it was too late, that it would throw itself forward, its bare legs wrapping themselves around his waist, its sharp teeth cutting into his shiny neck. Again and again it bit into him. A nuzzling, intimate, searing pain beneath the mackintosh's collar, followed by a spurting fountain of blood which pulsed with every beat of his heart. For a few agonising seconds he remained standing. A greasy lock of ginger hair had come away in his hand. He fell clutching it, nails digging now into his shoulders as its mouth burrowed deeper into his neck.

71

It was just after midnight when Miller and Estelle heard the sound of distant gunfire. It ended as abruptly as it had begun. Five shots, maybe more.

'What do you think that was?' asked Miller.

'Could be anything,' replied Estelle nervously. The creatures she'd seen were out there, but in his room she felt safe. In the morning things would be better. Then they'd have their chance to escape. She couldn't stay cooped up for another day, not with what she knew was going on around her. He'd help her get away; he had to, though she felt she'd yet to win him over to her side.

Miller got up from the chair and stroked his chin reflectively. 'I think I'd better have a look. You want to come along?'

'Dressed like this?'

He looked back at her from the window, thumbs and forefingers daintily stretching the lace hem of her negligee indecently high across her thighs. 'You need to put your gown back on.' It was time to break the spell she'd been weaving.

Estelle wasn't keen to leave the room, but as he had the flashlight she reluctantly did as she was told and followed him out into the corridor. 'We'll just check on the fellows in the lobby and then see if Ferradas is awake.'

'Shouldn't we wait till it gets light? It's the darkness I don't like. The idea that he could be out there.'

'Who?' asked Miller.

'Sam, maybe Leavis.'

'You afraid of them?'

'Not really.' It was another lie, and one which compounded her earlier one.

'Nurse,' he called. There was no answer. He thought of checking on Garret, but could do without the aggravation. Besides, he'd seen her lock his door and he was probably best out of the way. They were five yards from the stairwell when the dull thumping started up again from the mortuary. The first hollow thud made them both jump. Estelle gripped Miller's hand tightly. 'You ain't going down there, are you?' she whispered close to his ear.

'You don't think we should?'

'Not unless you're looking for trouble.' She smiled tentatively up at him, trying to hide how frightened she felt.

They went into the entrance hall. Like the nurse, the Brazilians had disappeared, though someone had left behind a lantern. 'There were two of them here before,' said Miller. He tried one of the main doors and it creaked open. 'Well, at least we can leave any time we want to.'

Outside the rain continued to fall. It was finer, almost invisible as the flashlight's beam swept down the stone steps to the sidewalk. There was enough light to pick out the park's entrance, the benches facing the hospital. Nothing stirred and the only sound outside was the soft patter of dripping water. At the flashlight's second sweep it stopped at the park gates. Estelle was the first to spot her, a woman standing just inside the park railings. It was no more than a silhouette, stock-still beside one of the benches. 'Hey,' cried Miller.

Estelle begged him to be quiet, tried to stop him stepping forward. She didn't want him to go over and yet he insisted. He needed to take a better look. 'Stay there,' he said, glancing behind, 'and keep the door open.'

324

When he got within twenty yards he saw that the woman's head was slumped forward, yet when the beam hit her face all the lassitude of waiting concentrated itself into a quick, nervous movement of the hand. It swiftly covered her eyes and yet the woman swung her head towards Miller. Her long, bedraggled hair fell to one side and a foot came forward. He could see that one of her stockings was around her ankle and that she was missing a shoe. Her legs began to move in quick, brusque jolts between the flower beds and towards the gates. She raised her chin slightly, as though sniffing the air. Her face, shining because of the rain, had that pinched, deathly look about it. From behind her a doll swung out. She was holding its hand as a child would, its chubby legs dangling from beneath its grubby lace gown. Only it wasn't a doll. Miller recoiled as the truth dawned on him.

'Are you OK, lady?' he asked. He didn't expect an answer, nor did he want to take another step towards her and her baby. Something deep inside made him keep his distance, as though sensing the unspoken threat which she represented. He heard footsteps coming from behind her and watched as a man in his sodden shorts and vest emerged out of the darkness, running up the path. He threw his arms round her, and it sounded as though he was sobbing. The woman had his chin on her shoulder, but her eyes remained fixed on Miller.

From out of nowhere someone brushed past him. He must have come down the hospital steps. It was one of the peons, carrying a machete. He strode quickly up to the couple, but stopped four or five yards away. He was gesturing with his machete, wanting the man to step away. The other Brazilian now appeared from the park, holding his rifle. Without hesitating he pressed the barrel of it against the back of the man. The man, after wiping his bare arm across his face, let go of the woman and allowed himself to be guided to the nearest bench. The one holding the machete gave the baby a cursory glance to make sure that it was dead before flexing his arm, swinging the blade above and behind and round, measuring how close he needed to be. The woman simply stood looking at him, a blank expression on her ashen face. The man on the bench sat with his head in his hands, while the other labourer started to shout at Miller and Estelle. They understood he wanted them to go back inside, yet neither moved an inch. It was obvious what was going to happen, but it was hard to believe he'd carry it through.

And then it happened. Even before his partner had finished his sentence, the swing of the machete had whistled through the air. When it struck her neck there was a soft, dull thump and a short, shrill gasp from the woman herself. She slumped to her knees, fell onto her side and then rolled, with her head hanging half off, onto her back. It was an ugly fall, a clownish imitation of a drunk falling down. But her ordeal wasn't over yet. With the methodical approach of a butcher he finished severing her neck then began to dismember her body.

72

Estelle was crying out for Miller to get back inside. It was too late to interfere and, without anything to defend himself with, he climbed the stone steps back towards her. In the entrance hall she wanted to know if he had the rifle she'd seen him arrive with in the morning. He hadn't. He vaguely remembered it had been taken away by Masterson. They spoke hurriedly by the door as they watched the man kneeling by the corpse. He was close to finishing his grisly task. 'I still got Sam's revolver,' declared Estelle. 'Garret was meant to take it off me, but he somehow forgot.'

'Where is it?'

'In my room. We should get it, shouldn't we?'

They took the lantern and the flashlight and, as quietly as they could, they climbed the two flights of stairs. It didn't take her long to produce it, yet she insisted on getting dressed and even looked pleased when Miller said he'd wait outside.

They found Ferradas in the first ward they visited and roused the Brazilian. One side of the watchman's face was still swollen, but he nodded when asked if he was OK.

'Are you sure?'

'I'm OK,' the Brazilian repeated. It wasn't convincing.

'Let me just have a look at your eyes.' Miller brought the

flashlight up to just beneath Ferradas' chin. His left eye was still all puffed up, but the right squinted back at Miller.

'OK,' Ferradas said again.

The agent shook his head but told the watchman he needed to get out of bed. 'You have to come with us.' Was he liable to become dangerous? They must have had good reason to do what they did to Bell, to the woman in the park. Or was it all just some kind of dreadful superstition?

Back in the entrance hall he quietly warned Estelle to keep an eye on Ferradas. 'I've got a few things I need to sort out.'

'You're not leaving me, are you?'

'I just want to make sure it's safe down at the dock. It's better if you stay here. I'll be quicker.' He wasn't sure if Alvarez was going to be given the job of taking him to Santarem, or if – as he thought more likely – the skipper would be heading back to Roeder's. Either way, he didn't see any point in hanging round. 'If the launch is there it should be easy for us to get away, or at least anchor out in the river until we figure out what's going on.'

'Shouldn't we all wait till dawn?' said Estelle. 'You saw yourself they're hacking folks up, chopping them to bits.'

'We don't know why they did it, unless—'

'It happened when they rioted. They say they turned on all the white folk.' She glanced at Ferradas. 'But there's more to be afraid of than just them with machetes.' Suddenly the bulbs above their heads started to flicker and ping. Under the electric light the watchman appeared to shrink into himself. 'See,' she said, oblivious to the Brazilian's reaction, 'things are being sorted out.'

'That may be,' said Miller, 'but all the more reason for me to take a look now before Masterson or anyone else returns. Why don't you get your things together and I'll be back as quickly as I can.'

'You promise you will?'

'I promise.'

328

Estelle, surmounting her hesitation, stepped towards Miller and lightly kissed him on the cheek. He held her as she did so, his hands resting briefly on her shoulders. 'If you want the revolver you can take it,' she whispered, thinking it the most precious thing she'd ever offered anyone.

'You keep it,' said Miller. 'I'm guessing you know how to use it.'

73

The rain had almost stopped as Miller descended the shining steps outside the hospital. Flashlight in hand, he hurriedly skirted the park and crossed over the road to the row of stores. The windows in the baker's and the general store had both been smashed, and each door had been forced open. He walked beneath what little cover the awnings afforded from the drizzle. It wasn't strange for it to be so quiet in the middle of the night, and yet there was a tension in the air, or at least something which tugged fretfully at Miller's mind.

At the doorway to the general store the agent hesitated. He played the flashlight's beam over the mess inside. Jars and bottles lay smashed, flour coated half of one wall, and there was the smell of garlic, beans and coffee as each had been trampled into the floorboards. Miller hollered from outside, and from behind the counter Tang raised his head cautiously. In his hand was a revolver. He squinted as the flashlight momentarily blinded him, but he'd seen enough that night to be wary of any visitor.

'You ill with fever?' he shouted, pointing the barrel at Miller, while his wife, who'd also been hiding behind the counter, switched on the bulb overhead.

'I'm not feverish,' said Miller, 'if that's what you mean.'

Tang was backing away to the door behind him, ushering his wife through. He didn't look too reassured by Miller's words.

'Where's everyone?'

'People sick,' replied Tang. 'You go back to hospital.' He waved him away. 'You find out.'

'Are you?'

'I stay inside. It still dark.'

'I've come for a machete, just in case.'

'Sure. Two dollar.'

With a shake of the head Miller pulled out the envelope Masterson had given him from his back pocket and put the dollar bills on the counter. The Chinaman turned and disappeared into his stockroom, closing the door behind him. Miller glanced at his watch. It shouldn't take him more than an hour to get down to the river, quickly detour to his house on Cherry Drive to pick up a few belongings then head back to the hospital. The dull thump of a box, things being moved round. 'You OK back there?' he called, just as Tang reappeared.

'You take.' Tang proffered the machete's wooden handle across the counter. 'You go.' Again Tang pointed his revolver at the agent. 'Go quick,' he ordered, his voice trembling.

Under the awnings Miller paused to run his thumb along the blade. It wasn't something he intended using, yet if there was a riot going on, or the undead were attacking the living, then he was ready to fight back. He started walking down Main Street, then followed the rails between the powerhouse and the sawmill and passed through the factory yards. The locomotive with its flatcars rested outside its shed and the steam crane and heavy tractors stood stock-still under the arc lights.

At the dock the river flowed lazily underneath the long pier and the smaller jetty at the edge of the clearing. The noise of the frogs rose and fell, but otherwise all was quiet. Not a soul to be seen. *Joana* was there, hardly moving on the sluggish brown water, but just about every other vessel had gone. 'Alvarez!' cried Miller. He tried again, but knew it was no good. Like the rest of the compound, he and his boy had disappeared. The jetty creaked underfoot as he made his way to the launch. He didn't want to step back on board but drew it gently towards him, his hand holding one of the upright struts. Dipping his head beneath the tarpaulin, his eyes adjusted to the shaded night. Apart from the two hammocks hanging limply from the cover's frame, everything else had been stowed neatly away. The deck had lost its varnish a long time ago and over the years the bare wood had been splattered with paint, diesel, fish blood and kerosene. Miller, bringing his flashlight to bear, stared at the dark blotches beneath one of the hammocks. Several flies circled above it.

He let go of the launch and straightened his back. The dock was bathed in the arc lights on the warehouse and the pier. He wanted to speak to the skipper Alvarez, hear his side of what had happened, see if he or anyone else had been given the job of going back to Roeder's, or whether he was delivering him to Santarem in the morning. The vegetation was creeping ever closer to the jetty and with his flashlight he could just make out the bow of an upturned canoe. It looked like it had been hidden or abandoned on the beach and was probably the one he and Garret had been on that fatal night just a week or so ago. He looked back again at *Joana*. If others had fled the plantation, what was to stop him from taking the launch right now? It was tempting – just to get away. In a couple of days he'd be in Santarem. From there he'd take a river cruiser up to the coast. Wasn't that what they wanted him to do? Yet God only knew what Masterson had planned for Estelle and her baby. No, he intended to keep his promise to the girl. And, to his way of thinking, Pinion still owed him an explanation, though out in the dark that didn't seem to matter as much.

Miller was so lost in his own thoughts he didn't hear the four pairs of feet descending to the jetty until the boards began to creak behind him. He turned, the machete clasped tightly. At first they were just silhouettes of different heights, but when the flashlight's beam reached their faces he saw it was Shriver, his wife and their two children. Shriver was clutching a revolver and a suitcase. The others too had cases, and looked alarmed to see Miller. 'Hey, fellow,' called Shriver, 'you want to drop that machete and keep the light out of our eyes.'

He let his arms fall, but kept hold of the machete. 'I'm not ill.'

'I didn't say you were.' Shriver and his family stopped five yards from the agent. They'd have to squeeze by him, but suddenly seemed reluctant to do so.

'You're not sick, are you?' asked Shriver's wife. 'I mean, your face . . .'

Miller lifted the hand holding the flashlight and stroked his cheek. 'Just hornet stings, that's all they are.'

'We got a motor boat tied at the end there,' explained Shriver. 'We just need you to step aside.'

'Can you tell me what's going on?'

'People are scared, that's all I know.' Shriver glanced nervously at his wife. 'I suggest you get away while the generators are back on. Lights won't stay on till dawn.'

'We waited for them to come back on,' said Mrs Shriver. 'Others will be making their escape now, while they can.'

'I guess we got room for one more if you want to come with us,' Shriver added.

74

At the hospital Estelle had left Ferradas at the door and had returned to her room, where she was putting what jars and packets she'd carried up from the kitchen into her suitcase. The fact that the electricity had come back on had reassured the few patients she'd seen, though only Ferradas had stayed in the entrance hall. There didn't appear to be any doctors or nurses on duty, and yet several families had arrived in the hope of finding some sort of sanctuary. A speaker from somewhere in the building crackled as she shut the lid to her case, static pitching through the corridors. Suddenly a voice broke through. Several words were spoken, too blurred to make any sense. Then an indecipherable word was repeated three times, each time louder than the last. The final effort twisted itself into an indignant scream that echoed through the building. A high-pitched whine, then a soft drumming as though something heavy was being bounced beside the microphone. Static reclaimed the airwaves, though threaded through it was a peculiar, wet, slapping noise.

Alarmed by what she'd heard, Estelle stepped out into the corridor with her suitcase and Colt 45 and went as far as the stairwell. Below her there was some sort of commotion and those patients who could leave their beds were walking out of their wards and returning to the entrance hall. There was a man shouting, calling for his wife, when suddenly the ringing of the fire bell began to hammer through the air. It lasted no more than a minute before it cut out, along with the lights.

Those on the ground floor began to scream.

75

Miller looked at his watch. It wouldn't start getting light for at least another two or three hours. In Cherry Drive the street lamp was blinking erratically while the dwelling at the far end sat quietly decaying in its forsaken corner. Tired of the darkness, Miller hastened inside his own bungalow. He turned on the light and started to gather some of his belongings together, including the framed photograph he'd brought with him of his daughter.

The bulb flickered and died as he was putting the last few things in his rucksack. 'Damn,' he swore softly to himself and was about to turn on his flashlight when he heard the sound of something shuffling out on the stoop. Picking up his machete, he crept silently towards the door. He'd left it ajar and from outside there wafted a stench too foul to be anything other than evil. He waited in the corridor, trying not to breathe, ready with his machete just in case whatever it was came inside. He didn't want to confront it, not after the cave, not after what he'd witnessed that night. Whatever it was seemed to be rooting like a hog, sniffing loudly and laboriously pacing up and down. Then, from somewhere a hundred yards down the drive, there came a hideous, almost inhuman yelping and shrieking; a man crying out in pain and anguish. From the stoop it was immediately met with a grunt of approval. Miller listened as the steps down to the path creaked in slow succession. The stench was receding, yet the shrieking briefly continued. The noise the man was making rose insanely high then collapsed into a guttural choking.

Miller knew it was too late to save whoever it was and didn't rush to the door. Instead he waited before quietly moving along the hall. Cautiously he leaned his head against the door. What little moonlight there was through the thinning clouds lit several dark shapes assembled over something which appeared to be sprawled out on the dirt road. As stealthily as he could, Miller inched out onto the veranda. Then, crouching low, he leapt down to the path and sprinted across the lawn to the corner of the next bungalow.

It was a child kneeling beside the man who'd been screaming. Its back was curved over yet it seemed to be lifting something to its face. Those watching over the grisly scene stood with a stillness akin to that of vultures waiting to pick the bones clean. One figure, lean yet otherwise as indecipherable as the others, appeared to turn its head. Miller quickly leaned back against the bungalow. But it wasn't Miller the figure was looking at. From the far side of the road, shadows were spilling out from amongst the trees, grotesque, monstrous shapes which defied description. It was as if hell itself had opened up. Miller tried to grapple with the hallucinatory vividness and power of what he saw, and yet nothing was as it seemed. There was nothing definable, other than their malevolence and their slow, shambling gait. The fear he felt was the same he'd experienced at the cave. His heart beat rapidly as he pressed himself against the wooden boards at his back. It was a convulsing, gliding, shuddering procession of a dozen demoniacal shapes.

Miller couldn't see what was happening, but he heard the figures stirring. The handle of the machete was damp with sweat. He stayed as still as he could, wondering when it would be safe to look again. From what he heard, the child seemed to take delight in being joined by the misshapen fiends. The thought, which had been at the back of his mind, of going on to Pinion's now seemed foolish, his desire for some sort of explanation paling into insignificance. The nightmare had followed him and the hell which he'd uncovered was running loose across the plantation. He had to get back to the hospital as quickly as he could. After a brief silence, he warily peered round the corner. The child and its hellish entourage had vanished, though two figures still stood above what was left of the corpse.

Gripping the machete tightly, he stepped out into the road. With all the stealth he could muster, he approached the two of them from behind. They seemed oblivious to him sneaking up and it would have been easy for him to hack at one and then the other, yet he hesitated to do so. For some reason they were not running with the pack. He edged round to the side, his machete raised, ready to swing it if they lumbered at him. But they didn't move. He glanced down at what was left of the man. He'd been mauled and pulled apart, yet there was no blood on the two silent sentinels. They simply stared straight ahead. Had a remnant of self-respect, dignity or decorum prevented them from joining the others? Did they cling to the last vestige of what they had once been and thus, from somewhere deep inside, abhor the thought of feasting on another man's flesh?

76

Nothing stirred on Main Street. It was easy to believe that he was the only one left alive, that every worker, engineer, manager, wife and child had fled the plantation. Above Miller the clouds were parting and in the watery light of the moon the palm trees in the park cut diagonal shadows across the street. The whole place had the feeling of a ghost town, of having been abandoned to ugly, distorted spirits who cavorted with the dead. The only lights, towards which he hurried, were shining dimly from lanterns in the windows and the entrance to the hospital.

Inside the air was moist with sweat. On the benches were slumped men and women, pale, feverish-looking individuals who seemed to be oblivious to the threat outside. Miller looked for Estelle and Ferradas amongst them, but neither was anywhere to be seen. Sitting on the stairs was a mother cradling her child. Both flinched as the flashlight's beam swept over them. The woman's dress was stained with vomit, but whether she was ill or beyond salvation was impossible to tell at a glance. Gingerly he brushed past them and made his way back to the room he'd been given.

Estelle stood up from the bed when he entered. She had her Colt 45 in her hand, but threw it down on the blanket when she saw the man she'd been patiently waiting for. 'Thank God!' she cried, looking up at him through damp lashes, brushing the back of her hand over her cheeks. 'I thought you were never coming back.' There was a fragile smile, a look of unspeakable gratitude on her face.

'We've got to get out of here,' said Miller. 'This whole place is swarming with the undead.'

'Of course, I—'

'Where's Ferradas?'

'I left him in the lobby. Something bad happened in there.'

A shriek rang out from somewhere nearby. Estelle grabbed her revolver and her suitcase and followed Miller into the corridor. A scuffle was taking place in the stairwell. The woman who'd been cradling the child was being held in what looked like a lover's embrace by a man who was a good foot taller than her. He lifted her like a rag doll, her feet dangling inches from the floor. Miller brought his flashlight up to their faces, only to wish that he hadn't. As the man turned his eyes from the light they saw blood spilling from the woman's neck. Half her throat had been bitten away. Her hands were clasping the man's shirt, but as her cries were overcome by a choking, burbling sound, she became limp.

Estelle, having dropped her case, steadied the Colt 45 she was holding with both hands and pulled the trigger. The bullet punched through the man's skull and sent him reeling into the wall. Their ears hummed with the noise and in the muffled silence they saw the woman fall lifeless to the floor. Her daughter, a child of no more than six, began screaming.

The attacker was on the floor, but Miller didn't hesitate. He went straight over to him, placing his feet either side of the man's head. As the man, merely stunned, started to raise himself up off the slippery floor Miller brought the machete down from above his shoulder. In an arced stroke that was as graceful as it was deadly, the blade descended into the neck below. It was a swing that by luck or judgement virtually

342

severed the head, so much so that it twisted on what flesh still held it attached. The face, albeit drained of colour and smeared with blood, was instantly recognisable: it was Garret. 'My God!' Miller exclaimed. He looked back at Estelle. She was still holding the revolver, though her hands were shaking. From above their heads the fire bells sprang momentarily into life – more a death rattle than a sustained alarm, a fading pulse of electricity triggering the final call.

Patients, drawn by the sound of the gunshot, had gathered on the steps above the bottom of the stairwell. Ferradas appeared amongst them and slipped through. He swore in Portuguese at the sight of the woman, her dress round her waist, one side of her face lying in a pool of her own blood. The child was kneeling beside her mother, hands paddling over her chest. Ferradas scooped up the child. '*Vamos*,' cried the Brazilian, ushering them to the double doors.

Miller wiped the blade on the back of Garret's shirt and briefly muttered a few words. Suddenly caught in the stream of patients coming from the floor above, Estelle allowed herself to be bundled through the entrance and out into the night. Miller followed, his beam illuminating the anxious faces of those already outside. There was a glimmer of light in the leaden sky, though the night seemed reluctant to depart. He grabbed Estelle's arm and steered her away. 'We've got to keep going!' he shouted to Ferradas, who was still carrying the child.

'You know I had to shoot?' Estelle was saying, appealing for Miller's approval. He was reassuring her while guiding her round the park. They'd stay in the middle of Main Street all the way down to the quay. He glanced to his left and could just make out the smashed window of the general store. Darker shapes seemed to be shuffling inside. There seemed to be shadows moving in every store. A dozen others from the hospital were running down to the river. Miller wanted to keep up, fearing that every craft was going to be taken, but Estelle couldn't run. He tried to quicken her pace by pulling, but that was met with a tightening of her grip and an unspoken refusal. 'I got stitch,' Estelle complained. 'I can't go any faster.'

'We've got to get down there if we're to stand any chance of getting out of this alive.'

Her stride was unsteady and he'd given up trying to get her to run. Both were sweating, as much from anxiety as from the growing humidity.

Miller caught the scent of something and hesitated.

'What is it?' asked Estelle, who'd stepped in front of the agent.

It was an acrid smell, drifting on what little breeze there was. Miller turned his head, but it wasn't the hospital which was on fire. It was ahead of them, down towards the dock. No flames were visible from where they stood, but plumes of smoke were billowing up into the sky; swirls of grey and then, as they started down the hill again, tinted with orange.

'It's the sawmill,' exclaimed Miller as the treetops parted. Willowing vines and countless leaves blazed with the fiery orange of the burning building. No attempt was being made to put it out. The fire had taken hold in the bowels of the mill and was climbing through the building, consuming the floors above. Golden lights, framed by windows of cracked glass, illuminated the ash which floated above their heads. As they approached, the heat became intense and they were forced across to the far side of the street.

'There ain't another way,' said Estelle, as though reading Miller's thoughts. 'We gotta get past it.' Ferradas was now forging ahead, his hands protecting the girl, keeping her head close to his chest. Others were veering from the relative safety of the brick powerhouse, preferring the heat to whatever lined its wall. They were a hundred yards or so away when they saw silhouettes of men and women, shoulders hunched over, just staring at the sawmill as though they'd never seen anything as beautiful. There was something about their stillness which made Miller mistrustful. The people ahead were running past, but those lining the wall appeared oblivious to the stampede passing by. One mannequin-like figure and then another emerged from a clump of trees which stood just beyond the powerhouse. The two men walked with a slow gait across the railroad tracks to those watching the fire. It was a group of about twenty now, all staring at the burning building, each head tilted slightly back, hands hanging by their sides.

There was something else in the air other than the acrid smoke. It was a stench that both of them had smelt before, the smell of decaying flesh. Miller tried to get Estelle to walk a little quicker. The others had run past the mute congregation with no interference, yet how would they respond to a couple who could do no more than walk past? As if in answer to his question, one of the heads slowly turned towards them. There, in the light, was the gaunt, expressionless face of a man already dead. The eyes were colourless and vacant and yet it seemed to see them. Several, as if in response to some silent command, began to break rank and stumble towards the sawmill, but the one staring at them turned its emaciated body towards the couple and began to lift its bare feet.

77

'It's him!' cried Estelle, and they watched in awful fascination as Halliday lumbered towards them, his shoulders swinging his carcass forward as though in a hurry to lay his outstretched hands upon her. 'Stay back!' she shouted, but her words had no effect. The fiery light from the blazing sawmill leapt and shuddered over the animated corpse as its ugly mouth fell open.

Forging against those who were now streaming down the hill, Miller pulled Estelle towards the fire. Yet in two yards Halliday had checked his progress and changed direction. Like the couple he was trying to intercept, those heading towards the river kept out of his path, while most of the living dead were stumbling towards the sawmill as though drawn to the flames which engulfed it. Main Street was nearly choked by the throng of people as they swayed past the pale, cadaverous troop blind to everything except the pyre of glass and timber. Spectral men in grubby overalls, somnolent women in filthy dresses, all crossing to the sidewalk, weaving their way through the tall grasses and abandoned lumber.

An American carrying his young son found himself between the outstretched arms of the agent and the woman he was trying to save. Estelle's wrist was torn from Miller's grip and he watched helplessly as she staggered forward several steps and then fell to the ground, her revolver sliding out of her hand and kicked beyond her reach. Miller, colliding with others, fought against the tide which was carrying him down to the dock. Yet by the time he'd made it to her side Halliday was there and Estelle was kneeling on her grazed knees, staring up into his pale and sunken face.

For a moment the man she'd once foolishly called her husband loomed over her, his gaze shifting as if wanting to take in her hair, her freckled brow, her almond-shaped eyes. Halliday's knuckles, cold and livid, brushed against her burning cheek before he forced his hand beneath her arm and pulled her to her feet. Miller managed to grab hold of Estelle's dress as Halliday clutched her to his chest. Unable to use his machete for fear of wounding her, Miller tried to wrench her away, yet his effort briefly stalled at the sight of the ghastly face. It had lost what grim determination it had had, a determination which the agent had mistakenly seen as anger. Before he could do anything else, Halliday had buried his head in her neck. Estelle felt him sucking the warm odour from her flesh, his mouth drily clamping down upon her scent as though eating the very air itself. It lasted no more than a second and then Halliday's face jerked away as though he was in danger of losing himself. He mumbled a word repeatedly, wearily. An attempt, perhaps, to say goodbye, though what he laboured to articulate didn't make any sense.

Estelle and Miller watched as he fell clumsily back, then turned and followed the men and women of his unhallowed kind who were making their final journey. Those who'd lost everything had nothing left to lose. They were redeeming themselves in their own eyes, putting an end to it all – showing a decency, even a goodness, which in many had never been absent but in abeyance.

Fearlessly, unwaveringly, he walked towards the burning sawmill. Only total annihilation would give him the release he

348

sought. It was the last conscious decision he was capable of making: annihilation rather than a living death. Rather than suffering the sins of their lives made manifest and the ignominy of slaving without the prospect of ever being set free, they were committing their one last rebellious act. In front of him the husks of men and women stumbled through the burning grass and into the flames. As dry as tinder, they briefly flared before collapsing to be consumed by the fire. Staggering a yard or two into the inferno, Halliday fell with his arms outstretched, buckling round as he burned as though vainly looking back to catch a glimpse of her face.

78

Dawn is breaking and west of Carsonville the rain is coming down again, falling darkly with a shimmering splutter into the muddy fields, hushing the swollen river. Inside his wooden shack sits Roeder, reading a paperback which is slowly disintegrating in the damp air. A kerosene lamp is burning behind his shoulder and on the threadbare rug at his feet crouch a boy and a girl absorbed in a game of their own invention; silent playmates ready to serve their grandfather while the rest of their family shelter in huts. In one corner of the cabin Roeder's two dogs lie stretched out. All is quiet, except for the roof of zinc and shingle which rattles with the rain. All is quiet until one of the dogs, a mastiff of black and grey, lifts its muzzle from the floor and sniffs. Its neighbour, sensing the presence of something in the air, something growing stronger and therefore coming closer, immediately does the same and almost as one they climb onto their long, spindle legs and trot to the door. Muzzles press against the wood of the door and floor, manoeuvring of heads to squeeze their black snouts into any gap. Nostrils flare, but what to make of it? To bark or to whimper?

The boy, now on his feet, points to a figure distorted by the rain-streaked piece of glass. Roeder reluctantly lifts himself out of the chair and places the novel spread-eagled on the cushion which still retains the imprint of his bony backside. He shuffles across to the window while the dogs begin to yelp and pace fretfully at the door.

At first he can't see her, but the boy persists and eventually, through the glass, he sees a pink apparition shifting through the sombre greyness of the rain. He fixes his eyes upon it and as he does so his thin frame shudders with a mixture of trepidation and delight, though why he cannot say. The figure walks between the guava trees, slow, delicate steps, the head thrown back, what's left of her dark hair plastered to the back of her velvet dress. Roeder, in his confused state, wonders if he should pick up his Winchester which rests on the chest of drawers. The boy wants to open the door, and with a gesture of his hand his grandfather shoos him out. The hounds and then the girl follow him. The girl tries to catch up with the boy as he races to the nearest hut, the dogs running towards the figure which continues to approach the shack.

Roeder watches spellbound as the hounds draw nearer. He's seen them tear animals in two and wonders with something akin to alarm whether the child is going to be set upon. Then, much to his surprise, they part and go round her, like a wave split by a rock. They keep running, bounding towards the forest, drawing together again as they head to the path. Yet this dripping stalactite which glistens pink and pale keeps moving ahead. He sees the hands clenched by her skeletal thighs, the dress clinging obscenely to her sparrow legs. The face is shining, skin drawn tight across the skull and jaws, the few teeth she has are bared. Her skin is white and her eyes stare vacantly ahead, yet she knows he is there, that he now stands on the porch watching her approach. Does he recognise her?

There's something behind the hideous grin which speaks to him. Not of sepulchres or graves, but of illicit love, of a night during which their destiny was fixed. He loves her for what he once was, for what they once shared. The rain drips from the porch as her feet, bandaged in leather, step onto the first step. She doesn't shiver but her teeth chatter, a slow tapping of tooth against tooth. Roeder steps back into the cabin and she follows with her slow, almost regal gait. He stops beside the chair and she stands in front of him. Behind her is the rifle, but he doesn't look at that. He deciphers her face, her figure, each scab and scar. The seeing eyes of the blind girl are upon him. She can smell him, the sweating flesh of a man steeped in sin. Her body is weak but she is driven by yearning, by an impulse long forgotten and yet never still. She raises her thin hands up to her dripping chin and feels for the buttons which she knows are there. The first one is missing and her fingers stumble over the cotton thread. They trail down to the next and are not disappointed. Roeder can almost sense the satisfaction she feels as her dormant fingers awaken and perform what was once a daily occurrence.

He wipes a hand over his bristled cheeks as she continues to unbutton. Despite the years of depravity, or perhaps because of them, he is not unmoved by the sight of the girl undressing. Her shoulders twist slightly and the heavy dress falls with a sodden thud to the floor. She stands naked except for a thin cord of grubby cotton which hangs almost comically from one hip down to just above the opposite knee. Frayed bloomers, which once fitted her waist, decorate her protruding bones. Her body is a sunken garden, blanched and blue. The skin over her ribs is translucent, her chest is a breeding house for beetles and maggots. Gone, other than in memory, are her insolent breasts pushing out delightfully plump curves in a weak-willed nightdress, the strawberry and cream flesh.

Roeder speaks her name, 'Larissa,' and her mouth widens into what was once a smile. Only his weariness and the dazed stupor into which he has fallen prevents him from crying aloud as Nascimento's daughter falls to her knees and pulls him roughly towards her. A fusion of the past and of the horror he has created becomes too much to bear. Still dazed, he tries to disentangle himself, but cannot. Her face rests momentarily against his bony thigh. A paralysis of fear stifles all attempts to cry out. The custodian of gangrenous emotions, constrained by death and its dark prison, begins her assault.

79

Downriver it was a morning of soft, invisible rain and the wind-stirred water lapped against the side of the wooden canoe they'd wrestled out from the undergrowth. They'd been too late for the launch and were now floating away from Carsonville, from the scent of death and the haunted faces of desperate men. They drifted beneath the dawn, her head nestled against his shoulder. He looked down at her: vulnerable, ignorant, a mess of wrong-headedness. But what shone through every pore, through her peach-fuzzed cheeks and half-shut eyelids, was beauty on the verge of blossoming into goodness. It was as desperate to bloom as he was to give himself over to the love a father feels for a child. Miller was tired and susceptible to feelings he'd suppressed for too long. The lump in his throat seemed to pull at his cheeks and eyes, and made smiling practically impossible.

'It's kicking,' she said. 'Here, you can feel it.' She took his hand and placed it over the taut material of her dress. 'Hadn't felt nothing before.' Her eyes glistened. 'Honestly,' she whispered, 'I wasn't sure if it was living or dead.'

'It sure is kicking.' Miller paused. The smile came eventually and was greeted by a gentle kiss on the edge of his jaw, as though she was aware of how fragile a moment it was. 'You'll be a good mother. Just let your heart do the thinking for a while.'

Estelle nodded. It was the way she was starting to see things, to make sense of the world. 'OK,' she agreed, 'but you're going to help me, aren't you?'

Miller smiled again. She was as poor at hiding her apprehension as she was at disguising her lies. 'I will,' he promised. 'Until you find yourself a decent fellow who won't settle for anything but the truth.'

'And you? What will you do if I find this fellow?'

'That's easy. Do what I've been promising myself for the last seventeen years. Take a trip down south and visit my daughter and her mother, Dolores.'

'If it's easy, then you shouldn't leave it any longer.'

Epilogue

Amongst the ruins of Carsonville, the natives who still inhabit the area speak openly of the strange things they have seen. They stand in baseball caps and grubby tee-shirts and point to where the bungalows on Cherry Drive are falling into ruin. There, they say, is the street which is haunted. At night a pale girl in a pink dress has been seen walking into the forest, looking for her lost love. In her hands she holds the wooden handle of a small vanity mirror. In the past, members of the tribe are said to have followed her. She walks only at night, beyond the crumbling building which once used to coagulate rubber and through the charred timbers of the sawmill. During the day she rests in the shade, but like a mule she sleeps standing up and with her eyes open, the mirror held close to her face as though endlessly gazing at her own reflection.